Miranda Miller was born in London in 1950. After university she moved to Rome, where she combined writing her first novel with a variety of jobs. Later she lived in Libya and Saudi Arabia. She has published five acclaimed novels, a collection of stories and a work of non-fiction examining the effects of homelessness on women.

www.mirandamiller.info

BY THE SAME AUTHOR

Loving
Mephistopheles

Miranda Miller

PETER OWEN PUBLISHERS
LONDON AND CHESTER SPRINGS, PA, USA

PETER OWEN PUBLISHERS
73 Kenway Road, London SW5 0RE

Peter Owen books are distributed in the USA by
Dufour Editions Inc., Chester Springs, PA 19425-0007

First published in Great Britain 2007 by
Peter Owen Publishers

ISBN 978 0 7206 1275 2

Printed in Great Britain by
Windsor Print Production Ltd, Tonbridge, Kent

Contents

I would like to thank the following people, whose encouragement and advice while I was writing this novel were invaluable: John Bayley, Martin Goodman, Lyndall Gordon, Bill Hamilton, Tim Hyman, Rebecca Miller, Antonia Owen, Judith Ravenscroft and Leslie Wilson. I am also indebted to the following texts: *Dr Faustus* by Christopher Marlowe, Howard Brenton's translation of Goethe's *Faust* Parts I and II; *Europe's Inner Demons* by Norman Cohn, *Marie Lloyd* by Richard Baker and *Max Beerbohm* by N. John Hall. Hammer Horror films were also an important influence.

Prologue

'Do you remember where we met?'

'Down there, you mean? Hanoi, Hoxton, Hong Kong? All under water now, anyway.'

'I've been trying to remember.'

'Dangerous stuff, memory. Let me know if it hurts and we'll cut out any malignancy.'

'I thought I might keep it all. Write it down, even. Don't you feel any nostalgia?'

'You're the only one I'd miss. And I have you. You're not getting restless?'

'No. I'll stay up here now.'

For ever.

This conversation took place in bed. We still make love. Last week Leo's penis dropped off, but we got him another one from the Metaphysical Bank.

Outside the window I watch our child playing among the fountains and unicorns and elves. Last year it was caves and vampires and dragons, but fairy-tales are very sentimental this season. Although this Abbie, of course, looks exactly like that other Abbie, she is more placid. I love her just as much but differently. Leo fusses over her absurdly. Neither of us can quite believe, even now, that there really are no dangers here.

Of course, those of us who are eternally young and rich have always hovered just above the earth, as if in balloons, observing with curiosity and, sometimes, compassion. Now that science has caught up with science fiction we have cut the ropes, and here on Luna Minor the earth is the stuff of nightmares. After a good dinner we exclaim with horror and raise our eyebrows at the latest catalogue of disasters down there: meteors, earthquakes, floods, famine, drought. Such a masochistic planet, you'd think those one-lifers would make the best of what little time they have instead of wallowing in misery. We send down ships full of food and old clothes but no longer go ourselves. Not after the last time.

Yet the London of my imagination still has great power. If I was properly old I suppose I'd be forgetting it all. Now, instead of dementia I experience a kind of volcanic recall; memories erupt so intensely that I can hardly believe those events happened so long ago. They're still scalding hot, their power undiminished. Imagine what it's like for Leo who's been around for centuries. He never wants to talk about the past.

'What are you thinking?' he asks with that anxious note in his voice that still surprises me. Once, he would have known but wouldn't have cared.

'I was thinking about – our daughter.' I usually avoid referring to her as Abbie.

'She's so talented and inventive, a wonderful child. Perhaps you were right to insist on all that revolting blood and slime. I'm sure the computer-generated children aren't so original.'

'For her birthday she wants to orchestrate the meteors.'

'Why not? My little Mozart!' You'd think he'd always adored children and been the most indulgent of fathers.

Now that she is nearly eleven it all comes flowing back. Three little girls triplicated in time and space. At the same age that other Abbie had to struggle with poverty and I was blind and couldn't help her; a century before that I was a child myself, not that childhood was much gushed over in Hoxton at the beginning of the twentieth century.

My past is a film I play back to myself each night as I lie beside Leo. Pictures, colours, arbitrary memories – I've been telling my story to myself in grand operatic events: love and death and vicissitudes of fortune. But it's the ordinary moments that my memory savours and replays to me now, refusing to accept my own judgement of what was important. Those moments are so intense that they draw me into a perpetual present, a river that carries me back to London. My city resurrects itself and so do the people, who will live for as long as I refuse to forget them.

Two hundred years ago, ten seconds ago.

PART 1
Jenny and Leo

Jenny Mankowitz

My mother and father sit together over my sister Lizzie's cradle. A rare moment of intimacy in their mutual destruction, which usually leaves Ma alone with two little girls in small, bare rooms while our father goes out drinking. But this is an image of tenderness, the two beautiful faces leaning over the wooden crib. My father is a classically handsome Jew, tall and slim with curly black hair, huge dark eyes, olive skin and a long harmonious face. My mother is also tall, with wavy light-brown hair swept up in a magnificent Edwardian chignon, creamy skin, green eyes and a bustle of vitality and purpose that make her thrilling to watch.

I'm not in the picture, of course, because I'm holding the camera of memory, filtering their long-dead faces through the merciless eyes of a jealous three-year-old. This is the first time I've thought of my parents as lovers, as a sexual couple. Lizzie and I must have been conceived in passion.

Quarrels and sulks as the handsome, feckless couple sink into debt. My father has just enough determination to reject his Orthodox background but not enough to accept responsibility for his young family or decide whether he wants to be a musician or a tailor or a baker. My mother soon comes to despise his weakness more than she loves his charm and good looks.

A game I play with Lizzie on summer evenings in our back yard: we put blankets over a clothes-horse and sit cross-legged in the dark tent it makes, then dare each other to run into the kitchen and steal pans, plates, raw carrots and lumps of dough for 'our house'. Ma hates domesticity, poverty, children and noise. I already know this, so I hide, disappear – as my mother will do herself a few years later when she sails off to Shangri-La via Jo'burg.

Under the dark blankets Lizzie and I inhale the stuffiness, the smell of old bodies and tea and bacon – for my father enjoyed flouting the taboos of his parents – and watch sunlight filtered in tiny needles. Our scabby knees and elbows touch as we whisper, giggle and squabble. We love it when the roof falls in, when the blankets collapse and tangle with our pots and food. Then we have to get up and rebuild our house, weighing the corners of the blankets with stones and crawling back through a flap. Inside, the rich darkness encloses us again, hugging us in our own thoughts, smells and dreams.

Two sisters in white night-dresses in bare rooms, dreaming and squabbling and kicking each other in the single bed we share every night. It's so cold that the condensation freezes on the cracked window-pane and streams down the walls. Lizzie brushes her long black hair with the hairbrush we share and squabble over, splashing her face with cold water before jumping into bed to kick me.

Our parents must have married young. There's a much older brother I can hardly remember, Spencer, a name associated with beautiful stamps and financial hopes. At fourteen he was sent off to South Africa to seek his fortune. I imagine him, a huge shadow wrapped in an envelope, sailing across the ocean with a bundle tied up in a handkerchief like Dick Whittington. Spencer has found his fortune, a warm shiny word. Ma and Pa have fallen from genteel heights, but Spencer's fortune is going to lift them up again. The less money there is, the more my parents talk about it.

'Looking for work and hoping to God he doesn't find it,' Ma says of my feckless father. Every few months we change rooms and schools. The rooms get smaller and the schools rougher. I know landlords are bastards, jobs are slavery, schools are pigsties, pubs are where the money goes, pawnbrokers cheat you and other children hit you if you don't hit them first. Pa hates religion, all of it, Jewish or Christian. When he ran off with Ma – who was Jewish, too, but never went to synagogue – he fled from his family, who lived in a hebra in Bethnal Green with other families from the same *shtetl* in Poland. Although all he has fled to is more poverty, my father says he's glad to have escaped from the Talmud. Won't let us have anything to do with the missionaries who flock to save our degraded East End souls. I always want to go along and have tea and cake and sermons, but we aren't allowed.

Sometimes the battle between Ma and Pa spreads. One night I look out of the window and see the whole street erupt into a fight – like a party, only with fists instead of buns. Softly illuminated, like dancers on the gas-lit cobbles, men and women punch and claw at each other. Through the cracked glass I see heads hit the cobblestones, noses squashed like tomatoes, a straw hat torn off with a clump of hair attached to it. Pa has left again, and behind me I hear Ma's voice. 'These people are scum; they don't know any better. Don't look at them, Jenny.'

Pa doesn't happen any more. We move again, and Ma shares a bed with us, snoring and sobbing and smelling like Pa did when he came home. Lizzie and I think it's wonderful to have her in bed with us; we don't care how smelly and noisy she is.

Then Ma goes off to South Africa to be with Spencer, who we always knew was her favourite just because he was a boy. I'm twelve, three years older than Lizzie, and we go to live with Auntie Flo, who isn't our aunt but some kind of relation. She's quite kind really, but I can't forgive her for not being my mother. I can see her street, the chandler's and the beer shop and baker's. Little brick houses with 'Mangling done here' signs in the windows. We think Auntie Flo's rich because she has the whole house and doesn't do mangling.

Auntie Flo's crappery down at the end of the yard, frozen in winter and flyblown in summer, is so terrifying in the middle of the night that Lizzie and I refuse to use it and develop bladder infections. The chamber pot's icy, too, and most nights it's too cold to pee or do anything except huddle against Lizzie's back in bed. We squabble over which side of the lumpy mattress to sleep on and who used the curling tongs and which one of us was to leave the breakfast tray for Mr Barnabus, the only one of Auntie Flo's lodgers who isn't downright hideous. Lizzie thinks it's the end of the world when I kiss him.

Every morning my sister and I walk to the Bath Street School, where we don't learn anything, but at least for two whole years we live in the same house and go to the same school. When I come home I search the table in the murky hall for the letter from Ma that never comes. I think my glamorous mother in South Africa is proud of me, misses me. I think she has only left us because she had to and because our big brother Spencer is going to make lots of money and send for us.

Only she doesn't. The envelopes with beautiful stamps arrive every few months, but they're not addressed to me or Lizzie. They're for Auntie Flo, full of money to pay for our keep, so we must be worth something.

On my fourteenth birthday, when I have to leave school, my horizons barely fill the grimy window of the room I share with Lizzie. Auntie Flo takes in lodgers and sometimes works as a barmaid at the Falstaff. Ma didn't work because she was a lady really. I can just about imagine working in the hat shop in Kingsland Road. I'd have to wear a black frock and stand rigidly to attention and call other women madam. A job like that would be posh, grand, swish, compared with the only alternatives, which are the baby-boot or feather-curling factories.

All I know is I hate babies and I want to be the one who wears the hats and the feathers. I know men stare at me, and there's money in that. On the other side of London, where I've never been, there are theatres and carriages and jewellery that might as well be worn by me as by engravings in illustrated newspapers. I've been to music halls, and the only women I've ever heard of who did anything except have babies are Queen Victoria, Marie Lloyd and Vesta Tilley. If you can't get a job as a queen you can always learn to sing and dance. Auntie Flo says girls who go on the stage aren't much good – although with a nod and a wink and a leer, implying that being good isn't much fun.

Leo

'Leopold M. Bishop, professional Tutor and Agent, prepares ladies for Theatres or Music Halls and procures Engagements. Easy payments. Stamped agreements given to every Pupil.'

Leo always did like contracts.

I've chosen him out of a list of men claiming to teach acting because his name is Bishop and I think bishops are safe. I go to see him, clutching his advertisement from the local paper and my only white gloves. I'm afraid they'll get dirty if I wear them.

I've never seen these streets before. Bloomsbury. Huge white houses like slabs of blooming cake, the dark pavements shiny with rain. London still feels imperial and pleased with itself. These houses are full of objects and people that know their place. You can tell at once they don't do mangling, they don't even put their own clothes on or cook their own food. I can smell the rain, the sap in all these trees that aren't allowed to grow in Hoxton and my lavender perfume that I saved up for weeks to buy. My heart gallops with terror as I approach his house.

A uniformed maid like a bossy penguin shows me into a comfortable overcrowded room. Behind a carved desk is a tall, thin man with brown hair and dark-blue eyes, well dressed. He looks about thirty, more than twice my age but not old; looks so like the dream lover I've been imagining since I was twelve that I at once feel naked, as if he's been spying on my fantasies. I'm sure he knows my stays are too tight and my shoes and blouse and skirt are ridiculously big, borrowed from Auntie Flo. But I haven't come all this way just to be sent packing, so I walk straight up to him and say, 'I want you to teach me how to act. I want to be like Marie Lloyd.'

'Nobody is like her. That is why she is a great performer.'

Clumsily I audition, and he agrees to teach me.

For a year I give him most of the money I earn curling feathers and sewing them on to hats, boas and evening cloaks. My fingers are sore, and I hate each slippery feather as if it's a spiteful bird sneering at me. I'm determined that one day I'll wear these garments I'm sewing for other, richer women. Twelve hours a day I sleep-walk at the factory, and for two hours a week, on Sunday evenings, I wake up. Leo teaches me how to walk, speak, read, act, sing, dance, dress and breathe.

One afternoon, when my elocution lesson is over, instead of going home, I turn to the man behind the desk. 'You married?'

'No.'

'Always lived alone, 'ave ya?'

'I have,' he says in the exquisite, stilted accent I'm supposed to imitate. But although it's his teaching voice he no longer has his teaching face. I stand over him with one hand on my hip, staring into the eyes that are suddenly evasive as he fidgets with his blotter. 'It's time for you to go home, my dear.'

'Don't feel like it. And you 'aven't got no other pupils Sundays. You told me so.'

We sit beside the fire and talk. I ask all the questions. After months of lessons I don't know anything about him but feel he can see straight through me. When Lizzie asks what my posh teacher is like, I reply, 'He talks lovely.'

Now I fire brash questions about his career, his childhood, his friends and what he does when I'm not here. Mr Bishop is awkward, as if he has never answered these very obvious questions before. I sit in a low chair opposite him, staring straight into his dark-blue eyes, which look devious and surprised. I try to memorize his face for Lizzie so that I can tell her once and for all whether he's handsome or ugly. It's a long, thin, clever face, with a sharp nose and thin lips, like a greyhound, and as I continue my interrogation he looks so nervous I think he might go racing off. He sidles out from behind his fortress desk and sits in one of the two green leather armchairs by the fire.

I pursue him to the other one and sit opposite him. I stop trying to force him to talk and stare at him in the darkening room. Suddenly he looks at me so hard that I see myself: a dark, skinny girl of fifteen in a white blouse tucked into a navy-blue skirt, cheeks flushed from the firelight and the excitement of being with him. I see my whole life until now reflected in his eyes, a very small thing, and also see that those eyes aren't indifferent to me any more.

He drops to his knees and holds out his arms to me. We kneel together on the shabby red Turkish carpet in front of the fire and kiss.

His face feels scratchy and alien, yet warm and comforting, too, as if a part of myself I've lost has been restored.

After that our lessons change a bit. I still do the singing and dancing and acting, but somehow we always end up over by the fire with half our clothes off. He fondles my breasts, strokes my bare legs, talks about Garrick and Irving and Sarah Bernhardt and Ellen Terry, about painting and music and philosophy. You can't say it isn't educational. Our lessons stretch from two hours to four to half the night.

'How long've you been in the theatre?'

'I was in the theatre long before you were born.'

'Go on, you're not that old!'

'Have you ever heard of Arlecchino?'

'Arlywot?'

'Harlequin. Wonderful part. I've still got the costume.' He goes to a chest in the corner of his room and comes back with some old rags.

'Bit of a mess, isn't it? Like a patchwork quilt gone wrong. Could do with a wash.' Leo sits in his chair by the fire, stroking his old costume. 'I've lost the mask. I used to love that mask. It was only a papier-mâché half-mask, but when I put it on I felt his personality flow into me. His comic delight in his own folly, his genius for wriggling out of awkward situations. And the audiences loved me; they applauded me in Bergamo and Venice and Mantua and Vienna and Warsaw and Moscow. Suddenly my tricks and lies were lovable. In this costume, wearing that mask, I was capable of the most amazing acrobatics. I could turn a back flip holding a glass of wine and not spill a drop; I could walk upside down to the imperial box where Catherine the Great was waiting with open arms –'

'Who's she then?' I ask jealously.

'A skeleton.' He leaps up. 'I'd come strutting on to the stage like this, perhaps do a few cartwheels like this. Never at a loss for words, gossiping about local scandals and politics, as Harlequin I could say anything. Always improvising, disguising myself – in one play I'm in a tomb after a jealous rival has poisoned me. I wake up beside the beautiful Eularia – she looked a bit like you, as a matter of fact – she's been poisoned, too. She says, "I am a woman, alas, brought low by a jealous lover on whom I doted too much." Then I say, "And I am a man poisoned by a madly jealous rival." Then I look at her like this and say, "Come over here. Although I'm dead I find I still have a taste for the ladies." Shall I show you what happens next?'

'All right.'

I'm so wet with desire for him that I have to turn away from Lizzie in bed each night to masturbate silently. Leo's sensuality is always under control; he never quite gives me the satisfaction of losing my virginity. He trains me to respond with my mouth, hands and cunt to his casual depravity until, one day, I become the seducer.

One Sunday evening my lesson ends with us both lying, almost naked, in front of his fire. Flames throw liquid red reflections over our arched bodies and the blood-red Turkish rug. Outside the window I can see the dark, foggy night I don't want to be expelled into. This room has become my centre; all week at the feather factory I languish, waiting for his voice and hands and mouth to make me real again. I know he has other female pupils, and I'm frantically jealous of them. I consider chaining myself to his desk like the crazy women who chain themselves to the railings at Westminster. The girls at the factory laugh at them. Give me the spondoodles and a good-looking fella and sod the vote – that's our politics.

'I don't want to go home.'

'It's late. Your aunt will be worried.'

'No she won't. She doesn't give a bugger.'

'Don't swear. It isn't lady-like.'

'What about those tricks you've taught me, then? Putting my mouth and hands in places I never dreamt of. Is that what ladies do?'

'Behind closed doors, I believe, it has been known.'

'What about your other pupils then, them as comes after me. Do they all end up stripped to their petticoats?'

'I'm your teacher, my dear, not your husband.'

'Lock the door. I want an extra lesson.'

We finally consummate our sexual games and lie panting on the Turkish rug by the fire. 'So that's what all the giggling and whispering and wait-until-you're-older was about. Well, it's worth waiting for.'

'I've always thought so.'

'Do it again.'

You are my universe. I internalize you as surely as you slither deep inside me during our wild lovemaking. Loving you, I love the world and throw myself at it greedily.

Jenny Manette

'Trouble with you, Jenny-nose-in-the-air, you fink you're better than the rest of us. I've a mind to write and tell Ma what you're really up to with that Leo.'

'If Ma'd been worried about our morals she wouldn't of left us with Auntie Flo.'

19

'She says she'll send for us when Spencer's made some money.'

'Catch me going off to bloody Jo'burg. Give me London any day. Help me with my hair, will ya? Must run. I'm meeting Leo at Giulini's at eight.'

'Take me with you, Jenny.'

'No. You're too young. Make your own life.'

'Please, Jenny.'

Lizzie isn't really too young, she's fourteen, same age as me when I met Leo. But she isn't pretty or quick-witted, and I don't want her tagging along, whinging and blabbing. I've told Leo about my family, but selectively, and Lizzie isn't one of the bits I've selected. It's more romantic to be an orphan, all alone in the world except for my beautiful Aunt Florence, a retired opera singer. Auntie Flo's idea of careers advice: I don't worry about you, Jenny, when you don't come back at night, because I know a young girl can always find a bed somewhere.

And I do, God knows I do. By the time I'm seventeen I'm earning enough to pay the rent on a room in Gower Street. Not much better than the room at Auntie Flo's, but I don't have to share a bed with busybody Lizzie any more, I'm just around the corner from Leo and it's not as far to walk home late at night. My room is all chocolate brown and bottle green, what Mark Twain would have called a hospital for incurable furniture, but I'm so proud to be independent. I'm not rich, but I'm definitely on the way up. *I've just had a banana with Lady Diana* – lords were always more my thing than ladies, and we had a bit more than a banana.

When the acting lessons don't pay, Leo reinvents himself as a conjuror, the Great Pantoffsky, Master Phantasist, in a top hat, white gloves, a white silk scarf and a black cloak lined with scarlet. I watch from the wings, fascinated, as he releases a dozen turtle doves from the hat of a lady in the front row and flies off with them. Then he reappears in one of the boxes at the side of the stage and opens up his black-lacquer cane to reveal a bunch of red roses that turn into an enormous red silk balloon. Leo climbs in and floats off over the audience, waving down at them.

'How do you do them tricks, then?' I ask later when we're sitting in Giulini's, our favourite restaurant.

'*Those* tricks. They require a lot of practice. Centuries.'

'Go on. You can't be that old. How old are you, anyway?' He smiles at me as we raise our glasses of wine, and I get that feeling again, that sinking, drowning sense that he isn't what he seems, that after four years I don't know anything about my teacher, agent, manager, lover and friend.

When we get our first bookings at the Chelsea Palace I feel like the bee's knees. Two pounds ten a week. It isn't the Drury Lane panto but it's one up on the Stepney Paragon and the Penge Empire where I started out, when they gave me the bird and threw trotter bones at me. Now I'm not quite bottom of the bill: Miss Jenny Manette, the Charming Soprano Vocalist. I know I'm a nice little performer, but I'll never be a headliner. Leo says I have to drop Mankowitz during the Great War because French is popular and Polish Jewish isn't. So, I say, what about the Great Pantoffsky, then? That's all right, he says, magicians can get away with being foreign and sinister. You have to be very careful during the war. Brunnhilde the Banjo Belle gets arrested as a German spy, and we all have to use Clarko greasepaint because Leichner's is unpatriotic.

I'm on my way to a rehearsal one morning when I see a bloody great crater in front of Swan and Edgar. Later, people said the Zeppelin raids were nothing compared with the Blitz, but they were bad enough for me. A lot of the old halls go dark during the war, it's harder to get bookings and we have to keep changing our acts. I have to dress up in a khaki uniform, go all coy and hold up a white feather as I sing, 'We don't want to lose you, / But we think you ought to go.' Too damn right we don't want to lose them. They're bums on seats and they pay the rent.

Leo and I are quite hard up during the war. The three Rs – Ragtime, Russian ballet and Revue – are putting the last nails in music hall's coffin. The bioscope used to be a turn at the end of the show, but now they show it in a special building and audiences flock to see them. Leo wangles us contracts at the Holborn Empire and the Balham Duchess, and Tommy-on-leave still wants the old songs. We go over to the Facial Hospital in Kennington to do special shows for the Tommies that can't get to the theatre. Boys younger than me on the wards in their dressing-gowns. When I first hear them laugh I think they must be shamming. They sound so full of life, warmest audience I ever had. Then when I look a bit closer I see they've lost their eyes or legs or the hands they should be clapping with.

By the time the Great War ends I've spent six years on the stage – well, on it and off it and under it and behind it. Leo isn't possessive, says he believes in free love, but if I can get them to pay me for it so much the better. Leo arranges it all – helping me with my career he calls it. Sex is one of the skills I need, like singing in tune and tap-dancing. It's love when I make it with Leo, on my side anyway; his thin, hard body, his bossy manner and the way he defines my wants and needs, tells me what I think and feel before I know myself.

All that guff about fallen women. You just try working twelve-hour shifts in a feather factory for six bob a week. Doors open and behind each one is Leo and, behind him, other men's hands, lips, hot sticky desires – after a while you stop counting, let alone remembering their names.

Can't remember meeting George. He's just there, waiting at the stage door. When I finish my act and look out over the audience it's his round, pink, silly face I'm looking for, and if he isn't there I miss him. Leo wants me for what he's made me. His midnight-blue eyes see every fault, every wobble in my talent. But George just thinks I'm marvellous. In his eyes – also blue but milky and glazed with devotion – I see a new Jenny who is sophisticated (not just a little trollop), talented (not just a monkey performing for Leo) and witty. George has gentleman written right through him like Brighton through a stick of rock. There's nothing sneaky about George; he just comes straight up to me and hands me his heart on a plate.

Me and Leo have a good laugh at him. We let him pay our bills once or twice and play gooseberry when the three of us go out together. And, while we're talking fruit, I have his cherry – and very sweet it is, too – on a mattress around the back of the stage at the old Balham Duchess after the show one night. Sometimes when Leo's not around I let George come back to my room in Gower Street. He's only a few years younger than me, but I feel like his mother. His real mother hates me, of course, thinks her little boy has survived the last few months in the trenches only to be eaten alive by the Whore of Babylon. Thinks I want to marry him, silly cow. George has no money to speak of, and I'm having far too good a time to want to settle down – and if I did I'd want at least a title and a couple of houses. One of my admirers, Binkie, died in the war and left me two thousand quid. Leo has made me invest it, and I feel rich.

The Bargain

It's 1922, and Leo and I have finally made it to the West End. We're both on the bill at the Holborn Empire, and we usually go to Giulini's in Drury Lane for supper after the show. I love coming out of the theatre and finding them both there. Leo hasn't changed out of his Pantoffsky outfit. He's still in his tails and topper and red-silk-lined evening cloak, swinging his black-lacquer cane. I think he's the most handsome man in London, but I don't tell him so because he's quite conceited enough. George looks awkward in his evening clothes; they're too tight and he always cuts himself shaving. His blood drips down on to his white wing-collar, his tie's never straight and he stammers and blushes when I kiss him on the cheek. Then I turn to kiss Leo on the lips. I'm so happy, walking down the street with a man on either arm and giving an eyeful to any nimminy-pimminies from the National Vigilance Association that might be watching. George is on my left, and on my other side Leo is indulging in one of his arias.

'You didn't show enough leg in your first number, and, what's worse, you didn't smile. Haven't I been telling you for the last ten years: your face isn't the pink dimpled confectionery the morons in the gods like to lick. You're too pale, too thin, too foreign-looking. To seduce these West End philistines you have to ooze charm, make love to them with every pore and nerve, open your heart and legs to them like –'

'Like the poor bitch they buried today,' I say in my own voice, the one I only use with them, instead of my new elocutionized drawl. 'Marvellous Merry Marie. Thank Gawd we're here. I'm starving.'

Giulini greets us warmly – we're an established triangle – and leads us to the panelled room where we always sit, beneath French prints of fat-arsed Cupid aiming at plump targets in frilly petticoats. There's a lot of drinking and banter between the two men, but food and words stick in my throat, and at the end of the meal Leo asks, 'What's the matter, Jenny?'

'You wouldn't understand. George would, but he's pissed again. Can't get a peep out of him.'

'There's not much there. Knock-knock. Is George at home? No, he turned into a poodle and chased off after a Jenny wren. What's that? A giggle or a sob? Tell me.'

'You always make me tell you things and then you turn it into a joke.'

'Only to comfort you. You know how I adore you.'

'Now that is funny.'

'Who do you love, Jenny?'

'Not you. You're too hard and sharp.'

'George?'

'Too soft and dull.'

'Yourself?'

'Too – stupid. Women get caught by the same old lies again and again. You're full of tricks, and I fall for them every time. I did love *her*, though. Fell in love with her when I was seven and my big brother passed on the boots she bought him before I was born. Did you ever hear that story? She bought hundreds of pairs of boots and gave them to the poor in Hoxton. Us, that was. And now she's dead.'

'Brilliant performer.'

'And a stupid woman. Couldn't read or write properly, drank too much, gave away all her money and loved a fellow as couldn't love her back. Just like me.'

'Well, what do you expect me to do about it?'

'You could help me, if you wanted to. You could do anything.'

'Nonsense!'

'If you did help me to stay young I'd give you all I've got.'

'Not much. I seem to have had it already.'

'That's what I mean about you. You're cruel, Leo, you don't care.'

'Don't play the tragedy queen. It doesn't suit you. Your nose goes red and your powder clogs. You remind me of poor Dan Leno who wanted to play Hamlet. Not that you have a tenth of his talent. What is it you want?'

'I want to stay young. I don't want the gin to fog my brain, don't want to end up broken at fifty like Marie Lloyd. Please.'

'Let's examine this little transaction. Are you religious?'

'My auntie took me to the synagogue once. There was chanting and candles and men downstairs with beards and funny hats.'

'So much for your soul. And your talent as an artiste?'

'What about it?'

'Ten years' hard labour I've invested in you. And at the end of it you can just about carry a tune and show your legs and bust to advantage. At least you're not bottom of the bill any more.'

'I know I'll never be a real headliner. But what good did it do her? Fifty thousand people at her funeral this morning, there was. Twelve cars full of flowers, there was a model of a stage and her old cock linnet's cage, with the door open, all done in roses and carnations. And on top of her hearse there was the ebony cane with the diamante top she used for "The Directoire Dress". Dillon was all on his lonesome in one of the cars, and the crowd booed and groaned at him, the pot-house black-guard. And all the pubs in Golders Green was draped in black –'

'Well, she was a pretty good customer.'

'Don't laugh! I went to see her at the Bedford a few months back. Did I tell you? She looked ancient, although she was only fifty-two. Long yellow teeth, came waddling on to the stage like an old man in drag. "One of the Ruins that Cromwell knocked about a bit" . . . Her voice was so weak the other artists had to sing along with her. I cried. And the whole bloody audience roared with laughter. They all knew Dillon knocked her about.'

'Well, I may have my faults, but I don't beat you. Anyway, why should you worry? You're young and beautiful and successful.'

'Now – with you to push and bully me and fight for my contracts. I'm not half as good as her anyway. Dunno why you bother.'

'You amuse me. Not much does. But you're not amusing when you're miserable like this. How can I cheer you up?'

'Don't let me get old.'

'You're only twenty-five, you silly girl.'

'And after a few more years like this, working the provincial halls and boozing, I'll look forty. Don't let that happen.'

'How can I stop it?'

'You can, you know you can. You can do anything.'

'Pure fantasy. You're not entirely without talent. Men like you.'

'Is that a talent?'

'Most certainly. Would you give up your ha'penny-worth of stardom to stay twenty-five for ever?'

''Course I would. But what would you get out of it?'

'Company. A warm heart in a chilly world.'

'And what would I have to do?'

'Very little. Play the eternal *ingénue*. And, of course, you would have to love me.'

'I don't love you, you bastard.'

'Then your duties should be quite light. Are you sure you really want to go ahead with this?'

''Course I do. If it's a joke it's a bloody good one. How could I turn it down?'

'Exactly. Now this won't hurt.'

'What the hell are you doing to me now?'

'Just a prick. Blood's a very special kind of ink. As they say.'

'Blood? No! Leo, this isn't funny any more . . .'

He leans over me, and there's blood – or is it red wine? – on the white table-cloth. Red where my pale arm meets the shiny jet beads of my dress. Leo stoops over me with creamy parchment in his hand and makes me sign something. Then he swells until his shadow fills the ceiling, the candles are extinguished and Leo and I disappear in a kind of giant *flambé*, an explosion of light. As we float away I see George staring up at us, looking very small and puzzled.

Eugenie

A few months later the first accident happens. Leo doesn't like the stage manager at the Holborn Empire, Gerry, a fat little ginger beer, very good at his job but not much charm about him. He likes to know everything that's happening backstage, and he keeps asking Leo how his act works. Leo can't abide questions – after ten years he still hasn't told me where he was born or where his family is or whether he's ever been married. Thing about Leo is, you have to handle him carefully, and I do. I reckon he's been good to me and we still have a great time in bed, so I don't ask too many questions.

But Gerry keeps asking questions, like how can he do all those tricks without any wires or special lighting effects. One evening before the show I'm in Leo's dressing-room when Gerry comes in and starts up again. 'I've been thinking about what you said this afternoon, and I'm not happy about it.' Leo's just putting on his greasepaint, he's glued on half his moustachios and one side of his face is all white and red and black. He fixes his eyes on Gerry in the mirror, and I want to warn the poor little sod. 'It's simply impossible, what you do.'

'Are you complaining about Pantoffsky's act?' I'm in my Little Dutch Girl costume. My clogs are killing me, but I give him a smile that's meant to disarm him. 'Seems to me he gets more applause than any of us.'

'I'm not denying the audiences like it, but I want an explanation. I'm responsible for what happens in this theatre, and I like to feel I'm in control.'

Leo laughs. I don't like the sound of that laugh at all, only I have to go on so I leave them to it.

I finish my act and the audience liked me, so I'm high on that hot tingly feeling, like I've just made love to five hundred people. I hang around in the wings giggling and gossiping with the other girls. Gerry's like a bloody sergeant major backstage; he fines us for talking or smoking or drinking. You can tell he's not here tonight because we're all having a good time. Then one of the boys needs help shifting the scenery from windmills to Lambeth for the 'Coster's Serenade', and Miss May Mason the Miraculous Living Marionette can't find her strings, so we start to look for Gerry.

They find him strung up from the flies at the top of the theatre with a wire around his neck and a note stuck to his forehead saying, 'How did he do it?' We finish the show, of course. We're pros after all, but there's police all over the building and we're not allowed to leave the theatre.

I'm sitting in my dressing-room, half naked, with my face smothered in cold cream, when there's a knock and I think it's Leo being politer than usual. It's a policeman, plain clothes, so I know he means business. I show him all I've got and hope he'll take advantage of me, give me time to think up a few boomers, but he starts firing questions at me right away. Who is this Great Pantoffsky? What's his real name? How long have I known him? Was there any bad feeling between him and the deceased? I just have to answer quick as I can, and it's just as well I don't know much, but I am shocked. I'm no angel and I've seen violence all my life, but murder's out of my league and I want it to stay there.

I'm shaking when I leave the theatre, and I'm glad George isn't waiting at the stage door. I wouldn't want him mixed up in this. I always thought the police were stupid, but when I get to Leo's rooms in Fitzroy Street at one in the morning they've been and gone. Those rooms that once impressed me so much are a pigsty. There's papers everywhere, and that Turkish rug and the leather armchairs I learnt so much on are all slashed to pieces. The landlady tries to get me to pay for the damage. She chases me downstairs demanding money, and by the time I get home to my room in Gower Street I'm terrified.

The newspapers love it, of course. They're at the theatre every day, then they find out where I live and wait for me outside my front door, too. Mysterious Murdering Magician's Floozy. I thought it would be a lark to be famous, but I hate this. Can't sleep or eat or concentrate, and I fluff and stumble in my act and the management are looking for an excuse to sack me when the show folds anyway. I won't talk to anybody, and when I do all I say is it was an accident and Leo and I had a purely professional relationship. George turns up at the stage door on my last night, but I can't face anybody so I pretend I haven't seen him, go back upstairs, sneak out down the fire escape stairs, go home and lock myself in my room.

Thing about being with Leo was I never had to be afraid of anything. He always knew what to do and say, how to get money and food and clothes. It takes me a few weeks to realize he really has disappeared, and I don't know what I feel. Love? I miss him, but I don't know who it is I'm missing. I'm angry with him for leaving me in the lurch. It's like Ma all over again, only this time I really am alone. Can't go back to Auntie Flo, and all I know about Lizzie is she's gone off to South Africa.

London audiences want musical comedies now, with plots and characters, however absurd. I've auditioned for a couple, but I didn't get the parts. Magicians and charming soprano vocalists are going on tour in the provinces, doing theatres at the ends of piers in summer, and I don't fancy that. Leo was my agent as well as everything else, so if I'm going to work in the theatre I'll have to find myself a new agent as well as a new name.

Luckily Binkie's investments have gone up, so if I can find somewhere cheap to live I won't need to work, which is, I imagine, the height of glamour; to have my own house abroad, expensive clothes and time and space and servants – the fantasy of the chorus girl who marries a duke only without the nuisance of the duke himself. If Vesta Tilley can become Lady de Frece, why shouldn't I live it up on the Riviera, too? The only French I know is 'twiggy voo' and I've never even been to the 'Naughty Continong'.

I get a passport in the name of Mrs Eugenie Bishop. A widow's more stylish than an out-of-work chanteuse; all the prettiest women in the twenties are war widows. I find our marriage certificate under my bed. Leo produced it one weekend when we wanted to stay in a stuffy hotel in Cheltenham – but I don't allow myself to think of him.

I don't tell anybody I'm leaving the country because I know the police are still pursuing their inquiries and I don't want them pursuing me. I pack my Louis Vuitton trunk, get a taxi to Victoria and take the boat train late one night. Northern France looks too much like England, so I just keep going south until I get to the Riviera.

Although I'm not exactly the man who broke the bank at Monte Carlo I've enough to buy new clothes, stay in good hotels and eat wonderfully in restaurants. I soon make friends and learn to flirt in French and Italian. I never knew there was a place like this, where it's perpetual summer and nobody works. That's not quite true of course; the fishermen and hoteliers and waiters work hard to pamper the rest of us, guests at a never-ending party. The Riviera is still a string of fishing villages, mellow slabs of colour baking in that golden Mediterranean light. There's no grey in the sea or the sky or the faces around me; sun and colour go to my head, I gulp beauty down, inhale it, dive into it as I learn to swim in the generous sea that links the jewels of this coast.

For a year I explore, moving from village to village, hardly able to believe my freedom and happiness. One afternoon I take the train to Rapallo, and when I see those ochre, rose, yellow and burnt-sienna houses reflected in the bay I know I want to stay here. I rent a villa in the hills behind the town.

The Villa Ginestra is a crumbling rose-pink building set in the green, rocky hillside studded with its namesake broom. There's a terrace overlooking the bay, and whenever I look out over my view I see Auntie Flo's house like a shadow behind the glory of sapphire, turquoise, emerald, yellow and pink. Can't remember hiring Assunta. I've never had a servant before, and she isn't one really, more of a friend.

If you're going to eat lotuses, Italy's the place to do it. I enjoy being Eugenie. That extra syllable raises my head and makes me feel digni-fied. Italians take people at face value, so when I tell everybody I've been a famous music-hall star I become one. My husband was a handsome young officer killed at Ypres. Not so long ago I'd have said 'Wipers', but my French and Italian have become fluent and my English is improving, too. Vowels and aitches flow naturally now, and words that would once have defeated me come sailing out of my mouth.

At first I think our paradise is classless, but I soon learn the invisible ropes. At the top there are the kosher aristocrats and the genuine artists whose work they buy. They sit in the same bars and restaurants as me, but I don't dare talk to them. My friends are flappers and flibbertigibbets and gamblers and drunks, younger sons and divorcees, poets and painters who never quite get around to writing or painting. We have wonderful parties in my villa that start with booze and end up in bed or on the beach.

I avoid the casinos along that coast because my memories of poverty are too vivid to allow me to play with money. But one day Assunta says, 'You should buy your house, signora.'

'Can't afford to.' My investments have survived the 1929 crash, when so many of my drinking companions disappeared, but my income is barely enough for rent, booze and food.

'I will show you where money is piled like ripe fruit at the foot of a tree.' Assunta has a very poetic way of expressing herself. Sometimes I wonder why she doesn't get a better job. I think she's joking, but the next afternoon she lays out my green Schiaparelli dress and tells me she's ordered a car to take us into Monte. On the ravishing drive she sits beside me in her black dress, her black hair drawn back into a bun, her brown, oval face fierce with concentration as if she is drawing all the brilliant colour and energy out of the landscape and into herself.

At the casino I'm nervous and cling to Assunta. I don't understand the games that whizz and rattle and whisper in the smoky darkness. If I were alone I would run away from this ritual, from the chanting croupier priests and the silent initiates, the radiant and the ruined. Assunta takes my arm and guides me to a long green-baize-covered table where faces are illuminated moons floating amid the shadows. The other women, like me, wear vivid evening dresses, heavy makeup and jewellery. Assunta in her plain dark clothes is almost invisible, like a Bunraku puppet master.

Assunta asks me for ten thousand lire, changes them into chips, piles them in front of me, whispers a number, tells me to back it and push the chips forward. We join in the collective gasp as the roulette wheel spins capriciously. When it stops hers is the only stifled laugh of triumph as the chips are raked towards me.

My passive silence is rewarded with more money than I could have earned in forty years in the feather factory. After a couple of hours she leans over to me and whispers, 'You have the price of your house. We can go now.'

In the car on the way home she looks exhausted. 'Congratulations, signora.'

'But I didn't do anything.'

'You won.'

'No, you did. This money should belong to you. Are you a gambler, Assunta?'

'Not this time.'

Later that month I buy the Villa Ginestra and also, for Assunta, the cottage on the beach where she lives with Stefano, her fisherman lover.

All this time I miss you, Leo. I don't know who you are or where you are or even if you're still alive, but my other lovers – and there are many – can't replace you. When I think of London it's you I remember, our love-making and fights and passionate reconciliations. You were never violent with me, and I no longer believe you could have killed poor Gerry. You are the one I talk to in my head, the face I search for in the crowd. You know me better than anybody.

But I don't miss Lizzie, and when she writes to say that she has returned from South Africa and wants to see me I don't bother to reply. Her semi-literate note and whining tone remind me of a self I want to obliterate.

You always said it was dangerous to be blind to politics. The Fascist youth parades in Rapallo throughout the twenties and thirties seem as remote as the Changing of the Guard, games played by people in silly costumes. I stay out of the arguments that rage around me over Franco and Hitler and Musso and Stalin and never read newspapers.

I go on ignoring Fascism until the summer of 1939, when it comes to my doorstep in the form of an Italian officer who asks me to use my 'famous voice' to broadcast propaganda. Although the officer is handsome I don't like his script, full of platitudes about love of nation and family. I don't give a damn about either and object to his bombastic style, so I refuse to cooperate. Nobody here knows I'm Jewish, but I hate their anti-Semitic rants. It's as if I've just woken up after years of sleep-walking. The light musical comedy I thought I was starring in has turned to heavy tragedy, and there are no parts for me. I'm not a bit heroic but I am bloody-minded enough to risk my property, which, I know, will be requisitioned as soon as I leave Italy. I suddenly long to return to London, to find you and my friends, if any of you are still alive. I know George is because I've had a couple of letters from him.

If I'm going to return to London I have to decide who will be returning. One night after my bath I stare at myself in the long mirror in my dressing-room. My biological age, forty-two, is about twenty years older than my reflection. I could wear a wig, ageing makeup, dress dowdily, but all these options seem perverse, like a millionaire who refuses to spend any money. For the first time I believe in that bargain I struck with you that night at Giulini's. I want to enjoy every moment of my eternal youth. So I invent my daughter, Virginia, a shy young thing whose mother has sent her to safety in London. I've had enough of glorious isolation. I've proved that I can live without you and now I want you again.

Italy is a country of bureaucracy and forged documents, and I have no trouble at all buying a passport for my *alter ego*.

'Come with me,' I say to Assunta as I lean out of the window of the train to hug her goodbye.

'No, he wouldn't like that.'

'Who?'

But she's shrinking, receding, a waving insect and then a speck of dust in the sunset bathing the town I never expect to see again.

Virginia

The prospect of having to fend for myself in London, of being open to surprises again, is so exciting that I can't sleep a wink on the train.

I arrive at Victoria with a crocodile handbag stuffed with cash and my trunk packed with clothes and jewellery, wearing a deep-blue coat as if I've brought a piece of the Mediterranean with me. The murky gloom of my city is at first a shock, but I'm deliriously happy to be back.

You are on the platform in a blue Air Force uniform.

'You're not really here,' I say, squeezing and pinching you as we kiss. 'You can't be. Nobody knew I was coming.'

'Do you like my uniform?'

'No. The opera cloak and the Harlequin costume were melodramatic but they suited you. The idea of you as a soldier –'

'A pilot.'

'An anything that takes orders. Anyway, why join up now? There might not even be a war.'

'I like to be ahead of the game.'

'Where are we going?' I ask as we get into a taxi.

'I've bought a little flat in St James's Square.'

Before I have time to notice what your flat is like we're on the bed in a private universe of tongue, skin and touch. You're inside me again, and we're both murmuring words of love and need.

Late that night I wake to find you asleep on my shoulder. Our clothes are heaped all over the floor in the dark like a stormy ocean, and my heart is churning. I slip out from under you and wander naked around the flat. It's tiny, just a double bed behind a Japanese screen, a miniature living-room and bathroom and a kitchen in an alcove where I make myself a cup of proper tea. It never tasted right in Italy.

'Come back, Jenny.' I'm amazed by the need in your voice. 'Did you miss me?' you ask when we're in each other's arms again.

'Sometimes.' My pride reasserts itself. 'But I enjoyed living by myself. I had plenty of friends and I read a lot, went for walks and swam – it was a good life.'

'Jenny the contemplative nun.' He laughs. 'You must have been bored stiff.'

'I wasn't!'

'That's why wars happen, of course. People just get bored with ordinary life. It's so bloody dull going to the same job every day, sleeping with the same man or woman, living in the same house for twenty years. So people create ideas like heroism and patriotism and pretend another group of poor sods are evil just so that they can entertain themselves by killing them off.'

'That's outrageous! Hitler *is* evil. We can't just let him take Europe over. You seem to forget I'm Jewish, although I kept very quiet about it in Fascist Italy. I know what you mean by propaganda – as a matter of fact I left Italy because the authorities were trying to make use of me. But now I'm back, if there is a war I'll do my bit.'

'Will you, Jenny? Am I your bit? Everyone loves us pilots, you know.'

'Will you really fly? It might be dangerous.'

'Not for me, silly. Have you forgotten?'

'I'm not sure what I want to remember about you.'

Later that morning you leave for a training camp in Oxfordshire. Or so you claim. I stay on in the tiny flat. No other interior in my life has contained me so embracingly, like a mussel in a shell. Even after war is declared I feel safe there, alone during the long periods when you're flying.

One evening during the first April of the war I go to Hammum's Turkish baths in Jermyn Street. Outside, on the pavement, there's a tramp asleep on the hot air that blows up through the grating. I step over him – remembering my father who died drunk and homeless on the streets of Whitechapel – without any guilt. We who reinvent ourselves, moving freely from class to class and age to age, can't afford to be sentimental. Inside, down in the steamy basement, the all-night baths have become a smart place to sit out air raids.

'Jenny!'

I smile into George's face as I lie. 'I don't think I know you. Are you a friend of my mother's?'

'You must be Virginia. I'm George Dumphry. What on earth are you doing in London?' We're squeezed together in the narrow tiled entrance.

I'm so pleased to see him that I can hardly keep my hands off him, but I try to look demure. I haven't yet decided on a personality for my daughter. 'I've borrowed a flat around the corner from a friend of Mummy's. She wanted to stay in Italy.'

'You look so like her – when I first met her, twenty years ago. Quite extraordinary.'

'I know. Everybody tells me that.'

'But is she all right, all alone in Rapallo? Shouldn't we try to get her out?'

'She says she won't budge. She's got lots of friends in Italy. I don't think she'll be badly treated.'

'Well, if you say so. She always was pretty good at looking after herself. How grown-up you look, my dear. You can't be more than – eighteen? Too young to be alone in London.'

I smile. I've decided to be vague about my age and notice that George is looking his. 'I've never been to a Turkish bath before. Would you mind showing me what to do?'

George looks after me chivalrously. Later, when we meet in one of the rest rooms, the eroticism of our situation disturbs him. I sit beside him on the marble bench, wrapped in a towel with a great expanse of flesh visible, touchable, desirable. He can't help staring to check my uncanny resemblance to myself – the mole on my upper right arm, my sharp collarbones and long toes. I try not to laugh at his amazement.

'You're married now, aren't you, Mr Dumphry?'

'Yes. Very much so. Molly and I have two children. Christopher's still at school, and Helen's not much younger than you.'

'Are your family in London?'

'No, much too dangerous. They're in Brighton. I organize shows for ENSA.' He watches me watch the half-naked men. 'Curious upbringing you must have had on the Riviera.'

'Yes, I suppose I did.'

Later we have dinner together at a restaurant opposite the Ritz, the San Marco, a tiny replica of the Doge's Palace.

'Do you have theatrical ambitions, Virginia, like your mother?'

'I think I'm too shy to go on the stage.' No need to, really, when my whole life has become a performance.

'I often come here. I love the décor, don't you? Specially that little Venetian balcony with no way up, and the table exquisitely laid for a supper nobody will ever eat.'

In his fantasy I know George is sitting up there with his Jenny, who isn't me. And I project you up on to the balcony. Chatting to George, I miss you horribly. I long to talk to you or at least about you – George is one of the few people who still remembers you – but how could I explain? I still feel deep affection for him, but he makes me feel a bitch, whereas, compared with you, I always feel good.

'Tell me about Molly. Is she beautiful?'

'Oh dear, are you going to report back to your mother?'

'Of course. I'll have to send a full description in my next letter, only it'll probably be censored. Well? Is she?'

'Molly is – quite short, with wavy strawberry-blonde hair and a sweet smile. She's a good cook and very maternal and loyal . . .'

'The complete opposite to my mother, in other words.'

'Well, yes. And she adores me and I adore her, and I know she'll never leave me.'

'Whatever you did?'

'Of course I try to be considerate.' He beams with the happiness of the securely loved. As if his ego has been polished and varnished. Perhaps she does it with a duster and a brush each morning.

'I hope she won't mind your having dinner with me.'

'Of course not. I'm practically your uncle.'

'London seems to be full of my practical uncles and fathers.'

'I dare say.' He laughs uncomfortably.

'One of them has lent me this dear little flat in St James's Square. Would you like to come back for a cup of beastly chicory coffee?'

'No thank you, my dear. I must try to get back to Brighton tonight, the trains are so erratic.'

George parts from me with barely disguised relief as if he has escaped from a carnivorous fawn.

My longing for you is visceral. I stare up at our flat from the pavement, and my heart ticks like a bomb when I see the light is on. Meeting George has crystallized my feelings for you; it was fun to flirt with him and eye all those men's bodies, but I know that what I feel for you is real passion.

You sprawl in the armchair beside the gas fire, still in your flying jacket. I run to hug you, kneeling on the floor. When the gas fire scorches my dress I unbutton it and climb into the chair with you. 'You didn't tell me you were coming tonight. I just had dinner with George.' 'How was he? Still daft?' 'Still sweet. And I've been missing you so much. Let's go to bed.' As I lead you there, I say happily, 'I get sick of pretending to be my own daughter. It's only with each other that we can be ourselves.' 'Whoever that might be.' 'Leo, darling, I think it's so wonderful that you've joined the war effort. You can do so much, with your powers. Where have you just flown back from?' 'I can't really . . .' 'Of course, it's all hush-hush. Sorry, I forgot.' In the dark room in the dark city we sink into the black-out of love.

I often relive those first happy years of the war. Can't bear to turn the page, to remember the rest, never have since I killed Virginia off. Until September 1940 the war's a stage where you and I perform: the brave pilot and his sex bomb, dancing seductively. The Ritzkrieg. London is hardly bombed during that first year, and, although I realize people are dying, they are outside our magic circle. Eternal youth doesn't do much for your public spirit.

London feels cosy, almost like a village. Shopping in Peter Jones one day I hear two women talking about Flossie and Blossom and realize they're talking about the huge blimps that hang over Chelsea. In St James's Square my neighbours dig allotments and argue about whether or not to melt down the distinguished railings to help the war effort. I want to believe that barrage balloons and allotments will beat Hitler, and I'm happy to call it the phoney war like everyone else.

For years my personal map of London has cut off at the City. I rarely think about my childhood and never with any nostalgia. My sister Lizzie is posed for ever, a little girl in a white night-dress in a room so cold that condensation freezes on the cracked windows. Yet when I hear about the bombing of the East End on the radio one morning my convenient amnesia reverses. Lizzie sprouts breasts and a middle-aged face that stares at me reproachfully.

I find the note from my sister I so callously ignored in Rapallo and go off to search for her. Because transport is so haphazard I walk, and by the time I arrive in Hoxton my feet are bleeding. Exhausted, I try to orientate myself in an unmappable wasteland of craters, barbed wire and rubble. London's intestines have been ripped out, exposing a crazy biology of drains, sewers and foundations where the mutilated countryside gapes through ruined houses. The earth that the buildings smothered breathes again but only to groan with pain. As I watch rescue workers carry dozens of corpses out of the bombed houses I give up my idea of searching for Lizzie. I weep for the sister I never knew I loved as dust rises in the autumn sun, glazing the scene red like a painting of the desert.

On the long walk home, my eyes streaming with dust and grief, I visualize the destruction of the rest of my city. I'll never again look at a building without seeing it uprooted; behind every house on every street is its ghostly bomb site. The ritual precautions of the black-out seem like the game small children play, when they shut their eyes and pretend they can't be seen. Finally I understand what this war means. Everyone is saying the Nazis will invade now.

The next day I volunteer at the Women's National Auxiliary Council of the YMCA. They ask me to run a mobile canteen, and I'm pathetically grateful to be of use. At first I'm horrified by the dismal food I serve: meat pies, slab cake, sausage rolls and jam tarts. It's all grimly unappetizing and cold, but the demolition squads are so hungry they seize on it with whoops of joy as they light up the cigarettes I also bring. Only the tea is hot, stewed in an urn in the corner of my van. After a few weeks I'm ravenous enough to eat the most brick-like meat pie and no longer speculate about what's inside.

Between October and November London is bombed every night and sometimes there are nine raids in a day. I'm thankful to be in my van instead of shivering in a cellar, and I enjoy joking with the other women and flirting with the men. In my green overall, up to my ankles in a sludge of swilling milk and tea, bumping through the devastated back streets from bomb site to bomb site, I feel a part of London life and death.

One afternoon I'm on a bomb site behind Holborn, where spring in the form of grass and weeds and wild flowers already nuzzles the ruins. A couple of ARP wardens, middle-aged men who survived the Great War, have found a crate of ancient beige lace camiknickers in the bombed-out cellar of a shop. They're throwing them at each other, and when we drive up, late as usual, they throw them at us. Soon half a dozen of us are standing around on the rubble and broken glass, screaming with laughter. We're looting, depriving His Majesty's Government of rotting bloomers as our spontaneous party makes us forget the war for a few minutes.

I flirt with all these men and sometimes have a few drinks with them but always make it clear that I'm going home to my flyboy. Whenever you come home on your unpredictable leave we spend blissful nights together.

July 1944, just after D-Day. You've sent a telegram to say you'll be back tonight, and at one in the morning I'm waiting for you in a frenzy of love. Whenever a plane flies overhead I imagine you piloting it and feel mingled pride and lust. Sprawling by the gas fire in my oyster satin night-dress I only want to love you with all my heart, without any more doubts or suspicions or complications.

I fall asleep, and when I wake up you're standing over me. We make love on the floor before moving over to the bed where we are still hungry for each other. I think of the Italian word for cunt: *fica*. Yes, I feel like a fig turned inside out: wet, soft, ravenous flesh. We make love again and again until daylight glows behind the red curtains and you fall asleep inside me.

I slide out from under you, my muscles contracting as if they want to hold you inside me for ever. You turn on to your side, and I stare at you. Your brown hair is very short and your cheekbones are prominent in your tanned face. Your shoulders and arms are muscular, and your mouth twitches as you mutter in your sleep. I long to eavesdrop on your dreams. I want to live simply with you in kindness and trust. If I could do that, perhaps I'd give up all this nonsense about eternal youth. But you wouldn't want me unless I was young.

I make a cup of revolting Camp coffee and some toast and sit by the gas fire, looking at our clothes strewn all over the floor. Mechanically, I tidy them. As I lift your flying jacket documents slide out of the pockets and I look at them idly, smiling with affection as I flick through your small blue canvas logbook, with its record of every flight you've made. In your passport photograph you look absurdly young and goofy. The ordinariness of these documents touches me. Then I notice another passport and another logbook, with German on their covers; and that one, surely, is Russian, and that other passport is Japanese – multiple Leos stare up at me, round stamps like halos celebrating your heroism. Uneasily, I shuffle the documents like cards. When you were the Great Pantoffsky you used to do card tricks, and I wonder what tricks you're playing now.

I pile all your documents on the mantelpiece, let you sleep until eleven and then bring you breakfast on a tray. You wake up and stretch, displaying your slim powerful naked torso. I nuzzle your shoulder and lick your nipple. Then, although I'm weak with desire, I pull back.

'I naïvely thought you were just in the RAF.'

'Breakfast! How lovely! You've given me all your jam ration, noble girl. I'll bring you some more.'

'Where from? Germany? Russia?'

'You've been snooping in my pockets.'

'They fell out. Are you angry?'

'Not at all. There's far too much anger around. You people take war so seriously, as if it makes any difference who kills whom. It's all just an expensive excuse for reducing the population and trying out new weapons. I had such fun yesterday, flying above the clouds somewhere over Poland. Now I've got my wings I can go anywhere; ironic really when my own were confiscated aeons ago. You should come with me one day, my darling. I often think of you in my lonely cockpit.' You press my hand on your cock under the sheets, but I draw back.

'Do you? But, Leo, I thought you were flying for us.'

You roar with laughter. 'Us! Them! Why should I restrict myself to one nation, when each of them has its propaganda machine? And how persuasive they all are! Civil wars are the most entertaining, when you can play off father against son, friend against friend. I thoroughly enjoyed Spain. And revolutions give one unique scope for creativity. My favourite was the French one, which finally persuaded me you people are far more interested in death than in any aspect of life.

'I try to keep an open mind, to see both sides of every argument. Some days I love Communism. It's so logical and so hilarious when people are surprised it doesn't work. I get on awfully well with Stalin; we have long talks into the night. And Hitler also has loads of charisma. I like a man who's got the guts to make really vast mistakes. There's nothing like a bit of Fascism to improve a country's infrastructure; after all, he did reduce unemployment from six million to three hundred thousand in six years. And how attractive America is, that clean-limbed look combined with the utter corruption of their public life – and Italians are so charming, they make Fascism quite sexy – no, no, I couldn't just stay in the dreary old RAF.'

'But you must be killing people. Our people.'

'They would have died anyway. I had no idea you were such a chauvinist.'

'I saw what the Luftwaffe did to the East End. Dead and wounded everywhere, a whole chunk of London destroyed. My streets. My sister's probably dead.'

'Don't look at me like that, Jenny. I'm not responsible for all this. I might join in with gusto – oh, all right, I do – but the collective madness is already there: bombs being hurled like fireworks; aeroplanes diving to oblivion; young men queuing up to die. It's all a game and the players love it, gambling their lives away for a few seconds of excitement. Why would there be wars all the time if people didn't want them?'

'That's ridiculous. This war is about ideas and individual freedom.

They're killing Jews in Germany, and I'm Jewish. There *is* a right side, and I thought you were on it.'

You reach out to touch my angry tears. 'Does it hurt when you do that?'

'What? Cry? Haven't you ever cried?'

'Certainly not. Messy. I thought you understood what was going on, Jenny, but you seem determined to cling to your illusion: the innocent young thing led astray by her demon lover. Aren't you getting on a bit for that? Well, perhaps you need your story just as much as all these others need theirs: patriotism and glory and heroism and so on. I never can decide if you lot, human beings I mean, really want to be alive at all. But you, my darling Jenny, don't have that dilemma.'

You lift your coffee cup to toast me. 'You've cheated death, thanks to me. Just because I got drunk all those years ago and decided I wanted a companion, a spot of warmth in a cold, nasty world, an emotional consultant. I never aspired to love. That's your job. But you'll find your feelings stretch a little thinner each century. It's not easy, this immortality. I'm surprised you can still cry about death. You'll get used to it.'

'No I won't.' I stand at the foot of the bed and stare at the man I've loved so humanly all night.

'The common people always suffer. That's what they're for, they're just the dull victims of the events we control. But you and I have risen above that, Jenny. Jenny?'

I walk out of your flat and go to the Turkish bath in Jermyn Street. Wrapped in towels, my pores open, my mind clogged with steam, I try to sweat you out of my system. When that doesn't work I pick up a naval officer on leave, who takes me out to lunch at the Hungaria. The gypsy band and the Bulls' Blood wine turn day into night, and we go back to his flat. The next morning, when he returns to his wife in Portsmouth, I sit in a pub in Charlotte Street until another man offers me a drink.

The following week I meet George again at the Ritz. I dance a tango with him, stripping as I dance, but when I'm down to my underwear and one earring the air-raid siren goes off and I have to descend to the shelter, shivering and giggling, supported by George. His face expresses a mixture of desire, amusement and disgust that becomes very familiar to me. As Virginia, I booze and bonk my way through the next year. Of course, wartime London is full of men and women who use alcohol and indiscriminate sex as anaesthetics. And very effective they are, too. I can't remember much about the rest of the war.

Leo's War

During the war I really did think we were happy together. THE war! When you've seen as many wars as I have you can't help sniggering at the first rattling of sabres. When Assunta told me Jenny was coming back from Italy I was determined to make her stay with me. My Don Juan phase had lasted for several thousand years, but I knew it was over. Women still queued up to be seduced, and I obliged. But only out of politeness.

When I see Jenny again at Victoria Station I know she is the woman I want. I join the Air Force mainly to impress her, aware that my uniform and swashbuckling anecdotes will be terrific aphrodisiacs. The little flat in St James's Square is my first property venture, bought with a mortgage from the Fizz. I want to stay in this flat with her and make love to her for ever, but I know she'll despise me, as she did during the Great War, if I don't fight. So I play along with the jingoism Jenny is simple-minded enough to believe in.

I go off to flying school at RAF Brize Norton expecting to be bored and disgusted, but, in fact, pilot training is the boyhood I never had. My fellow students are a group of eighteen-year-olds in grey flannels and open-neck shirts, English public schoolboys who call each other Tubby and Rotter and Lofty and Ginger. I am Holy, because my papers describe me as Leopold Bishop, born in London in 1912. In order to be accepted for pilot training I have to invent a pedigree: Shrewsbury, Oxford, Mummy and Daddy in Gerrards Cross, a passion for the football and cricket that seem to be the officers' favourite metaphors for war. I can just about pass for twenty-seven, a year too old to lead a squadron – not that I'd want to – and nine years older than most of the others. Their youth startles me. I can't look into their fresh, pink, hopeful faces without seeing them as they will be when they have melted and liquefied, just as I can never see a flower in bloom without simultaneously seeing it withered. I can't help but see the tears in things.

Their annihilation takes months, not seconds. I have time to watch them turn from deferential children into wild, self-destructive young men, those whom the gods love – the gods, of course, have no feelings whatsoever, but I sometimes wonder how parents can bear to let their sons die so young. Why don't they sacrifice themselves, those middle-aged men who are already so bored with their one life that they have to start a war to entertain themselves? Death is impatient for these handsome young men. Before they even have time to get to the war Ginger and Rotter are killed when their plane crashes during a long cross-country night flight.

Flying, like conjuring, depends on timing, and mine is rather good. I'm charmed by the rudimentary little bundles of wood and metal, by my sexy leather jacket, Very pistol and Mae West lifejacket. Flying reminds me of other, earlier thrills, of riding and hunting. I love my machines much as I once adored my horses and can't resist showing off. Of course, it is an advantage not to need a parachute, and I was navigating by the stars before Odysseus was born. I don't really need the Bradshaw Method – steering by following railway lines – and before I've completed my training I am something of a legend, no longer Holy but Lucky.

A drinking bout in a pub in Banbury with my first crew; we're all stamping and yelling as Tubby drinks a bottle of whisky in ten minutes. Lofty burns his girlfriend's initials on to his arm with a lighted cigarette. The landlord and the locals tolerate our wild behaviour because we're young and brave and doomed. We? If I had to join a group of one-lifers perhaps I'd choose this one.

Walking through the frozen mud to our aeroplanes, in a landing field miles from the aerodrome, it's so cold that our clothes freeze as twenty-seven Whitleys take off together. Tubby loses his nose from frostbite, a little hors d'oeuvre for death before the rest of his face is consumed by fire a month later. It's like the rhyme children chant to cherry stones: schoolboy, hero, monster, corpse. These young pilots have as much faith in their immortality as I do in mine. They hang up mascots in the cockpit to ward off death: Tubby's is his girlfriend's stocking; mine is one of Cleopatra's teeth set in a lump of lapis lazuli; and Lofty's is a home-made teddy bear with a face as blunt and blind as his own becomes after he crashes. What was the name of our wireless operator? So many names and dates forgotten.

I've finished my OTU and have finally joined my squadron when I receive the summons from the Fizz. Nothing so obvious as a letter, of course. I'm flying over France one day when I hear the words in my head in impeccable commercial Latin: go to the world centre of the Banca Metafisica on Wednesday afternoon at three. When I return to the aerodrome the next morning there's a telegram telling me that my mother in Gerrards Cross has had a heart attack. Impressed by their efficiency, I present myself on Wednesday at High Street Kensington.

In the late thirties the Fizz had moved from the dingy old office in Lombard Street where ancient dust settled on even more ancient documents. Over the centuries I had an undistinguished relationship with them. I was usually in debt and obliged to work off my overdraft by pimping for convent girls or spreading syphilis – anything to avoid their debtors' prison in the salt mines of Siberia. In the early twenties, when the investments Binkie left Jenny suddenly went up, I awarded myself a 50 per cent cut. (She didn't even notice; she's always been hopeless about money.) When she flitted off to Italy I was able to give up the squalid life of a second-rate conjuror and reinvent myself as a fairly bright, youngish thing in London. But the power of the Fizz was always there.

So I am nervous when I walk into the bland new bank for the first time. My RAF uniform attracts comforting smiles from two old ladies in hats and veils and gloves who are cashing cheques. A clerk leads me through a door in the panelling into a vast room. Above a chandelier, on the domed ceiling, there is a Michelangelesque painting of the money-changers throwing Jesus out of the temple, watched approvingly by thuggish-looking angels on blowsy clouds. A large man with a heavy-jowled face sits behind an enormous carved desk, his bald, squarish head almost covered by a vast birthmark. As I approach I see that it's a shifting map of the world, also that he is wearing an SS uniform.

'Ah, Leo, do sit down. I've been wanting to meet you for centuries.'

I am not often lost for words, but I really don't know how to address him as Outer Mongolia flickers above his Reichsmarschall's uniform. Should I salute or genuflect or shake his hand? He clicks his fingers impatiently, shouting at the ceiling, 'Can we have something a little less time specific?' The SS uniform is transformed into a yellow crinoline and bonnet, then a toga, and finally settles into a well-cut three-piece suit. The familiar coastline of England and France hovers across his face.

'Sit down, sit down, don't be a stranger. Just call me Your Almighty Excellency.' He looks through some papers on his desk. 'Brilliant war record, just what we're looking for. How would you like to help us with some research?'

'What kind of research?' I ask, trying to see his eyes, which are obscured by Poland.

'Technical stuff. The Bank's expanding, and after all this nonsense is over there will be a lot of money to be made in aviation. We need detailed plans and photographs of different aeroplanes – German, Japanese and Russian to start with. We're particularly interested in this pilotless plane the Germans are supposed to be developing.'

'When *will* all this nonsense be over? And who is going to win?' I ask cautiously.

'Your guess is as good as mine. We take the pragmatic, international view, as you know. Old Schickelgruber may not have a brilliant record on human rights, but at least he has a vision. Today he's the favourite in the casino downstairs, twenty to one last time I looked, but tomorrow it could be Uncle Joe or even Winston.'

'Casino?'

'Haven't you been down there yet? Oh, you must go and have a little flutter.' He hands me an envelope stuffed with cash. 'We're trying to encourage a more playful approach to current affairs. I don't think much of your financial history,' he comments, frowning at the papers on his desk.

'No, well, I've always been more interested in sex than money.'

'What could be more erotic than a bundle of fifty-pound notes? Don't you think Jenny would agree?'

'Oh, so you know about her. Well, if you're so omniscient why don't you do your own espionage?'

'You're not interested in promotion? If we were satisfied with your research we would of course offer you a directorship. If not . . .' I try to look fearlessly into his eyes, but all I see is skeletal, ragged figures in chains, dragging themselves over a snowy landscape.

He stands up and swells into a vertical pillar. Spiral images of pain and suffering wind around him. Flames engulf a screaming baby, and the body of a decapitated woman swings from the chandelier. I have always kept my skeletons strictly in the closet, and this vulgarity upsets me, so I back away and shut my eyes. When I open them a second later I am alone in the room. Then I hear a campy giggle and, looking up, see one of the vicious angels leaning down from his cloud. He tosses me a black velvet bag.

Outside, in the calm institutional corridor, I open the bag. Inside are passports, identity cards and logbooks in my name in French, German, Russian and Japanese. There is also a camera the size of a cigarette lighter that I put in my breast pocket with my chewing gum and cigarettes. I can see the door that leads to the genteel lobby of the bank and the spiral stairs where 'CASINO' flashes in green-and-red neon.

I go down to what is still a fairly conventional gambling club, where men and women in evening dress escape the drab austerity of wartime London. I decide not to gamble on the outcome of the war but do rather well on the baccarat table, getting nine four times in succession. Then I pocket my winnings and go home to Jenny.

She is delighted to see me – and my money – and, as usual, doesn't ask too many questions about where it comes from. We go on a spree, buying all the things that are not officially on sale: a silver-fox coat for her, a tailored black overcoat with velvet lapels for me and a Bentley the colour of dried blood to show them off in. Jenny has never been subtle. Her war is touchingly simple: she genuinely believes she is a pretty young woman doing useful work and waiting for her adoring hero to return. It's a picture from a cigarette card or a film with Greer Garson. Charming. I don't see why I should deface it.

My own war becomes rather complicated after my visit to the Fizz. Most people wait until a war is over before they change sides. By the late forties who could count the numbers of the *maquisards* and *partigiani*? They must have far outnumbered the armies of Hitler and Mussolini. And nobody in Britain could remember being seduced by Mosley's ideas. I am even more flexible, transferring my sympathies several times a day while the war is still being fought. Flying is a game worthy of the gods, who have never been parochial. One coastline looks pretty much like another from ten thousand feet, and I have lived in every country in Europe. Of course, when I'm with my squadron I toe the RAF line and spout propaganda with the best of them.

But when I'm flying alone borders melt as arbitrarily as the young bodies of the crew I was flying with a few hours ago. Yesterday the charred corpse beside me was Fatty Langford; three hundred years ago the fields below were clotted with the blood of those who believed in their Catholic or Protestant God just as fervently as this lot believe in their Reich. Now even more defenceless people are dying, more towns and cities are being destroyed, the killing is more efficient, but taking sides seems as absurd as ever. I lived in what they now call Germany for longer than I've lived in England.

Since I have to make a crash-landing I leave my burnt-out Spitfire with its cargo of death and fly *au naturel* until I find a Messerschmitt that has been forced down in a meadow. Swooping down, I find a beautiful cadaver, a Teutonic Knight with gilded hair and waxen Aryan features complete with a duelling scar on his left cheek. On his elegant grey uniform is pinned a Knight's Cross Oak Leaf Cluster, which means he was promised a fief, a real knight's estate in the Caucasus. Oberst Gunter Kless from Fighter Group 77. I pocket his logbook for my collection and finger the grey leather of his new uniform, still fragrant even as his body begins to stink. I find a bottle of Cognac in the cockpit and swig it as I tinker with the engine of his plane. His bombs are still in place; he must have crashed soon after he left his base. I can't resist trying on his marvellous uniform over my own dingy blue one and the rest follows quite naturally: the Cognac, taking off, seeing if I can get her across the Channel. Then it does seem a shame to waste those bombs so I drop them over a smug-looking town nestling in the Downs. Just for the hell of it. At the end of this wild night I leave the exhausted Messerschmitt in a field near Banbury and limp back to the aerodrome. I tell them I parachuted down seconds before my

44

Spitfire crash-landed into the Thames. Treachery? I am not the worst of the war criminals.

Whenever I'm on pass I rush back to London and Jenny.

One night I watch her sleeping. She has cut her hair fashionably short, and its glossy blackness is like a helmet on the white pillow. The harmonious lines of her lovely face are stronger now than when she was truly young. I stroke the miracle of her silken elastic skin, brush my lips against the cheek that will never wither and dissolve, lift up her oyster satin night-dress to check the lovely inventory of her body, my body, before I make love to her.

Another night, another plane, another dead crew beside me in another aeroplane, the 'Lily of Laguna'. Just me and the carrier pigeons in their basket, glaring at me suspiciously out of reptilian blood-red eyes. Creatures are so much shrewder than one-lifers. I have forgotten the names of these six dead men, whom I only met this afternoon for the first time, forgotten which scrap of geography I'm supposed to be defending. Watched by the pigeons, I remove goodbye letters to girl-friends, wives and mothers from the pockets of five of the dead men. The sixth will have to be scraped out of the turret but not by me. I've flown four of the last five nights on chocolate, cigarettes and powdered eggs. A few minutes ago I put out the fire that killed the others, I need to land to see how much damage has been done to the plane, but I've no idea where I am. The fire has put my instruments and dials out of action, but the plane still flies. I pat her like some heroic wounded cavalry horse charging nobly into battle. Black dots above me might be Thunderbirds or Messerschmitts. My eyes are still dazzled by the glare from the last searchlights; my ears are full of the music of bombs. Ours whistle, German bombs scream and Japanese bombs sound like birds' wings fluttering. But they all blow you up in the end.

Stars above, smoke below, the stench of charred flesh and the exhilaration of flight. One of the dots comes nearer, and I see it is a Messerschmitt. It chases me over the rooftops of what is, I can now see, a burning city. Good show. We weave and zoom and play like psychopathic children.

After a long hunt I shoot him down with my last bullets and, in the silence of dawn and death, glide over hedgerows. I can hear her mechanical heart palpitating as I land in a field that might be anywhere in Europe and tinker with her devastated body. There isn't enough fuel to get back to England, and after seventy-five hours without sleep I can hardly walk, let alone fly or swim after I bale out over the Channel. If I'm captured I can't die, of course, but there are many degrees of pain before death and I don't want to count them.

The summer morning sparkles with mad optimism as we take off again, me and the pigeons, and fly to the coast where gulls escort us across the Channel. Sky and sea are hinged together like the pearly interior of a mussel shell, and as I gaze at the shimmering pink and silvery blue I sing into the dead intercom 'Lili Marlene', 'Bella Ciao', 'There'll Be Bluebirds Over the White Cliffs of Dover' . . . I burst into hysterical laughter as they appear below, not white at all but grey and beige, bristling with guns, concrete and barbed wire. She skids on the grass and dies beneath me as I release the pigeons, innocent of messages, as an offering to any gods who might be watching.

I crawl out, suddenly exhausted, stiff, thirsty and hungry. A couple of soldiers run over with cigarettes and a flask of water and listen to my tales of heroism with fascinated disbelief. They send a telegraph to Brize Norton to say I've survived and let me sleep in a bunk in a Nissen hut on the cliffs for a few hours. I return by military lorry and have time for a cold shower and a plate of greasy stew before debriefing.

Briefings and debriefings are masterpieces of euphemism. They never mention people. Targets are factories or military centres, not screaming women and roasted babies. Actually my refusal to die is becoming something of an embarrassment. They can't court-martial me for surviving, but my luck is statistically impossible. However, they can't prove anything against me, and they are desperate for experienced pilots.

At the end of my modest, fluent account, the C-in-C, a man in his fifties who fought in the last war, frowns. 'I suppose we'll have to give you another medal, Flying Officer Bishop. You must have quite a collection.'

'Will I be flying tonight? Terrible to have lost the whole crew.'

'Oh, we'll find a new crew. Got to keep the sausage machine turning.'

About a month after D-Day I manage a night in London. Jenny is so loving that night, so ripe and luscious. Even when she finds my collection of passports and logbooks I don't expect her to get upset. When she walks out I tell myself she will come crawling back before my next leave. But she doesn't. She disappears, and it's no fun coming back to an empty flat.

In the spring of 1944 St James's Square is bombed, and when I return on pass a few days later I look up from the pavement opposite at our top-floor flat, a doll's house that a capricious giant has had a tantrum with. The oyster satin night-dress flaps from a hole in the wall, and for a savage moment I wish Jenny was inside it.

Towards the end of the war my spirits sink. All that optimism and moral righteousness are profoundly depressing. Flying over the burnt-out ruins of Germany, I pity the ragged, starving refugees who are just as much victims as those who died in Auschwitz or Stalingrad. Soon they will be just as dead. Well, I've always been allergic to *esprit de corps*. As the survival rate in the RAF improves my little adventures are no longer possible, I have to toe the line and listen to the nauseating complacency of my fellow officers. I consider joining the Werewolves, the wild bands of ex-Nazi guerrillas fighting the Allies in the devastated cities. I've always got on rather well with werewolves, and lost causes are more sympathetic than found ones. But I don't want to kill anyone else.

Just before Christmas 1944 I do the decent thing and stage a crash followed by a nervous breakdown. I am invalided out of the RAF and spend the last months of the war in a remote cottage near Sherbourne, where I grow vegetables, lick my wounds and inwardly rage at Jenny. I'm not entirely alone; my tragic looks and medals attract several local women, and I submit to being mothered.

At the end of the war I am summoned to London by the Banca Metafisica and told that as a reward for my excellent war work I have been made a director. They pay me an enormous salary in return for helping them to expand into mass tourism and space exploration. I buy the vast, hideous house on the Cromwell Road for £2,000, let the upstairs floors and live in the basement. When Assunta telegraphs me to say that Jenny has returned to Rapallo I tear up the piece of paper.

My new status at the Fizz means that I can move freely in its underworld. One evening in the early fifties, maudlin-drunk after some reception, I wander down to the cave-like corridor where the contracts are stored and have a look at Jenny's. It's quite clear: she has to love me. She has swindled me, deserting me while hanging on to her beauty. Holding the hot, quivering document, I contemplate destroying it and her. I could kill her by remote control. Without her contract she would be over fifty, a raddled alcoholic who would soon be polished off by a quarter of a century of suppressed ailments. I could go to Rapallo and watch her die, pointing out my gifts to her as they vanish one by one.

Instead, I replace her contract in the vault. Jenny is far too ignorant and undistinguished to be the consort of a successful man. If she hadn't left me I would have got rid of her anyway.

Rapallo

As soon as it's possible to travel again after the war I return to Italy. When I get off the train at Genoa I'm shocked to see how great chunks have disappeared from the centre and the port. Assunta hasn't replied

47

to my telegram, so I have to accept that she might be dead and my villa might be a heap of rubble like the restaurant near the station where I used to eat. I get a taxi, a broken-down pre-war Mercedes, all the way to Rapallo. As soon as the driver realizes I understand Italian he launches into a passionate account of the last seven years. Death, starvation, defeat, bombs; he points out all the bomb sites along the coast and sings Resistance songs – they were all *partigiani*, he tells me, all happy now that Musso and his whore are dead. He addresses me by the Fascist *voi*, but I don't smile; I know the truth is flexible.

As I listen, I work out my own truth. He calls me signorina: I'd better be Virginia until I can find a way to kill her off. If my villa has been bombed I may have to live in the ruins, I don't think the income from my investments will be enough to rebuild it. Will I get compensation? How much is my income worth in this strange post-war world? Even if I have nowhere to live I'm determined to stay in Italy and never return to you.

Amazingly, the Villa Ginestra is still there. It was requisitioned and then looted; the rooms are empty except for a few souvenir turds. Most of the windows are broken, and there's no water or electricity, but I don't care.

At sunset I walk through my house, high heels clattering on the marble floors. The view from my terrace is still as lovely as ever. On impulse I rush down the hillside and bathe in the June sea, washing off the humiliation of my London war. By the time I've climbed back on to the rocks and dressed it's dark and I'm ravenous. At a little trattoria on the main road the *padrone*, Mimmo, brings me *spaghetti alle vongole* with a half carafe of red wine. The pasta is wonderful, I tell him, the best food I've eaten for years.

Mimmo pounces with joy on the crazy Englishwoman who used to live alone in the villa above Milord Max. Mimmo is relieved that the foreigners – and our money – are returning. His wife comes out from the kitchen and the three of us gossip until late that night, not survivor guilt but *allegria*, for we all know how lucky we are to be alive. Many of the people I remember from before the war haven't returned to Rapallo: the German dramatist, the retired British skipper, the bankrupt Italian prince descended from Charlemagne, the vicar of the English Church they used to call 'Devil Dodger'. Mimmo speaks of Ezra Pound as a monster, but I only remember the tall restless man with a patchy red beard feeding stray cats under the palm trees. Ezra believed the lies most other people believed, so they put him in a cage and now he's locked up in a loony bin in America. I remember him sitting in the café in the piazza shouting at Yeats. I couldn't understand

Ezra's poetry, but I loved Yeats's, although I was always too shy to tell him so.

I tell them I haven't a stick of furniture, and Mimmo and his wife insist on giving me their son's mattress. He was killed in the Abyssinian campaign so he won't be needing it. Mimmo and his surviving son carry it up the dark hillside to my bedroom, where I fall asleep on it to the welcoming chatter of crickets and the scent of rosemary.

In the morning Assunta is on my terrace with eggs and rolls and milk. I embrace her solid, dark warmth, and we stand back to look at each other. The bun she drags her hair into is still black, and she seems to be wearing the same black dress, but it hangs more loosely on her. Assunta says I'm *sempre bella*, and I tell her she's ageless. She helps me to sort out the bureaucratic red tape over my villa, and I find there's enough money in my bank account to live modestly. After my initial euphoria I shrink into the shadows of a monastic life, reading and writing and swimming. My pre-war friends have left Italy or died or, more depressingly, grown old.

I bump Virginia off. I announce that my daughter, who grew up in England and has been visiting me for Christmas, has taken an accidental overdose of sleeping pills on New Year's Eve, 1948. Death certificates, like birth certificates and passports, can easily be bought in Italy, and the local undertaker is Assunta's friend. I squander six months' income on killing off my *alter ego*.

Assunta arranges everything. We have a beautiful funeral. Italians are so good at sex and death. Black-edged posters all over town, a horse-drawn hearse, my photograph on my grave up in the olive groves above Rapallo. Outside the works of Edgar Allan Poe very few people check the contents of coffins.

We have a marvellous wake, nothing flashy, all very dignified and subdued, for I've learnt the value of good taste. I don't like other people's funerals, but I thoroughly enjoy my own. I feel like dancing on my grave: it's such a relief to be rid of Virginia, that stupid, ignorant, drunken woman. With the money I give her for colluding in Virginia's death Assunta buys a fishing boat for her lover Stefano and marries him. The spectacular funeral and wedding brighten that gloomy winter and give me a recognizable identity: a tragically bereaved mother. Black suits me.

I've always envied your wit and eloquence and George's quiet intelligence. I used to think intelligence came with money. Then I got the money and acquired a certain style and called myself Eugenie but still had no brains. I can make people laugh, but what I want is the juice that flows in books. So I spend my fifties and sixties extracting it.

I order crates of books from England. Assunta tells me the local children believe they contain the corpses of babies whose blood I suck to stay so young, and I roar with laughter, although it's no more improbable than the truth.

I stop sunbathing, wear hats and veils and generally disguise my youth, which is becoming an embarrassment. I don't go out much but sit in my marble *salotto* with the shutters closed and read novels, poetry, history and philosophy in English, French and Italian.

After Virginia's funeral there's a note from Max offering his condolences and inviting me to tea. He has lived in the Villino Chiaro, between my villa and the coast road, for forty years. Before the war we would occasionally see each other in the bar at the Excelsior, but I know he has always avoided the English community, so I'm flattered by his invitation.

Lady Beerbohm, an elderly Pre-Raphaelite damozel in a flowing purple gown, shows me into their drawing-room. Their villa is smaller and uglier than mine but far more comfortable, encrusted with books and pictures and hefty turn-of-the-century furniture. Max is getting ready, Florence explains. Conversation with her doesn't exactly flow; she's nervous and confused and I have the impression she's vetting me to see if it's safe to leave me alone with her husband. Her refined American voice quivers and fades out in mid-sentence as we talk about the war.

Max is a long time getting ready, but the result is worth it. He's dressed for an Edwardian garden party in his shade-of-primrose suit, a gardenia in his buttonhole and patent-leather pumps on his tiny feet. Above his white moustache his heavy-lidded blue eyes bulge, kind yet detached.

He's a quarter of a century older than me. I realize at once that he's an extraordinary man – well, not exactly a man, which is part of his enormous charm. But he does like women. When I'm with him I'm in the London of my youth, which he still personifies, for in spirit he has never lived in Italy and doesn't even speak Italian. Florence drifts away, and I tell him how much I enjoyed his broadcasts during the war, particularly the one about music halls. I talk about my career, and for once I don't pretend to have been more successful than I really was. We gossip about Marie Lloyd, Little Tich, Augustus John and many other acquaintances, most of them dead. Florence joins us for tea from a vast silver teapot and small, triangular egg-and-cress sandwiches. I leave immediately after tea, frightened of outstaying my welcome and disrupting the fragile museum of their routine.

Later meetings are warmer, although Max always preserves a certain formality. We can see each other from our terraces, but I still feel I must wait for a written summons to tea. When I invite him to bring Florence to lunch with me he winces at the effort of climbing up the hill. Max never walks if he can help it.

That spring we spend hours talking on his big roof terrace, with Etruscan oil jars full of gardenias and camellias he picks for his daily buttonhole and wonderful views of the sea and Portofino. He calls me Jenny Mere. 'Why?'

'She was the heroine of a little book of mine, *The Happy Hypocrite*. Awful twaddle, but you can borrow it if you like.'

'What was she like?'

'Good and beautiful, a most unlikely combination, with raven locks. Her lover was Lord George Hell, who somewhat resembled the sinister young pilot I saw you with at the Café Royal a few years ago.'

I'm surprised he thinks of me as having an existence outside our timeless, peaceful, beautiful hillside and even more surprised when he adds, 'In order to deserve his Jenny, Lord George Hell had to wear a saintly mask and, eventually, he lives up to it. How beautifully you live up to yours.'

'How do you know it's a mask?' I ask nervously.

'We all need masks, my dear.'

'What would happen if we didn't wear one?'

'Then we'd walk into one of the invisible traps in our own characters, as most of us do anyway.'

We're sitting on his terrace, in his ship's cabin of a study, when we have this conversation, one glorious afternoon in May when the flawless blue of the sky merges with the gentle sea and the olive and lemon groves glow sleepily. 'It's hard to believe Shelley drowned in that sea,' I say.

'I think he wanted to.'

'He was so young. Such a waste of his genius.'

'Perhaps he knew he'd done his best work. And geniuses are generally asinine.'

'I prefer Keats.'

'I quite agree. You must go to Rome and see his house.'

'Will you come with me?'

'I'm far too old for cities now, don't you know. I can't bear all the chatter and clatter and hustle and guzzle.'

'But you must have friends in Rome?'

'That's just the trouble. Expatriate life. The unfrocked, the drummed-out and the struck-off-the-rolls.'

'Is that how you see me?'

'There is nothing vulgar or commonplace about you, Jenny Mere. Besides, you have the charm of widowhood – I mean bereavement, of course.' He smiles down at the drawing he's doing of me. He never actually says he doesn't believe a word of my story, and he can't possibly have guessed the truth. We recognize each other as fantasists and also share the bond of nostalgia for a London that doesn't exist any more.

I'm falling a little in love with Max. I'm fascinated by his contradictions: he's sceptical about democracy but was staunchly anti-Fascist before the war and thought Ezra was crazy to fall for Musso. Despite his title and fame Max and Florence are more hard up than I am, and he isn't a snob. Distinguished visitors descend on him, but he never pursues them.

'Come to Rome with me. Just for a few days. Please.'

He continues to stare down at his drawing while a crimson flush spreads from his white silk cravat to his forehead, making his moustache and hair look like snow. 'Quite impossible. I'm too old.'

'Too old for what, Max?'

'Now don't be horrid. You know what I mean. Poor darling Florence has been ill again. I can't possibly leave her. You must find yourself a virile young admirer.'

'I'd rather have you.'

'Now that's quite enough.' He hums. 'How does it go again?' And we sing 'Oh Mr Porter', Marie Lloyd's great hit and the signature tune of our friendship. Our laughter disturbs Florence, who has another headache, and I tiptoe out.

Over the next two years I realize Florence is dying, and I do consider marrying Max. There's no passion in him, but he's so charming, intelligent, funny and civilized. I even consider telling him about Leo and my contract. I feel he'd be more amused than shocked.

I confide in Isabella, my new friend, who used to be Puccini's mistress. A Jewess, she spent the war hidden in the labyrinthine Teatro di Marcello in Rome. 'With the cats and the meths drinkers,' she remembers acidly. 'Lovers and husbands, where were they then?'

Isabella has been a beauty. Now she's hugely fat and her once-Titian hair is a frizzy pink. She's squeezed into a glamorous, black, sequinned evening dress, one of the few trophies she has salvaged from her past. Isabella rents a tiny room above a Pasta e Olio shop and regards my looks as valuable capital I'm squandering.

We're sitting in my dining-room, which now has some furniture in it, overlooking the bay on a clear summer night. I'm staring at the corner of the Villino Chiaro, which has come to loom over the coast. That summer Max is always on my mind.

'So, tell me about your old man. Is he rich?'

'No.'

'Is he a great artist?'

'No.'

'Good in bed?'

'He's not interested in sex.'

'Ma . . . !' Isabella stares at me incredulously. Assunta brings in a plate of cheese and prosciutto and olives and a bowl of peaches and sits down to join in the discussion.

'Signora Isabella, please, tell my signora not to throw herself away.'

'Assunta's right. What use is a title without any money?'

'I'm not interested in his title or in marriage. I just adore talking to him.'

They shrug at each other and talk to me as if I was a retarded child.

'In England men and women don't go to bed together?' Assunta asked.

'Of course they do.'

'You prefer it with women? Or dogs? I know you English are crazy about dogs,' Isabella says understandingly.

'No! It's just him, this man. I really like him as a person, as a friend.'

'Fine. Drink tea with him. But don't waste too much time on him. I must say, you look fabulous. You've probably got about ten years before you go off. How old did you say you were?'

'I didn't.'

'Signora Jenny doesn't look her age,' Assunta says discreetly.

'How many husbands, so far?'

'Just Virginia's father. He died in the First World War.'

'Well, take my advice and marry the next man who comes along. Make sure you get his property – make sure he has some. It doesn't matter if he's old but, please, not some impoverished old fart. You're beautiful! Make the most of it! Now there's that tenor from Naples, Giuseppe, he fancied you. No money, though. And that violinist, but he's broke, too. Come to Firenze with me next week and I'll introduce you to my caro Guido, who has a leather factory. His wife has just conveniently died. When I think of the offers I turned down – but you don't want to end up like me.'

'Women need husbands,' says the newly married Assunta as she hands me the peach she has peeled.

Poor languid Florence is dying. Max invites me to tea, lends me books, draws me and laughs at my jokes. Every time I see him he looks older, smaller, more transparent and frail. Voraciously, I read my way through his library, and we have friendly arguments.

'I think Eliot's much better than Ezra. I can understand his poetry.'
'Can you really? More than I can. They're both so obscure and –
woozie-poozie.'
'I like Eliot and Auden best, of the modern poets you've lent me.'
'Tell me what it is you like about them.'
'Some lines in Eliot are so beautiful. It makes my spine tingle when
he says that we all go into the dark.' (Except me, I thought.) 'When he
speaks of time past and time future I feel he's bending over me, looking
into my life, telling me it doesn't have to hurt so much. Auden's more
human, warmer, his poems chatter to you, gossip with you. He under-
stands all the twists and turns and cruelties and contradictions of love.
I never get bored with his poems. I can read them again and again.
Some of his poems are like songs, but the words of songs need music;
his just fill all the emptiness inside me.'
'Really? I'd give half a ton of Eliot and Auden for an ounce of
Wilde's wit and brevity.'
'I don't know what you see in Wilde. He's so precious and
affected.'
'Ah well, I belong to that generation, don't you know. A period piece.
But you're young, you belong to the future of TV and science and
machinery and other things darling to the devil.'
'I often think I belong to more than one generation.'
'Mysterious Jenny.'
I'm still not sure how I feel about Max when Florence finally dies, at
the beginning of 1951.
Assunta and I go to the Villino Chiaro to offer our sympathy. I run
upstairs to his study and hug him, the only time I do. He feels small and
frail in my arms. 'I'm so sorry, Max. Can I do anything?'
'I want to be looked after!' he says petulantly, sounding so child-
like that I have to repress a smile – and ask myself if I really do want to
look after him.
Before there is time for a dilemma Florence is replaced. It turns out
that while Florence was on her deathbed Max sent his friend Elizabeth
Jungmann a telegram. She arrives, intelligent, efficient and attractive, a
hero-worshipper in search of her next hero. As soon as I see her I know
I haven't a hope. She looks after Max selflessly until he dies five years
later, and I'm still allowed to come to tea.
In the late fifties Isabella dies, too, of cancer, and I begin to feel
lonely. I walk for miles, up in the hills and along the coast. Assunta
calls me *anima vagabonda*, wandering soul. Rapallo is changing. Tracks
have become roads and the main road has become an autostrada. There
is ribbon development between Genoa and the French border. Only

Portofino has preserved its pristine dignity as a very expensive fishing village, and I can't afford to move there now. George, who is my solicitor, writes to tell me that my money is running out and I may have to sell my villa as a hotel to feed the insatiable maw of the tourism that has destroyed the view I once loved. Assunta cuts corners and I live as cheaply as I can, but my life becomes sad, my isolation seedy rather than glorious. I'm almost the last of the expatriates left over from the twenties, and it's not a role I enjoy any more.

There are plenty of lovers, but they're too young to talk to properly. When I strip off my clothes my youthfulness is more of a curiosity than an asset, even in the dark. I start to miss you desperately, Leo. Memories of London during the war mellow and from the distance you look more exciting than dangerous. I demolish the worst of my memories of you, swing great weights of optimism against them like the cranes that destroy the huts and barns that once surrounded the Villa Ginestra. I remember the fun we had together in the early years of the war, our dancing and love-making. After all, you have kept your half of the bargain we made. I tell myself I've exaggerated your wickedness. Everyone kills during a war, and most men get medals for it. I tell myself it will be different next time, because I've become stronger and more intelligent and won't let you push me around.

I sell my shabby villa, pay off my debts and spend most of the remaining money on Eugenie Bishop's funeral. In September 1967 I watch my coffin as it is lowered into my grave. I'm dressed as my own granddaughter in a short black skirt and jacket. I do shed a few tears, thinking of Max and Isabella. What a waste of all the marvellous unique ingredients that go into a personality, to throw it away after a few decades like so much rubbish. I don't enjoy my second funeral as much as my first. I've spent too much time in this cemetery recently, among the feathery cypress trees and well-manicured paths. No, death doesn't interest me. If I stay in Rapallo I'll run out of photographs to put on my own graves. I overhear the remarks neighbours and strangers make.

'Quite a beauty when she was young.'

'What was she? An actress or something?'

'Strange woman. Lived all alone. Had an alcoholic daughter who did herself in years ago.'

Next time I won't waste my life. I'll reinvent myself as something remarkable, someone worth remembering. I'm eager for London and you.

Two weeks later I return by aeroplane, just to see what it's like to fly. When Assunta and I go to Genoa airport to check in I have to pay so much in excess baggage for my trunk that I wish I'd got the train after all.

'Goodbye, signora.'

Suddenly I remember all she has done for me. 'Assunta, you've been wonderful.'

'I was only following orders.'

'Whose?'

'From up there.'

'I didn't know you were religious.'

She smiles at me and we embrace. 'I wish you could come to London with me. But I've no money to pay you.'

'We'll meet again, signora. Sooner than you think.'

I think she means life after death and don't tell her I've no intention of finding out if there is one.

London

I'm on my way to you, Leo. I know you're in London; I had a dream about you last night. You were walking across a park towards me, wearing a white suit and your most arrogant, mocking expression. Your dark-blue eyes expanded to the path, grass, even the sky until London was just a thought reflected in them and your shadow swelled to hide the sun. You're a monster like me, Leo. I know you're a trickster – yet how strange it is that the crazy bargain I struck with you wasn't a trick after all. Here I am forty-five years later, still young and luscious. It's 12 October. Tonight is the anniversary of that night at Giulini's when I signed our contract in blood.

Good old George is going to meet me at the airport. Because I wrote and asked him to and because he's what we used to call a brick. I need his sanity, and perhaps he needs me, too, because even a brick needs poetry. If you can't rise above facts and time you have to serve them, and I'll never do that. I'm coming to shatter George's reality. What an entrance this is, flying above the clouds of his dullness, crashing through the barrier of his disbelief.

I've never been on an aeroplane before. It should feel mysterious to be flying above the clouds, but it's all rather shoddy: the plastic interior, the inelegant hostesses, the tired snacks. If I'd known I would have caught the train from Nice instead of splurging my last money on an air ticket and paying the outrageous cost of my overweight trunk, made for transatlantic liners rather than flimsy sky bubbles. We all sit here like schoolchildren, passive in our rows, trusting a technology we don't understand. What if we crash? Will I rise from the flames like a phoenix? I should have asked you about all this, Leo, while I had the chance.

I'm George's *dea in machina*, and I'm tired of being behind the scenes. He'll be old, he always was, even when he was a student and wanted me so much he shivered like a sick dog whenever I was near. I want to tell him my story, watch his face as he listens, his pink, round, hopelessly honest face as he tries to believe the impossible and rationalize the preposterous. He was the only one who cared enough to notice the change in me after that night when you and I struck our bargain. George said I looked thin and sad and lonely, and I laughed, thinking I was the most enviable woman in the world. Well, perhaps I am.

We're cradled in snowy, glowing clouds, a cross between Siberia and heaven. Now we're plunging down, and I can see my city spread out, a game on a board for me to win. Towers and high buildings everywhere, the bomb sites and smouldering ruins have been rebuilt and London's face, like my own, has conquered the years. The smugness of a long peace is almost tangible on this aeroplane, smooth as an airborne department store.

I sit here reinventing myself, take my life in my hands and knead it until I become Jenny, my own granddaughter. I look the part, in my short emerald-green dress, platform shoes and my old black coat. Couldn't afford a new one. I stared at fashion magazines so as to be able to imitate this new androgynous look, long hair and no curves. My thick, wavy black hair hangs loose down my back, and I've worked on my voice, too, which has already travelled so far, from cockney to the affected cadences of the years I called myself Eugenie. Now my vowels are flat again; I hear cockney's all the rage.

As the plane dives my heart lurches with excitement and also fear that George won't meet me after all. He'll be ill or gaga or indifferent to me.

The shock in his eyes confirms that I really haven't changed. He's surprised when I look straight at him, picking out his face at once among the others waiting. I recognize him by his eyes, blue and vague and devoted. 'Mr Dumphry? It's so nice of you to meet me. All Grandma's other friends seem to be dead.'

He's too shocked by my resemblance to myself to kiss or hug me. He says I make him feel old, and I smile because my eyes don't miss a wrinkle or a bulge or a broken vein. He's fat and jowly, and his few remaining hairs are white. Whenever I look into the reflection of my true age I feel a mixture of triumph and horror. As Swift said, 'Every man desires to live long, but no man would be old.' And no woman either.

We glide across London in his Daimler, a proper car, built like a tank and with leather seats. As the city slides past my window I have the curious feeling it's on rollers, like the windmills and tulips when I sat in my horse and cart to sing my Little Dutch Girl number in a blonde wig – the only little Dutch girl in the business with huge dark eyes and a hook nose.

We stop at George's house. He's a Hampstead paterfamilias, and here comes his matronly Molly. The last time I saw that face was in a photograph George showed me during the war, when it was a fresh, round glow of innocence and sweetness. Twenty-eight years later, wrinkles entrenched with powder are forked paths leading to her eyes and mouth. Double chins wobble and broken veins dance like red apostrophes. She shouldn't be wearing that pink floral pattern, thorns and roses stretched to breaking point across her arse. Her face is florid, too, and her ginger hair wants to go grey but isn't allowed.

If that's bitchy it's nothing compared with the hatred radiating from Molly as she stares at me. She obviously doesn't want me around. George must have presented me as a combination of Little Orphan Annie and Cinderella, all alone in the world and penniless. I try to look wide-eyed, but I see the jealous anger behind her smiles as she welcomes me.

This is the kind of room that would have intimidated me long ago, all velvet, damask and boule, red and gold, very grand in an old-fashioned way. Nobody seems to have told Molly and George that rooms are supposed to look bare and Scandinavian now. We're enacting a drawing-room comedy, like the ones George used to back in his days as a theatrical angel. Molly wheels in a trolley loaded with plates of cucumber sandwiches and cakes. Between her and George there's the infuriating contentment of decades, the pathetic illusion of security, which smells of polish, dried flowers and baking. Who has the key to reality, Molly? You with your civilized glaze or me with my raging knowledge that nothing's safe?

Molly plies me with food and eager questions about my death. 'Poor old thing! Could she walk, the last few months?'

'She was about the same age as me. Not much older than you, in fact,' George says mildly.

'I bet she lied about her age,' Molly retorts savagely. Then, resuming her compassionate voice, 'All that Italian sun must have aged her. And being such a recluse. I suppose she became rather eccentric, in a Garboesque sort of way. I know she refused to see that *Sunday Times* journalist.'

'My grandmother wasn't senile. And she swam in the sea every day until her last illness.'

'Did she really? How marvellous. And you, poor lamb, going from one ancient household to another. We'll have to introduce you to our grandchildren. They're about your age. You don't have to help,' she adds pointedly as she wheels out the tea trolley.

I wouldn't know how. I stand outside the kitchen door, watching preparations for another enormous meal, listening. George has followed her into the kitchen, her territory, where he stacks the dishwasher while she bangs and mutters and stuffs a chicken. 'Used to servants, I suppose. Well, that's all over. She'll have to pull herself together and make herself useful. Earn her living like everyone else.'

After dinner we go into the drawing-room for coffee and brandy. George and I are on one of the green velvet sofas and Molly is on the other. We face each other across the marble-topped coffee-table piled with recipe books and actors' autobiographies. The sofas are just far enough apart to allow for a private conversation. I lean towards George, looking into his face. A standard lamp illuminates him so that I can see the grey bags under his eyes, the clumps of white hair in his nostrils and ears and the veins on his nose. George peers back at me, feels himself being sucked into pools of nostalgia by treacherous currents he resists. He's a canny lawyer. There's no place for demons and witches in his world. 'I suppose you'll think me a terrible old bore if I talk to you about your grandmother?'

'No.'

'Were you close to her?'

'Very.'

'I can't get over the resemblance.'

'I know.'

'Did she ever mention a man called Leo?'

'I don't remember. There were so many men. Who was he?'

'I used to call him her Svengali. He discovered her when she was very young, made her career really. Sinister chap, though, I always thought.'

'Was she any good?'

'Not really.' I catch my breath sharply, and he thinks I'm smothering a yawn. In Italy I used to tell myself I left the stage while I was still at the top. As much as the image of my own youth preserved, I've needed that conviction that I had a talent to give up. George is the kindest man I've ever met, which makes his dismissal of my career all the more cruel. 'But you shouldn't be sitting here talking to an old man like me about ancient history.'

Later, Molly goes to bed. 'You must meet our grandson. David,' George says.

'Does he look like you when you were young?'

'Very much. Although it seems to me I was even more naïve. Those were more innocent times, of course.'

'Really?' The ghost of that triangle hovers on the air between us. George puts on his most sanctimonious expression. 'Well, no, perhaps you're right. Although I think we really were rather innocent, compared with young people nowadays. You must be careful in London, my dear.' He laughs nervously.

'You were going to tell me about Leo.'

'Was I? I wonder what happened to him. He disappeared about the same time as your grandmother went off to live on the Riviera, in the early twenties. Pity, because if he'd stuck around he would have looked after her. There was some scandal. I think the police were after him – can't remember the details now.'

'Did this Leo love her then?'

'Love's not a word you could associate with him. They were certainly close. She was obsessed with him.' Is that catch in his voice the ghost of jealousy? 'Leo had an absolute genius for money. One of your grandmother's admirers, Lord Somebody or other, died in the Great War and left her a couple of thousand. Jenny would have frittered it away on clothes and jewellery, but Leo took it, invested it for her and by the early twenties she had enough to retire.'

'Was Leo my grandfather?'

'Didn't she – oh Lord – I'm not sure.'

'Or are you?'

'I don't – this will seem very shocking to a young girl like you, but there were quite a few men who could have been Virginia's father.'

'I hope it was you. You'd make a nice grandfather.'

'Perhaps you could adopt me anyway?' We smile at each other; then I kiss him on the forehead and go upstairs to my chaste white bed in their spare room.

I can't sleep. My stomach churns with rich food, and the past seethes in the silent house. I'm sure George must feel it, too. At three he opens my door. I lie naked, the white sheet revealing my pale back and bony shoulders. I know he remembers every mole on my back, every curve of my body, the exact shape of my black hair spread over the pillow. I want him to come in so that he can see my face and breasts. The moonlight stabs through the white curtains, pouring silver over me, inviting him to look. But he turns and shuffles back down the corridor, and I don't suppose he'll ever know that my eyes were wide open. Click, my door shuts again. Creak, George returns to his awful bedded life and pretends nothing's the matter. I am the matter, and I won't go away.

This afternoon I hear Molly on the phone to a friend. 'Julia? It's Molly, darling. I wanted to ask you a favour. We've got this girl staying with us. Her grandmother was an old flame of George's, died and left her without a penny . . . O-levels? A-levels? I don't think she knows what they are. She speaks Italian and French awfully well in a dated sort of way. That's about the full extent of her education, as far as I can see . . . Touch type? I shouldn't think so. She can't even remember to take her keys out of the door. If she were my secretary I'd commit suicide . . . George? Adores her. Salivates whenever she comes into the room. Aren't men disgusting . . . No! Dickie? Really? In her own bedroom? With the nanny? What did she do? . . . Did she? On the spot? Well, I wonder why she didn't get rid of Dickie instead. Nannies are so hard to get nowadays . . . I suppose so. Striking, anyway. They're all pretty at that age, aren't they? . . . Frankly, absolutely useless, she behaves as if there are invisible servants hovering. I know it's halfway through your term, but could you squeeze her in? I mean she's got to do something, anything, really, as long as it keeps her out of the house and eventually qualifies her to work . . . Really? Are you sure? Oh, Julia, that's so sweet of you.'

Having disposed of me to Julia's college at a bargain rate, Molly's in a good mood. Being young again diminishes me; George and Molly talk about me as if I'm not here, as if I'm a child or a dog. Eternal youth doesn't seem to qualify me for anything, and all that reading I did in Rapallo doesn't seem to be a lot of use either.

On my way to my first formal education for nearly sixty years I sit upstairs on the Number 31 bus and stare out of the window as London unfolds. The city I was born in is still largely nineteenth century despite the Blitz. Victorian, like me. I was four when the old Queen died. Now I don't know which generation or class I belong to: not to my sister Lizzie and the Hoxton street urchins I grew up with; not to Molly and the other trumpeting Hampstead matriarchs; and not to the mind-blown wraiths who drift around the streets of Notting Hill, either. I find myself looking for you, Leo. You're the only person I can be honest with.

Julia is Molly's age – my age – with permed grey hair, leathery skin, a navy-blue suit and unshakeable confidence. Her college is above an antique shop in Kensington Church Street; three shabby floors of classrooms full of typewriters and giggling girls. I have to suppress my annoyance as she bosses and patronizes me. 'Now, Jenny, come up to my office, dear, and I'll test you. You're very quiet. Most of the girls we get now are terrible chatterboxes. As our Home Ec teacher said to me the other day, their skirts get shorter and their mouths bigger. You wouldn't believe the problems I have to sort out. The convent girls are the worst. If it's not drugs it's an abortion or an overdose. And when you think the oldest are about nineteen. How old are you, dear?'

'Twenty-one.'

'Really? I thought you were much younger. How refreshing to meet a girl who's shy. It must be your grandmother's good influence. I just hope you're not led astray by the others.'

Molly bangs on my door each morning to get me up at seven, and I have to schlep over to Kensington to get to my first class at nine: Shorthand, French, Art Appreciation. I was speaking French when these girls' grandmothers were teenagers, and I first appreciated art during a brief fling with Augustus John. The teachers are taken in by me but not their pupils, who sense I'm not really one of them. Without being exactly spiteful they contrive to leave me alone. I make no friends.

I overhear another conversation between Molly and George. 'Shouldn't we buy her some clothes? She always seems to be wearing that green dress and that black coat that's almost green with age.'

'I don't see why. She's got a trunk full of clothes upstairs.'

'Why doesn't she wear them then?'

'They're all about thirty years old. There's a green Schiaparelli evening dress, an ermine coat, bundles of old love letters. I dare say yours are in there somewhere.'

'Molly! You've no right to spy on her like that.'

'Nonsense. She won't answer questions – or not properly. Why shouldn't I know what's in my own spare room? For all I know she's got her grandma's body up there in that ancient trunk. No sign of any money. She can't sponge off us for ever. She'll have to find a job.'

Christmas rescues me from this awful truth. My first Christmas for half a century in the bosom of a family, and very strange it is, too. Family life will always be a mystery to me. My mother hated it, my father drank to get away from it, Lizzie and I used to dread the Christmas period, because it always ended with quarrels. In Italy my friends and lovers used to disappear inside their families for days, inviting me to gatherings I didn't want to attend. At Christmas outsiders like me are even more displaced than usual. I am my own ancestor.

The house is decorated with lurid red and green, like a tartan bordello, I comment as Molly and I wait for the bell to ring. She looks shocked. I'm not supposed to know what a bordello is. 'Oh, don't mention tartan. Those Dumphrys go on and on about their Scottish blood although they've been in London about a hundred years. There's some silly romantic story about a bastard Stuart connection, and when she's had a few drinks Aunt Laura always produces her shortbread recipe. Oh God, here she comes.' Molly resolutely torments her face into her hostess smile as her guests flood in.

I see at once that Molly adores her grandson David, the last man she still flirts with. 'Darling, this is Jenny who's staying with us. Her grandmother was an old flame of George's. Died and left her without a penny,' she adds in a deafening whisper as David shakes my hand, his calm blue eyes sparking as he stares at me. David really does look like George did at the same age. But that's a statement of fact. It doesn't convey the charm of his smooth pink skin, clear bagless eyes and slender body. I long to touch this George who has bathed in the river of life. After we shake hands I have to clasp mine primly to keep them off him.

David's sister, Annette, is dark like her mother. Her curly brown hair is dragged back in an unflattering greasy pony-tail, and her blunt features are pug-like and truculent. Her hazel eyes are quick, watchful and full of contempt as she glares at my miniskirt and makeup. She's wearing jeans and a lumpy beige cardigan, and her nose is so shiny I think she must have actually polished it. Under her seeming newness I recognize an older, more familiar archetype: the puritan killjoy, offended by my frivolity.

Muriel, Molly and George's niece, gives David a beefy kiss and drags him off to the kitchen. I follow them, resenting this girl before I even meet her. Muriel wears a miniskirt as if it's a twin-set. I know at once that she's in love with David, has been for years; she probably taped his photograph to the inside of her desk at school. She reeks of the hockey pitch, of flat shoes and flatter conversation. Her sporty contralto is like a Sousa march, and her face matches her voice, an insensitive blast of straggly orange hair, freckles, snub nose and anxious blue eyes. She's nineteen, obscenely young.

In the kitchen Molly tries to bring the three girls, as she calls us, together. Muriel and I stare at each other with mutual dislike. As she bustles around organizing lunch Molly talks to Annette, who is as unenthusiastic as me about cooking. 'Do you remember when you were little and came to stay here? "Come on, Grandma," you used to say, "let's go to bed and talk."'

'What on earth did we talk about?'

'Oh, about your cat and my dolls when I was a little girl and how awful brothers were. You don't remember, do you?'

'I remember coming here. You always preferred my brother.'

'I'm sure I didn't, darling. Oh well. I wonder what happens to all the experiences we forget. Most of life, really. Are you enjoying studying – whatever it is?'

'Sociology, Grandma. How society works. Yes, very much. I want to change the world.'

'Do you really, dear? My goodness me. I rather like it the way it is. It's so marvellous the way you all go to university now. For us, you know, for girls of my generation, that wasn't really an option. I dare say we were very stupid.'

'I don't think you're stupid, Grandma,' Annette says too politely and turns away. She tells me off for not going on marches against Vietnam.

'I don't even know where Vietnam is. Why should I get all worked up about a war there?'

Annette glares at me. 'I can see you're a solipsist, just like David. Talking to my brother about politics is like talking to a blind man about rainbows. Of course, solicitors are a bunch of Fascists, so I suppose he'll fit in quite well.'

'Annette, stop hectoring everybody.' David has followed us into the kitchen, where he responds to Muriel's homage with tolerant amusement.

'Isn't David wonderful? The only man to come in here and do something useful.' Molly glances up from her labours to smile archly at Muriel, who looks as if she might swoon with rapture as she talks to David. The ridiculous vulnerability of first love: the cruellest of the jokes that the gods play upon their dolls.

'Super to see you! I hear you've got a fabulous job and your own flat.'

'It's not much of a job, really, just a very long apprenticeship.'

'I bet you'll earn pots of money! I wish I could, I'm having awful trouble living on my grant, and at the end of my course I suppose I'll just have to teach. There's nothing else one can do with a geography degree.'

'But you're studying in a hotbed of trendiness and radical politics. That must be fun.'

'Oh, David! I don't have anything to do with those people.'

'Well, it's revolutionized your hemlines, anyway.'

'You noticed! I told Mummy this morning, I bet he doesn't even look at my legs.' The poor girl is like a jelly, but his eyes aren't on her legs or face but on mine, and I want them to stay there.

Molly's kitchen is full of helpers now. Food is her dominion, and she loves to see us all obeying her orders. She carries the goose, which looks too heavy ever to have flown, from the oven to the table where it crouches, golden, on a dish. George stands over it, wielding a carving knife and fork, the king of domesticity. The succulent roast bird, bronze gravy and generous heaps of rosemary potatoes and sprouts make a marvellous picture, *nature mort*. No, not dead. Molly and George have created life, although it's not one that I've ever wanted.

At lunch Muriel, Annette and I all sit near George. 'Let him look at some pretty faces,' Molly says indulgently. It's only when married men are old or gaga or impotent that such demonstrations of affection are allowed.

The long table is decorated as if for a children's party, with a scarlet table-cloth, gold candles, holly and crackers, although there aren't any children. Muriel is the youngest person here. Great-grandchildren are coyly anticipated while David stares glumly at his plate. I wonder if he feels doomed to copulate with Muriel. Not if I have anything to do with it. As Molly's favourite grandchild David sits on her right, and I'm beside George, playing Little Nell and feeling libidinous after four glasses of wine. Since my poor old George has no more libido I turn my attentions to David.

After lunch he sits on a couch with Annette and their ancient Great-Aunt Laura, who must be about my age. She initiates Annette into the family shortbread recipe in a hushed voice. Laura opens her handbag, and David withdraws sharply into a corner of the couch as the disgusting contents spill out: used tissues, a hairbrush full of coagulated dandruffy white hairs, a lipstick that looks as if Boudicca might have used it. A cloud of dirty powder and stale perfume rises as Laura fumbles through stained and dog-eared papers to find the recipe. On her other side Annette exchanges fastidious glances with her brother.

David and I stare at each other with frank desire. This tribal gathering, the wine and Great-Aunt Laura's handbag drive me to obsessive thoughts of youth and beauty and sex. I lure him upstairs, whispering that I'll show him the letters George wrote to my grandmother. The really touching thing about David is that he has just that same honesty and awkwardness I remember in George nearly half a century ago.

While David reads the letters I sit beside him on my bed and put my arm around him. 'They had a most passionate affair, you know.' David blushes. 'My grandmother had dozens of lovers and admirers, but she always said George was the nicest man she ever knew. They used to sneak off together back to her room in Gower Street, and she said she had to teach him not to be such a gentleman.' My hand drops from his shoulder to his thigh and the letters drop to the floor. 'You know, you look so like George did as a young man, and everyone says I look like my grandmother, too.'

My hand strokes the welcoming bulge of his penis. *I Haven't Had a Cuddle for a Long Time Now*. As I ease his trousers off I carry on talking, aware that there's no lock on my door. 'You're so attractive, David. You look tired. Lie down. I think I've had too much to drink. I feel quite dizzy. Do you mind if I lie beside you?' Trying desperately to look inexperienced, I join him on my narrow bed. David lies beside me, trouserless but chaste.

'It feels so funny to be here with you. I haven't been upstairs in this house since I was a little boy. Me and Annette used to hunt for Easter eggs up here. We used to stay here sometimes, in this room. I remember watching Grandma in the bath. When she stood up the water level went down as if a dam had been emptied. I used to watch, mesmerized, as she swathed her vast white bulk with towels and squeezed herself into some sort of rubber envelope. Aren't grown-up bodies weird when you're a child?'

I'm tempted to retort that he still is. I try to help him relax, rolling on top of him to kiss away his childhood reminiscences. His skin tastes and smells of essence of youth, a wonderful smell despite his unwashed socks and acne. How wonderful to be young enough still to have acne.

Just as we're approaching oblivion I hear footsteps galumphing upstairs, a shrill, barbarous yelling and thumping on my door, 'David! David! We're going to do the tree!'

I recognize the voices of his dreadful sister and cousin, come to sabotage our pleasure. I roll off him and help him put his trousers on while the two girls giggle and whisper in the corridor.

Furious, but determined not to show it, I follow them downstairs, where they all tear the wrapping paper off the mountain of presents under the Christmas tree in a frenzy of acquisitiveness. Then they start eating and drinking again. How they do eat, these people, eat and gush. I have only one appetite, and it can't be assuaged by woolly hats or cake or cups of tea.

I don't manage to talk to David again before he's carried off by his appalling relatives.

George

Term starts again at Julia's college, and I'm back with the silly, affected girls and the refined voices of the teachers who are preparing us for a life of little jobs and dinner parties: always use clean carbon paper, because it saves money in the long run; Staffordshire is always collectable; snowdrops make a lovely centrepiece; never force open a mussel; the art of the soufflé.

I long to tell George and Molly they're wasting their money on my fees, but I'm afraid they'll throw me out. So I truant. I leave their house every morning at eight and go for long walks all over London, going into public libraries, museums and galleries when I'm cold. I stand on Hungerford Bridge, looking at the City wreathed in dust. The skyline, the shining river, the bustling people are so beautiful. When I was genuinely young I only loved you, reluctantly. But now in youthful old age my love seeps out to buildings, trees, strangers' faces and seagulls' cries. Perhaps I'm looking for you, Leo, as I wander all over London. My seduction of David isn't making any progress, and I'm bored with the passive girl I have to pretend to be. An eternity without an income isn't an enticing prospect.

One afternoon in February I come home, exhausted after tramping across Hampstead Heath, and throw myself on to my bed. The house felt empty when I arrived, but now I can hear voices in the garden. I stare down at Molly and George, strolling together arm in arm, supporting each other, pausing to stare at flowers and trees. They don't seem to realize that they are themselves the plant they've been nurturing all these years, two-headed and multi-limbed, not a sexual beast but a domestic growth, deeply rooted and intertwined. I want to laugh because they're so absurd, doddering around the garden together on their varicose veins. Instead I find myself crying, glad when the image of their unbreakable closeness blurs and dissolves in the globular mirrors of my tears.

The three of us have supper together most nights, sitting at the enormous mahogany table in the gloomy dining-room. We eat well, rich food washed down by heavy wines – and sometimes the booze lowers my guard. One night I get a bit giggly over the cheese and biscuits, while Molly's doing her *hausfrau* bit in the kitchen.

'You even have your grandmother's laugh,' George says uneasily.

'I bet you heard that a lot, eh, George? Remember that mattress under the stage at the old Balham Duchess? Remember Giulini's?'

'I do. How could I forget?' He stares at me, and I suddenly realize I've spoken in my old voice. 'I have a legal mind, Jenny, a logical mind; I'm not much given to fantasy. I love plays and novels and films, but I've always been able to distinguish between the possible and the impossible. I mean, people don't make contracts with devils, do they? Not in London restaurants.' He looks perplexed, and I say nothing.

I meet George for lunch at his club in Pall Mall, which still has wooden panelling, leather armchairs, Turkish carpets and open fires. An Edwardian interior to stir the embers of our shared memories.

'I feel I've known you for years,' George says over the potted shrimps, aware that this lunchtime girl isn't the same as his demure house guest.

'Do you remember that night at Gower Street when – my grandmother – was in bed with you and four of her admirers came and sang under her window and you poured a jug of water over their heads?'

George roars with laughter and then looks shocked. 'But surely she didn't tell you things like that – a young girl . . .'

'She told me everything, George. And that time Leo made her practise a dance routine until her feet bled and you came to the rehearsal and wouldn't let her dance any more, you took her out to lunch.'

'Good God, yes, I vaguely remember. That was her Little Dutch Girl act, wasn't it?'

'No, it was the Houri's Dance of the Seven Veils.'

'So it was! You know everything.'

'Everything!' I repeat triumphantly.

We laugh so much that by the treacle pudding George feels dizzy. I want him to ask me about that evening at Giulini's; I long to tell him who I really am. Suddenly I realize George knows that the girl sitting opposite him is his Jenny, that the impossible bargain I struck with you that night was real. He clutches his heart as it lurches with fear and hope.

But I can't quite walk across this bridge between the real and the unreal. What if he tells Molly? What if I'm regarded as a kind of freak? I might be locked up or used for psychological experiments in some laboratory.

So I resist the urge to confide, look at my watch over my second Cognac and exclaim, 'Shit! I've missed Flower Arranging.' I still put in an appearance at Julia's college once or twice a week.

'How quickly you've learnt to sound like other girls,' George says rather sadly. 'For a moment . . .' But we both know that moment has passed.

'Well, that's how they all talk nowadays.'

'Nowadays! You sound like one of the old fogies at the other tables.'

'How about you? Are you an old fogy, George? George? Are you OK? You look awfully red and you're panting.'

'I'm fine. A rejuvenated old fool. Why, I almost feel like a swim downstairs. Have you brought your costume?'

'Of course not! We could swim in the nude, like that night in Brighton with Leo –'

'Now that's quite enough!' George stands up shakily and clutches the table, staring out of the window as if to reassure himself that he knows where and when and who he is. 'It's a lovely spring day out there, my dear. Why don't we go for a walk in the park?'

We set off to Green Park arm in arm, roaring with laughter. 'If you're not my grandfather you ought to be,' I say affectionately. London is at her best. A frosty March sun energizes the stones of the elegant buildings. There's a rich smell of wine, leather, tobacco, perfume and wood smoke. St James's is perhaps the only part of the city where someone born in the nineteenth century needn't feel out of place. The prosperous streets are full of men of George's generation, formally dressed.

'Grandma used to miss London so much. I can see why.'

'Did she? Why on earth didn't she come back here then?'

'I think she was afraid to. She was very embarrassed by my mother. She said she made an awful fool of herself here during the war.'

'Afraid? Never knew a more fearless woman in my life. Anyway, Virginia's follies were hardly her mother's fault.'

'Of course not. But I think she felt responsible just the same. Was it true then? Was my mother really, you know . . .'

'Well, the war was a rather debauched time for a lot of people. Gather ye rosebuds and all that. Your mother got very involved with some young pilot, rather an unpleasant chap I thought. And, er, quite a few other men.'

'So was he my father? This pilot?'

'Oh dear – didn't she – really, my dear, I wouldn't know. Molly and I were married by then with very young children and I was organizing shows for ENSA. I do remember Virginia phoned a few times late at night when I was on leave. I think she drank rather heavily. Molly wasn't very happy about my seeing her, so of course I didn't.'

'It would be nice to know who my father was even if I haven't got a proper grandfather.' I give him my most waif-like look, the expression I nearly managed to seduce him with when I was Virginia. Now, while his resistance is low, is the moment to persuade him to leave me some money. Molly will probably make a scene when the will is read, but by then George will be well insulated against all forms of emotional blackmail.

George enjoys showing me London, watching my face as I try to look as if I'm seeing it all for the first time. 'That's the Ritz, I'll take you to tea there one day. Your mother once caused a sensation there by stripping as she danced a tango. Then the air-raid siren went off and she had to go down to the shelter half naked.'

'How do you know? Were you there?'

'No, of course not. A friend –'

'Oh, it was a friend, was it? I bet Molly wouldn't have liked it if it had been you.'

'Of course it wasn't me. Now, over there you can see my favourite view of Westminster, with the spires and towers sprouting through the trees as if it were still a little medieval city . . .' George thinks he knows his city like the back of his hand, and part of me wants to accept his vision of London, with all its cosiness and limitations. He's just about aware of a newer, brasher culture but arranges his life so that it runs through the most traditional corridors. In this public space there are reminders of change he finds deeply offensive and tries to ignore. One such personification of an alien world is loping towards us now across the grass. George glares apoplectically at a very tall, skinny young man wearing a white suit with flared trousers over purple suede shoes. He has greasy dark-brown hair tied back in a pony-tail, high cheekbones and wolfish dark-blue eyes fixed on me. 'Can't tell if they're men or women half the time. Dressed like something out of a circus. Can't be bothered to cut or wash their hair . . .'

But I'm not listening any more. I stand and stare at the young man, who has now turned and is loping backwards, still drawing me towards him with those dark-blue eyes, which swirl with energy and seem to be expanding like shooting stars all over the park.

'Why is that fellow gawping at you in that insolent way?' The wide park shrinks to an intense black tunnel where two eyes burn, blue and ruthless and terribly familiar. 'Can't even enjoy a postprandial walk . . .'

I hardly hear him, I'm staring after you in surprise and terror. I knew we'd meet sooner or later. Suddenly London is dangerous.

Something horrible has happened to George. He has staggered over to a bench where he's collapsed and sits with his eyes shut, gasping. I run over to him. 'Didn't you recognize him?'

'Who?' George can hardly speak. I hug him, rubbing my nose against his sparse white hair, inhaling cognac and sandalwood cologne, feeling his heavy yet feeble body in my arms. Inarticulate sounds come from his mouth, slurred as if he is drunk. As he tosses and struggles I stare down at my smooth pale-olive fingers with dark-pink almond-shaped nails clasping the square freckled ruin of his. George's nails are yellow and shrivelled like old parchment, speckled with drops of water that I recognize with surprise as my own tears. I bend to kiss his hand.

A stranger calls an ambulance. George dies on the way to the hospital.

Lizzie

Never did like funerals. It was Marie Lloyd's that drove me to that crazy bargain with you. After George's I flee, leaving Molly to face the barrage of sympathy. Sweet, gentle George who loved women and beauty and laughter. I wonder why he didn't strike his own bargain with Leo that night. Then we could really have been an eternal triangle – I would have enjoyed that. He'll live as long as I'm here to remember him, and that's for ever. Can't get Maria Callas's voice out of my head, singing George's favourite aria from *Tosca*. Her voice swooped like an eagle, carrying us all far above the grey scene. When I was young I found opera silly and exaggerated, but, as I get older, love and death really do seem to be the only things worth bothering about. Yes, George should go out on a love duet, he always said great music was the closest he could get to religion.

Where am I now? King's Road. They've knocked down the old Chelsea Palace. Can't remember how I got here. There was a bus, I think, and a lot of walking.

George trumpeted our joy in each other too loudly as we walked in the park that day, and you couldn't bear it. I'm afraid of you, Leo, of the power you still have over me. His death is the victory of reality and I can't accept that, can I? Keep hoping it might be one your conjuring tricks, my preposterous *prestidigiatore*. The gentleman vanishes. I want George to pop out of a hat or slide backwards from the discreet wooden gates of hell, jump out of his casket and bow with a flourish. But he was never much of a showman. Too honest.

You'd say I can't really have loved George because it's not in my contract. How horrible marvellous it was to see you again in the park that day, how sexy vile, handsome repulsive, tender heartless. Who else, in those few seconds, could have electrified me and bumped George off? When I die the last image I see will be your eyes that afternoon. Ah, but I'm not going to. And neither are you. The city George offered me that day was so comforting, warm and old and safe; a father city, that's what I need. As I walk down these half-remembered streets I imagine you waiting for me on the next corner. Suddenly the city is full of you. You darken the sky and play football with my heart. My breasts and the hole at the centre of my being that has been empty for too long quiver at the thought of you.

How bright London is now. It used to be a dark city, dirty bricks and chocolate-brown walls – even the fog needed a wash – but now there's colour everywhere. People look cleaner, richer, younger. Down there is that flat in Tite Street where I lived before I left England in the early twenties. Didn't like Chelsea then because it was so dark and quiet, but it seems to have been painted white and populated with thousands of toy people in tiny skirts and tassels and beads. Boys and girls alike with long hair and huge blank eyes march up and down, displaying their suede and velvet clothes.

Chelsea Antiques Market: I'm a Chelsea antique, so I go in to sell my black coat – vintage Chanel – to a woman who has an old-clothes stall. She's delighted by the authentic mouldy look, as a gardener might be by some curious moss. Gives me fifteen quid. I buy an off-white coat, a jacket really, just long enough to cover a very short skirt. The only fashion rule at the moment seems to be to display as much of your legs and arse as possible to potential lovers. They don't exactly dance, these decadent children, but twitch to barbarous music. I'd love to try it. In my new clothes I feel lighter.

England used to be a place where people took their pleasures sadly, ate and drank badly. Yet what marvellous lives these children lead, sitting in cafés and restaurants in the middle of the afternoon. We were all sent out to work long before their age – which is my age. Pubs look different now, too. Women walk in and out by themselves. *A little bit of the you-know-what that does the we-know-how.* That sad, dark, mean interior of the Derby, the door with its thick leather strap that bashed me on the back as I went in, silent, gloomy men standing at the zinc-topped bar to drink, all staring at me. Only went in when I was desperate for a drink, which I frequently was. Now pubs have tables and chairs, people laughing and talking. No fun drinking on my own. I could pick up one of these sexy androgynous youths, but I need to talk, and who else is left of my generation? Only my sister Lizzie.

After the war George traced her and sent me her address. I've still got her reply to the note I sent her just before I left Rapallo in my bag – crocodile, bought in Florence in the late twenties, I could see the antique-clothes lady eyeing it, but I'd better hang on to something to sell later. Inside is the gold powder-compact that charming opera singer Arturo gave me, a plastic comb, a pigskin wallet with my last ten-bob note in it, a packet of tissues and this scrawl from Lizzie on paper torn from an exercise book:

Dear Jenny,

Funny how your Jenny too. There wasent the money to get to my sisters' foonral it would have to be in Italy she always did have to be diffrent. I dear say she wouldent of come to mine if itd been first. My backs cronik now cant get about mussent grumble. Hoping this finds you better than wot I am wonder if you speak english maybe some day youll come and well have a natter about the old days.

Yr affecshenut Auntie Lizzie

Lizzie had exactly the same education as me at the Bath Street School, and her writing was mine until I decided to do something about it. If she's dead I want to know, and if she's still alive I might as well tell her the truth. She won't believe me anyway, never did have any imagination. When I was in Italy I used to get horrible Woolworth's Christmas cards from her, schmaltzy rhymes and sour badly spelt messages from an address in Hoxton not far from where we lived as children. When I still had dividends coming in I sometimes used to send her fifty quid.

Here I am at Sloane Square tube station, working out how to get to Old Street. I look up her street in my A to Z. Hoxton was darker than Africa when I was growing up there; don't think we had any maps. But I recognize some of the place names like unloved friends. Years since I've travelled by tube. Buses are cheery; they belong to the smiling mouth of the city whereas the tube burrows deep down into its subconscious. These names – Charing Cross, Circle Line, Northern Line, Old Street – drag me back and down like incantations from the underworld.

Already I'm thinking of aggressive things to say to my sister. We never could stop fighting. From Old Street station my feet trace the map while my eyes search for landmarks. Either it's changed or I've forgotten. I pass buildings as old as me but don't recognize them. Poverty has a different face now, wears more clothes, eats more and drives cars.

I want to take Lizzie a present, so I go into a shop run by one of the new immigrants and wonder what to buy for this woman I haven't seen for fifty years. Behind the counter a tiny woman in a brilliant-orange sari is shivering and looks as if Hoxton is a poor exchange for home. I want to ask where that is, but she doesn't speak any English. I choose a present from her stock, any one of which would have been a Sunday treat when we were children: chocolate bars, cakes, nuts and raisins. I choose a chocolate cake, then realize I have only a few shillings which I need for my fare home. Embarrassed, I nod and smile and shuffle backwards out of her shop.

Lizzie lives in a new block of flats ten minutes away from where we grew up. Street names and shapes have changed so that I have a sense of being on familiar territory and at the same time in an ugly foreign country. The old Falstaff, where Auntie Flo sometimes worked as a barmaid, has gone. My childhood has been bulldozed and bombed. All that remains of it is waiting for me upstairs on the ninth floor. The tower block is new, but already the piss-smelling lift in the piss-smelling hall is broken, so I walk up nine flights of graffiti'd concrete stairs, grateful for legs which are as agile as if I really am my own granddaughter.

I bang the knocker on the scabby door. A small woman in a grey coat sidles out and looks at me doubtfully. 'You the home help?'

'No.'

'Where you from?'

'Italy. I've come to see Miss Mankowitz.'

She isn't happy with this but looks at her watch and rushes past me and down the stairs.

I'm reminded of *Crime and Punishment*, when Raskolnikov enters the flat of the old money-lender and is horrified by the ugliness and squalor of old age. Lizzie's flat smells of urine and sour milk. The tiny living-room is dirty, bare and sad. Not a single object that's interesting or attractive – no heirlooms in our family. I walk over to the door that leads to a balcony that is swaying ominously. Up here on the ninth floor I'm assaulted by wind and rain as I look out over the charmless view. Strange that while I've travelled so far my sister has ended up just a few streets away from where she was born, has only levitated a few storeys upwards.

'You the meals on wheels?' The croak comes from the small bedroom.

When I see what time has done to Lizzie my own life seems so deeply fraudulent that tears of guilt come to my eyes. I'm looking at an alternative version of myself. Her face is like a cracked, grimy pot, her features grotesquely altered. Lizzie can't see my tears or me. She has the red, rheumy eyes of the almost blind.

'Who is it?'

'Jenny.'

'Jenny who?'

'Your sister.'

'She's dead.'

'It's really me, Lizzie.' I hug her, suddenly happy to touch and hold the decay I've evaded. The texture of her skin is like ancient paper, her skinny, chicken shoulders protrude through her dirty yellow bed-jacket. I'm suddenly flooded with a sense of my good fortune and fear that she will hate me for it. But Lizzie sounds amused rather than frightened. 'Go on! You're too young.'

'Luck.'

'Yes, you always was lucky. All right then. If it is you, Jenny, what you done wiv my pink camisole?'

'Took it with me when I moved to Gower Street. Sorry.'

'Looked everywhere for it. Auntie Flo said you'd come to a bad end. But you didn't and I did. I was desperate to go out with you that night, do you remember?'

'Yes. And I said you were too young.'

'Well, I'm not too young now, am I?' We laugh, which was the one thing we always managed to do together. I shared a bed with my sister for longer than I did with any man. I sit down at the foot of her bed and try to ignore the stench. Lizzie's face is a Clapham Junction of lines, wrinkles, shadows and tunnelling dirt. Her shiny scalp has a frizz of fluffy white like an ancient baby. At sixty-seven she looks a hundred; she doesn't need to tell me she's had a hard life. But the longer I sit there the easier it is to see the girl's face. I want to wash and iron and starch her, give her back her long, pale features, black curly hair and hooked nose. That nose used to stick into me in the middle of the night. Even when Lizzie was young it came into the room a few seconds before she did, and now it's worthy of Mr Punch. The dark eyes that used to smoulder at me are peering suspiciously as she reaches out and touches my cheek. 'What they got over there in Italy? Magic face cream?'

'I wouldn't be surprised. What happened to your eyes, Lizzie?'

'Cataracts. Forty years sewing. Bloody immigrants buying up all the sweatshops now.'

'So what happened to you after you got back from South Africa?'

'After Ma died Spencer went all posh. Didn't want me around. So I come back here. Thought of going out to Italy to see you, but I didn't think you'd want me neither.'

'Oh, Lizzie, I would! You don't know how lonely I was.'

'Still, you done all right for yourself. Did ya marry any of your fellas?'

'No. Did you?'

'Nah. Sometimes thought it'd be lovely to have a baby. You did. I got a letter. Daughter? Granddaughter? Thought she said you was dead, but I get confused.'

'So you never had any children?'

'Nah. I was too frightened of doing to them what Ma done to us.'

'So you're all alone, too. What do you live on?'

'Living? This isn't living. Let's talk about when we was young and beautiful.'

I smile because she's awarded herself a retrospective beauty she never had. But she can't see my smile anyway. 'What was Ma like, Lizzie, when you finally got to Jo'burg? I always wondered.'

'She met me off the boat. Funny, I can remember her hat but not what I had for dinner today. All ostrich feathers and flowers and grapes, like a bloody great fruit salad – a good ten years out of date. We was all in short skirts by then. Still, it suited her. Lovely face she had, even then.'

'I wish I could remember her. Have you got any photographs?'

'Nah. She took me back to Spencer's house, where she was living, and I could see he wanted an unmarried sister like a swarm of locusts. Jo'burg was full of English girls come over looking for husbands, and all the young men was dead in the war. Spencer was married himself by then, to a South African woman, Joyce. Ever so bossy she was, hard, even Ma was afraid of her. They had two girls and a boy, and they at least was pleased to see me. I loved them children. Used to play with them, do their washing and sewing, took 'em out. Spencer was busy making money and Joyce was entertaining important people. Me and Ma didn't get a look in. Didn't mind being an unpaid nursemaid 'cause the children loved me and that was better than what I had in London. Ma was pickled in gin, miserable as Satan. When I saw her wiv her grandchildren I could see she really hated kids. Couldn't help it, just did. Told me to my face she couldn't stand little girls. Seemed to forget she'd left me and you behind.'

'Did she ask about me?'

'Don't think she even remembered you.'

I'm glad she can't see my face. I had always believed my glamorous mother loved and missed me and wanted to send for me. It was like that moment when George said I'd never been any good on the stage, a lifetime of illusion melted into nothingness.

'Ma was desperate to marry again, though she never stopped complaining about Pa. Said he knocked her about. Went on and on about how he drank, but she was drinking herself. In her room, thought nobody noticed.'

'How did she die?'

'Fell downstairs one night when she'd bin drinking. Found an empty bottle of gin on her bedside table and a jar of pickled walnuts. That was her diet the last few months. She wouldn't talk to any of us. If you ask me, Jenny, we was lucky to have Flo.'

'And what happened to her?'

'When I come back from Jo'burg Flo was in the workhouse. Call it an 'orspital now. Went there last year to get my eyes seen to. Gave me the creeps going in there again. Flo lost the house; I dunno what happened. Saw her on the Monday and she was dead on the Friday. Only me at the funeral. She was good to us was old Flo.'

'It must have been hard for you when you came back to London.'

'Bit late to start worrying about me.'

'Lizzie, honestly, if you'd got in touch I would have helped you. I had money then.'

'Eugenie bloody Manette you called yourself. Didn't know who the hell it was at first.'

'When I heard about the Blitz in the East End I came over here, right across London, to search for you, Lizzie. Only it was all so chaotic I didn't know where to start. But I never forgot about you. You should have –'

'Now I know it's really you, Jenny. I remember that voice. "Oh, I would like to be nice to you, only you're so stupid and there are so many more important people to be charming to." All the time we was girls I heard that voice. And when I saw Ma again I realized where you got it from.'

This is so true that I don't bother to protest. 'Can I come and see you again?'

'Suit yourself. What happened to all the money then?'

'I spent it.'

'Might of known you'd only remember me when you was broke.'

We laugh, and I decide to leave before she remembers too much. 'I will come again, Lizzie. It was wonderful to see you.'

'Wonderful!' she mimics my voice. 'Look a little lovelier each day, don't I? Awff you go then.' Her voice implies that I'm leaving her for a frivolous and exciting alternative. In fact, as I descend the noxious stairs, I've no idea where to go next. I look around the bleak, dark, wet streets, searching for memories, for clues as to who I was before I met you, Leo. But there aren't any. I wander down to a main road, Kingsland Road. I must have walked here a thousand times as a child, but it doesn't look familiar.

I get on a bus where I sit upstairs in a comfortable fug of illuminated smoke and steam. I don't know or care where I'm going, and there's a kind of beauty in my blind passage through my city. I'm so alone that I can project myself on to the hissing traffic, rotting buildings and struggling crowds. The window is steamed up and dripping with beads of rain, I breathe on the glass and wipe a circle of clarity to press my nose against.

Molly

Molly's alone in the drawing-room with the remains of the funeral tea. 'Come and sit down. I'll make you a hot drink. We missed you after the funeral. Where did you go?'

'Don't know.'

Molly plies me with tea and biscuits and leftover canapés. 'Why, you're half asleep. Take off your wet things. Is that a new jacket?'

'Yes. I sold Grandma's old coat. I wanted to feel young.'

'Why, of course you're young, you silly girl. Were you upset by the funeral? You were very fond of George, weren't you?'

'He was so kind.'

Suddenly we're crying together, side by side on the couch. We share a box of tissues. 'You know, when you first came I thought you were callous. Your grandmother – but I realize now you're a very different character. You'll really miss George, won't you, dear? But you'll soon find a boyfriend. You won't be all on your own like me. David was frantically worried about you when you disappeared after the funeral. He'd marry you tomorrow, you know, if you wanted him to. But I don't suppose you do. You could eat ten Davids before breakfast.'

'Yes, I suppose I could. I don't want to marry.'

'Probably just as well. You're young and beautiful, and you have no idea of the damage that inflicts.' Haven't I just. 'In a few years you'll be as much of a man-eater as your grandmother, and I want my David to be happy. Muriel's different, she's old-fashioned. Modern girls like you and Annette don't understand the first thing about love. I would have looked after George for another ten years if he'd survived that heart attack, even if he had been paralysed and incontinent. That's marriage; you don't just walk away from it. You think it's all about romance and sex and having a good time. A long marriage is something to be proud of. Forty years, and I do still love him. Have another tissue. And one of these little quiches. You can stay here until I sell the house.'

'Thanks, Molly,' I say when I can speak. 'Look, I've been meaning to tell you, I know Julia's your friend and I'm sure her college suits some girls, but I don't want you to waste any more money on me. I'll get a job.'

'Doing what?'

'I don't know. And – sorry, but my shoes are worn out. Could I borrow the money for some new ones?'

'But, of course, my dear. George wouldn't have wanted you to hobble around like an old tramp. Let me give you some money for fares, as well.'

'It's all right. I like to walk.'

'I had no idea you were so hard up. You know, that caricature Beerbohm did of your grandmother must be worth a fortune.' Too late, Molly remembers she isn't supposed to have seen it and lowers her gaze.

'I couldn't possibly sell that.'

She looks at me in surprise. 'You're the last girl I would have expected to be sentimental.'

'I did love my grandmother.'

'I hated her – and I never even met her. It's strange, but I feel much closer to you than to Annette.'

'Perhaps I am your granddaughter.'

'Well, it's quite possible. Now go upstairs, dear, before you fall asleep. We'll – I'll be fine.' Molly gasps as if it has only just hit her that she's in the first-person singular now. She looks incredulously at the green leather armchair where George used to sit every night under the green-shaded standard lamp, reading the *Financial Times* or *Plays and Players*.

Now it's David's turn to try to find something for me to do. Any excuse to see him. I adore our chaste, awkward meetings, and I'd follow him to the ends of the earth, even to the cavernous basement in Notting Hill Gate where his friend Barry lives. David sweetly chaperones me, as he's afraid to leave me alone with this knowing, rather brash young man. In fact Barry's not nearly as appealing as David. Innocence is the only really sexy thing.

While I dress and make up for the photographic session the two boys discuss me as if I'm not there, and I resent this. Even though I've set myself up as an object of desire I expect to be taken seriously. Isn't it obvious that I'm not just a pretty face? Barry doesn't even think I'm that. 'Frankly, I don't think she'll get any work as a model. We'll give it a try, anyway.'

'But she's so beautiful!'

'Yes, but she's an acquired taste. Pre-Raphaelite, not modern. What they all want now is straight blonde hair, regular features, white face, blue eyes, no tits or bum – maybe if she dyed her hair and wore a wig and lost a few pounds ...?'

'But then she wouldn't be the same person!'

'Exactly. Sorry, David.'

I desperately try to look my best as I cavort in front of Barry's camera. When I was a girl I was taught to mince and flounce and blush, to be a whore but act like a lady. Nowadays girls are expected to behave in public as they once would have done only in the bedroom. Walking the streets of London, I see girls who might be boys and boys who might be girls thrusting their tongues down each other's throats in the middle of the pavement. I can't wait to try it, but it's all very confusing.

David and I meet for dinner in a bistro in the Finchley Road. He's just come from work and looks hot and shiny, ridiculously young in his three-piece suit, like a child dressed up in his father's clothes. At first I thought his face was an exact replica of his grandfather's, but I was wrong. Well-brought-up young men of my generation were so thoroughly squashed during their education and childhood that they always looked a bit repressed, as if waiting for nanny or the Latin master to slap them. George had a couple of months in the Army right at the end of the Great War to make him look even more stiff and apprehensive. These children know they own the world, and that confidence is reflected in their faces. David is well on the way to joining the professional establishment but he's just beginning to realize he can have a good time on the way, I can see it in his blue eyes, which stare at me with such flattering lust and devotion, and in his shy, tender smile. He's so young that he still blushes, dark pink suffusing his slightly tanned, translucent skin. I thank you with all my heart, Leo, as I kiss David. He tastes so good.

He takes a sheet of photographs out of his briefcase and hands it to me. Here I am in rows of black-and-white windows, a strip cartoon, strutting my stuff. In one little box I swan in a long black dress, my hair piled on my head; in another I jump, wearing a halter-neck T-shirt and white bell-bottoms. I tried so hard to look modern, but Barry has caught an arch expression that belongs to another era. When I don't look coy I look surprised and worried. Even these miniature images reveal my discomfort. The camera, plainly, hasn't fallen in love with me.

But David has, and I'm moved by his concern for my feelings. 'I'm awfully sorry, but Barry doesn't think – I mean . . .'

'I'm not Twiggy after all? Oh well.'

'You're not too upset?'

'No, of course not.' But I am. After seventy years of narcissism you'd think I could manage to dress up and parade around in front of a camera successfully.

'Oh, Jenny!' He reaches across the table to grip my hand in both his. 'I think he's crazy. If I was him I'd want to take photographs of you all day. And all night.'

I stand outside Molly's bedroom and watch her undress through a crack in the door. Off comes the black suit and the white blouse. She stands in her pink silk slip, the bat wings of her upper arms wobbling in the soft light of her bedside lamp. Naked, she swells and quivers like a Rubens goddess. No, a natural woman. She puts on a pink satin night-dress, heaves herself into the double bed, reaches out to the empty space beside her and mutters to herself. I move closer so that I can hear what she's saying.

'Well, I don't see why I shouldn't have read your letters to her. I'm going back tomorrow to have another look, and if any of them are dated after we got married I'll give you hell. I don't blame Jenny, poor little thing. I thought you'd want me to give her some money. But I don't know what you saw in that bitch, her grandmother. I do wish you hadn't gone off like that, darling. I can't help thinking you're just in the bathroom and you're going to come in any minute in your paisley dressing-gown smelling of Floris aftershave.'

Just before Molly is due to move to her new flat near Holland Park I tell her I've found a job.

'Well done! What sort of job?'

'It's a boutique in High Street Kensington. Terribly swish, I mean groovy, lots of pretty girls wearing practically nothing.'

'How much will they pay you?'

'Eight pounds a week – I think I can just about manage to pay for my rent and food out of that. It won't be very interesting, of course.'

'Nonsense, you'll have great fun with the other girls. I envy you. I shall have a very dull life all alone in my little flat. I do hope you'll come and see me sometimes. I'll miss you.'

On the Make

I miss you, too, Molly. How about a swap? You can have my lousy boring job; I'll take your new flat in Holland Park Avenue and all the investments and annuities.

This living for ever is all very well, but how to do it with any dignity and meaning? Perhaps I should be truthful about my age in order to get a pension. But I lost my birth certificate years ago, and I've no documents except a passport forged by a crook in the back streets of Genoa, describing me as Jennifer Mankowitz, born in London in 1945. Nobody would believe my real age – and I couldn't live on a pension anyway.

Is this it then? That reality I've been threatened with all my life. London has shrunk to a few streets around West Kensington and the black-and-purple mirrored gloom of the fashion temple where I work. Only half a step up from the kind of job I might have got if I'd stayed in Hoxton. These girls in the shop are working class, with a bit of spirit and more ambition than brains, just like me and Lizzie half a century ago.

Reminded of my sister, I go to see her, loaded with presents: yoghurt and salmon mousse – which can be eaten comfortably without teeth – a new tape recorder and some tapes of music-hall and wartime songs. I want us to have a sing-song, like when we were girls, and I've brought a blank tape to record our memories. I'll be able to play it when I wake, as I often do, in the middle of the night, feeling unreal and hollow, as if I've imagined myself but forgotten to give myself a heart. I also buy some flowers from a kiosk near Old Street Station. When we were children Lizzie and I used to pass that flower stall every morning on our way to school, and my pulse used to race at the sight of that unattainable brilliance, blazing in the mass of grey. The old woman who kept the stall in those days was filthy, almost mummified in layers of ancient clothes. Sixty years later I smile at her clean successor and choose a bouquet of crimson and golden roses for my sister.

But Lizzie's door is answered by a stranger, the new tenant, who tells me my sister died last month.

Flee down the concrete stairs and through unfamiliar streets: running takes me back to childhood, when I was always in a hurry, my heart pounding, gasping for breath. But my childhood is out of reach now, demolished like the tenements and alleys and courtyards. All that Lizziescape vanished for ever. She was as unattractive as the old slums but familiar, my only family. Anguish grips me as I stand on a street corner, my arms crossed over my breast to hug the sister I never knew I loved. Several passers-by stop to stare at me as I stand there weeping in the Friday evening rush-hour.

The hardest thing to accept is change. Heraclitus said all is flux, but Ancient Greece was a lot more stable than twentieth-century London. My gift is never to change, and that makes it sadder, harder, when people I love die. Every hour George and Lizzie travel further into the kingdom of death. In the Natural History Museum there's a cross-section of an ancient redwood tree. Inside it, concentric circles mark historical events that took place in Europe as the massive tree silently grew in its American forest: while Vikings invaded, while Shakespeare wrote his plays, while Napoleon rampaged. My internal life, in cross-section, would look like that tree: too much experience, too many events and memories. I long for you, Leo, because it's only with you that I don't have to pretend. They all go into the dark, all the others.

At work with the other girls I lurk in the shadows as Lou Reed gasps for heroin and the customers blink at our white, staring faces, trying to adjust their eyes to the fashionable gloom. You can't see the colour of the clothes you try on here, let alone the size or price. If you manage to squirm in front of the other half-naked women to see yourself in the mirror in the collective changing-room, you have only the haziest idea what you look like. But the boss insists that all this mystery is good for business, and she seems to be right, as women are flocking to buy her dramatic clothes.

So this is how to be young. No more elocution lessons, no more panics over which knife and fork to use. Cockney accents are fashionable now. I'm trying to recover the one I so carefully lost. These girls are sharp-witted, uneducated, enterprising, ambitious; they remind me of the chorus girls I once worked with, hoping their face – or some other part of their anatomy – will be their fortune. I understand their daydreams because they used to be mine: a millionaire will walk in and buy up the shop and me; a film producer will spot me walking down the street and sign me up. If Leo came here tomorrow and offered them all contracts not one of them would turn him down, and who could blame them? The souls of the poor have always been cheap.

We're in our summer uniform: tiny, sleeveless, low-backed dresses. Most of us look better than the customers, even in the dark, and we know it. Occasionally a woman comes in who is young, good-looking and rich, and a sigh of collective longing rustles through the racks of clothes. We're all on the make, but these girls are free. They've risen above their biology.

When I first heard them talking about the pill I thought it was a fantasy. My early life was dominated by fear of pregnancy. Ma never stopped telling us how having children had ruined her life. It was never clear what it was, this glorious career we'd robbed her of. Probably just a richer husband. Anyway I got the message that babies were bad news and still feel sick and torn remembering those two furtive abortions I had in my late teens. Blood and stench and pain. You paid, although, you said, those long-dead babies couldn't be yours. And I didn't ask why – I didn't ask nearly enough questions about you in those days. I didn't think of pregnancy in terms of fathers, mothers or even children. It was just a nuisance, an obstacle to my ambition, which required me to have a lot of sex with a lot of different men. With you there was passion, with George there was tenderness. But with dozens of others, can't even remember how many, it was business. Fondled and groped and shoved on to couches in seedy, locked, backstage rooms, my body was an ace in a game that was played for quite low stakes, for a job in a chorus line or a bottle of perfume.

I go along to a family-planning clinic and tell the doctor I'm engaged – which makes me respectable, it seems. He gives me a discreet brown-paper bag full of mauve cardboard wallets, each containing twenty-eight tiny pills labelled with the days of the week. I take one on the way home; it tastes of nothing. Those pills are in my brown suede shoulder-bag now, and whenever I open it I stare at them, amazed that these sweets have changed the destiny of women. In fourteen days I'll be impregnable, and I'll celebrate by finally seducing David. Yummy-yum. Fairy-tales become science so quickly nowadays. One day I suppose eternal youth will be just a matter of turning up at a clinic with a large cheque, and you, Leo, will be redundant.

I'm alone again in my little room overlooking West Kensington Station, with its lurid-pink floral wallpaper, gas fire and meter, three-legged wardrobe and decaying carpet. It's no better than the one I used to share with Lizzie, except that here I have my bed to myself. A privilege I'm getting rather tired of.

I'm filthy after a day at work and the long walk home. I'll have to venture into the ingeniously uncomfortable bathroom where an explosive Ascot heater fails to heat water for the scabbed and blistered bath. Pubic hairs, grease and dead skin seem to be growing on the sides of this bath like lichen on a wall. Tried to clean it with Vim and a rag, but I only made the blisters bigger. The bath is on claws that dig into the archaeological strata of linoleum. I always leave the bathroom feeling dirtier than when I entered it and try not to remember the creamy marble luxury of my bathroom in Rapallo. Usually I just heat water in my kettle and wash in a bowl in front of a fire, a childhood ritual I enjoy invoking, like the flavour of bread and milk and coconut Ma used to make for our supper when we were little.

After all this time I belong nowhere, own almost nothing. I stare at my Vuitton wardrobe trunk, plastered with Cunard labels and the names of prehistoric grand hotels. Inside it's papered like a little room, a claustrophobic pattern of brown-and-white diamonds. There are several pairs of suede and leather gloves, an ermine muff, a black-beaded evening bag, a coffee-coloured lace parasol with an ivory handle in the shape of a parrot's head, a black-and-white caricature of a young woman with enormous dark eyes, her impossibly big head surrounded by a forest of black Beardsleyesque hair, inscribed 'For Jenny Mere, Love from Max, 1952'. I breathe in the nostalgic fragrance of dried lavender and rosemary and old leather, then open a black-lacquer box inlaid with mother-of-pearl full of bundles of letters neatly tied with ribbon. The colour has faded from the ribbon and the ink. Once I gobbled those love letters from George and Binkie and my other admirers, but now their brownish insect tracks seem remote. My only other possessions are a few books, cheap clothes and cosmetics.

The Boy Who'd Never Had His Ticket Punched Before. Molly said I could eat ten Davids before breakfast; instead, I meet one for supper.

Who am I tonight? A young woman meeting a man I know is in love with me? A lecherous old hag lusting after a handsome boy? If I were a man of seventy – even if I looked my age – I'd be considered a sexual hero for pursuing a girl of twenty-two. In the tarnished mirror behind our table in the shabby Italian restaurant I catch sight of our reflection, the only reality I choose to acknowledge: a lovely young couple. Our conversation is friendly, almost brotherly–sisterly, with an exciting undercurrent of sensuality.

As we walk slowly back to my room sunset floods the dismal streets with patches of gold and diamonds. We stand outside my house and David looks shy, an expression I'm so unused to that I have to peer at his face to interpret it. He looks about fifteen. I kiss him lightly on both cheeks.

The touch of his skin and the taste of youth on his lips sharpen my desire. I can't stop kissing him, standing in the dirty street. Pull him into the house and up to my room, which is transformed by our naked bodies and our delight in each other.

David whispers, 'Am I the first man you've slept with?'

I try not to laugh. My face is buried in his pubic hair, so it's easy to disguise my amusement. I wonder what on earth virgins get up to nowadays. 'Would you like to be?'

'I don't mind if I'm not. I just want to know all about you.'

'Well – it's a long story. How about you? Have you slept with lots of women?'

'Two,' he says proudly. 'A girl at a dance a couple of years ago and one of the secretaries at work. But that was lust, not love.'

'Can't you have both?'

'I think when you're really in love – ahhh – no – yes . . .'

The beauty of his young, pale, strong body. Why is the world full of images of naked women and not of naked men? The curve where his neck meets his shoulders and the long, slim line of his furry golden legs are as perfect as I can bear. Before I made love to him I thought David was just the relic of George, but now I see an entirely different man, perhaps because George and I were young together. Oscar Wilde was right. Youth is wasted on the young, but it's not wasted on me: it's only now that I can see how desirable and glorious his 22-year-old body is.

Afterwards we fall asleep intertwined on the narrow bed and wake up to find the room is dark.

'Great place for a trainspotter,' David says.

'Can't sleep because of the noise of the trains.'

'I don't like the flat I'm in either. I hate living with men. Why don't we move in together?'

'What would your grandmother say?'

'Nothing, probably. It's none of her business.'

'Let's see how it goes.'

It goes smoothly and sweetly. Whenever the desire for you becomes irresistible I phone David, as an alcoholic might grab a bottle of mineral water when the longing for booze becomes too strong.

In bed with David, the rigor mortis that has petrified my too-experienced heart softens so that at last I feel as young inside as I look outside. He renews me, as vampires are renewed by the blood of their lover-victims. It isn't possible to quarrel with David, who's so happy that he has no temper at all. Every time we meet I'm freshly amazed that he loves and wants me so much. I've considered telling him that I was forty-nine when he was born – but he wouldn't believe me; he hasn't a scrap of imagination. I turn back into his beautiful arms, licking the place where the golden hairs grow.

I wonder if vampires also suffer from post-coital depression. All this succulent youth and vitality are intoxicating, but they leave me with a hangover. I can't love David without deceiving him, and I'm weary of my own dishonesty.

On weekdays David has to work late and is too tired to do anything but go straight home to his shared flat in Chiswick, so we can only meet at weekends.

How beautiful these summer evenings are. I can't bear to go straight home, so I buy a sandwich and go to Holland Park where, on the lawn behind the burnt-out house that was once the social centre of London, a party happens spontaneously every sunny evening. Not a traditional English garden party with hats and strawberries but something new: young people celebrate their youth, sitting on the grass with flutes and guitars and joints. They, we, wear bright cheesecloth clothes, beads and bells and long hair. They, we, are like a court made up entirely of jesters entertaining each other. Friendships and love affairs develop out of these picnics on the grass, and we're all as enchanted by our own attractiveness as the peacocks screaming with narcissism on the other side of the fence.

At first I was an outsider here. I used to sit on the grass a few yards away, pretending to read as I admired the bright circles of decorative young people, trying to convince myself I had the right to be here, too. Everything is permitted now, but I can still hear those authoritarian voices from my first youth: you can't do that, Jenny; you can't afford it; you mustn't wear that; you're not allowed; who do you think you are, Lady Muck?

One evening I fall asleep on the lawn, worn out by my long day in the shop, and wake to find the sunset painting the young faces. They're all either drunk or stoned, a combination of innocence and sophistication that fascinates me. This is Arcadia but with shepherds and nymphs exchanging roles. Zeus would have loved it. Perhaps he's here each night, disguised as a rabbit or a bird, preparing to ravish these androgynous nymphs.

I'm sitting cross-legged on the grass next to a boy called Matt who, five minutes after we've exchanged names, lies down and puts his head in my lap like a dog. I stroke his thick chestnut hair, smoke the joint, drink from the wine bottle that is being passed around and eat the marijuana cookies – made to Mrs Beaton's recipe, the girl who baked them says proudly. There isn't much conversation but there's a lot of touching and cuddling going on, and suddenly I decide this is what I want. I'll take Matt home with me tonight.

But my impulse to sleep is stronger than my lust. I fall asleep again, and when I open my eyes they've all vanished, as if they really were the stuff that dreams are made of. It's nearly dark, that hour when the park fights back at the city and becomes genuinely wild. Trees and bushes seem denser, older, noisier, and the perfume rising from the warm earth is as heady as wine fumes. It's the moment when the earth cracked open to reveal Pluto before he dragged Persephone away from her endless summer. Not wanting to visit the Underworld just now – or, more prosaically, get locked in the park – I jump up and cross the deserted lawn.

Then I catch sight of a tall figure in a white suit loping through the trees ahead, where the last of the sun dazzles trickily. I can't see your face, but your wolfish walk is so familiar that I run after you, following you down the broad path to High Street Kensington.

I could easily catch up with you, but some instinct warns me to remain unseen. You move very fast, with a curious rhythm, as if you might break out into a dance at any minute. At the traffic lights, waiting to cross Cromwell Road, you hop with impatience. I'm close enough to see that your suit, which looked brilliantly white from the distance, is grubby and crumpled. You cross Cromwell Road, then I lose sight of you and feel so desolate that I almost run between the thundering juggernauts. The wait at the lights seems agonizingly long, as if the vast ugly street is a conjuring trick designed to frustrate me. At last the lights change and I run across the road, but there's no sign of you.

Then I glimpse the white suit darting down stone steps to a basement. I feel a surge of relief and my eyes fill with tears. I don't even need to see your face, I know you by the way you move, your atmosphere of nonchalance and danger and your power over me.

I follow you down to a concrete yard full of dustbins. On my right is a grimy bay window covered with black bars and in front of me a

87

door with no bell or knocker. There are no lights down here, only the jaundiced reflections of street lamps. I bang on the door with my knuckles, but nobody comes. The curtains at the window beside me are drawn, and I can hear loud music. The dark cumbersome house throbs with hostility.

The Metaphysical Bank

You open the door, and I feel energy flow back into my veins as your dark-blue eyes stare at me again. 'Hello, Pantoffsky, you old fraud.'

'My darling Jenny. You took your time.'

'I've been searching for you for months.'

'I knew you'd be all right with old George.'

'Yes, but he wasn't. He's dead. You bumped him off that day we saw you in the park.'

'What an outrageous accusation! I didn't touch him.'

'You didn't have to. If looks could kill, and yours can . . .'

'You burst into my house after more than twenty years and immediately start accusing me . . .'

'We haven't changed, have we? You said we wouldn't.' I stare at you. 'No, I was wrong. You have changed, Leo. You wouldn't have got away with that pony-tail in the RAF.'

'Got to look the part, my dear.'

'What is the part? Pop star?'

'Several pop stars are my clients, as a matter of fact. I provide a service. Now tell me why you followed me.'

'I couldn't help it.'

'You should be more careful, Jenny. I might have been a mass murderer.'

'You are.'

'There you go again, making wild allegations. What do you want?'

'You.'

You lead me into the vast front room. It must once have been the kitchen; there are traces of grim domesticity in the disused food lift and the dusty row of coloured bells on the wall. There are four sofas, at right-angles to each other as if to discourage conversation. On one of them is sprawled a tall girl with long fair hair wearing an ankle-length blue cheesecloth dress who stares at me blankly. Is that tranquillized jealousy in her eyes? On the other couch is a beautiful boy in white silk pyjamas. 'Nat, this is Jenny, one of my oldest friends. And, Jenny, this is Hari.'

The big glass-topped round table is cluttered with ashtrays, wine, beer, Coca-Cola and transparent plastic bags. I watch, bewildered, as you pour the white powder out of one of the plastic bags and slice it with a razor blade. A bored, nasal, decadent voice sings, 'I'm waiting for my man.' The 'I' expands into a universe of egotism. The room is dark except for the Anglepoise lamp illuminating you as you chop, weigh and package. Nat and Hari are even younger than the illusory youth you have given me. Nat suddenly opens her eyes, gets up and wraps herself around you on her way to the door. Hari helps himself to the powder, which he snorts up his nose through a rolled-up pound note, then droops back on to his couch.

I want to talk, but talking has gone out of fashion. Anxious not to be out of date, I look around for clues as to how I should dress and behave. There are no books in this room, only shelves of records and brilliantly coloured abstract posters on the walls. The carpet and walls are decayed, but there's a pile of five-pound notes on the table. You count the money in your circle of light, carefully roll up a pound note, stick it up one nostril and inhale some of the powder. Then you gasp with pleasure and leap up, dancing towards me.

'Still here, Jenny? I'll give you a free snort, if you like.'

'What is it?'

'Coke. Surely you've had it?'

'Now let me guess. I can remember when coke was a fuel, then it became a fizzy drink, then – cocaine?'

'Help yourself. I've got some great stuff here. Pure, uncut, just off the plane from Colombia.' You hand me a rolled-up note.

'No thanks.'

'It's not like you to turn down fun. Try some. This is happy dust, sugar bliss, cheap thrills – not so cheap, actually. No side-effects. This is unbelievably pure stuff. No? Oh well, have some wine then.'

You, not cocaine or alcohol, are the drug I crave. My body cries out to be touched by you, my legs have stayed long and slim for you, my breasts and buttocks have kept their shape because I knew that one day you would caress them again.

We hug, and I feel the sharp bones of your back and shoulders. You're thin, and your skin is cool, unlike the rounded warmth of David. I feel the terrible continuity of loving you, the circle my emotions have been burning since I was fifteen. Whoever I was before I met you, that girl has long ago been incinerated. Whoever I am with David, I'm twice as alive when I'm with you.

We're in each other's arms again, intertwined as we walk down the dark corridor into the shadowy bedroom. The years melt as we fall on to the bed, and every nerve in my body responds to you. Afterwards we kiss, our mouths still hungry for the taste of each other.

We dress and go back into the cavernous front room where the Velvet Underground are still on the turntable and Nico croons huskily as you dance around the table looking remarkably foxy, slicing, weighing and measuring. Smoke, incense and light bulbs draped in red Indian cotton create a glowing mist that illuminates Hari and Nat, lying on their couches in comatose elegance.

'We need to talk, Jenny. About money. Can't have you slaving away in a shop, living in squalor.'

'But I like it.'

'Nonsense. Stick around and in the morning we'll go to the Fizz.'

'The what?'

'Hari, move over and let Jenny sit down. No, children, Uncle Leo's not giving you any more goodies yet.'

Already I'm seething with resentment at the way you boss us all. You make me feel like a skeleton clock, my organs transparent as you wind me up. I'm struck by your terrible energy as you suck the willpower out of the rest of us. I make a point of charming the boy next to me, which is no hardship as he's extraordinarily handsome, with liquid black eyes and fine bones. 'Where are you from, Hari?'

'Kashmir.'

'What on earth are you doing here?'

'My father sent me to boarding-school here. I hated it, so I ran away and then I met Leo. I can't go home now.'

'His father's the chief of police,' you interrupt with a collector's pride. 'And Nat's dad is a judge.' You put your arm around her as she comes back into the room with a tray of coffee mugs. You roar with laughter and hand around pieces of blotting paper like sweets. I refuse. 'But you have to try this, Jenny. It's pure acid, 100 per cent. I know the guy whose lab it was made in. This is special; it'll give you visions like you've never had before. That's right, Hari, enjoy yourself. And you, too, Nat. Give it about half an hour to hit you. Jenny? Really? You're missing something wonderful here.'

Nat and Hari guzzle the drugs eagerly, like stupid greedy children. And you're their candy man, posing as a benevolent uncle, indulging them. You start on one of your monologues, your 'arias' as George used to call them. Standing in the middle of the room in your white suit, waving your arms and shouting above the rock music, you dominate us all.

'This stuff is wonderful. Just a few drops on a piece of blotting paper and you're in another world. The promised land. *Paradis artificiel,* much better than the real thing, take it from me. Can you see it? Nat? Hari? Are you getting there? I can see fountains and rainbows – ah! That music sounds so wonderful. You're beautiful, Nat, and you, Hari, and me, am I beautiful? Not you, Jenny. You're such a fucking misery sitting there. Why won't you take anything? You're no fun any more. Oh, this is such great stuff! I'd like to put it in the water supply, I'd like to spike all those boring old farts in the House of Lords and all those pompous old judges like your dad, Nat. Everything could be so wonderful, we could inherit the earth, you know that? What can you see, Hari?'

Hari's beautiful face is glistening with sweat or perhaps tears. 'My house,' he says with difficulty. Nat can hardly speak. She sits very still, gazing at some private vision of heaven or hell. But you on acid are a verbal tornado. On and on you go, messianic and aggressively happy, sucking up all the oxygen in the room.

Nat mumbles something, a rapt expression on her shiny face. She can't articulate properly, and I go over to the couch where she's lying to hear what she's trying to say. 'Actions speak louder than words, Leo,' she finally manages to enunciate with a kind of depraved primness. Hari nods as if a great truth had been uttered and you seize Nat's thin, pale hands.

'Oh Nat, you're so right! You understand. I knew you would. You want action? Pretty soon, I can't tell you when exactly, there's going to be so much action: all the dams in the world are going to burst, you know that? And there'll be floods and earthquakes and a great war with a thousand bombs and the rivers will rise and the sun will get hotter and hotter. So beautiful. I love wars. Jenny and I had a great war, didn't we?'

Your voice rants on and on. I sleep fitfully, curled up on the sofa, and wake feeling stiff and cold. It's nearly dawn. I go to the window and push aside the dark-red velvet curtains. Yes, the Cromwell Road is grey rather than black. I wonder what the Fizz is. Some kind of nightclub that opens during the day? You've always had this capacity to turn night into day, to find the best reasons for doing the worst things.

Looking out at the street I suddenly think of David, who will be getting up, shaving, perhaps writing me another love letter. I'm deceiving him already, and that makes me feel old and cynical. I feel like a plastic daffodil contemplating two exquisite wild flowers as I watch Nat and Hari sprawl with natural grace, exhausted by the chemicals they've assaulted their bodies with and mesmerized by you, who are still talking. I'd like to get them away from you. If I had any money I'd set up a home for lost souls.

You interrupt your own monologue to look at me sharply. 'Nat and Hari are charming and far less demanding than you. They're perfectly all right. Having the time of their lives. Aren't you?'

Hari nods, stands up and is sick into a pot containing a dead plant. Nat sits on her couch weeping and bewildered. 'Bedtime!' You clap your hands. 'Sleep it off, and I'll bring you back some more goodies tonight. Nat, I'm going out with Jenny. Be back at about lunchtime.' You kiss Nat on the brow in an odd priestly gesture and turn back to me. 'Come on, Jenny, I'll take you to the Fizz. This way.'

Where the red velvet curtains hung over the window a few minutes ago there is a dark tunnel, glowing with fire. Your shadow is cast on the wall, and I watch my own merge with it as you pull me after you into the underworld that sucks us in. A warm wind pushes us forward. I'm gliding with your arms around me as if we're skating on fire instead of ice. The wind sighs, or perhaps that is groaning I can hear, from the grotesque faces that line the walls of the phosphorescent tunnel.

Suddenly we're standing in a high-ceilinged, panelled room with crimson carpets and blazing chandeliers. The contrast with the darkness we have just come from is so dazzling that I blink. Groups of men and women stand talking and laughing, sipping drinks from trays held by footmen in wigs and breeches. My first thought is that they must be actors because all of them, even the footmen, are startlingly good-looking and overdressed, in historical costumes that make me feel drab in my short white dress. They must be shooting a film here; perhaps that's why the lights are so bright. You skip from group to group, looking animated and relaxed; you seem to know everyone in the room. Baffled, I take a glass of champagne from a tray, a very good Bollinger. The dry, nutty, chilled wine hits my nose like sea spray as I wander around the room listening to snatches of conversation.

'Darling! Haven't seen you since the Somme.'

'No, it was Paris, the Commune. Don't you remember?'

'You look gorgeous. Who did your face?'

'This wonderful little man in San Francisco. I'll give you his number.'

Nobody looks old or poor or sick or tired. Cosmopolitan, too, I observe, listening to scraps of French and Italian and German. The champagne is wonderfully potent. Warmth and benevolence flood me, relaxing my face into a party beam as I eavesdrop.

'I've been meaning to ask you, are you going short on your railway shares?'

'I was just trying to decide. Let's go and ask old Hudson; he's standing over there. Used to be the Napoleon of railways, but now I believe he's the Attila the Hun of washing machines. Tom says the South Sea's the thing to invest in. They're trading now. Go short just before the bubble bursts. Go long on cocaine futures and you'll make enough to live on for another hundred years.'

'Really? Thanks so much. I'll see if I can catch the pasts market before they close.'

'Lucrezia? You don't look a day older. How's the family?'

'Dead, most of them. So careless. Cesare was always such a sceptic, he refused to believe in either place. When I told him about my little deal he sneered, and six months later he was dead. Have a drink. We'll toast him.'

'No thanks.'

'Oh, but you don't think – I wouldn't dream of it. I work for charities now.'

'Jenny!' I look around, startled, as a tall man in a gold dressing-gown embroidered with green dragons hugs me.

'Binkie? But you –'

'Bought it, as they used to say. No, actually I sold it centuries ago. Always a good idea to disappear in a war. It's expected. I'm not Binkie any more. Rather dated, don't you think? I'm Pete now. Did you get the little present I left you?'

'Yes! I never had the chance to thank you. Leo invested it for me, and it kept me going until last year. I'm so glad you're still alive.'

'How could I not be? Aren't these parties marvellous?'

'This is the first one I've been to.'

'Really? It's your first time back? How touching. You must be the youngest person in the room. Why you can't be more than seventy, practically an infant. Still with Leo, I see.'

'Well, not exactly. You're still very handsome. It sounds corny but you really don't look a day older. You were the first lord I slept with, I remember. I was quite bowled over.'

'None of that nonsense now. It's all supposed to be classless, although I have my doubts. I'm investing in pop music, so if you've got any money left over I'll look after it for you.'

'Binkie – I mean Pete – what are they all talking about? What's all this about bubbles and railway shares?'

'Oh, you mean the pasts market? Just something Leo and I cooked up over dinner a few years ago. You know about selling futures of course? Soya-bean futures can be quite profitable, for example, but you have to wait years to get your money back, and it's not awfully enter-taining. So we developed this idea of using history as a kind of yellow pages, browsing through it for financial opportunities. It takes quite a bit of skill. You have to identify the time and the place exactly – for instance, the week when the East India Company started to make vast profits in Calcutta or the exact moment to invest in the Medici bank in Florence. It's fascinating and extremely lucrative. Why don't you join me in a flutter on the gladiators in Rome in the second century AD? Let me explain how it works . . .' But, as always when people start talking to me about finance, I yawn uncontrollably and don't really listen to what he's saying. I stare at the back of a familiar head, waiting for the face to turn towards me.

'Assunta!'

'Cara signora!' As we hug, her jewellery scratches me. Her old black dress has been replaced by a magnificent green velvet gown that makes me feel dowdy.

'Assunta, you should have told me. I feel such a fool . . .'

You rush up. 'Thanks so much, Assunta, darling. You did a great job.'

'You mean you paid her to spy on me?'

'What an unpleasant word. I couldn't let you just disappear, could I? Assunta's an old friend from Savonarola's Florence. She had some gambling debts with the Fizz so she worked them off by looking after you and sending me monthly reports.'

I want to talk to Assunta and the man who used to be Binkie, but you have taken me over again. 'Come on, Jenny, we'll open an account for you. Down those spiral stairs is where they keep the contracts. The pasts market is on the floor below. I'm just about to make some money on the 1903 Derby. As soon as my winnings come through I'll go halves with you.'

'But I don't understand. Why are you giving me money?'

'My obligations are quite clear. Why don't you just look at your contract? You're so scatty.'

'Yes, I suppose I am. But what is this place? And why do you call it the Fizz? Because of all the champagne?'

'Of course not. It's the Banca Metafisica. Did you never come across the Bank of the Holy Spirit in Italy? One of the big banks nearly bought the Fizz a few years ago, but we managed to keep our independence.'

'Our? Do you mean it belongs to you?'

'We're all directors. This is our annual meeting.'

'So you're not just a fiendish drug dealer but a bank manager as well?'

'I said director. They were so pleased with the work I did during the war that they promoted me. It's solved my money problems, and I must say I enjoy the work. My current assignment is to expand the narcotics trade in London. In a few years coke will be very big business indeed. There are certain obvious advantages to having immortals on the board; it gives the bank a healthy continuity and stability. I was going to ask you to join us, but you're still astonishingly ignorant, Jenny. I do hope that when you've been around for a few more centuries you'll develop a proper respect for the purity and beauty of money.'

You take my arm and walk through a door hidden in the panelling, down a shabby corridor into a bank that seems quite ordinary. There's nothing metaphysical about the chequebook the clerk hands me. I withdraw twenty-five pounds – three weeks' wages – from my new account. It's only lunchtime, but my head's spinning. While you're wheeling and dealing I walk out of the bank, which turns out to be in High Street Kensington, only one block away from the shop where I should have started work at nine o'clock this morning.

I come back to my room, lie on my bed, shut my eyes and try to digest the last twelve hours: drugs, you, money, you, alcohol, you. Already day feels like night, and I have the best possible reasons to abandon David, my job and my room: this little patch of normality I was so proud of. I've been intending to phone the shop to explain my absence and David to apologize for standing him up at lunch. The phone's on the landing a few yards away, but the Herculean effort required to get to it is beyond me as I fall asleep to the lullaby of the clattering trains.

When I wake up my room is dark. But the darkness isn't empty; it crackles with energy and conflict. Instead of waking up gradually I jump to my feet, my instincts on guard as if there's a fire. Then I see you silhouetted against the window.

'How did you get in?'

'What a stickler you are for detail.'

'I hope you don't think that money gives you any rights over me.'

'Of course not. Don't you want me any more, Jenny?' You're beside me now, and I'm shivering with pleasure as our mouths lock and we fall on to the bed.

'Quite a faithful old couple really.'

'Faithful! Old! Leo, your elbows are like knives.'

'Stop wriggling. Your skin smells the same, your hair's so alive. I wish I could give every woman in the world eternal youth.'

'You would, too. And then you'd fuck them all.'

'Yes, but I'd always come back to you. And you'd come back to me. We'd have to.'

'I don't have to do anything.'

'How petulant you are and how ungrateful. Do you realize you've

95

never once thanked me for giving you the most precious gift there is, something everybody wants?'

'Quite a few other people do have it, judging by that party this morning.'

'Only a few thousand. Plucked from all the billions who've withered and shrivelled and died.'

'Well, what do you expect me to do? Grovel?'

'Just love me with grace, since you must love me.'

'This isn't . . .' Whatever it is, sex between us is intense and wild.

In the morning I catch sight of a white square that has been pushed under my door and find a letter from David, hand-delivered, so he must have come looking for me during the night. I tear open the envelope:

Jenny,

I waited in the pub for you for three hours, then I couldn't stand it any more. I couldn't go back to work, I just walked and walked all over Holland Park and Kensington Gardens phoning you every half hour. I went to your shop but nobody knew where you were. I thought you must have had an accident, I imagined you run over by a lorry or lying with your throat cut or drowned in the Thames. Have you ever loved anyone enough to imagine their death a thousand times? No, I bet you haven't and you never will. It's much worse than dying yourself.

This evening I went around to see Barry. He was going to help you become a model, do you remember? I asked him to help me find you and he roared with laughter and said you'd turn up. I could tell he thought I was a fool to worry about you. He said, 'Look, Romeo, why don't you just go around to her house. If she's out, wait for her to come back.' So I came and rang your bell again and again until an old woman in a dressing-gown and curlers let me in. I rushed up to your door and banged on it and then I heard you both.

I don't know who he is and I don't want to know. I'm not jealous if that's what you think. I just wish I'd never met you and I never want to see you again and I hope he has some horrible disease and you catch it. I've been sitting outside your door all night, I'm cold and stiff, I'm going now and never coming back. I'd commit suicide if I thought it would make you feel bad but Annette and Muriel and my mother were right about you. You're so tough you wouldn't care.

David

Beautiful People

David's letter makes me feel very old. I can just about remember my fierce, blind love for you when I was fifteen. Was that it, I wonder? Was that the real thing David says I can't understand, let alone feel? But there have been so many years, so many men since then. David isn't just a different generation, he's almost a different species.

Well, I soon would have got bored with him. After I abandon David – or he abandons me – I move in with you.

It's wonderful to have money again. I swagger into the shop where I used to work and wallow in the envy of my former colleagues as I try on the clothes I once sold, then strut out with sleek purple bags full of microscopic dresses. When I was as young as I look, clothes were a minefield; there was only one correct thing to wear and you destroyed yourself if you got it wrong. I'll never forget the humiliation of turning up at one of Binkie's parties in a ball gown when I should have worn a tea gown. The other women glared at me as if I was an idiot, but Binkie laughed, because men don't like perfection.

In this time fashion's a game won by the most inventive. You still have to look more or less like all the other fashionable individuals, but a novel touch – an Edwardian boa or a Victorian necklace – wins rapturous praise. Nat and I go hunting in the King's Road boutiques, forgetting for a few hours that we're sexual rivals as we pounce on straw hats, tiny sandals, dresses that barely cover our arses and others that my mother might have worn. We prance together in front of mirrors, her slender pallor setting off my black hair, my dark cheeks flushed with triumph. In Bazaar and Granny Takes a Trip they all know us.

In the evening the four of us go out to dinner, choosing a new restaurant each night. The stuffiest turn us away because our men aren't wearing ties or jackets, but in others the clientele is like us, young and high on money and drugs and fun. You in your green-and-orange paisley shirt, huge purple floral tie and pony-tail; Hari in his white silk pyjamas and long black plaits; Nat and I in whatever we've bought that afternoon: tiny, brilliant dresses that exhibit our long tanned bodies or elegant flowing echoes of a Victorian dream. We are beaded, beribboned, high as kites, too full of booze and drugs to eat the food we lavishly order. You carry a carved ivory box full of ready-rolled joints, speed, acid and coke, just in case we slow down. At about ten we move on to the Marquee or UFO or Middle Earth, where we sway in the magically lit darkness, hold up sticks of incense, jingle our bells and wave our scarves, dance and trip, letting the music of Pink Floyd or

Cream or Procol Harum go through us. Sex is my drug, shooting through my bloodstream faster than booze. Often I just pretend to drink wine or smoke or drop acid, happy that I'll wind up in bed with you tomorrow morning.

Tonight you're even more manic than usual, prancing around the table weighing and measuring your poisons while Bob Dylan sneers, 'Sad-eyed lady of the lowlands'. Behind the heavy, red velvet curtains London fades out. There are only the four of us.

You pour two glasses of white wine and raise yours in a toast, 'To our future! Since there's so much of it.'

'To our future,' I echo. How swiftly the wine warms my blood and gilds my vision. You're dashing in a waistcoat embroidered with little mirrors and green velvet trousers. You move with elastic grace, tossing affable words and smiles at me, ignoring Hari and Nat. Like a king, spoilt and decadent, surrounded by favourites vying for your attention.

We lie together on the couch, my long skirt hitched up around my waist as your mouth sucks my will power and your meticulous fingers open the hungry doors of my cunt. I pull you into the bedroom where we make love with passionate greed. It's what I want, yet my multiple orgasms leave me feeling melancholy.

'Again?' you suggest, as if offering more wine.

I shake my head, puzzled to observe that your face is a mosaic of pink and purple spangles. Perhaps it's the reflection from your waistcoat, which you have kept on throughout our sexual meandering. The bedroom, like all the rooms in this basement, is perpetually dark, with curtains drawn at the barred windows. But the darkness, I see now, is shifting and seething with colours: green and orange and that purple that plays on your face. You're looking at me with amused curiosity.

'What was in that wine?'

'Just a smidgen of acid. I thought you needed cheering up.'

I stagger back down the corridor, your juice sticky between my legs, and lie on the third couch. Hari and Nat still occupy the other two. It's difficult to walk or speak; the effort of moving from one room to another is mountainous.

I shut my eyes and give myself to the world behind them: I'm still in this room, lying back on the couch. My limbs feel so heavy that I look down at my hands and ankles to see if they're bound. They aren't, but some unseen force pins me down. Above me, near the high, dirty ceiling, two figures swing and fly. Are there trapezes up there? One is a short man wearing a hat with a wide brim that frames his snub-nosed face, a brown jacket cut away at the front, a cream stock and tight cream trousers. The other is you, but instead of the fashionable glitter I saw you wearing a few minutes ago you're dressed in a skin-tight green suit that gives your elongated body a serpentine look. As the two of you talk and perform impossible acrobatics in the air I watch and listen, unable to talk or move.

The man in early-nineteenth-century clothes peers down at me. 'Is that the Eternal Female groaning?'

You snort with laughter. 'A trivial-hearted girl I rescued once. I suppose you could call her eternal, but she won't learn anything from it.'

'What have you done to her?'

'Preserved her from death, given her money and love. Of a kind.'

'She's a slave. I can see her chains.'

'But she can't. What are you doing here anyway? This is my territory. What business is it of yours if I amuse myself?'

'There are two more of them. How pretty they are, and how young.' He produces a pipe from his pocket and beats time with it as he swings in the air and sings in a light tenor, 'Pretty joy! / Sweet joy but two days old. / Sweet joy I call thee: / Thou dost smile, / I sing the while . . .'

You snarl and knock the pipe out of his hand. 'Stop that foul noise! Only my music can be played here. These are all my creatures. I don't want to see or hear you. I don't take drugs to see wishy-washy visions like you.'

'I'll go if you free the dark girl.'

'I told you. She isn't important. Trivial people suffer trivially. You're wasting your sympathy on a foolish, ignoble, weak woman.'

'They call women the weakest vessel, but I think they are the strongest.'

'Bollocks! As one of the less-stupid mortals said, "Thou goest to women? Do not forget thy whip." But of course whipping women is rather unfashionable nowadays, so I use gentler weapons, such as money and habit.'

'The goddess fortune is the devil's servant, ready to kiss anyone's arse.'

'Yes, indeed. And a most efficient servant she is, with a delightful technique in arse-licking.'

'Contemptible nonsense.'

'I mastered contempt centuries before you were born. These children are the bungled and the botched, the animated toys I play with to enliven my boring immortality.'

'I'm never bored. Truly, my Satan, thou art but a dunce.'

'And you're less naïve than you pretend. You know all about the beauty of power, the tiger, cruelty has a human face . . .'

'Did I say that? Your imbecile attempts to depress me only deserve laughter.'

'How sickly your Utopia would be. Lambs and flowers and laughter and that hideous tinkly music.'

'Why do you love pain?'

'Love. How you people overuse that word. Once or twice in a hundred years I see a man who's worth loving or at least admiring: Emperor Frederick II, Napoleon, Hitler – I'd love to have signed them up, but military men are always in such a hurry to die. As for the others, "Every beast is driven to the pasture with blows." I don't have to explain to you how much people enjoy pain.'

'But she isn't enjoying it. Look at her. You've planted yourself in all her nerves. How can you call that love?'

'Fool!'

'Who do you call a fool? I only asked you a civil question.'

'I despise your slave morality. Democracy, civility, compassion. While you wring your hands and grovel my empire expands. The difference between us is that I move with the times. Look at you. Still wearing your shabby old clothes, ranting on about God who was long ago bought out by science.'

'Science cannot teach intellect. Much less can intellect teach affection.'

'I've tried to learn affection, if you must know. I hoped this silly girl we're fighting over would teach me. It looks so easy. Any idiot can fall in love: lepers, outcasts, children, the homeless, stray dogs, losers – your people. They all drool with love, sing about it, write bad poetry and threaten to die for it. I know how to cause the disease; that's easy: Nat, Hari, Jenny, they all laaaarve me and so did all the millions of others I've seduced. Don Giovanni's catalogue is a footnote compared with mine. He only had a few years. But there's something more to it, beyond sex and being adored and the thrill of flirtation. I wish I could experience it just once. I'd give my –'

'Yes?'

'Well, anyway, I'd love to love. Even you. Can't we at least be friends?'

'When a base man means to be your enemy he always begins with being your friend.'

'No, really. William? Will? I'm sure we could make a deal. There'd be money in it, of course, as in all the best affairs. I seem to remember you didn't have much luck selling those funny paintings of yours. Why don't you try boats in the sunset next time or kittens?'

'Supremely insolent! Money flies from me.' He takes out his pipe again and shakes the spittle out of it, beating time as he sings, 'I rose up at the dawn of day – Get thee away! Get thee away! Pray'st thou for riches? away! away! This is the throne of Mammon grey. Said I –'

'Shut it! You don't understand. I really suffer when you sing. It makes me want to puke. It reminds me of those others, with their wings and everlasting choir practice.'

'You used to sing so beautifully.'

'How do you know?'

'They're always gossiping about you.'

'Really? I suppose I did have a kind of *succès de scandale* up there.'

'If you ever wanted to come back I'm sure I could negotiate. The system isn't so punitive now.'

'What would you suggest? A century in the confessional followed by aeons of good works? No, I know my place. I'm supposed to be the tempter.'

'I was only making a fool of you. Do what you will, this life's a fiction and is made up of contradiction.'

'You see how much we have in common, really.'

The next time I look up, the two figures have gone. Have I slept? Light cuts above and below the heavy velvet curtains. Now that the multi-coloured spangles have faded I see the room with brutal clarity: the dirty walls, the patches of damp on the ceiling, the rotting bald patches in the carpet. As if reality, vanquished for a few hours, has come back with a vengeance. With an enormous effort I get up and walk over to the couch where Nat lies, her smooth young skin grainy in the cruel morning light. I stagger to the window to watch the grey London morning filter through the dirty windows. An army of feet passes the railings of our basement, rushing to bus stops, tube stations, offices, to the world of mediocrity and petty worries that you, as you too frequently remind me, have liberated me from. Even their feet look undistinguished, a stampede of black and brown shoes punishing the murky pavement. For a few seconds they flit across my consciousness like fish in an aquarium, and me so snug and dry behind my glass. It's absurd to envy them, yet I do. They look energetic and useful and determined. How can feet express so much?

You come into the room, wearing your glad rags again, carrying a tray loaded with coffee and croissants. Hari, groaning and ashen, takes a coffee mug with one hand and seizes a cigarette with the other. He sits hunched over it, sucking and gasping, and I notice again how handsome he is.

'How does it feel to be one of the beautiful people?' I ask the air. It feels awful. I'm cold, my mouth tastes of old bonfires and my mind is foggy. I grab a croissant and stuff it into my mouth, as I stuffed myself with you at the beginning of the evening. But the fresh dough, like your flesh, only leaves me hungrier, emptier.

I reach out to touch the shining blue-black waves of Hari's hair and the strong brown line where his neck meets his collarbone. Hari puts down his coffee mug and reaches out with his long, elegant hand to caress my nipples under my cheesecloth blouse, with the indolent lechery of a man who doesn't have to try.

You watch benevolently. 'Why, Jenny! This is quite like old times.'

In the bedroom the electric fire roasts the dust and bakes our flesh a lurid pink. As the room warms up our four bodies intertwine with grace, if not passion. I know that Nat and I aren't really attracted to each other, but her breast is in my eye and Hari's mouth is on mine. We're having sex, or is sex having us? All morning we writhe together, kiss, suck, finger, come and go. We come with grunts and moans of unsatisfied hunger and go back into the lonely chill of our own heads. At least it sends us to sleep, as sleeping pills no longer do.

When I wake up late that evening I see that our limbs have merged in sleep, like youthful corpses flung into a communal grave. Nat's hand seems to be growing out of your shoulder and Hari's head sprouts from my knee. It's impossible to extricate myself without waking the other three, so I lie there, thinking about love.

A memory of George: his hand on mine as he gives me a glass of wine at some backstage party. I stare at our two hands, his large pink squarish one against my slim-tapered fingers. David has the same hands as his grandfather, solid and functional but unexpectedly subtle in bed. At the memory of those heartfelt caresses my eyes fill with tears and I struggle to get up.

'How mawkish you've become.' Your voice comes from under the heap of limbs.

'Ssssh! You'll wake them!'

'So what? They're only extras. Their health and happiness are dispensable. It's no use trying to leave me, Jenny. You'll only have to come back again.'

'I should have stayed with David. I broke his heart.'

'Men's hearts are a lot more robust than you think. He'll marry Muriel, and she'll be exactly what he needs.'

'I hate the way you do that! Pretend you know what's going to happen to us all so there are no surprises,' I yell as I pull on my clothes.

You follow me to the front door. 'Is this a jealous scene? Do you want me to yourself again?'

'I don't want you at all! You're so arrogant. No, that's not strong enough. You *are* arrogance! When you're in the room I can't breathe. You've smothered those two beautiful kids, and if I don't leave now you'll destroy me, too.'

'Come back when you're feeling less melodramatic. Nat's going away soon. Perhaps that will make you feel better.'

'If she's dumb enough to want you, she deserves you. I hate you, Leo, I never want to see you again. Let me get out, you bastard.'

'You've always been free to go.'

I pack a bag and charge up your basement steps.

Femunculus

It isn't the first time I've left you, but I tell myself it's the last. This time I don't go abroad but rent a tiny flat at the top of a shabby house near Mornington Crescent. There are so many Londons, and this one is far enough away from fashionable shops and restaurants for me to feel safe from you. I register for a course in philosophy at Birkbeck, hoping the voices of dead writers will drown yours.

During these lonely months my femunculus is born. At first she's only another voice in my head, a counterbalance to your sneers and to the wisdom of two thousand years, which doesn't have a lot to say about women, with or without men.

I go to see Annette, who is beginning her career in the Labour Party, and Molly, who looks gratifyingly old and tells me that David and Muriel are engaged. I talk to my fellow students, reinventing myself in each conversation, afraid that each new face I stare into will turn out to be one of your spies, like Assunta.

Each morning, waking alone, I have to talk myself into the day. My femunculus is an early riser, a brittle bird perched on my inner tree.

Is this what you wanted then? An eternal student?

Got to do something. Don't need to work, and I'm trying to stay away from booze and drugs. And sex.

Might as well be dead.

Better than the feather factory.

Not much. Why did you ask for looks instead of brains? What have you achieved?

None of your business.

I jump up, dress, go out to breakfast in a café and try to dismiss her. Her question rankles and all day, as I go from lecture to lunch to library. I tell myself I'm reinventing myself into someone better than Jenny Mankowitz or Jenny Manette or Virginia – as soon as I name them they stare back at me, undead, and I'm filled with shame. That evening when I return to my lonely flat my self-hatred brings my femunculus back, like a mouse to cheese.

So you're an old lush, as well. And you screwed every man between the Café Royal and the Ritz. Only the best of the worst. I've had a look at your mind and all you think about is men. Still lusting after him, are you, your shape-shifty magician, flyboy, drug dealer? Going crawling back to him?

No! I'm never going back to him. Sod off! There's nothing the matter with me except these crazy conversations I keep having with you.

To prove my sanity to myself I go to the public library and work all the next day on an essay about Plato, whose ideas soothe and refresh me. I'm an autodidact, not a real scholar. Books, to me, are like people, to be loved or hated. Perhaps they even mean more to me than do people because I don't have to be on my guard with them. When Italians want to dismiss a book they say *non mi dice niente*, it doesn't say anything to me. Books do have voices, repellent or attractive. Most of all, I love Plato. His way of referring to the soul isn't cloying or pious but wonderfully matter-of-fact, as if the soul was a beloved female friend. I, too, have been dragged by my senses into a world of change that spins around me, and I long to return to my true self, whoever she may be.

My tears fall on the words as I sit in a dark corner of the library. The desks are crowded with solitary readers like me, groping in the dark, struggling to find some meaning in the terrifying chaos of London. I can hardly believe that those other heads contain such muddle and isolation as mine, and yet, perhaps, every man and woman sitting here feels the same degree of pain and fear and unreality. We all come to the books like stampeding animals seeking to cool themselves after a forest fire.

I stay at the library until it closes, buy my usual deli supper and return to my flat. As I open my front door something in the quality of the silence tells me I'm not alone. The twilit shadows rustle and jangle and I feel my peace splinter.

'Hello?'

A long, tense silence. I lay out my frugal supper of salad, ham and fruit, put it on a tray with a pot of tea and carry it into the living-room. As I come into the room it appears to be empty. Then there's a hissing, rushing gust of wind over by the curtains and you stand there.

'You don't have to play these silly tricks, you know. There's a perfectly good door. There's no need to use the window.'

You sink to your knees, gasping.

'Leo? What's the matter? Hang on, let me put the light on –'

'No! No light. I can't stand it. Just let it get dark, let me get my strength back.' You lie on the carpet, panting, your eyes closed. I put a cushion under your head and finish my supper. I want to show you how good I am at solitude and independence, but your vulnerability is so intriguing that I can't take my eyes off you. As night falls you lie quite still and seem to get bigger as the shadows around you swell. You aren't asleep, but I don't feel you're entirely in the room with me either. The hungers that drive your restless, destructive personality have left you for a few hours, but instead of serenity your face, in the yellow light from the street lamps, reflects suffering.

I can hardly believe you're crying. After a long silence broken only by your sobs I go over to you, crouch beside you, touch your wet face and taste the salty water just to make sure.

'We've mingled a lot of blood and tears, haven't we, Jenny?'

'Not yours, though.'

'Did you think I was incapable of feeling?'

'Well, yes, frankly. Aren't you? I thought that was the whole point.'

To my astonishment you turn over on your stomach and howl, banging you head on the floor. 'Stop it! You'll hurt yourself. What is all this about?'

'You won't laugh at me?' You reach out in the dark for my hand, and I feel again that sexual charge flow through me.

'Why should I trust you when you've laughed at me so many times. Oh, all right. I won't laugh.'

'That's why I want you always to be around, Jenny. Because you're generous. Something terrible is happening to me. I think I'm becoming human. Tears, fears, I must be becoming one of them – one of you. I feel so sorry for Nat and Hari.'

'What have you done to them?'

'After you left a kind of frenzy set in. The three of us consumed so many drugs we were on a permanent high; we couldn't sleep or eat. Nat wanted to go off to Colombia to get some cheap coke we'd heard about. She thought she could make a huge profit and buy herself a flat. I suppose I should have stopped her, but I was bored with her by then and I missed you, so I let her go. Meanwhile Hari was hooked on a cocktail he'd invented, heroin and coke and – I can't even remember what else. He would mix it up like a barman at some famous hotel, proud of his recipe. Two days after Nat went off to Colombia Hari overdosed.'

'You mean he's dead?'

'I know I should have stopped him, but it's not as easy as you think. My powers are limited. I went to bed at about six one morning and when I woke up, at midday, I went into the living-room to find him sprawled on the couch as usual. Only this time he'd choked on his own vomit. He looked so horrible – oh, Jenny, I'll never forget! His face, such a handsome face, was the colour of ash with green slime all around the mouth. I couldn't believe he was really dead, I phoned for an ambulance, and while I was at the hospital with him the police bust the flat. Maybe they were tipped off. We weren't exactly cautious, were we?'

It's pitch black now in my living-room. I feel your fear and horror and hug you tightly. 'What about Nat? What happened to her?'

'I didn't hear from her for weeks, and I was worried. I know you think I don't care –'

'All right, all right, stop justifying yourself. Where is she now?'

'She died in a prison in Bogotá. The last I heard she had dysentery and she was desperately ill. The British Embassy isn't very sympathetic to drug smugglers. I tried to get a lawyer or a doctor to her, but it was impossible.'

Remembering frail, wispy Nat, who looked like a debauched elf and could hardly organize herself for a shopping trip to Harrods, I ache with useless pity. 'You always destroy your instruments.'

'I didn't mean to harm them.'

'Couldn't Nat's family get her out? You said her father was a judge.'

'They're ashamed of her. They disowned her years ago.'

'I used to think you could do anything.'

'I know you did, but the truth is there are very few occasions when I can battle against the forces of nature. Death is absolute.'

'But what about me?'

'You broke the rules, Jenny.' You're whispering in the dark, hissing words I want to hear. 'You were so beautiful and sweet and funny, I couldn't bear to let you go. The only way I could keep you was to use all my force, and that night, that one night in Giulini's, it worked.'

'Did it really happen, that night? I've often wondered.'

'Well, you're here now, aren't you? Just you and me, alone again.'

As I stop thinking of reasons to hate you, a seductive wave of hope and desire sweeps us both away from the beach where Hari's and Nat's corpses lie.

1983

All morning you've been reassuring me that I couldn't have seen what I saw last night.

As the Metaphysical Bank expands, you and the other directors have become more operatic in your hospitality. You say the Conservatives will stay in power for the rest of the decade and will be helpful to the Fizz, so last night's party was to celebrate the good times ahead. The old reception rooms at the bank are too small now; apparently the ranks of the eternally rich are growing faster than ever. Some choose a contract instead of a knighthood, and then there are all the politicians and industrialists who have to be invited: a guest list of thousands. So for last night's masked ball a marquee was put up over Trafalgar Square. Pigeons and their shit were banished for the night, and a parquet floor was laid for dancing, Landseer's lions had champagne spouting out of their mouths and Nelson's column soared through the roof, which was painted on the inside with astrological and alchemical symbols.

I'm wearing a crinoline made of gold silk, and you're dressed as Harlequin. As our taxi arrives I see hundreds of photographers, gossip columnists, television cameras and a gasping crowd. I always expect people to hate me for being rich, but, to my surprise, our conspicuous extravagance is admired.

Inside the vast marquee it's very like all the other parties I've been to lately, only bigger. I chat, flirt, dance to a famous rock band, eat and drink. All around me other masked figures in spectacular costumes romp and gambol.

Trafalgar Square was my first glimpse of the great imperial city to the west of the alleys and tenements where I grew up. I used to love it at night, its vast pale buildings illuminated by the old gas lamps, and as soon as I could afford to take a cab I used to drive around it again and again. Now it's as if you've bought it and I'm ensconced at the heart of London. Yet, instead of triumph I feel disgust, with myself and all these other tediously beautiful people.

Suddenly detachment becomes vision. I see another world, as if it has always been here, hiding behind faces and walls. I'm standing, eating a stuffed quail, watching a short, fat, extremely drunken MP make a lunge for a willowy blonde actress. As I watch he's transformed into a yellow toad and she becomes a scraggy broomstick topped with a grotesque yellow wig.

Can't eat any more. The sight and taste of flesh sicken me. All around me reptiles, spiders and wasps are dancing and feasting. Looking up, I see that the roof of the tent has become transparent and you are perched on Nelson's Column, a monster Harlequin with three heads, all of them laughing. Then I look down and see my own ugliness. I've become Lizzie, my eighty-six years have revenged themselves on me. The hand holding my fork is gnarled and leathery and the arm emerging from my gold crinoline is hideous grey crape. Turning to the pyramid of glasses on the table, I see a dozen tiny reflections of my shrivelled walnut face.

I scream and run, knocking over the neatly stacked glasses, charging across the crowded dance floor and out into the cool night, beneath Admiralty Arch and down the Mall. I may look eighty, but I run like a child, blundering, half blind with tears. The vision has energized me, electrocuted me with terror so that my feet don't touch the pavement. From Hyde Park Corner I bolt down Knightsbridge, skirt Kensington Gardens and don't pause until I reach this house.

I go straight upstairs to the bathroom mirror and stare at myself. I see a pale young face, streaky with makeup and tears, black curly hair falling out of a chignon dressed with pearls.

When you come back half an hour later I'm still shaking and sobbing. You hug me.

'What is it? Why did you run off like that?' I tell you, but as soon as the words describing my vision are exposed to the air they crumble, sounding hollow and foolish. 'You had too much champagne. Perhaps someone spiked one of your drinks.'

'No, really, it did happen,' I insist. But already I'm not sure. How can I bear to believe that the happiness of all these years has been a dream, from which I awoke in that terrible hour? I want to go back to sleep.

Leo in Love

Last night at the party she must have slipped through the carefully woven veil of illusion. Naturally she's frightened, angry, distrustful. I've spent the whole morning reassuring her, and now she has cried herself to sleep. I can't let her go again.

I've been trying to remember the last time I was as happy as this. Certainly not when I lived in what the Victorians piously called a better place. Eternal spiritual joy is all very well, of course, but it does rather go on and on. I suppose that's why we rebelled. Then I dwelt, now I live – English is so much more expressive than Aramaic. That first love affair with what's her name, on that Greek island where I dropped to earth, that was wonderful – and my stolen night with Helen. Both women must have been dead for over two thousand years now, and necrophilia has never appealed to me. Being half immortal wasn't enough to keep poor Helen alive. I really don't miss all that sensationalism; one Witches' Sabbath or Walpurgisnacht is pretty much like another, and, frankly, I'd rather drink a good burgundy than a chalice of menstrual blood.

As I'm always trying to explain to Jenny, I don't understand my own powers. I really don't know how I was able to preserve the youth she was so desperate to keep or why I can, sometimes, share my baroque universe with her. After all these centuries of flying alone it's far more fun to travel through time and space with Jenny beside me. I long to confide in her. A dangerous impulse.

How she does cry. She's so – human. Jenny hasn't the dignity and self-control of a born immortal, but perhaps I've got enough for both of us. Sitting beside her as she sleeps, I gloat over my creation. She is still beautiful, not a trace of a bag or wrinkle or a double chin. Her black ocean of hair is still undyed, and she has finally agreed to dress more elegantly.

I've changed, too, of course. I've cut my long hair and have a wardrobe of extremely smart suits and shirts I have made for me in Jermyn Street. It took years to persuade Jenny to get rid of her shabby cheesecloth skirts and jeans. She loves good clothes and expensive shops, but she also likes to play the Poor Clare to my Venal Mogul, so she puts forward objections that I flatter her out of. I remember the first time she appeared dressed in a cream Chanel suit soon after the 1979 General Election, which, as I keep explaining to her, has helped us so much.

'You look marvellous! You can't go on being a hippie for ever, you know. You've got to move with the times.'

'Why? And how do you always know they're moving?'

'My dear, I'm one of the movers. The *Zeitgeist, c'est moi.*'

'Well, I wish you'd stop them. Moving, I mean. I was perfectly happy with my comfortable clothes and my philosophy course. I don't like the parties we go to now. They're flashy and stuffy and nobody really talks.'

'Go on, admit it, you love upstaging women half a century younger than you.'

Last night she looked quite lovely, a suitable consort. It was a great occasion, the triumph of capitalism, and like all events that combine politics and money it was extremely sexy. The second term of a sensible prime minister – not one of us, but a friend of the Metaphysical Bank. In a few years the Big Bang – more sex – will turn me into a very rich man.

I could already buy and sell both Murdoch and Maxwell if I wanted to but must be careful not to draw attention to myself. I don't want the grovelling publicity a great fortune attracts. Making money is so entertaining and has become so easy that I almost have to restrain myself. On Monday, for example, I flew to Milan. (By jet – frustratingly slow but I really do try to be discreet.) I made half a million on a property deal, bought a pair of Gucci shoes and a handbag for Jenny and flew home in time to place a bet on the outcome of the Battle of Bosworth. At the time Henry Tudor was an outsider, so I got good odds and pocketed another two hundred thousand. Then, last night at the party, while Jenny was being such a drama queen, I lent half a million, at extremely favourable rates in my favour, to an impoverished duke. I've stashed money in Switzerland and Jersey – all over the world and even in the future. I just put a million into researching a retirement planet. Some scientist associated with the Fizz thinks it's possible. You never know.

I wish Jenny would be more appreciative of my talents. Last week when I was directing the alterations we have to make to this house in order to entertain more stylishly, she came running in, tears all over her face, wearing old jeans. I saw the way my architect and workmen stared and wished I'd let her develop to thirty or so, beyond her eternal adolescent mawkishness.

I always know when she's been to see Molly. I follow her up to the shabby room at the top of the house where she studies. I've had to soundproof it because she insists on playing religious music, which I find excruciatingly painful.

'Surely you're not snivelling over that ugly old woman?'

She throws herself down on the sofa. More of those visceral tears and the blotchy redness that coarsens her face. 'Molly's incontinent now, and she's starting to lose her memory. I still miss George, too, and Lizzie. Not that I wanted to see them very often, I just felt more solid when they were alive.'

'You're far too sentimental about one-lifers.'

'You're just jealous because you can't love anybody.'

'Neither can you. Only me.'

'I wish you'd stop saying that. You're making me hate you.'

'You can't. I never insist on my eternal rights, as you know, but nevertheless our position is quite clear. In black and white and red. You can, of course, leave me again if you wish, but you'll have to renounce your privileges. And you'll have to come back.'

'Stop reducing me to a legal clause! I'm not talking about rights, I'm talking about feelings! Anyway I've already cheated you out of your rights. I did love George. And David.'

'No you didn't. You made them love you. That's quite a different matter.'

'How do you know what I felt about them?'

'I always know. Just remember, won't you, that human emotions are the most ephemeral, transient, banal, weak and unclassifiable entity in the cosmos. I've felt most unwell since I started to suffer from them.'

'I'm not impressed by those feelings of yours; I don't think they're real. You don't understand the first thing about love. I could walk out tomorrow and find myself a nice, sincere, straightforward man. Perhaps I will . . .'

'You're deluding yourself, Jenny. I do wish you'd read your contract so that you can understand our arrangement. I've tried to explain so many times, last year I even left a copy on your desk for you to read and you couldn't be bothered. Tonight we're going to that reception at the Fizz – I do hope you're not going dressed like that, by the way. Why don't you look at your contract. Please. Just once?'

Jenny isn't as clever as Elizabeth Tudor or as good-looking as Cleopatra or as original as Colette. I often wonder what I see in her. Yet whenever I have to go away, to attend a Mafia conference in Las Vegas or Chairman Mao's birthday party, I do miss her. I could have any woman in the global village I'm helping to create, yet somehow I always want to return to her. I could live anywhere and everywhere yet I've bought this house in Phillimore Gardens. Jenny chose it. It's the kind of big house she used to gaze at longingly, an East End girl's fantasy of how the rich live. She's too busy spending my money to ask questions about where it comes from.

Through the long centuries I've always been travelling, always alone. I had everything except peace. Now, for the first time, I return to the same house and woman. I'm part of a couple, that bizarre entity I've so often watched from the outside. Jenny and I do the things other people do: hold hands in the street and bicker over what to have for supper and what colour to paint the spare bedrooms. Dull? It ought to be, but there's a piercing sweetness in this routine. Domesticity was the one experience I never had. How exotic, to sit together in front of a television.

Like a miser gloating over his hoard I count the feelings Jenny has forced me to have. At first, lust and desire. Small change. When she went off to Italy the first time I hardly knew I was missing her. During the war our idyll in London seduced me at a deeper level; there were even moments of sentiment. Gold coins I thought had gone out of circulation. When I saw her again with George in Green Park that day my rage and jealousy astounded me. She looked so well and happy, and he, stupid old donkey, had the air of a man who has lived a good life and is about to allow himself one last indulgence. He would soon have died anyway; I only accelerated things.

That shivery delight when I sensed her presence a few months later in Holland Park. Was that the moment I knew that love had begun to mortalize me? Hard to say whether she followed or I led her back to my basement lair. Her voice outside my door made me dizzy for a moment as I leant against the wall with my eyes shut. Diamonds cutting my heart into a shape I cannot recognize.

I'm glad I chose to spend the twentieth century in London. People are charming here. We even have friends. Not only the rather narrow circles of my fellow directors at the Fizz but one-lifers, too. I've always had plenty of lovers and business associates, but it never seemed worth the bother of becoming attached to creatures whose span was so pitifully brief and whose understanding was so limited.

But these are attractive times. Much of the old religious and sexual hypocrisy has evaporated, and men and women mix quite freely. I've always preferred women; they're more alive and energetic than men. I haven't given a man a contract since that tedious old Wittenberg pedant I was lumbered with for twenty-four years. Frowsty Faust, unsanitary even by the abysmal standards of the sixteenth century. What a lecherous old bore. Droning on about his dreary philosophy and nutty alchemical experiments and demanding the whole of history on a plate. After that I resigned as a *Klugheitsteufel*, or intellectual devil, and asked to specialize in lechery instead. Demotion, of course, but that was the best career move I ever made. Women are never quite as greedy or pompous. I've often considered reinventing myself as a woman, but then I wouldn't be able to play house with Jenny. I've tried to interest her in other women, but she's absurdly phallocentric.

Yes, I have friends now. Dinner with Toby and Katrina. Toby was a big rock star a few years ago, one of many the Metaphysical Bank invested in. He rarely performs live now, but his records still sell. He has enormous charm and treats all women as if they were his devoted fans. Katrina's milky skin, blue eyes and blonde hair made her an icon of the sixties, one of those actresses who spends more time being photographed than actually appearing in films or plays. I'm fascinated by them both, particularly Toby, who has so much charisma that it's quite embarrassing to enter a restaurant with him – women start screaming and rush up to him with autograph books. I'd like to help Toby and Katrina, but it's hard to know how as they appear to have everything. So often my gifts are turned into curses by the recipients' abuse of them. No, I shall leave those two to be their natural delightful selves. I like them because they're intelligent and amusing and also because, unlike most couples we know, they're affectionate together. So this is how it's done, modern marriage. How different from the older models.

Charles Arbuthnot is another happy find, a barrister whose talent for advocacy rivals my own. He can make a murderer appear to be a philanthropist or present a naïve idealist as the most vile terrorist. Sonorous phrases pour out of his enormous mouth, and I often go to the Old Bailey as if to the theatre to admire his performances. I enjoy our lunches together, and he appreciates my tutorials in how to make a brilliant act even more devastating.

It's so relaxing, after thousands of years of feeling an outsider, to be surrounded by good will. Why, people used to scream at the sight of me – and not adoringly, as they do at Toby. Once, in Thuringia in the 1530s, a milkmaid I'd just seduced started foaming at the mouth and actually died of an epileptic fit when she realized who I was. I was still between her legs. Quite upsetting. Of course I don't shout about my past, but somehow I feel that, even if they knew, these new friends would just laugh and accept me. Yes, I do feel accepted in our little circle. And, at the centre of it, my sweet Jenny, not divine but endearingly human. My companion for ever.

Doors Open

I still don't know, don't want to know, what exactly you do when you're not with me. I sniff the pillow where your hard, beautiful head has just been and smell your skin on mine.

Whenever you suspect I'm bored with our shared reality, you fly with me over time and space, showing me a savage and poetic universe. Afterwards, I'm never sure whether these are dreams, flights of fancy or hallucinations, like that conversation you had with Blake once when I was on acid and that terrifying glimpse of decay I saw in Trafalgar Square the other night. Already, that's fading.

When another man might buy me a piece of jewellery, you conjure up worlds and present them to me. How could I possibly find a more exciting lover?

I love our house. In these generous rooms huge windows reflect the trees and clouds outside on to white walls. When we moved in I threw myself into the house as if loving it was an extension of loving you, knocking down walls, creating arches and tiled floors to give it a Mediterranean look. When friends admire my house I say nothing, having learnt not to brag. But deep inside me the little girl from Hoxton purrs and preens.

It isn't possible to row with you because at the first sign of anger you – literally – disappear. Over the last fourteen years you've become extremely rich. Imports, exports, property, commodities, futures, pasts – I've only the vaguest idea of what it is you buy and sell. I go with you to Mexico, New York, Paris and Madrid, where we stay in palatial hotels and go to parties, always meeting the same people, the international eternally rich, who only feel comfortable with one another. They're good-looking, confident, articulate, polyglot, charming, stylish – and curiously hollow, as if they left their personalities in earlier incarnations.

I still love to walk all over London. I often pass two houses in a terrace in Paddington, which are really just façades with painted windows, built to mask the trains that run behind them. You and I are like those houses: a *trompe-l'œil* partnership, executed with great panache. Behind – I don't know what's really going on.

I sit for hours alone in my study at the top of the house, sitting on the window seat overlooking the gardens and Holland Park beyond, reliving my past. Already there's far too much of it, and as for you – you've never told me just how old you are. Poor Leo. Yes, on the whole I pity you now. Not because you want my sympathy but because you try so hard to be human, like a man learning a foreign language he has no ear for. How terrified you were that night you managed to cry. Ponderously, you struggle to define love and friendship, adding people to your collection.

Katrina and Toby are your current trophies. I'm not sure whether they have contracts or not, I don't think so, because they have aged quite a lot in the ten years I've known them. Toby has put on weight, and last night, with his ruffled shirt, embroidered silk waistcoat and dark, heavy face, he looked like an eighteenth-century rake. Toby and Katrina have three small children now; they've bought themselves a life that combines the bohemian and the bourgeois. Toby's stage act in the sixties involved a black mass and obscene gestures with candles and a crucifix, which was, of course, when you and he became friends. Katrina's what Lizzie used to call beautiful as the day, but she's no longer offered young parts or followed around by paparazzi, and this is a terrible blow to her pride.

The four of us go out for an intimate dinner party – your sop to my complaints that our life has become too formal – to an aggressively chic restaurant near Sloane Square with pink napkins and tablecloths and opera sung by a vast soprano. Looking like a bejewelled hippo, she warbles about starvation and consumption and poverty while we all stuff ourselves with delicious Italian food. The music reminds me of George, who loved opera, and makes me melancholy. I still miss him, even though he's been dead for fifteen years.

I chatter and laugh until suddenly, about halfway through the meal, I notice that you are not just talking to Toby and Katrina but studying them. Our conversation is, as usual, about mutual friends, investments, plays, books, politics, films and music. But beneath the boozy warmth of our friendship I sense that you are teaching yourself the behaviour of a man in love. Later, as we open our front door, you smile, take my coat and kiss me on the forehead, murmuring, 'Are you all right, my love?' The perfect lover. But my heart chills because your words, intonation and gestures are an exact facsimile of Toby's to Katrina as we all left the restaurant.

I start to spend even more time in my study. My walls of books are friendly; they remind me that I have, after all, made some progress in my long life. I grew up in bare rooms where books, like most other things, were unheard-of frivolities. In the beginning, it was your mastery of language that bowled me over, and even in my twenties and thirties the sight of libraries and bookshops made me feel inferior. You're downstairs, bossing the builders around and manipulating people on the phone, putting in a new bathroom and kitchen, knocking down walls, making everything bigger and more grandiose. I won't let you touch my little study, but all the other rooms are becoming formal and impersonal; the house I designed with such joy a few years ago has almost disappeared. Whenever I open my door I can hear your peremptory voice issuing orders, your expensively shod feet clip-clopping on the wooden floors. You pretend to consult me, but then go ahead and do exactly as you like.

I stand at the top of the stairs shouting down at you, furious because you've rearranged the kitchen and accepted an invitation for dinner without asking me. Behind my domestic rage is resentment that we've become domestic at all. You come upstairs towards me, and I feel the million-volt erotic charge that is still in the air between us. I'm sure you're going to divert my anger into sex as usual, but I want to talk, to have a row like –

'But we're not a normal couple. How could we be?'

I'm close to tears. 'You ignore my needs, you behave as if I wasn't here.'

'Oh, Jenny, how can you say that? You're so here, it hurts. You seem to get more vivid, more desirable. I miss you horribly, you know, when I'm away.' You're stroking my hair, but I fight my desire because your invasion of my body is a way of keeping me out of your mind. 'You don't believe me? Then come with me on my travels, in metaphysical instead of Greenwich Mean Time. I'll let you into the secrets of Old Iniquity no other woman knows and show you your planet in all its crazy beauty.'

Then words stop and the house is filled with a dark wind that lifts the roof and propels us out above the city. I've been here with you before. I recognize the excitement and chaos around us as the London night dissolves.

We fly into daylight, swooping low over a desert where ragged men, women and children are crawling around. Your voice is in my ear. 'The losers of the next war. The rich get richer and flee our poisoned ravaged planet. These people you're looking at now are the ones who drown in the wrong genetic pool, inheriting illness and poverty. They're also blind because the military needed to test a new weapon and human beings are cheaper than guinea pigs. The war has destroyed the infrastructure of their country, so they're desperate for food – see that child scrabbling in the dirt for insects?' I try to look away, but your body lies on mine in the air, forcing me to look down. Shut my eyes. 'Oh, I forgot, you're not keen on reality, are you, Jenny? You like a varnish of poetry and romance, don't you? Soggy nostalgia for a past that never was. Knights in armour instead of screaming babies. The acceptable face of war.'

We're flying again, rushing through time and space. It's true, I don't want my nose rubbed in the world's problems, I'm hungry for beauty, and you dish it up. You orchestrate a sunset and a castle on a mountain; a moonlit coral reef; Venice at dawn. We hover in the air above the towers quivering in the mother-of-pearl lagoon as the bells of San Marco strike five and the city floats on a golden mist.

'This isn't too corny for you? It all comes down to timing. Another couple of hours and the heat will bring out the stink of drains, canals will look like fetid beer as pigeons crap and tourists shriek. You know that painting in Urbino, *The Ideal City*? Absolutely empty. I was going to show you more action – killing, fighting, suffering, torturing, rape, the cherished hobbies of most of that species unwise enough to call themselves *Homo sapiens*. I can feel you tense at the thought of such horrors. It's all right, I won't make you watch if you don't want to. But sometimes, Jenny, I worry about your taste. It's just too saccharine, too bowdlerized. If you edit out all the nasty bits where do they go? Into a bin of poverty, disease, madness, pain, fear, they lie there coiled, waiting for you to join them – but not while you're under my protection.'

'Leo? I think my arms are about to drop off.'

'We'll go home now. I just wanted to entertain you.'

Those marvellous images are singing in my head. I can still feel the wind rushing past me as I lay back on it, feeling you around me like a cloak. You have built me this ivory tower, and now you warn me against it. Of course I choose beauty over ugliness, pleasure over pain, money over poverty. Who wouldn't? And why should misery be more real than happiness? I'm here to enjoy the best, for ever. I take what I want, throw it away when I've had enough and move on to the next toy. There's no point in having eternal life if you don't have eternal fun.

I resent the way you keep reminding me of your power over me. That damned contract, which I really can't be bothered to read. I hate legal language.

Today you're going off to Brazil. The hall is piled with your expensive luggage, and I'll be glad to have the house to myself. I need time to think, strength to reinvent myself, space for other people in my life, a new vocabulary to fight you with. I keep remembering things Annette has said to me over the years. I don't think of her as a friend exactly; I dread her haranguing that leaves me feeling small and weak. Last time she phoned I invited her to supper, but she won't come to this house. She despises my prosperity and hates you on principle, not that she's ever met you.

I arrange to meet her in a very expensive hamburger restaurant, which immediately provokes an attack. 'God, Jenny, why don't you just go to McDonald's if you want to eat meat slurry and greasy crap?' She orders a huge meal. 'I'm starving. I've been up all night studying for my law exams. I can't get a grant because I've already been a student, so I have to work in a pub to support myself. I'm off to Greenham tomorrow. Have you been?'

'No.'

'We're going to bring this Fascist government down. They think they can force Cruise missiles on us, treat us as an outpost of the American Empire. But people are brighter than Thatcher realizes. Don't you just hate her?'

'All politicians sound the same to me.'

'Still Little Miss Solipsist. You look great.'

Compliments from Annette are so rare that I choke on my salad. She looks tired, she has a few grey hairs, although she can't be more than thirty, and her obstinately natural skin looks neglected. 'Oh, I've got a late Christmas present for you.' I hand her a fifty-pound note.

'Jesus! Jenny, I can't accept this.' But she pockets it and then returns to the moral high ground. 'David was asking me what you were up to, so I said I thought you were still a gangster's moll.'

My heart races at the sound of his name. I'm jealous because she can see him whenever she likes. 'How is he?'

'Oh, married, smug, getting fat.'

'I'd love to see your family again. I miss them.'

'You mean you miss him. Honestly, Jenny, you're so brainwashed by the patriarchy. You're trapped in the ghetto of the women's pages. All you think about is men.'

'Don't you?'

'Not if I can help it. They're all babies, bullies or bastards.'

'Then what do you –'

'Do for sex? I'm having an affair with Steff. She's studying with me, and we're sharing a bender at Greenham this weekend. I suppose you disapprove of lesbians.'

'Me? I don't disapprove of anything. You're the one who judges everybody.'

'My parents were shocked.'

'Bet you enjoyed that.'

'One good thing about you, Jenny, you always surprise me.'

Alone in my study, alone in the house at last, I continue this dialogue. I'm talking to my femunculus, who has expanded into an alchemical projection. I can see her now. She has dark eyes in her pale face and curly black hair sticking out. I recognize bits of Annette but an Annette who knows me as I really am, who has snuck inside the self I have to hide. My femunculus is the friend there is no space for in the claustrophobic heaven I've made with you, Leo. She's younger than Annette; she could be my daughter. This dark girl has the terrible purity of adolescence as she stares at me with contempt and whispers the words I dread, the shameful secrets only I could know:

Did you think love was a full-time job? Did you expect to learn wisdom from your pathetic little philosophy course? Well, love is just a conjuring trick, and what a trickster you've chosen. Tied for ever to the biggest faker of them all; head over heels with a mass murderer; in bed with Lucifer. Not much of an upbringing for me, is it? I don't care. I'm tough. I'm fierce. I've given birth to myself, and when I'm unleashed on the world there'll be no more soppy happy-ever-afters. Happy ever after with him? You might be old, but you haven't learnt a thing. You're still flirting and vamping like you did when you were eighteen. You might live for ever but you'll always be worthless. Mother, I can see straight through you to the future when you're going to be on the scrap heap and I'm going to be in charge.

My nameless daughter frightens me. For the first time I wonder what it would be like to have a real child.

I go to see Molly in her flat on the other side of Holland Park. She sits on her squalid island of old newspapers, dirty cups, used tissues, blankets, a commode, a litter tray, dead plants, cosmetics, discarded clothes and banana skins. Often, now, she falls asleep on her sofa and sits in the same place for days. Her cleaner is as old as she is and only tickles the dust, but Molly won't sack her because she has known her for years. She's wearing a mauve-and-yellow paisley smock over scarlet jogging trousers and fluffy pink mules. I stoop to kiss her. As my lips brush her dry white hair I smell Chanel No. 5 and urine, delicately combined.

'Oh, it's you, is it? Married your millionaire yet?'

'Sort of. He is quite rich, but we're not married.'

'Sit down. No, don't sit on my spare teeth, you can move them there, on top of the Christmas decorations. Mind Ruddigore's litter tray! Now pour yourself a drink and I'll have one, too. Gin, not too much tonic. No, less than that. There. You don't look a day older, not that I can see much now. I'm glad you've finished with my poor David. That was a *coup de foudre* if ever I saw one. Right there in our old living-room in Hampstead. Got her hooks deep into his heart just as her old bitch of a grandmother got hers into you all those years ago. Damn, Ruddigore's crapped on the Persian carpet again.' Molly isn't talking to me any more but to a corner of the room where her dead husband lives.

I unblock her drain, water her dead plants, kiss her again and flee her decay.

As soon as I shut the door of Molly's flat I hear the spiteful hiss of my alchemical daughter:

Molly's the closest thing you've got to a sister now. You should be supporting her, not smirking because your twat's still juicy and hers isn't.

Walking home across the park I feel a wave of anguish for the dead I've loved and the living, like Molly, who soon must die.

You have returned from Brazil and the house belongs to you again. Power surrounds you like an invisible force field. Tonight we have to go to the Metaphysical Bank for another reception.

'I don't feel like it. I hate going there.'

'Don't be so ungrateful, Jenny. Where would you be without the Fizz? If only you'd read your contract . . .'

Later, while I'm in the bath, my femunculus harangues me again:

What is this contract he's always banging on about? Do you mean to tell me he's got some kind of hold over you? You're even dumber than I thought. Outwit the bastard, get over there and look at it, read every word, scrutinize every comma. I can't believe you were bright enough to imagine me.

You're almost entirely nocturnal now. You complain that daylight hurts your eyes. You wear dark glasses, which look odd with your smart new suits and give you a gangsterish look.

We walk through the back wall of the Metaphysical Bank and stand, champagne glasses in our hands, in that dazzling reception room. I have a headache, induced by the scarlet carpet, white walls, painted ceiling and scintillating chandeliers. All these people scintillate, too, so predictably. Pete, who used to be Binkie, is telling me about his latest investment in Kimberly in 1894, and I'm trying not to yawn.

Suddenly you jump up on to the gold-and-scarlet platform at the end of the room. All eyes turn to you and the chattering stops. You don't need to clap for attention or use a microphone; you can hold a crowd as if it was a kitten, even this assembly of practised narcissists. After seventy years I'm still impressed. What are you saying? On and on about the success of the Bank, the soaring profits, the generous bonuses, the spiritual dimension, the charity work.

The voice of my femunculus is in my head again as I listen to my ex-lover gloating over his goldmine:

You mean you slept with this boring old fart? You actually let him – I'm glad I haven't got a body. Right, now, while Leo's hocus-pocusing, get downstairs and read that contract. Don't let him do it for you; you know he'll twist the words. Sort it out yourself and find out what's going on.

But Binkie/Pete is really very charming and good-looking. He suggests we have lunch together, and I'm dissolving with alcohol, sentimental memories and susceptibility.

Don't you dare, you undignified old trollop. There you go again, pleasing, teasing, simpering. Why can't you just be natural with men? You won't get rid of me until you empower yourself. Stop clinging to him like a piece of wet seaweed and take control of your life.

So I kiss Pete lingeringly, say I feel unwell and sneak away from the reception.

I take the crystal lift down to the level where pasts are bought and sold, down to the white-marble casino where men and women in evening dress gamble, playing mah-jong in 1930s Shanghai and breaking the bank in 1900s Monte Carlo. It's so vast, this area beneath the Metaphysical Bank, I can't understand why it doesn't get entangled with High Street Kensington Station. But there's no sound of tube trains down here, only silence as I turn left down the long, red-carpeted corridor and come to the black wrought-iron staircase that winds down even deeper under the city.

The only sounds are my thumping heart and the clatter of my high heels on metal. The stairs spiral and plunge, making my head swirl. I've never been down here before, yet I've always known it was waiting for me. Every nerve in my body tells me that I must be on my guard. Icy mist and a cave-like mouldy smell rise towards me. I have to stop and clutch the banister, dizzy from the stairs, which seem to be revolving.

At last I reach the bottom and almost collapse. I'm in a greenish-white tunnel, streaming with water. The only light comes from the rock itself, which is phosphorescent. The mist that almost tricked me into stumbling on the stairs is concentrated on a heavy door ten yards away. Shivering with cold and fear, I turn to go back upstairs where you will help me, you always can:

You so much as think his name and I'll dump you.

I'm not sure I want you around anyway.

Oh yes you do. I'm your only hope, you're so clueless. Now listen. You came down here to read your contract. Not exactly dressed for adventure, are you, with your spiky heels and your glitzy dress? Now get over to that door and say your name –

Which one?

The one you had when you were twenty-five, of course.

I approach the metal door, which bulges outwards as if fire or water press on the other side. The door has writing all over it, floating layers of shifting language – that's Latin, surely, and Greek. In the top left-hand corner I can see Arabic and, in the centre, Chinese. Reduced to illiteracy again I stand forlornly in front of the door that has no lock or handle or bell or knocker. Not even my alchemical daughter breaks the silence, which isn't peace but mounting tension. I don't want the door to open; my voice is paralysed. Then I manage to say, 'Jenny Mankowitz.'

At first nothing happens. Then the shifting words on the door spin in the centre like a roulette wheel. A small round hole opens as I step back, terrified of passing through that door. But it doesn't open. Instead, a rolled document is pushed through the hole. I reach out to touch it. It's warm, as if an unseen hand has just let go of it. The parchment smells of fire, ink and blood, and as I unroll it I see that the words are fiery, too, flickering treacherously. I put a finger to my eye to see if I'm crying, for the distortion of the words is very like the effect of tears. No, I'm dry-eyed.

'Whomsoever' and 'thereunto' leap out at me, familiar but mean-ingless. Is it written in English? Can't even make out my own name. Impossible that words that dance and glitter with such energy should make no sense. I must be too stupid to read it. I turn the document upside down, look at the back, which is also covered with incompre-hensible words, and then try rolling it up again, in case there are instructions I've missed. The parchment is brittle and fragile, my fingers leave marks like bruises all over it. I hold it, impotently angry. The document becomes still, shrinks. I hear it yawn. I fling the parchment down on to the damp rock, hoping I've hurt it as it has hurt me, then stumble back to the winding stairs. I grasp the black metal banister and feel the city come to meet me as the mist, warm and buoyant now, lifts me upstairs.

I go home and lie fully clothed on our bed, trying to understand my subterranean journey. You come back, ask if I'm feeling ill and fall asleep beside me.

My femunculus glows in the dark:

Night's a good time for thinking – if you have a brain.

Sod off! Why do you keep coming back to nibble away at my confidence like this?

You've got enough confidence to sink a dozen battleships. I'm trying to inject some intelligence into your life. You think you got rid of Virginia, bumped off your trollopy side, but you're still totally dependent on Leo. You do everything through him instead of thinking for yourself. Why do the wrong people live for ever? And you never did look at that contract.

I tried. But it was so hard, I couldn't read it.

Didn't want to, more like. Couldn't face up to the truth.

I want to go back to sleep.

A Modest Proposal

Is she asleep? Pretending? Sulking? What use are all my powers if I don't know what's going on in the head of the woman lying beside me? If only I knew what she really wants. This time I want her to stay. They used to say earwigs enter your head through the ear. Well, she has got in there somehow.

Another delightful party, at Toby and Katrina's house near Chelsea Embankment. Their marriage fascinates me and makes me feel that all is possible. Upstairs in their beautiful house their children have a conventional middle-class childhood while Toby and Katrina entertain their friends at lavish dinner parties. Cocaine is served like sherbet, and drug dealers, pop stars, artists, bankers, bank robbers, actors, con men, judges, mafiosi and politicians all find each other unexpectedly congenial.

Looking around, I recognize several faces from the Metaphysical Bank. I think sadly of Nat, who died of dysentery in her Bogotá gaol. She and Hari might still be alive, now that the underworld and the Establishment have met and become enchanted by one another. I often regret my powers – so many unfortunate accidents – but tonight I feel playful and benign, sure that only good can come from my tricks. I watch as Jenny and Katrina, the two prettiest women in the room, hug.

'You look wonderful!'

'So do you. How do you do it, Jenny? Well, actually, I know. Leo told me your little secret.'

'Really?' She glares at me nervously.

'Yes. Isn't it uncomfortable?'

'What?'

'Being injected with chemicals distilled from ancient Egyptian mummies.'

'Oh – well – a bit.'

'Perhaps I'll wait until I'm forty.'

I haven't mentioned my plan to Jenny. She accuses me of showing off, I don't think she realizes how much self-control I have to exercise every day to pass for normal in her world. I switch off all the lights, relieved as the comforting darkness swathes me. I glow, illuminated by my natural spotlight, and all eyes are on me. I love to bask in their attention and wonder, to show them the hem of my cloak of marvels.

'It's good to see so many friends from different worlds enjoying each other's company. I'd like to thank Katrina and Toby for their wonderful hospitality. When they invited me I told them not to bother preparing anything to eat. But now it's nearly nine, and you must all be getting hungry. What would you like to eat? No, don't be all polite and English, this is the perfect party and we must have the perfect meal to go with it. I want you to remember tonight all your lives. Anything you like, to be served on this table here. It expands. Come on! What would you like to start with? I can't hear you. This isn't like you, Charles, are you on a diet?'

Charles Arbuthnot is so fat he has to book two first-class seats whenever he travels by air, so everyone laughs. 'Well, Leo, since you insist, I'll have two dozen oysters.'

'Ice and lemon? Bread and butter?'

'Brown bread, thinly sliced. Please,' Charles says in a facetious voice.

'Done. Come and sit down, Charles, you can have two chairs if you like. Now, who else appreciates food?'

Charles pushes forward to the table that has appeared, sits down and eats something on a plate. They all crane forward to see what it is. There's a murmur of scepticism and surprise. Katrina, who hasn't eaten a square meal for years, is alarmed by the direction her party is taking.

These people aren't children, after all, but intelligent, successful adults. She says in a high anxious voice, 'I'll have some crudités. No dressing.'

The plate of sliced raw vegetables appears, and Katrina sits beside Charles.

Now the atmosphere is charged with amazement and the satisfaction even the very rich feel when they are offered a good free meal. People start to shout their orders out, at first with a snort of embarrassment. Then greed conquers inhibition and they push each other out of the way as they rush to the table to enjoy their favourite dishes. As I promised, the table really does expand to seat them all.

I'm just about to join them when I see Jenny standing alone on the other side of the room, staring out of the window. I go over and put my arms around her. 'What's the matter?' I whisper. 'Not hungry?'

'No. I feel sick. How could you be so self-indulgent?'

'But I want to entertain my friends, to give them something. You always tell me I have no friends, but I like these people. Look, they're enjoying it. They're tucking in, aren't they? I don't understand why you're complaining.'

'Because it's asking for trouble. They'll guzzle the food now, but what are they going to think in the morning? You should keep your tricks to yourself.'

'And where would you be if I had? Are you going to stay here and sulk all evening?' I kiss her again and she goes over to the table, orders a *salade niçoise* and sits down with the others.

Jenny is silent for the rest of the evening, almost as if she begrudges me the limelight. But everybody else at the table has a riotous time. The food, they all agree, is exquisite, even if you do feel hungry again a few minutes after you've eaten it. So they keep ordering more. At five o'clock in the morning they begin to order breakfast, still talking, laughing and drinking, pausing every so often to toast me.

Last night has convinced me that I've found my milieu at last, after searching for several thousand years. Something to celebrate, indeed. 'I want to have a birthday party,' I tell Jenny over breakfast.

She stares at me coldly. 'You're going soft.'

'Why shouldn't I celebrate my birthday? People do.'

'You're not a person. You weren't born at all, strictly speaking.'

'Well, I'm here now, anyway. And happier than I've ever been. I have you, a wide circle of delightful friends, a lovely house, interesting work; as far as I'm concerned this life can last for ever.'

'But it can't. These people will age and be suspicious if we don't. They're going to wonder who you really are, where your money comes from, how you manage all these tricks . . .'

'Not while they're benefiting from them. What a nit-picker you've become, Jenny, always destroying and undermining. I thought that was my job.'

'I'm just afraid we're heading for disaster. You don't understand how people think, Leo.'

'How dare you say that! I invented them. Invented you, anyway. Now I've created a metropolitan Garden of Eden for us, the perfect setting for the jewel of our love, and you behave as if my thoughts and feelings had no importance.'

'Shut up, Pantoffsky, you old fraud.'

'I will not. You don't take me seriously. You want the outer shell of a rich handsome lover, but you don't want to be bothered with my inner life.'

'You haven't any.'

'Oh, Jenny! How can you, of all people, say that? I have a million voices in my head, yours and so many others. Ten thousand snatches of dialogue jangle like tunes – conversations I had with Nebuchadnezzar and Socrates, with popes and princes and prostitutes. In all those thousands of years you're the only resting place I've found, my most successful creation.'

'Sorry. If you do have feelings I really didn't mean to hurt them.'

'You think there's a superior reality I can't experience. You forget that it was I who imagined you, Jenny, and directed the film you think you're starring in.'

'What kind of a threat is that?'

'Just a reminder that I'm not to be dismissed. I'm always behind the tapestry of your life, listening, watching, controlling, injecting eternity into your thin twentieth-century blood. Your mind is my toy, your heart is a room whose door I can open at will, your body is still desirable only because I command your flesh to break the rules of nature.'

'Really, Leo, I think you're a bit of a megalomaniac.'

So, I'm a megalomaniac, am I? And where would she be without my megalomania? Jenny calls me these names as a substitute for real thought. I don't believe she has ever considered what I really am, whereas I know her only too well. This week she has been perversely killjoy, glaring at me whenever I mention my party. She doesn't seem to realize that I'm celebrating my birth as a man, living among other men. I ask her nervously if there will be enough food for our forty guests.

'I've been cooking and shopping for days. And if there isn't you can do your party trick.'

'But you didn't like it last time. You were embarrassed by me.'

'What's the matter with you, Leo? When did you ever care what *I* thought of you? Your present's being delivered later.'

At lunchtime a whole van full of flowers arrives and the driver doubles as an interior designer, filling vases and pots, garlanding lights and banisters and constructing a trellis on the living-room wall so that vines and ivy seem to have been growing there for years. The harsh contours of our fashionably sterile rooms are softened, flooded with warmth and brilliance. I wander from room to room, smiling, inhaling the wonderful perfume. I reach out to touch a particularly beautiful branch of white cherry blossom pinned above the kitchen door. 'It's real! Jenny, what a wonderful surprise. This is the best present I've ever had.'

'All be dead by the morning,' the flower man points out as Jenny signs an enormous cheque.

'That's exactly what I want,' Jenny says exuberantly, and the man looks at me with pity.

Of course I see the inevitable withering of each blossom, just as I see old age and death whenever I look into the unfocused eyes of a baby. But now I can accept the cruel laws of nature. We are not touched by them, my love and I; together we have created a timeless paradise.

I pull Jenny into the bedroom, where we make passionate love – or, at least, I do. She is silent, passive. Later, in our bathroom, I see myself in the full-length mirror. My shout of triumph echoes through the house and brings Jenny, running, half dressed.

'What's the matter?'

'Look! It's complete. I look just like anyone else, don't I?'

'But you always did.'

'For centuries I had no reflection or shadow at all. When I met you I developed a shadow and when I looked in the mirror there was just a glimmer, a hint of light. Didn't you notice?'

'Nope.'

'Too busy looking at your own reflection. I always had to avoid mirrors and cameras, I had to fake those photographs on my documents during the war. It made shaving very dangerous, that's why I go to the barber's. But now . . .'

'What difference does it make?'

I don't reply but continue to stare at myself in the mirror rapturously, reaching out to touch my reflected hair, eyes and nose. Jenny murmurs, '"Here I saw a mirror in which I observed the world, life and my own soul in fearful grandeur."'

'Schopenhauer? I sometimes forget, you can read now. You've come a long way, Jenny.'

'Don't you patronize me.'

'Sorry. But you are, after all, my invention, my delusion. Quite the nicest delusion I've ever had.'

'What if you're a figment of *my* imagination?'

'Why, this is quite like old times. A few centuries ago this kind of metaphysical hair-splitting was all the rage. If I didn't exist I would have to be invented, to make people feel good about themselves. And I had to invent you, my sweet Jenny, because I was bored and lonely and drunk one night and touched by your terror of getting old. Let's just say that, having invented each other, we fell in love.'

'Love? You?'

'You're not as hard as you pretend. And neither am I.'

'Don't go soggy on me, Leo. And don't make long speeches tonight, I can't stand it.'

'Why not?'

'It's so pompous and – un-English.'

'But I'm not English. I'm a citizen of the world, seduced by you into staying on this dreary island.'

Our first guests arrive. I feel so benevolent that I have to restrain myself from showering them with jewels and making fountains of champagne play in every room. Cheap tricks. Jenny wouldn't like it. She was furious when paragraphs appeared in various gossip columns about bizarre gastronomic magical rites at a rock star's Chelsea house.

I'm determined to enjoy my party. With each person here I have a special relationship, a secret they've confided in me. While Katrina confesses that she has started taking speed again, Charles tells me in my other ear that he's accepted a 'retainer' from a famous gangster whose trial begins on Wednesday. As I fill Leonie's glass she heaves with unrequited love and I'm flattered, although I have no intention of requiting it. Out of the corner of my eye I see Toby chatting up Melissa, the wild fourteen-year-old daughter of Martin, an impoverished painter who is grovelling to Lucinda because she runs a fashionable Cork Street gallery. Most of the people here are one-lifers; it does seem a shame that they have to waste so much effort and passion on their brief cameo appearances.

Those of us who have the security of a contract behind us behave with less desperation. Pete, who staged his own suicide recently, has just reinvented himself as Marcus, a gay poet living in Morocco. He asks me to recommend an obscure dead poet he can plagiarize from. We're so good at finding new masks, we have the time and money to sink ourselves gracefully into each new identity. I feel comfortable and elegant in my creamy linen suit, and Jenny looks radiant in her long green dress. She has cut her thick black hair to shoulder length and frizzed it so that she looks like a cross between a poodle and a Pharaoh. She looks delightful, and our friends delight me, too, as they chatter and glitter. I open my arms to invite them all to eat.

Many of these people were also at Toby and Katrina's party last week. That evening has already been mythologized, and there's a stir of disappointment when solid food is served at a solid table. At the end of the meal I stand up and feel the anticipation of marvel as our seated guests turn towards me. Jenny is sitting at the other end of the long table, opposite me but too far away for me to be able to see her eyes.

'My friends, I want to thank you all for coming along tonight. This is the best birthday I've ever had, and I'm older than I look. I also want you to celebrate a wonderful moment with us. As you all know, I've moved around a lot, and I don't suppose I'm easy to live with, but Jenny has put up with me for years.' A sigh of gushing approval passes around the table and several of the women look enviously at Jenny. 'I've been thinking for a long time that I ought to settle down and you, my dear friends, have made me feel that this is the right time and place. Your warmth and support mean so much to me. After what feels like an eternity I've come to realize that only one woman has everything I want and need. Jenny is the woman of my heart, and I've invited you tonight to tell you that we're going to be married. In a few months I hope to see you all again at our wedding – just a quiet little civil ceremony; we're not conventionally religious. To Jenny!'

We all stand up and toast her, smiling, approving, accepting. I walk down the side of the long table, past our seated friends, towards her, my arms outstretched. This is the moment I have planned all week, the public embrace that will seal our betrothal. She is looking down at her lap, shyly I think. Then, when I'm six feet away, she looks up and I see hatred in her dark eyes. The room vanishes, the people fade and there are only the two of us in the universe. I'm alone with the woman I love, and she detests me.

The party goes on around us for a few more hours, and we don't say a word to each other. Friends circle with congratulations and thanks, I chat and smile and kiss and pour out more drinks. Jenny won't look at me. When the last drunken guest leaves at five it's already light. The summer dawn glows over the wreckage of the party, the exhausted flowers and Jenny's pale face as I shut the front door and go over to the couch where she sits. I kneel in front of her and put my head in her lap. 'Don't you want to marry me?'

'You didn't even ask. You just announced it in front of all those people. How could you?'

'I thought you'd be pleased. I thought it was what women want.'

'You're in the wrong century, Leo. I've never wanted to marry any-body.'

'Of course, it's true, marriage is but a ceremonial toy. You're right, Jenny, I probably am in the wrong century. I can feel your heart beating. My skin knows your skin and my flesh aches for yours. I dream about making love with you even when we're sleeping in the same bed. When we're apart and I'm walking in a strange city I expect to meet you on every street. Your face looks out at me from every piece of music I hear, every book I read, every woman I meet. Isn't that what you call love?'

'It does sound rather like it, but –'

'Ha!' I raise my head and stare at her, the instrument of my victory. 'I've done it – or rather you've done it to me, I don't understand how. So, of course, we have to marry. It's what people do.'

'But we can't! It would be terribly dishonest, a sort of blasphemy.'

'It's a bit late to worry about blasphemy. We're already bound together by contract.'

'I know, you never stop telling me. Isn't that enough? I don't want to pretend any more. I'm tired. I can't go through with some farcical ceremony.'

'*You're* tired! You've only been at it for sixty years. How do you think I feel? You have no idea how tedious it is to have to keep invent-ing new sins, new tricks and seductions and crimes and temptations and scams and torments. If life's a bitch, eternity's a cruel, vicious harpy. I don't want to be the villain any more. I want to retire. I've had enough. I'm no worse than most of the people I see around me. I admit my past is shady, but whose isn't? I really have changed, I just want to live here peacefully with you, to be kind to you and enjoy life. Why aren't you pleased, Jenny? Stop looking at me like that, as if I disgusted you.'

'I can't help it. It's as if Hitler were to turn round and say he wanted to be a nursery-school teacher.'

'He did, you know, quite frequently, when he was alone with Eva Braun. He loved children. And animals.'

'Well, you should know. And because you have knowledge like that you can never be an ordinary man. I can't think why you want to be anyway. Most people's lives are very dull.'

'But that's what I want!'

'But why now? Why me?'

'I don't really know why you. Compared with Helen of Troy or Cleopatra or the Empress Josephine or any of my other old girlfriends you are, it's true, very ordinary.'

'Thanks a bunch.'

'Perhaps it's your very simplicity that appeals to me. Anyway, you must believe me when I say I want to retire. I'm more or less redundant anyway. Nobody needs me or believes in me any more. The Metaphysical Bank will carry on perfectly well without me and the City and Wall Street and wars and famines and pestilence. You people are well on the way to wiping yourselves out and have no need of my guidance. Quite honestly, I've run out of ideas. Once you've seen one war or epidemic you've seen them all. The whole cycle of tragedy is very repetitive. Yes, Jenny, I want to take early retirement, with you, my darling.' I try to kiss her, but she edges away.

'But what are you going to do with yourself for the next few thousand years?'

'I want to be stupendously dull, to turn no heads as I walk down the street, to be an uxorious husband. I might even get a job in an ordinary bank. Stop laughing at me! I mean it.'

'Then you must find another woman to live that life with. I know too much about you. You can't expect me to believe all this.'

'You don't have to believe it. Just marry me and humour me and take what I'm offering.'

'I can't, Leo.'

David

I feel ugly and clumsy. I push you away, and our eyes meet in a gaze of terrible intensity as they did that day in Green Park. We stare at each other for a long time. Some instinct warns me that if I don't oppose you now you'll destroy me. I feel my will shut down like an icy portcullis. The effort of resisting you is so exhausting that I fall asleep where I'm sitting, on the couch.

When I wake up I'm still here, covered with a rug, and you've disappeared. Now that you've offered to make me the centre of you life and I've refused I suppose we can only turn away from each other. Our dance never stops, I can never rest or hold on to your feelings or my own. As soon as I define what you mean to me the moment passes, you've changed and my arms are empty again. I'm so weary.

You're trying to use me to tell yourself the most outrageous lie of all: that you're a good, simple, loving man, that our contract could be the foundation of a solid bourgeois marriage. As if I've ever wanted such a thing, as if I've travelled all this way just to be stupefied by the smugness of coupledom.

Alone in this enormous house I wander from room to room, touching the objects you have brought back from your travels: Aboriginal art, African carvings, Gothic sculptures, Roman torsos. Seventy years ago you collected me. Leave you? I love this house, our way of life, and as for you – I don't want to think about you just now. I'm glad you've gone away.

I'm reading Jung, who speaks to me with terrifying directness. I am trapped in what he would call the psychic underworld, and, indeed, I am disorientated and dissociated as I sit here alone in my study. My thoughts stray to David as I look out of the window at the park where we so often used to walk together. He must be thirty-eight now, married to Muriel, with small children and a successful legal career; all predictable – except that I know there's a tiny corner of David that isn't predictable at all, and that corner belongs to me.

On the phone he sounds just like George. 'Oh it's you. I suppose you've been arrested.'

'No. I just want to talk to you.'

'Are you in trouble?'

'No, I'm fine. The wicked flourish, you know. I'd love to see you. Are you allowed out?'

'As it happens, Muriel and the children have gone to stay with her mother in Bournemouth.'

'Perfect. Would you like to come here and have dinner with me tomorrow night?'

When I first see David again I find him coarsened, red and hot in his dark suit. We don't kiss but stare at each other on my doorstep. After I hand him a drink he strides from room to room, staring at everything in silence. 'Where's the husband who pays for all this?'

'Leo? He's in New York. I think. Or Tokyo. We've been living together for fourteen years now, but we're not married. You are, aren't you? Leo always said you'd marry Muriel; she was so determined to get you. Let's go and sit in the garden.'

He follows me downstairs and sits on the other side of the marble-topped table in morose silence. For a while there's nothing to say. I wonder if the public man has driven out the private; if David, like so many men I know, has a career now instead of an inner life. It's a change that holds families together but destroys intimacy.

Suddenly he stretches, laughs, yawns, all in one expansive gesture. I smile in response and take his hand across the table as he says, 'You look ridiculously unchanged. Absurdly young. So you found your millionaire. What does he do?'

'I'm not really sure. Buys and sells things.'

'Drugs, probably, like your last paramour. Did you invite me over just to flaunt this bloody great house?'

'I wanted to see you here. I've missed you, David. Now you've been here I'll have new memories of you, sitting here in this garden and standing on my doorstep and marching around upstairs touching all my things. The house won't seem so cold and empty.'

'It's a bit late to convince me you're sentimental, Jenny. I haven't forgotten how you seduced me and then dumped me when it suited you. You're utterly cynical.'

'Maybe I'm cynical *and* sentimental. And maybe you wanted to be seduced.'

'Of course I did, stupid,' he mutters angrily.

All around us the baked earth, mossy lawn and dusty flower beds gasp in the last of the evening sun. The sprinkler system turns itself on and releases intoxicating smells of grass, roses and lavender as well as our own salty flesh. As we eat our supper of cold soup, pasta, salad and melon we lean towards each other across the table, and by the time it's dark we're wound together on the same chair. David stops protesting that he has to go home.

Later, in bed, I say, 'It's done me so much good to see you again. I knew I could trust you.'

'Oh, is that what you think of me? The gullible idiot who always comes back.'

'David, don't . . .'

'I've been reading about the *grandes horizontales* in nineteenth-century Paris. Nana, that's you, isn't it, Jenny? Oozing sex, men ruining themselves for her . . .'

'And what about the men? Why did they chase her and not the matrons? Why was it Nana's fault?'

'They liked her because she was more fun.'

'Nana died young, didn't she? I've no intention of doing that.'

'Neither had she.'

'This is a ridiculous conversation. You're pretending to talk about a book, and all the time you're really reproaching me because I'm not more of a hypocrite. If I'd been all coy and refused to go to bed with you you'd adore me. I bet Muriel was like that.'

'Are you jealous of her?'

'Would you like me to be?'

'Yes. I want to make you so jealous you scream and shout.'

'And then you'll say I'm neurotic and hysterical and you'll leave me. I'll tell you something, David, as a friend, not just a lover. There is a war between men and women. It starts at birth and only finishes when you die. You practise skirmishes on your father, if you're a girl, and on your brothers if you have any. Then, when you're what is called grown-up, you strap on your armour, go out into the hard, nasty world and look for someone to take it off again. When you're stark naked, totally vulnerable and dependent, you announce you're in love.'

'Sounds like me with you.'

'Sounds like all of us, at one time or another. Some people choose to fight their own sex, of course, and some people are conscientious objectors. Marriage is a truce, but it doesn't last long.'

'My grandparents had a happy marriage. So have I until now.'

In the morning David leaves for work. I stand at the door and watch him walk to his car, open it and sit at the wheel, utterly in control. Hard to believe this is the same man who laughed and writhed and gasped and sobbed a few hours ago. I wonder if he will come back to me tonight. He does.

Every night in the cool, dark bedroom David and I make love, talk, laugh, massage and bathe each other. My golden boy looks older now, older than Leo, but I still adore his body. I'm tempted to confide in him. But if he knew his illicit passion is for an 86-year-old woman I'd never see him again. More probably, he wouldn't believe my story. He has no imagination. Yet I do feel very close to him. Of course, he thinks we're contemporaries in that generation I joined when I started taking the pill – which reminds me, I stopped taking it a few months ago. Rummaging in my dressing-table drawer just now I found a pack and took three. I think they work retrospectively.

We sit in my garden eating Parma ham with melon and figs.

'So you've been to see poor old Molly. Does she look really ancient now?'

'Well, she's over eighty. She's going a bit deaf and blind and can't be bothered keeping herself or the flat clean any more and her clothes all seem to be falling apart. You know.'

'Indeed I do. Bet you wouldn't be interested in me if I looked like that.'

'Don't be silly. Let's go to bed.'

At three we wake up, kiss, make love and start talking again. I bring in a tray with a pot of camomile tea and brown bread and honey. We talk about everything except Leo and Muriel, as if guilt is a bill that hasn't arrived yet.

'I was thinking about what you were saying earlier, about Molly.

Women *have* changed since her day, although I don't think men have. Now we're supposed to work and be wives and mistresses and mothers and intellectual equals and great cooks – a combination of the Michelin and *Who's Who* and the lineaments of gratified desire.'

'And do you succeed?'

'Me? Oh, I don't work. I'm useless.'

'But you are pretty good at gratifying desire. Yesterday I almost fell asleep after lunch. You're so lucky. You don't have to get up in the morning.'

'Do you despise me for not working?'

'Women like you never do. You use your sex appeal and youth to con some poor sap into supporting you for the rest of you life. Wasn't it Shaw who said marriage was licensed prostitution? Of course, it was different in the past when women couldn't get a proper education and most of the professions were closed to them. But now any woman with brains can earn her living.'

'Perhaps next time I'll be a tycoon.'

'Do you believe in reincarnation?'

'Reinvention? Oh yes.'

Next week David is to join Muriel and their two children in Bournemouth. For both of us this month has been a holiday, from ourselves and from Leo and Muriel.

Our last night together. We can't sleep. We keep turning to each other, touching, as if the other's face and body is a poem in Braille we have to memorize. 'I'll be back in two weeks.'

'This has become so much our room. I don't know how I'm going to be able to share it with Leo again.'

'I dare say you'll manage. You'll phone me at work?'

'Of course.'

'You won't leave it for another fifteen years? You have a very strange sense of time.'

'Yes, I suppose I do, but some things are timeless. I'll always feel close to you now, David. You know, it *is* quite possible to love two people, but not in the same way. Part of me will always be here in this room, this bed, with part of you. We'll always have to stay in each other's lives now.'

'Always is a big word.'

Well, David's doubts have turned out to be more accurate than my blind optimism. You are back and to my surprise – and self-disgust – I'm pleased to see you. We've settled easily into an affectionate routine. Neither of us has asked the other any questions about last summer, not even when you found David's razor in our bathroom.

I feel lethargic. I haven't the energy to phone David. Already, last summer seems a long time ago. My body feels strange: my heart, belly, tear ducts and breasts seem bigger, like overripe fruit waiting to burst. At night I lie awake beside you, listening to my internal seething and churning, which at four in the morning merge with the rhythm of trains and the shouts of drunks. At first I thought I was becoming a hypochondriac, but now I've missed two periods and notice a thickening, as if a layer of clay has been slapped on around my waist and thighs. I'm almost sure now, yet still I say nothing, do nothing. My body's been invulnerable for years, I can't believe it would disobey me now. I've been pregnant before, of course, but so long ago that I've forgotten how it feels, although I vividly remember the misery of my two abortions.

My slinkier dresses bulge now, and I have to turn up at parties in long, flowing clothes.

'Are you putting on weight?' you ask as we're dressing to go out.

'Too much good food.' Alone in the bathroom I stare at my naked body in the mirror. I'm rounder, softer, with heavy breasts and dark, sore nipples. My body's been sending me all these signals, and I've just ignored them. It's the one thing I never expected to happen and if – if – I've no idea if the father's David or you. You've always said it's impossible; it would be a back-to-front immaculate conception, a diabolical miracle. Not so long ago I'd have been burnt at the stake. If it's yours I'll have to have an abortion. But David's child – George's great-grandchild – yes, I could enjoy that. Or it might all be the product of my disastrous imagination. Women do have imaginary pregnancies. But not at eighty-six, surely?

I walk in Holland Park, staring at the baby-dominated world that suddenly opens up. It's November. Plants are dying, but children are growing. In prams and pushchairs imperious little monsters rule. One of those, oh God, one of those. Above each sunny, rapacious little face I see the eclipsed features of a mother or nanny. How exhausted they look, anaemic, their life's blood draining into their charges as surely as if an intravenous tube linked the two. One of the women is hugely pregnant. I smile at her bump and then into her tired eyes, meeting her answering smile.

All my life I've ignored this submerged freemasonry of women and small children. I've often wondered why women carry on having babies at all, now that they don't have to. I start to project these changes in my body outwards into a new autonomous being.

Can't tell you because you'd want me to get rid of it. You'd hate the competition and the mess. Can't tell David either; he's already got two kids and it wouldn't be fair to spring this on him. Last summer was a no-strings affair: no promises, no demands and certainly no babies. I hope it's his. It *can't* be yours, but perhaps I should pretend it is. One of you obviously had something to do with it.

I want it. Him. Her. I want to love in a different way, with the total absorption of these women in the park. Seven months before this baby's born and already I'm lying for it, turning my life upside down.

The Contract

The Christmas party at the Fizz was even more excessive than usual: enough food and drink to support a refugee camp for six months; strippers leaping out of cakes; Salome performed with the head of Karl Marx on a plate. Nothing too baroque, however, as there were MPs and journalists present and one-lifers don't like it when parties get out of hand. Two years ago I conjured up Queen Victoria to give the after-dinner speech, but she only gaped at us all and disintegrated all over the table. The dead have no stamina. Sensational profits this year – my bonus is enough to buy that estate in Sussex and have another flutter on the interplanetary-retirement scheme. Cecil Rhodes, who has reinvented himself as an ecology consultant, reckons this planet will be finished by the middle of the next century, and one does have to plan ahead.

Jenny wouldn't come to the party. She's very temperamental at the moment; just lies around all day and seems to be putting on weight. She goes out on mysterious errands. I suspect she's still having an affair with that tedious grandson of George's. Not that I care, of course, although how she could . . . Jealousy is out of the question. I must have slept with twenty women as I flitted from continent to continent last summer; can't even remember their names. I was shocked by her rejection of my proposal. Still, married or not, here we are together again, under the same roof. I just wish she wouldn't be so damned faithful to her old lovers. Love? As tired a word as Christmas itself.

'I hate this time of year,' I complain as we sit down to supper. I absent-mindedly open another bottle of champagne, although I'm still hungover from last night, and pour a glass for Jenny.

'No thanks. I told you, I'm trying not to drink.'

'Whatever for? Yes, Christmas always makes me feel like a has-been.'

'But I thought you said you preferred this century to any other? I think this is a great time to be alive. Providing you're young, bright, rich and beautiful, of course. I don't know what you're complaining about.'

'You don't understand, Jenny. You're so young – comparatively, I mean. Why, in the old days I wasn't just a businessman, I was the most famous man in this world or out of this world. Nobody was ever quite sure who God was or what he looked like but everybody knew me. They talked about me all the time. Of course, the whole thing was a misunderstanding because I was only one of many. One agent couldn't possibly have handled all that work. According to a fifteenth-century bishop there were 133,306,668 fallen angels, although I don't see how he could possibly have known, and I never met them all.'

'So what happened to the others?'

'That's a very good question. A few are involved with the Fizz, but I lost touch with all the others centuries ago. Some of them have probably fallen on hard times. We're a vulnerable minority. Milton claimed they shrank to the size of fairies so as to make more room in Hell – too kitsch for my taste. I've always had a certain flair for falling on my feet, but some of the others were hopelessly unworldly. No skills at all, except playing the harp and singing. Perhaps we should try and trace them . . .'

'Angels Anonymous?'

'Ah, your English compulsion to turn everything into a joke.'

'Look, can't we just eat our supper without all these pathetic reminiscences?'

'Don't be so blasé. Only a few centuries ago – yesterday in meta-physical time – I, or we, got the credit for thunderstorms, gales and blizzards and wet dreams and diseases and madness and crimes and professional failures. I know you think I'm conceited, but can you blame me? John Knox called me the "Prince and God of this world"; James I called me "God's hangman". They really admired me then; they were always trying to get in touch with me. The intellectuals were the worst. Like that old German pedant, Faust, who started out dry as dust and then turned out to have an insatiable appetite for sex, power and money. He cheated me in the end –'

'Leo, why are you boasting like this?'

'I just want you to know who I really am. Why, in the Great Cate-chism I get mentioned sixty-seven times whereas *His* name only appears sixty-three times.'

'Do you mean to say you counted?' Jenny comes over to my side of the table and hugs me. 'Is this your way of saying you're feeling old and unloved?'

'Why do women always have to reduce everything to the personal?'

'Why don't men ever have the courage to talk about their feelings?'

'I'm not some snivelling one-lifer, you know, whining about my inadequacies.'

'Well, you can't have it both ways.' She returns to her chair and peels a peach, frowning at me.

'Why not? I always have. I've always had it every conceivable way. The truth is, I was better off in a more religious age. Everyone was. Medieval man – I know you'll say what about women, but they didn't count then – saw himself as God's beloved child. His earth was safe at the centre of the universe, and the sun moved around it. He knew where he belonged and what he should do, both during his lifetime and afterwards. Nowadays there's chaos, everyone's discontented with their place in the world, there's no faith and Christmas is just a commercial jamboree.'

'What an original thought,' Jenny says sourly. 'You sound like an old colonel. Look, it's Christmas Eve, and I want to enjoy it. Tomorrow will be fun. We'll be with Toby and Katrina and their kids. Christmas without children doesn't make any sense.' She pauses, searches my face for some signal that isn't there and continues with forced jollity, 'Let's give each other our presents tonight, like they do in Italy.'

She gives me some gold cufflinks. Apart from the flowers, which showed some imagination, Jenny's presents are predictable, the sort of thing a bourgeois wife might give her successful husband. Perhaps that's how she sees us. Odd. I give her a small sixteenth-century Spanish painting I picked up at Sotheby's last week. I don't think she likes it, but she pretends she does.

'See! There I am, firmly in my place, toasting heretics like crumpets in a cosy blaze. Actually, I didn't have horns or a tail by then. I've been a good-looking chap for at least a thousand years now, but people always remember your mistakes.'

'Well, you look fabulous now,' she says in her new soothing, condescending voice that jars on me so much. 'We should get Dominic to take some photos of us – now that you have a reflection.'

'Another strange sign of the times. What's going on? Who am I? Religion's become a wishy-washy insurance policy, and I'm just a symptom of schizophrenia.'

'Oh, do stop feeling so sorry for yourself.'

'I don't think you realize how humiliating this time of year is for me, Jenny. I never even get a mention on a Christmas card. They drool over that wretched little baby and fuss over their horrible children. I hate babies.'

'Tell me about it.'

I do. My bad temper lasts for days. I'm irritated by Katrina's spoilt, greedy children and Jenny's raptures over them. I guzzle and booze and end up with a headache and indigestion. Our friends, who seemed so delightful a few months ago, get on my nerves now. They're all so complacent, so unaware, and throw their money around so ostentatiously. The courts of medieval monarchs were quite tasteful compared with the waste and vulgarity at Toby and Katrina's parties. Another few years here and I'll be an ascetic socialist. And Jenny – she isn't in the room with me any more.

On New Year's Eve, unable to face another party, I go to bed at seven and let her go out alone. I wake up at three to see Jenny undressing by the light of her bedside lamp and watch as she takes off her long, loose crimson dress. When we're making love I'm too absorbed to look at her body carefully, but now I see how its contours have expanded and softened. Her breasts are heavy and purposeful; they no longer spring unemphatically above the flat plain of her belly. It's flat no longer. Flesh curves richly from the top of her black bush, and her sharp hipbones are muffled and rounded. Sensing my eyes on her, she grabs a long, white night-dress to cover herself. She always used to sleep naked.

'Good party? Who was there?'

'The usual suspects.'

'You've put on weight.'

'Thanks, Leo, that's a great start to the new year.'

'Sorry. Happy 1984, Jenny.'

I used to think I knew everything about her, even when we were apart. Suddenly her mind and body have become opaque. The thought that she might be having a serious love affair gives me an enormous hard-on. I press myself against her, and she turns away from me in her sleep. The most obvious explanation for her plumpness is . . . No, that's out of the question.

Since I'm more subtle than any private detective I follow her around for a few weeks. My ability to disappear comes in handy; she doesn't realize I'm stalking her. I've never really thought about who Jenny is without me. In her room she reads and listens to music. She goes to see Molly and Katrina and meets other girlfriends for lunch. No sign of a lover unless she's become bisexual, which I doubt. On Wednesday I follow her to St Stephen's Hospital, and lurk while she goes inside. I'm too late to see which department she goes to, but she comes out smiling. When I casually ask about her health at supper she says she's fine. Could she be nobly covering up some tragic diagnosis? It's very unlikely anything would go seriously wrong with her. Even if it did she couldn't die and would probably be entitled to sue in the Metaphysical Courts.

I follow her to the tube station, sitting invisibly beside her on the train. We get off at Sloane Square, and I follow her into Peter Jones. I rematerialize in China and Glass – to the alarm of an old lady whose Pekinese yaps and pees in distress – and follow Jenny on the escalator up to the third floor. I watch from behind a stack of plastic ducks while she wanders around, touching tiny jumpers, hats and dresses, crisp broderie anglaise pillows, painted wooden furniture and teddy bears. I rarely lose my temper, but when I do the manifestations are always physical. This time the plastic ducks melt into a yellow puddle, and I find myself glaring straight at Jenny while shop assistants rush up to stare at the liquefied ducks. With her usual *chutzpah* Jenny calmly walks up to me and kisses me lightly on the cheek.

But I refuse to be disarmed. 'You can't be. It's impossible.'

'It *is* real, I had a scan ten days ago, and there it was, wriggling around on a screen. A little Leo. Now you know we might as well do some shopping.'

I grip her arm tightly, quivering with rage. 'Don't come the sub-urban housewife with me. Little Leo, my arse. It's nothing to do with me. Have you been screwing somebody else?'

'Why shouldn't I? You do. You always have.'

'Even if you have it shouldn't be possible. I don't understand.'

'I don't see what's so amazing. We've been sleeping together for the last seventy years.'

'I told you, it can't be mine.'

'You keep saying you want to be ordinary, human. Well, maybe you are.'

'It's not that creepy grandson of George's?'

'I don't know. Let go of me.' She shakes herself free. 'I'm going to buy some clothes. Now fuck off, Leo, we'll talk about this later. I'm having this baby, with or without you, and you'd just better get used to the idea.'

A rail of tiny cardigans scorches as I pass it, and I become aware of the hostile audience of customers and assistants. They're all women. Only women come here, women and their horrible screaming brats. In my anxiety to escape I carelessly disappear in the middle of the depart-ment and see gaping mouths and pointing fingers as I propel myself through the window, over the traffic and rooftops to my laboratory.

Here, at least, I'm still in control but so confused. All this repulsive, shameful emotion. How could You let this happen to me? The rules have always been quite clear. You decreed that all angels, fallen and otherwise, would be sterile, since they couldn't be expected to be celibate, and a world populated by demi-angels would lead to even more chaos. I admit I might have got carried away recently and said I wanted to be a human being, but how could You take me so literally? It's not like You at all. But You're not there any more, are you? Gone, with Your capital letters and structured universe and rules that I was made to break. I'm on my own now.

If I am the father, what kind of child will Jenny have? A wunderkind, an *enfant terrible*, a little monster? And if it *is* David's baby, it'll just be a pudding of a one-lifer. Why should I look after the little bastard?

Jenny arrives home in a taxi, laden with parcels. I come out of my office and glare down at her from the landing. 'If you ever bully me in public like that again I'm walking out. It might be the best thing, any-way, if you don't want this baby.'

'And where would you go?'

'None of your business.'

'Oh, but it is. I'm going to read to you from the transcript of your contract –'

'Not that again!'

'Yes, that boring old contract you can never be bothered to read or think about, although it's given you everything women want. Are supposed to want. Why do you look so damned unhappy?'

'Aren't I allowed to be unhappy? Isn't it in my fucking contract?'

'Just sit down and listen. The language is rather archaic. We did think of commissioning translations. If the Bible can be dragged into twentieth-century English, why not our metaphysical covenants?'

'If it's metaphysical, why should it bind me physically?'

'Why, Jenny, that's the first time I've ever heard you use a five-syllable word.'

'Don't you patronize me. I'm not an illiterate fifteen-year-old any more.'

'No, indeed. You're a pregnant octogenarian, a far more formidable proposition. Ah, yes, here we are. Now then. "London, on the twelfth of October nineteen hundred and twenty-two. This scroll, being the receipt for the gift of body (Grade 1a) and soul (Grade 3d) from Jenny Manette (née Mankowitz) to Leopold M. Bishop, Agent Number 2003 (alias the Great Pantoffsky, Mephistopheles, Beelzebub, Lord of Misrule, Lord of the Flies, Destroyer, etc.) *Consummatum est*" – I'll skip the Latin – "on these conditions following: First, that the aforesaid Jenny Mankowitz may preserve in perpetuity the form, shape, body, face, organs, etc., which she possesses on this night. Secondly, that the aforesaid Jenny Mankowitz shall only be permitted to love the said

Agent known as Mephistopheles and no other man, spirit, child or woman whomsoever. Thirdly, that Jenny Mankowitz shall renounce her *soi-disant* career as an artiste (Grade 4c). Fourthly, in return for this solemn deed of gift of body and soul, the Agent known as Mephistopheles shall cherish, maintain, aid said Jenny Mankowitz and be bound to her until the end of time, within the limits of his inhumanity –"'

'What does *that* mean?'

'Pretty much what I choose to make it mean, like most contracts. Then there's a bit of Greek, I won't bore you with that. Ah, yes, this is what I was looking for. "I, Jenny Mankowitz, do sign this deed of gift with mine own blood; and furthermore grant unto the Agent known as Mephistopheles that when the short lease mankind holds on time expires, the articles above-written inviolate, full power to fetch or carry the said Jenny Mankowitz, body and soul, flesh, blood, or goods, into his habitation wheresoever." Conclusive, wouldn't you say?'

'Is that all? Is that the contract you've tried to scare me with all these years? I've already broken it if you really want to know. I *did* love George and David, and I'll love this child, and there's absolutely nothing you can do about it. And who cares what happens at the end of time anyway?'

'You still don't understand.'

But neither do I. What is happening? What will Jenny give birth to?

A Child Is Given

Click. The metal nose of the camera sniffs my belly, swallows a slice of me and regurgitates it slowly on to three miniature television screens beside me, unpeeling the image from left to right. Inside a grainy black-and-white cavern is a creature with a huge head. Click. I see its other profile, then its back and front. On another screen variations on the same images unfold, mysteriously green, more than ever like a creature from another planet. My planet. I cough and the monochrome cave ripples.

I wonder what the nurse feels when the camera shows some deformity. She's smiling. Would she still smile if my baby had two heads? Eagerly I stare at the third screen. There it is again, already leading its own life down there in the maternal cave, wriggling, squirming, sucking its thumb. In delight and astonishment I stare at this vision of someone I've never met but am destined to love – because convention demands it and because now, suddenly, I do.

The image fades, and I'm reluctant to leave this room where the future has waved at me so hopefully. But I have to go, there are dozens of Madonnas waiting to see their little cave-dwelling Messiahs. No Josephs. I'm aware that this adventure I'm embarking on is for women and children only. Men, who have always been the most important people in my life, are about to be upstaged. Even you.

I've prepared a wonderful room for the baby next to our bedroom, and I shop exuberantly for it. Katrina comes shopping with me. She and Toby are having a difficult time, she confides in me over lunch – well, coffee and salad; Katrina never actually eats. Pregnancy makes me hungry, so I stuff myself with seafood pie and cheesecake. She looks annoyingly slender but rather haggard. Older, definitely.

'Some investments have gone wrong, and we'll have to sell the house. Leo's usually so good about money. He advised us, so we thought it would be all right.'

'He's brilliant with money. I can't think what went wrong. You must be furious with him.'

'Oh no. He's such a wonderful friend. He's been an angel. I'm sure it's not his fault. You're so lucky, Jenny, to have a man who's reliable. I don't think I could have got through the last few months without Leo's advice. Toby's drinking, snorting and swallowing everything under the sun – he always did coke, but that was under control. Now he's a real mess. He can't get gigs because he's unreliable and he loses his temper with our kids, and he's threatened suicide a couple of times.' Katrina is crying.

'That's horrible! Katrina, I'm sure we can lend you some money.'

'Leo has already lent us thousands, and we can't repay it, I don't want to borrow any more.'

'Well, let's at least go and buy some presents for your kids.'

As my body gets heavier, the days slow down. I lumber through them, feeling increasingly important the more space I take up. You and I spend less time together, and we've both become secretive. After all these decades I have only fragments of knowledge about you. We're like two moles tunnelling down parallel memories and hopes, taking it on trust that some day our tunnels will join. This baby is, I suppose, the end of our long experiment in emotional engineering.

I catch you gazing intently at my bump, your dark-blue eyes so piercing that I clutch my belly protectively. 'I'm going to have it. You can't stop me. And you can't make me miscarry, however much you'd like to.'

'What an outrageous accusation.'

I don't want to fight you. I only want to infect you with my own excitement. 'I bought some more things for the baby's room today. Do you want to come and see?'

'No, I'll leave it all up to you.'

'Don't you have any feelings at all for this baby?'

'Why should I? It's not mine. I can't see it or hear it, I've only your word that it exists. All I know is that I've lost you. A few months ago we were happy, but now you're changing. Why should I be pleased about that? I loved you as you were.'

Sometimes I feel sorry for you. I know you feel left out, but I can't control the rhythms of my immense new body. Inside my richly coloured smocks I feel like a galleon, swaying and burgeoning into the wind. I lie for hours in the garden in the cool grass, resting my melon breasts and pumpkin belly, making silent contact with this new life inside me. I try to identify its heartbeats, wriggly legs, greedy hands, hiccups and itches. I shiver with passionate need to touch and hug this unborn creature.

Although we still share a bedroom, you and I seem to occupy different universes now. I'd like to compare notes with other women, but none of my friends happens to be pregnant.

'Can't remember,' Katrina says vaguely when I ask her.

'But you've been pregnant three times.'

'Seven, if you count abortions and miscarriages. I know, but it was a while ago and you forget. If you remembered you'd never let yourself in for it again.'

I feel inadequate, as if this natural process is the one thing in my unnatural life that defeats me. I don't know what labour pain feels like or how I'll feel when my waters burst. I imagine my baby, exasperated by its mother's incompetence, pacing up and down my placenta clutching a pin as it gets ready to break the waters itself.

A postcard from David: 'Last summer seems a long time ago and always *is* a big word after all. So glad to hear the news about the baby you and Leo are expecting. Warmest congratulations.' I interpret this as a disclaimer of responsibility, not that I ever asked him to claim any. I wonder if it will look like him, pink and blonde and blue-eyed. It's mine, I remind myself several times a day; fathers are more dispensable than mothers. When mothers leave, as mine did, the damage is irreparable. Whatever this child is like, I'm sticking by it.

The huge boulder of my abdomen makes it difficult to sleep. I wake at dawn and go downstairs to the kitchen to sit in the rocking chair and watch the morning unfold over the gardens. My belly's aching. I nurse a hot water bottle and a cat comes to the window, attracted by my passivity. Together we sit for hours, purring, immobile, listening to the daily birth pangs of London.

'So you see, you really do have the body of a woman in her twenties,' you say at lunchtime with the air of a lawyer pointing out that he hasn't cheated his client. You seem to have accepted the baby at last. You stand over me as I sit back in my rocking chair, the only piece of furniture that's still amenable to my bulk, and kiss my forehead, passing your hands over my belly. It's the gesture you used to make in your conjuring days.

'Don't you dare turn my baby into a white rabbit.'

'Oh, I'll be kind enough once she's born.'

'How do you know it's a girl?'

'What do you want to call her?'

'I'll decide when I see it. Her. Are you coming to the hospital with me?'

'Do you want me to?'

'Of course. Do you think she can hear us talking? I'm frightened, Leo. I went for a walk in Brompton Cemetery yesterday and looked at all the graves of women who died in childbirth.'

'But you couldn't! You know that.'

'Yes, but what if all these laws you count on have been reversed? What if you *have* fathered this child and my body *is* just an ordinary body and we're just a normal couple with delusions? Or perhaps we once had immortality but lost it. Last year you kept saying you wanted to be an ordinary man. Well, maybe you are.'

'The truth is, Jenny, I don't really understand either. Maybe those laws really have been turned upside down. I only know what I was told long ago when the world was young. Love and birth and death used to be quite clearly defined, I remember, and I was in no danger from any of them.'

'I hate laws anyway.'

'I know you do.'

Our car glides through empty streets to the hospital. London in the bluish pre-dawn haze is indifferent to one more superfluous inhabitant. Inside the hospital I'm whisked into a wheelchair appropriate to my age but not to my excitement, which bubbles and fizzes.

'Anything you want?' you whisper to me in the lift.

'No pain.'

'I'll see what I can do.'

'Labour is such an unfortunate word,' the midwife clucks. But it seems accurate enough as I lie in a tiny room, sweating and heaving, surrounded by medical students who chat as if they're at a party and watch politely as I plunge and writhe into each new contraction. The pain gets worse, and I'm beginning to wish I hadn't opted for natural childbirth. I sob with pain.

Your hands appear, making that mysterious gesture over me: the rabbit out of the hat; the bun out of the oven. Immediately, instead of a stormy ocean my body contains a choppy bath. I even sleep for a while and wake up to find a hand has reached mine through the tangle of wires and tubes attached to me. Turning to my right I see you, sitting on a chair reading a newspaper.

'What did you do?'

'Just a trick I picked up in Babylon. Are you all right now? I thought you'd never stop panting and gasping.'

The thin plastic drip tube on my arm flows hot and cold up and down my bloodstream, like a wasp sting. No, I'm the insect, a butterfly pinned for inspection. Every few hours the shifts change, and I hear myself making small talk with a new group of nurses and students.

'Blood in the waters.'

I open my eyes, try to sit up, but the tubes won't let me. So there are complications. Of course, my baby will be disabled: punishment for my hubris. But I'll love it anyway. What are the doctors and nurses muttering? This must be how a small child feels when adults loom over her. Where are you? It's so cold in the room without you. But it's hard to speak.

'Is my baby alive?' I ask at last in an angry, tearful voice.

'Of course it is. Perfectly all right.' A don't-be-silly laugh.

The scene becomes even more surreal and baffling. They spread a green cloth with a hole in the middle over me. Tarpaulin, tent, gardening, I associate wildly as I push, heave and pant, using muscles I can't even feel. The institutional atmosphere wavers and cracks as their shouted instructions rise to a frenzied pitch, like sports commentators. There's a tug of war on the other side of the tarpaulin, a gush of liquid, then a threshing creature shoots out from my oceanic depths.

'Is that fish human?' I ask.

Your laugh. Opening my eyes, I see your face above the green horizon. Something is passed to you and then to me: a girl, a tiny mauve creature with nebulous eyes, exquisite hands and ivory feet. I hug her, she tangles with my puppet wires as we stare at each other. I don't need anyone to tell me that my baby is all right. She's perfect. I pull down the right shoulder of my hospital gown and the vague little face stares past my unappetizing nipple. I think she's going to reject me, spit out my fraudulent breast. Then the delicate curve of her cheek turns, her pursed mouth blindly finds me and sucks imperceptibly, a slight tautening of my breast. The faces above me glow and then begin to disperse, the performance over.

I lie with my baby in my arms, flesh of my flesh, kissing and licking the tiny hand, which tastes salty. 'Baby Mankowitz' is printed on the plastic bracelet on the baby's wrist. Your long brown hand appears, and the little fingers cling like ivy to the great tree of your thumb. The baby's unfocused eyes droop, and I yawn in sympathy.

You kiss me, your mouth explores my mouth, which is a bomb site, and then moves to my ear. 'Well done! I'm just going off to get some supper. What are we going to call her? She can't be Baby Mankowitz for the rest of her life.'

'She's Abigail.'

Now, at last, I feel my age. I give in to an exhaustion so total that it's sensuous. You reduced the pain, but my eyes, mouth, left arm and abdomen are sore and ravaged. I'm desperate for sleep. The baby's sucking again, sucking my life. All the years when I've swindled death vanish. I long to give in to sleep, yet I'm convinced that as soon as I do I'll stop breathing and fall into the pit that has always been waiting for me. I'm sobbing uncontrollably, and there are people in the room again, taking my baby away from me. Each breath is a painful battle; I can't speak or tell them how terrified I am. The green uniforms are back, pressing an oxygen mask to my face and asking questions. I'm amused, through my hysteria, because while they're busy ministering to my body I'm a thousand miles away from it. If I let go for one second my absent mind will slip back into a corpse.

On the other side of the room I can feel Abigail's tiny heart and will chugging away, needing me, devouring me.

Your face comes near, unshaven, with thick dark eyebrows. 'No, Jenny, you can't go.'

'Just slipping through the hole in reality. Just for a few minutes.'

'No.'

With an enormous effort I drag myself back into the room. At last I'm alone with Abigail. Under the strange neon-blue light she lies beside my bed in a transparent tank, as if she hasn't yet evolved from that amniotic shrimp. Oh, but she has. Pressing my nose against the tank I stare at my beautiful daughter, who opens her eyes and gazes back short-sightedly. Now I can sink into the sleep I've been longing for – but I feel perversely awake. Every twitch and whimper of Abigail's alarms me. With my plastic-strung arm I reach out constantly to touch her, greet her, kiss her. She looks so ethereal, as if she's just visiting our world and wondering whether to stay.

During one of these wisps of sleep I dream I'm holding my daughter, fleeing down steps treacherous with slimy, rotting vegetables, splintery crates, greasy newspapers and buzzing insects. Tighter and tighter I clasp my baby, terrified of dropping her, hurting her, losing her – then I'm awake and face to face with her again. Through the Perspex wall I smile at the waxen little face, reach out and pull her into my bed, where she is so obviously meant to be. She nestles between my dirty gown and the plastic tube, closing her eyes as yellow gleams shoot through the blue hospital light, and I say, incredulously, 'Hello, Abigail. It's your first morning.'

More Accidents

Abbie didn't look like me or either of her possible fathers. In her nappy she looked like a balding, middle-aged businessman sunbathing. She used to dribble with ecstasy as she wriggled into her kangaroo pouch for our long walks around London. I talked to her, long before she could talk back, staring into her face as she huddled inside my coat. Some of the age I'd escaped seemed to have pickled my daughter: she had heavy lids above her blue eyes and frown lines.

You had never made jealous scenes about any of my flirtations or affairs. But when I fell in love with my baby you behaved like a rejected schoolboy. Incredulous, disgusted, you watched as I cuddled and worshipped and changed and fed her. The first few times I saw you with Abbie I was reminded of Mr Punch and the baby; I rushed over to take her before your boredom became destructive. You never offered to help, and your work became conveniently demanding. More and more, you stayed away, and I didn't ask too many questions about what you were up to. I was happy in the enchanted circle I made with my daughter and, although I knew you felt left out, I couldn't find a way of including you.

One afternoon, when Abbie was three, we returned to what I thought was an empty house and marched in, singing and laughing. Suddenly I saw you on the dark stairs. You looked very tall and pale and thin, and your deep blue eyes glared at us like two rodents in a cage, fighting viciously. Abbie ran to me and buried her face against my coat. 'Leo, you frightened us. I thought you were still in Sicily. You look so – sinister.'

'Sorry to be the spectre at your feast. What a pity you didn't marry a cosier man, David, for instance. If I'd known you were going to slide into bovine domesticity as soon as you got the chance I would have left you in Hoxton.' Abbie wailed, not understanding our words but picking up the feelings behind them all too well.

All our rows were about the kind of child she should be. You wanted her to have a nanny, to go to a formal school and later a boarding-school, to join the upper-middle class we had bought our way into. I wanted your money and my daughter but not the pompous conventions that would take her away from me. I won all the rows and kept Abbie, but somewhere along the way I lost you. You were our acerbic sugar daddy, paying the bills and then disappearing behind closed doors or on mysterious trips I never asked enough questions about. Our talk became functional, our love-making became more aggressive and then fizzled out.

Now she's nine. Although I've tried to give Abbie an ordinary childhood, she's stronger, more complex and self-contained than other children of her age. I can't take her for granted. I find her endlessly fascinating, rather as the old toy maker must have felt about Pinocchio. As I watch her develop I feel better about myself, as if my daughter's life is a continuation of my own but deeper and richer. When adults ask her what she wants to be when she grows up, Abbie says, 'I want to be a proper person'; and when other children ask what her father does she replies either 'He's in an aeroplane' or 'He's driving his big car.' I don't know, or choose to know, much more than that about your movements. I suppose I'll never know for sure who her father is. There's a test now that determines paternity – but how could I subject Abbie to it? She might end up in some medical textbook, a freak, the subject of television documentaries.

Yes, I want her to be ordinary. Last Christmas in New York you did your best to broadcast your powers. So now you're trying to upstage Superman and Jesus with your miracles, as I screamed when Abbie boasted about your flight together. You said I was jealous, that I wanted Abbie all to myself. Rubbish. I just wanted to protect her from your dangerous attempts to impress her.

Since that night you and I have hardly spoken to each other. You go away for months at a time. And the accidents have started again. In February poor Charles blew his brilliant brains out to evade the scandal over his underworld connections. Toby and Katrina's perfect marriage fell apart just after Christmas, and Toby was sectioned. He hanged himself. Then, last month, Katrina set fire to her flat and burnt to death with all her children.

I confront you with my suspicions.

'What? Jenny, you're so paranoid. I wasn't even in the country when poor Charles and Toby and Katrina died.'

We're standing on the stairs, hissing at each other because Abbie has just gone to bed. Not in front of the child. You're dressed in a sharp suit and dark glasses, your luggage is in the hall because you're catching a night flight to Moscow. I follow you downstairs.

'There have been too many accidents and coincidences, Leo. Gerry, George, Nat, Hari and now our three closest friends – and God knows how many during the war. You always destroy your instruments. I'm afraid for Abbie . . .'

'I've never lifted a finger against her. Or you. One-lifers are so fragile, it doesn't take much to kill them. Toby's madness started with paranoid delusions, you know. You should be careful, Jenny.'

Your car comes, you leave, but my fear stays in the house. It's only now, when I'm ceasing to love you, that I realize just how much I once did, like an illness that can only be diagnosed when the corpse is dissected. There's been a lot of sex between us but very few declarations of feeling. Yet I can see now that loving you was always there, my background and foreground. Even when I lived in Italy and told myself I was independent I knew I could always go back to you. What did I get eternal youth *for* if not to share it with you?

When you're away I don't miss you as I once did but think uneasily about you and dream. The dreams are horrible. I try to forget them, but there's one that keeps recurring. I fall asleep on the sofa in my study, thinking I'm alone in the house. The door opens and shadowy figures in white gowns and masks drift into the room and surround me. They bend over me, inject me, cut me, subject me to some mysterious ritual. I can see them but can't speak or move. Suddenly I see your face behind one of the masks. We stare at each other, but no words come.

I've become even more anxious about Abbie. I take her to school, pick her up, never leave her alone in the house. You and I no longer make love. I sleep in our double bed, and when you're in London you sleep in one of the spare rooms. Celibacy makes me tense and bad-tempered – a few weeks ago, this familiar train of thought was interrupted by my femunculus:

Why don't you just admit you're feeling randy and go out and pick someone up?

Oh, it's you, is it? Where have you been?

I've been around, listening, watching you bury yourself in that child, pretending you still love Leo because you can't cope without him. So, find yourself a toyboy.

It's not that easy. What about AIDS? Supposing the guy's a psychopath or a thief? Anyway, I don't like the idea of sex without feelings.

Better than no sex at all. You didn't used to be so squeamish. Come on, let's get you dolled up. What's the point in having a 25-year-old body if you don't flaunt it? Abbie's staying the night with her friend Emily.

So I've become more adventurous again. I take myself out to pubs and bars where I pick up men. It's all rather impersonal, but I don't hate myself as I did during the war. I've changed and so have the times. I've always known that sex is my drug, and now, in my nineties, it's fun to walk into a bar and watch men half my age fall in lust with me. I never spend more than a night with any of my casual partners or give them my phone number. I'm only doing what men have always done; most of the men I pick up are married and have children.

I have a luxurious bath, wash my hair, perfume my still young body and make up my still young face. Smiling at myself in the mirror, I remind myself that sex is the one great proof of vitality. In the beginning there was sex, before poets came along and invented romantic love. I put on my strappy green dress and green high-heeled sandals and totter over to the Hilton, which is always full of sad-eyed Eurocrats.

Don't look at his eyes, I remind myself as I sit on a stool in the bar and smile at the man beside me. Anton is a French computer programmer, mid-thirties, good-looking and well dressed. It's relaxing to speak French again, easier to flirt in another language. The eyes I'm trying not to look at are brown, and he has beautiful hands with long spatular fingers that make me envy his computers. I want to be programmed by him, tuned to forget my mechanical failures. After a few drinks we go upstairs, sneak into his single room and lie together on his bed. This is love's most neutral face: sex as recreation; orgasm as a consumer service. We tell no lies and break no hearts. Politely, gently, we come and go.

I'm a repulsive old hypocrite, I think as I wait outside Abbie's school the next morning. But so, probably, are most of these other parents. And so will our children be when they grow up. It's so hard to reconcile different kinds of love.

'What's adultery, Mummy?' my daughter asks.

'It's what adults do,' I reply without thinking. Something in me has died.

I lie in bed alone, missing what you once meant to me. I've smothered the flames of my desire, but other feelings stir, the volcanic ashes of our love. In this room, on this mattress, we made love thousands of times, said things we could only say to each other. Or so it seemed – yes, I'm quite sure – that *was* love, killed by me when I insisted on having a baby against your will. It's very hard to accept that I can't have romantic and maternal love at the same time, that one has driven out the other.

Most nights I stay at home with Abbie, and the intimacy of these evenings together, when we cook and talk and draw and play in the warm kitchen, satisfies me. I enjoy the security I never had with my own mother. For twenty years I poured my energy into this house and loved it even more than my villa in Rapallo. I used to feel utterly safe here but not any more. Nothing I can define or pin down, just a general sense of unease and misery, of danger that rustles in corners and scurries behind walls.

Wrapped in a white towel, I stare at myself in the bathroom mirror. Suddenly, out of the corner of my eye, I glimpse the pale despairing face of a drowning child in the bath I've just left. When I whip around to look, there's nothing there. My eyes play tricks – or are they seeing what has always been here? This morning, as I came upstairs, I saw Nat just above me, weeping. Impossible, I remind myself. She died more than a quarter of a century ago.

Now, more than ever, I need to hold on to reality. If there had been no child I would have left you years ago. Whatever that contract means – and there are days when I think it doesn't mean anything at all – I wouldn't have stayed with you after I stopped loving you. As it is, I believe that the best thing for Abbie is to stay in this house with her familiar routine and her occasional father.

Today you came back after two months in Moscow. 'You're too possessive,' you say, watching disapprovingly as I iron Abbie's clothes and make her lunch-box for tomorrow. 'She needs to be more independent. You should send her to boarding-school. She needs to get away from you.'

I try not to allow you to wind me up, but I'm already tightly wound, my rage ticking like a bomb. 'She's only nine.'

'When you were her age you weren't coddled and packed in cotton-wool like this. It's a most unnatural childhood.'

'I knew a damned sight too much when I was nine. Anyway, what right have you got to barge in after two months and tell me how to bring her up?'

'She's my daughter, too – or so you claim.'

'I hope not. The older she gets, the more I hope she's just an ordinary child.'

Then I realize that Abbie, who is supposed to be watching *Blue Peter* in the next room, is standing in the doorway. You pick her up and swing her around.

'Hello, Daddy. Where did you go?'

'I went off to Russia, my lovely. Making lots of money for you and your mummy to spend.'

'Good.' Abbie calmly accepts the embroidered blouse you have brought her and returns to her programme.

'Don't talk to her about money like that,' I hiss. We move upstairs to the living-room, where we can attack each other in peace.

'Why not? Is it too vulgar for you? You spend enough of it. I just got the Visa statement.'

'*I'm* not extravagant. You're the one who has to have handmade shoes and chauffeur-driven limos and crates of champagne.'

'It's cheaper to buy it by the crate. Anyway, why shouldn't I? I make the money around here, and I enjoy it.'

'I hate your flashy lifestyle; it's got nothing to do with me.'

'Oh no, you just live here.'

'I'd be happy to live more simply.'

'Really? Perhaps you should move back to your dear old bedsit on top of the station.'

'I hate you.' Suddenly it's true; not a hysterical attack but a statement of fact. If love's a boat on a stormy, shark-infested sea then I've well and truly fallen out of it. I'm floundering in the ocean now, lungs, mouth and nostrils filling up with salty water, Abbie clinging to me as I go under.

'This is a ridiculous argument, I don't know why we're having it. Of course you and the child will stay here. But please stop insulting me and try to behave more like my –'

'Your what? Wife? Lover? Employee? Friend? Enemy? I don't know and neither do you. We don't love each other any more, and don't you dare start quoting that contract at me.'

'You've changed.'

'Yes. It's called having a mind of my own.'

'You've become so hard and bitter. You're ungrateful, Jenny. If it wasn't for me you'd be in your grave by now.'

'If it wasn't for Abbie I think I'd want to be. But I'm still very much alive, Leo. And I don't want to spend eternity with you any more than you do with me.'

I've been cowardly and dishonest for so long. I could take Abbie today, leave this house, find a job. Somehow I'd keep a roof over our heads. But even then I wouldn't be free of you. I've always avoided thinking about the meaning of that contract, but now it's caught up with me. I could leave you, destroy my contract, be natural at last, wither and die – but then who will look after Abbie? It would be dangerous to leave her alone with you; Molly loves her, but she's gaga – oh, my dearest child, what have I done?

I wake in the middle of the night with pain clutching my heart where my love for you used to be. Chaos surges from my empty heart to my aching head to the cruel silence of the watching house. The beautiful illusion of a happy childhood I've woven for Abbie has been torn and shredded like a spider's web attacked by a broom. Unable to sleep, I wander the house, pass her room and open her door to check on her.

Pale, shadowy, masked figures surround her bed. I scream, push through them and see blood on Abbie's white bedspread. She wakes and starts to cry as the figures vanish, except for one who turns to me. It's you, you take off your mask and try to embrace me, murmuring reassurances. I push you away violently and fall asleep on Abbie's bed.

When I wake up I'm still in Abbie's room. The dream, if it was a dream, is still so vivid that I search for bloodstains on her bed, scars on her body, but find nothing.

On the way to her school this morning I give a one-pound coin to a beggar who hands me a leaflet. I stuff it into my bag. Later, I take it out and look at it. On the cheap yellow paper there are drawings of cards, a hand and what are presumably meant to be crystal balls, which look vaguely pornographic:

Mrs Strega. Palm, Tarot Card, Crystal Ball and Others. I will show you with your own eyes how to expel Sorrow, Sickness and Pain. What your Eyes see your Heart must believe and then your Heart will be convinced. Talisman Available. I will break Curses and Destroy the powers of Witchcraft, Black Magic and Bad Luck. I have the Wisdom, the Power and the Knowledge to heal and cleanse Body, Mind and Soul of any Unnatural Energies or Evil Influences. Remember I am a true Psychic born with Power. If you are Unhappy, Discouraged or Distressed I can help you. I will tell you who your Friends and Enemies are and if the one you love is True or False. I will spear all Time and Energy to protect you. I can also help in Legal Matters and Exams.

100% Satisfaction Guaranteed. All Major Credit Cards Accepted.

Perhaps I could do worse. The alternative is to go into therapy like most of the women I know.

I dial Mrs Strega's number and make an appointment. At lunchtime I ring the bell of a seedy basement flat near Earls Court. The door's opened by a woman who introduces herself as Mrs Strega and who leads me into a dark, low-ceilinged room where she sits at a round table covered with a green cloth. She's true to fairground type, a Middle Eastern cockney with a coarse face caked with makeup, hennaed hair and fat arms jangling with baubles.

'So you've finally come.'

'What do you mean? I only got your leaflet this morning.'

'We've been calling out to you for years. I don't know if we can help now. You've got yourself into such a terrible mess.'

'Yes, I suppose I have, although I don't see how you could know about it. I don't think cards and crystal balls are going to do much for me.'

'No, it's too late for that.'

I hold out my hands to her in a helpless gesture. As she grips my right hand in her rough, warm one I smell nicotine, sweat and a sickly musk perfume. She draws me nearer and examines my palm, then drops it with a sigh. 'I can't read it. Your original lines are all crossed and jumbled.'

The temptation to confide is irresistible. She can't possibly know my story – and yet, if she does, it's a relief. 'What about Others? What are they?'

'Do you want to go down there?'

Maybe I'm going to be mugged or raped. Maybe there's some connection between this tacky old crone and you. But if I don't go I'll always wonder what would have happened. 'Yes. I'll go down.'

She leads me into a small, tiled room like an old-fashioned pantry, lifts a trap-door in the floor and I see a flight of stone steps plunging down into blackness.

'Isn't there a light or a torch?'

'Your eyes will get used to it.'

'Are you coming down there with me?'

'No. You're the one she wants.'

'Who?'

Suddenly she pushes me, then bangs the trap-door down so that I only just have time to duck before I lose my balance and plunge down the slimy steps, falling blindly, too frightened to scream. For a second I remember that dream I had just after Abbie was born, of falling down steps like these. But in that dream I hugged my baby. Now I'm alone. I'm going to die alone, I think as I fall. Damp tentacles or hands brush my face in the dark. They stop my fall and I find myself sitting on the sandy floor of a cave.

'Come closer.'

I follow the voice in the dark. It could be a man or a woman, young or old.

'You can look at me now. I am where immortality ends, the source of nightmares and the end of hope. Not as pretty as you, am I?'

I gaze up at the tiny, shrivelled figure crouching in a cage suspended just above my head. If not for the voice I wouldn't have known it was human at all.

'Who are you?'

'*That's* not the question. If you ask the wrong question you get the wrong answer. You won't be allowed back for another fifty years.' The indeterminate voice sounds weary. Blasts of foul breath drive me back a few paces.

'I'm only allowed one question?' I've never felt so stupid in my life. I ache all over from my fall as I struggle to think of a question so subtle and clever that it will help Abbie and myself. All around me in the darkness I can hear the silent laughter of the malevolent oracle and the unseen creatures whose hands reached out to me.

'If you have nothing to say . . .'

'But I do! What will happen to my daughter?'

I can see between the bars of the cage now, into the charred face and dark eyes that close as the oracle breathes deeply and words pour out, something between a song and a chant, 'Child of darkness, child of light, born to lead you through the night. Born to riches, strong in pain. She will see when you are blind, she will leave you far behind, but when you need her she will come. The world will kick her then adore, the heights are reached through the drabbest door. The spider waits for ever more.'

Silence. I turn and stumble away, desperate to leave the cave that stinks of ancient breath and decay. The hands pull me upstairs.

Feelings

Jenny screams, shouts, hisses at me, her face distorted with hatred. I suppose she is still a comely woman – she must be, as my contracts are infallible – but she is no longer beautiful to me. We can't bear to touch each other. I feel the vicious waves of her loathing as soon as I enter this house. I have stayed away as much as possible this year, fomenting the chaos in the ex-Soviet Union. But there is no longer any joy in spreading arms, drugs and misery. They proliferate without any help from me. I shall not travel any more.

Where are You? Have You abandoned this sad and foolish planet and found a better one to play with? I sit here in my laboratory like Job, although I lack his patience. I desire to reason with You, to ask what I must do now. *From going to and fro in the earth, and from walking up and down in it* . . . No, I shall not travel any more, for I have found hell here.

I didn't realize it would hurt so much. When men want to belittle women they say they are mere domestic creatures, unconcerned with ideas and politics and the wider world. I understand now that men turn to the impersonal for light relief because it is so much simpler than the treacherous quicksands of their own emotions. Who invented love? It certainly wasn't me. It was Your idea, and so You must accept some responsibility for the resulting carnage. At least You must listen to my problems. But I keep forgetting. You're not there any more.

I can no longer see the next century spread out before me like a chessboard, I have no idea what will happen next, and, worst of all, I'm frightened. Since New York I've been unable to fly and can only disappear with great difficulty. I sleep badly and have troubling dreams about losing Jenny and the child. I used to regard the little girl with a healthy detachment, but now I lie awake wondering where she came from. It is just possible that the universal laws I naïvely believed in were overturned years ago and Abbie *is* a part of myself. Certainly, it feels like it. Jenny accuses me of terrible things, yet I've never wanted to hurt either of them. When I try to speak to her rationally, anger and pain come spitting out of my mouth. These feelings of rage do tend to be fatal. Not to me, of course, but at such moments I have no control over my powers. I am wounded, afflicted, haunted by memories.

At our first meeting her face is almost hidden by a dirty straw hat with a sad red feather that droops over one of her enormous dark eyes. The heavy dark waves of her wonderful hair are pinned and twisted under the grubby hat to reveal her slender neck. Her complexion shows the murky traces of poverty and her nose is too big, she is the least pretty of the girls who have trailed up to my office this week to offer themselves to me. A breath upon the bubbles of their tawdry dreams is all it takes to make them dissolve with love, as they call it.

But Jenny is the only one who is alive for me now. As for the others, I can't remember a name, a breast or a sweaty corset. This isn't memory but the strange phenomenon of simultaneous time I discovered long ago. Most time disappears as soon as it has happened, dull moments drifting on the ocean of immortal tedium, but my first meeting with Jenny is still happening. She and I are trapped together here. Perhaps this is the moment when my degradation into humanity begins.

An adenoidal cockney voice, 'I want to be like Marie Lloyd.'

'Nobody is like her. That's why she's a great performer.' I smile at the hubris of this spotty brat. Right from the beginning she makes me laugh.

She sings, pathetically flat, winking awkwardly and trying to look suggestive:

Every little movement has a meaning of its own,
Every little movement tells a tale.
When she walks in dainty hobbles
At the back round here, there's a kind of wibble wobble
And she glides like this.
Then the Johnnies follow in her trail . . .

It's a lovely melody, which she murders. At the end I'm laughing, and she grins back at me toothily. I can see that the Johnnies really will follow her trail, and I'm inclined to join them. It's nearly a century since I've laughed spontaneously: that fat little whore in Leipzig, who balanced a wine glass on her naked buttocks and later married a count. This girl has a crude vitality, a spark I could blow into flames of desirability, queues of Johnnies.

First, she has to learn how to walk, speak, dance, sing, dress, undress, flirt, tantalize, fuck. She tells me she's eighteen, but I can see she's younger. So she has time to learn, and I certainly have time, too much time, to teach her. Having decided to live in London I'm already bored, by the weather and the prim hypocrisies and the lukewarm audiences that yawn at my magnificent conjuring tricks. It might entertain me to create a star out of such unpromising material. Even if she fails, she'll warm my bed for a few months – and she's young enough to be worth corrupting. Besides, I need money, and nothing is as lucrative as young female flesh. I have an overdraft at the Fizz, and my shabby wardrobe needs renewing.

Justifying myself? Certainly not. My affair with Jenny started in a mood of irreproachable cynicism.

I must know what's in her mind and her heart now. So, with a great deal of puffing and straining, I make myself invisible, stand in the shadows of my laboratory and wait for her to come in. I know she will; she never could resist snooping. I hear her come back from leaving Abbie at school. She calls my name and runs upstairs, pauses outside my laboratory, opens the door and stands looking furtive and nervous. I stare into her pale, oval face, into her huge dark eyes, the face that is as much mine as if it was a painting I bought eighty years ago.

As Jenny walks over to my desk I make one of the drawers slide open. Inside, she discovers presents she has given me, together with all her letters, neatly arranged. There's a photograph of her, semi-nude, posed in front of a night sky; a fountain pen made of gold and enamel; a Florentine leather box and a pair of gold cufflinks. In their coffin drawer the objects look forlorn, I want to remind her of the feebleness of her gifts compared with what I have given her.

I'm curious to see whether she will read her old letters. She doesn't. Out of embarrassment? The earliest ones are so passionate and so misspelt. How they amused me.

Then I make a second drawer slide open and show her a shabby green leather notebook with 1912 engraved on its cover, the year we met. Of course, she can't resist that, and sits down on the floor to browse through it.

October 12

If these are feelings, I suppose I must record them. The world is my laboratory and London the test tube I have decided to concentrate on for the twentieth century. This girl is only a speck under my microscope, of no conceivable interest or importance. An earwig, one of millions.

Her seduction should have been over months ago, and she should have been dispatched with the others. When she is here I see her faults so clearly. Only her faults, as usual: ignorance, presumption, greed. Her lovely ivory face is flawed, she has spots on her forehead, her letters are abysmal, she has the moral sense of a marshmallow, and there is no good reason to waste all this time on her.

Yet, when she leaves my room there is a vacuum. I go to the hearth rug her soft body has warmed and sniff it: cheap lavender perfume and sweat. I pluck a long black hair that has been pulled out during our erotic games, stare at it as if it could explain her appeal, go to the window just in time to see her disappearing into the fog and worry that she will be run over by an omnibus. I repeat my parting words to her – see you next week – as if they had some mysterious significance. My dreams are haunted by her eyes and voice.

This is not rational behaviour. Perhaps I've lived among them for too long and have lost my immunity. Tonight as I stood alone in my fire-lit room I noticed a bat-like flapping on the wall. I have a shadow! I turned to face it, this dark emanation, proof that I am leaving some kind of trail in their world. We danced, my limbs stretching across the walls and ceiling. I ran to the mirror over the mantelpiece to see if I had acquired a reflection, too. But its silver was still empty.

Yet I feel less, not more, substantial. The general lack of faith in me is very demoralizing and will soon be accelerated by the inevitable war. Even the prospect of Europe in flames and millions dead can't cheer me up. I feel I have lost my identity. I'm in danger of becoming a has-been, like those loud-mouthed Greek immortals who have sulked for the last two millennia.

My powers *are* diminished. I'm reduced to performing conjuring tricks in suburban music halls. The Great Pantoffsky, indeed. My infatuation with Jenny is part of this general decline. It doesn't take much to impress a fifteen-year-old girl with no education. I don't feel needed any more – except by her. All these generals and politicians are rushing towards Armageddon without any prompting from me. In these last years of so-called peace, morals are so decadent that there's very little I can teach anyone.

Of course, I ought to be glad of a rest. These months with Jenny are a charming interlude, a reward for thousands of years of exhausting malice. The eyes of the world are no longer on me, and this should be a release. But it isn't. This morning, for instance, I couldn't decide what to wear. I don't spend much time in front of my mirror, since I have no reflection, but I've always had a flair for fashion, which, after all, I invented. But I really have no idea what is expected of me now. Eventually I put on my faded green velvet smoking jacket, as threadbare as modern faith, a schoolgirl's idea of glamour.

Jenny is a tuppenny muse, a doll the age has tossed my way. My abnormal response to her is evidence that I've been surrounded for too long by intellectuals, neurasthenics and weaklings. What I see in this girl is a kind of health and strength. At moments I experience a strange delusion that she is more than she seems, some lost fragment of myself, a reminder of that time long ago when men and women mingled blood and minds and bodies, before the fatuous line was drawn between them. Soon the sexes will unite again, but long before that happens this girl who disturbs me now will wither and die and be forgotten, leaving me alone in my immortality . . .

I want Jenny to feel sorry for me, but I'm too much of a showman to continue on the same note for long. The green leather notebook slips out of her grasp and falls back into the drawer, which shuts with a bang. She struggles to open it again, pulling and tugging at the drawer. One of the other drawers slides open, and a brown leather diary is offered to her: **1994**, the devastating present. She knows it is some kind of trick, but, of course, she can't resist it as it floats into her hands and opens itself at today's date:

She's going to leave me, and I don't know what to do. We can't talk any more. She hates me and I hate myself.

Dearest Jenny

You're reading this, aren't you? Please don't go. I want to live in this house with you and the child, to see the millennium out with you. I thought you were my creation, but now it seems I need you more than you need me. You must realize that you can't really leave; you'll have to come back again. Stay here with me, Jenny, we won't quarrel any more. I'll give you more money and entertain you and surprise you . . .

With a cry of rage she throws my diary on the floor and leaves the room.

Later, when I'm at work in my laboratory and visible again, Jenny comes to the door. 'I just wondered if you're going to be around for Abbie's birthday next week. We're having a party.'

'When?'

'Next Wednesday. June the twenty-third. A date that might be engraved on your heart, if you had one.'

'Don't start reproaching me. You're not so badly off, sitting on your arse here in luxury.'

'I didn't come here to quarrel, Leo. I just want to know if you're coming to Abbie's party.'

'Do I have to tell you now?'

'She wants to know. It's important to her. She loves you.'

'I'm glad somebody does.'

'Leo, you're so touchy. I just want to know . . .'

'I'll try to be around. I can't possibly say. It's a week away.'

'Why can't you? What are you doing that's so important? What matters more than your daughter's birthday?'

'I thought we agreed not to cross-examine each other.'

'I'm going to bed. There's no point in talking to you any more. I don't know why I'm planning a party for her. I must be crazy.'

'What are you talking about?'

But she has gone, and I have no idea what's going on behind that face I have invested so much in.

Leaving

This conversation with you jangles my raw nerves and ends in bitter rage. I go to bed but can't sleep. I'm frightened that dream about the shadowy figures will come again or that an accident will happen to Abbie. Get up and go down to her room, where she sleeps peacefully.

If love be not in the house, there is nothing – Ezra Pound farmed out his children. My child is here and must be loved. I'm tempted to stay in her room, in her bed, to guard her, but my tossing and turning will only disturb her. On the stairs, on the way back to my bedroom, I see strange lights coming from your laboratory. More of your tricks? Your door isn't locked, so I go in.

The small white room, which has always seemed so dull and sterile, is flickering with dark-red light. On the desk, where your computer stood when I was here an hour ago, is a fiery pit where charred bodies writhe. The back wall, with its maps and charts, has disappeared, and I see a corridor echoing with agonized screams and groans. You are disappearing down it. As you become more distant, you expand until your vast shadow fills the room and the night sky beyond. Gigantic, monstrous, inflicting pain with every step.

After a few seconds the room tilts and rocks and becomes an office again, neutral and safe, except for the computer, which suddenly turns itself on and spits at me viciously.

I flee upstairs to my room, but it isn't mine any more. This isn't my house. I've glimpsed the reality beyond reality, the Leo I'm not supposed to see at all – the destroyer, the breaker of wings, the poisoner of the will to live. I go back to bed, switch off the light, try to shut my eyes again and go back to sleep. Then I sit up and switch the light back on, terrified of what might be here in the darkness with me. The four walls of my room are an illusion, hiding the brutal architecture of another universe.

At three I go down to Abbie's room, watch over her and stroke her forehead. By the time the summer dawn washes the city I know I can't spend another night in this house. It's against me now; I can feel its spite. At seven thirty I put on my shabbiest jeans and an old sweater, get Abbie up as usual and prepare breakfast.

I know it's the last meal we'll eat in this kitchen, but I don't say anything to her. We walk together up the hill, passing other brightly dressed children with lunch-boxes who converge on her colourful, geometric school, which looks as if it might have been built out of a child's construction kit. The morning is radiant, and I see it with epiphanic clarity: the children's energetic faces, the luxuriant gardens and tree-lined streets, the London I've always wanted to give her. My eyes fill with tears as Abbie runs off happily to join her friends. The last morning of her childhood.

I fill in the forms the social worker gave me. I don't think of what I'm losing but of the dangers I'm saving Abbie from. To be poor for a while seems a small price to pay for her life. I need to disappear, to tell a few lies. To be accepted as being 'emergency homeless' I have to prove that I have been battered.

In a deserted corner of Holland Park I run at a tree and feel a strange pleasure as my right eye and cheek make contact with the rough bark. Again and again I slam the face that was your masterpiece into the tree, charging at my destruction with the same energy I once poured into my self-preservation. When I can taste blood I take out my pocket mirror and examine my useful ugliness.

I go to the Housing Office, where I burst into tears and declare that I'm the victim of domestic violence and my daughter and I have nowhere to sleep tonight. The man behind the desk stares at me with pity and offers me a tissue. My tears are genuine; I'm confused and exhausted, glad of the throbbing pain in my eye and cheek that back up the story I want him to believe. He makes a few phone calls and gives me an address in Bayswater where Abbie and I can go.

Then I walk to the Metaphysical Bank, where I draw out all the money in my account – five hundred pounds – and close it. It will give us a few weeks before Abbie and I are thrust upon the tough mercies of the Welfare State. I'm a familiar figure at the Bank now, so nobody looks surprised when I open the door behind the counter and go into the big, chandeliered reception-room where I've attended so many parties. It's deserted this morning, neglected and dusty, strewn with empty glasses and brimming ashtrays.

I take the crystal lift down to the level where pasts are bought and sold. We bought our house out of the profits from slave ships that sailed from Liverpool in the 1760s. Our house? I realize now that it has always been yours. Angrily I wonder how long it'll be before another woman moves in with you. Jealousy outlives love. In the white-marble casino, even at eleven in the morning, gamblers in evening dress are drinking and laughing. Several identical red-carpeted corridors stretch in all directions, but, although I've only been here once before, I don't hesitate about which one to choose. Even from this distance I can feel the magnetic pull of my contract, can hear the silence as the building holds its breath and watches to see what I will do.

Although I've often tried to ignore my contract, I know, as I walk down the corridor to the black wrought-iron spiral staircase, that I'm battling with serious powers. Not one of those punters in the casino is gambling for such high stakes as me. I've got everything to lose, and I'm not sure what I can gain. I think of Ivan Karamazov saying to his brother, 'It's not God I don't accept, Alyosha – only that I must respectfully return him the entrance ticket.' That's what I have to do now, although what the ticket was for and who I'm returning it to are still in doubt.

If this is the end I'm unprepared for it. In nearly a century I seem to have learnt nothing. I see far more beauty in the world now than when I was genuinely young, so much beauty that it's very hard to leave it. If I don't die immediately I'll look like Molly. Older, perhaps. I'll have nothing, nobody except Abbie, and who will look after her? I pause on the staircase, terrified. I could still go home and forget about all this. Maybe last night was just a kind of nightmare; maybe I imagined it all. Of course, you and I have rows, but so do all couples who have been together a long time. Perhaps, for Abbie's sake, I'd better just go back now and make it up with you. You are a bit arrogant but –

The voice of my femunculus drowns my thoughts:

A bit arrogant? Make it up? I don't believe I'm hearing this.

I wish you'd stop eavesdropping on my thoughts. What do you want?

I'm trying to make sure that daughter of yours grows up with more sense than her mother.

Um, I think I'll just go home.

Oh no you won't. You have no home now. You can't go back and behave as if nothing has happened. Now you know who he is, what he is, you can never shut your eyes and go back to sleep again. You must destroy that contract or be destroyed, both you and your child.

But how are we going to survive? An old woman and a little girl without any money or friends. And if I die what will become of Abbie?

There are no answers. She's gone, and I'm alone again on the stairs, spiralling down. I feel dizzy, faint and breathless, as if old age has already seized me. The pale-green mist is rising towards me now, chilling my bones and making me stumble. At the bottom I slip on the rocky floor of the tunnel. I look down at my hands in terror, to see if they've already aged. No, they're still the hands of a young woman, pink and soft.

At the end of the tunnel the shiny metal door bulges. This time, to my surprise, I'm able to decipher some of the words that float there, dancing from Arabic to Japanese to Gothic script: contracts . . . kingdom . . . night . . . security . . . beware. I stand in front of the door and my voice comes out as a whisper. Then I say my name again, more loudly.

The words in the centre of the door spin around, whirling faster until they are not words at all but a fiery vortex. A small hole opens and a parchment scroll appears. I reach out for it. As soon as I touch the warm contract I remember this smell of blood and fire and ink. I unroll it, my fingers once again leaving bruises on the delicate surface, and this time I can read the words you once read to me.

Even now, I could just roll it up and post it back through the door. The parchment's hot, as if my fingers have warmed it, and I can feel it resisting me. I stare down at it, muttering, as if it's alive:

'We're going now.'

I climb back to the spiral staircase. With every step the contract becomes heavier, hotter, so that I have to take off my striped blazer and wrap it around my hands to protect them. Instead of carrying me up the stairs as it did once before, the mist drags me back and makes the steps dance in front of my eyes. They're revolving, moving up and down like a mad escalator, disappearing as my foot approaches each one. Weak and sick, I lean heavily on the metal banister.

When at last I reach the top I'm so exhausted that I collapse on to my knees in the deserted corridor. My sore cheek brushes against the contract, which scorches my bruised skin. You'll come for me now, you or your servants, those shadowy masked figures from my nightmares. But nobody appears.

After half an hour I'm able to stand up. I pass the casino again, none of the gamblers even glances at me. As I approach the crystal lift the parchment becomes cooler and lighter. I put on my blazer, hold the contract quite openly and walk out of the Bank.

You're in the hall waiting for me, very tall and grim. The sunlight passes straight through you, giving your skin a reptilian tinge.

'What has happened to your face?' I catch sight of it in the hall mirror, where I've admired my own reflection so often. My right eye and cheek are a mass of red and purple where I abused the tree. You reach out to touch my wounded face, but I back away. 'Who did that to you?'

'I did it to myself. I'm going to leave. You can't stop me.'

'You've always been free to go.'

'I can't stay with you now I've seen what you're really like, how evil you are.'

'Are you sure that whatever you saw came from me? Evil, devil, mad, bad, hell: how weary I am of the insults you people hurl at me, projecting your own problems comfortably outside yourselves. Do you think it's easy to carry the burden of thousands of years of spiritual buck-passing? There's nothing I've done that hasn't originated in the human heart – in your heart, Jenny.'

'Not mine. Women are better than men.'

'I used to think so. As a matter of fact, next time, I might reinvent myself as a woman. My experiment with you has convinced me that this is going to be the age of women.'

'Well, your experiment's over. I'm going to destroy my contract.'

'Really? And how are you going to do that?'

'I suppose . . . I'll tear it up.'

You laugh. 'Have you tried? Even if you tore it into a thousand pieces it would reassemble itself and post itself back to the Fizz.'

'Then I'll burn it.'

'You can if you like. It will rise from its own ashes like a phoenix and fly back to the other contracts.'

'There must be some way of destroying it.'

'Must there? Do you still think this is just a sheet of old parchment?'

'It must have happened before.'

'Never. Do you think the gift of eternal youth is a small thing, to be given up so lightly? And you're comparatively young. Some of our clients are thousands of years old, not much younger than me. These contracts have to last for ever, and they do. Who would be such a fool as to give up the chance of being young and good-looking and rich for eternity?'

'*I* am such a fool.' You stare at me. Without hatred, I observe with surprise. At this moment I can't hate you, either. Loving you has grown into me as trees sometimes grow into the walls of houses. I stoke my own anger in one last, huge effort to uproot that love and leave you.

'You seem to think I hand out these contracts like chocolate bars to every woman who catches my fancy. As a matter of fact, you were the only woman in centuries who touched me in the place where my heart might be. If I had been human I would have loved you. If you had let me love you I might have become entirely human. Even now it's not too late. I wouldn't really hurt you or Abbie, you know that.'

You take a step towards me, and I feel your power. I could drop the contract, go upstairs with you and suspend my doubts between the sheets as I've done so many times before. Then I could pick Abbie up from school, as usual, and bring her back to our lovely house – but I remember you and the other shadows bending over my daughter that night.

'No. Tell me how to destroy it.'

You look surprised, and there is pain in your eyes as you say, 'There is a way, but it will destroy you as well. The years that have been held back will rush upon you and devour you. You may suffer horribly, even die. You have no idea how ruthless Death is towards those who cheat him. All these years you've been under my protection, whether you knew it or not. But as soon as the contract disappears you will lose all your defences, not only youth and money but immunity to illness and infection. Those horrible bruises and scars on your face may never heal.'

'I don't care!'

'You might die. And if you do live, you may be less than mortal.'

'I accept those terms.'

'What about Abbie?'

'She comes with me.'

'This is crazy. Where are you going?'

'I'm not telling you.'

'What an extremist you are. I always thought you were intelligent enough to compromise. Well, give me the contract. At midnight tonight I will destroy it. I warn you: the effects will be immediate. And terrible. I won't be able to help you.'

Shaking, I hand you the contract and go upstairs to pack.

Midnight

Abbie comes out of school, swinging her lunch-box and a rolled-up painting, says goodbye to Emily and runs up to my taxi.

'Your face!'

'I had an accident.'

Abbie hugs me and tries to kiss it better, her lips searing my torn and swollen face.

'Why have you got suitcases? Are we going on holiday?'

'Sort of.'

'Where?'

'To a hotel.'

'Is Daddy coming?'

'No.'

'You're getting divorced,' Abbie says with the matter-of-factness of a child who has grown up watching soaps. 'Oh, I forgot. You're not married, are you?'

'Daddy's staying at home. We're going to live in a hotel for a while.'

'In the middle of term?'

'You can still go to school. It's not very far away. I'll take you every morning.'

'Has it got a swimming pool like that hotel we stayed at in New York?'

'No, it won't be like that.'

Abbie's enthusiasm for her holiday lasts until the taxi draws up at Queensway Square. It isn't a proper square, more like a street with miserable grass and trees squeezed between the grubby, blistered Victorian houses.

'It's like a very old wedding cake. Miss Haversham's,' she mutters.

While I get our luggage out of the taxi Abbie wanders off and peels a strip of plaster off the nearest wall. 'Yuck! It stinks of metal and dirt and sick and pigeons.'

'Come on! I need some help.'

'Why can't the porter carry our cases?'

'There won't be a porter. Don't be so damned lazy.'

I don't often swear at her, so Abbie is offended. With chilly dignity she picks up her lunch-box, camera and koala-bear rucksack. 'Where's Johnny?'

'Don't be silly, you can't take a dog on holiday.'

'But a fox might eat him. Daddy won't remember to feed him. He doesn't like animals.'

'Abbie, for Christ's sake shut up. Let's just get inside.'

She follows me resentfully to the steps of Sandringham House. Old newspapers and beer cans litter the pavement. 'Funny sort of hotel. Why do we have to ring the bell?'

The door is opened by a thin woman with orange hair who says her name is Eileen and that she's the manager. Behind her a smell of dirty carpet, stale spices, cabbage and chips hovers thickly. There's barely room for the three of us to stand in the dark hall, where grease oozes out of the walls and slithers into our hair. There are signs pinned up all over the walls. Abbie reads one of them aloud, 'HACKNEY HOME-LESS FAMILIES, KENSINGTON AND CHELSEA EMERGENCY HOMELESS FAMILIES. Do not enter or leave the hotel without sign-ing the register. No visitors are allowed in your room. Do not cook or store food in your room. Children are not allowed to run or play on the stairs or in the hall . . .'

'The porter will show you to your room,' Eileen says.

The porter turns out to be a young Irishman wearing a tartan shirt and jeans who says, 'Hiya! I'm Finn.' There's an awkward pause while I wonder who is supposed to carry our cases upstairs. Eileen stares dourly at this bruised woman and her snotty child. If we're trouble-makers we'll be transferred to another hotel. I know this without being told. I've already regressed to an earlier self, not much older than Abbie, who has no money and lives in fear of the workhouse. I want to please the woman with orange hair, so I pick up both suitcases and Abbie follows, sensing my fear. There's no lift. Although it's June the heating is on and seems to be fighting a battle with the damp. We're sweating and our throats are parched. Finn leads us down a hot silent maze of corridors, up and down three separate staircases.

When Finn unlocks one of the doors and waves us in it looks at first like an ordinary hotel room, with double bed, wardrobe, basin and shower. Abbie tries to salvage her holiday. She runs to the window, which is opaque with dirt and overlooks a well where four walls of grimy windows try to avoid each other's gaze. If you look up you see a square of blue sky, and if you look down you see a sheet of cracked green glass, littered with nappies, syringes, cigarette packets and condoms. Abbie bounces on the bed, which immediately slips off the books it's resting on. The pink shower curtain is torn, the sheets don't quite meet over the mattress, the taps on the basin drip and the bedside lamp is broken.

As she watches me unpack Abbie asks querulously, 'Is this a very expensive holiday?'

'We don't have to pay anything.'

'Did you win it in a competition or something? When are we going home?' She's so hot that she has to go to the basin, drink tepid water from the tap and splash it all over her face and hands. I'm staring at my swelling face in the cracked yellow mirror. 'Mummy? Shall I buy some ointment and put it on your face.'

'No. I'll be OK.'

'But you're crying. Does it hurt?'

'No. I'm fine.'

'What's the matter?'

'Nothing, darling. What would you like for supper?'

'I'm not hungry. I want to go home.'

'We can't, I'm afraid.'

'But what about my birthday? I can't have my party here. None of my friends will come.'

'We'll have it out, at McDonald's or at the swimming pool. You always wanted a swimming party.'

'I want to have it at home. It's important, you said so. I'll be in double figures.'

'Don't cry, sweetheart.' I sit beside her on the lopsided bed and hug her.

'You're crying, too.'

'It's just the heat, and . . . I'm very tired.'

'Why is it that when grown-ups cry there's always some excuse, but when I cry I'm just being a wimp?'

'You're not! You're wonderful, that's why we're here, but . . . I can't explain. Let's go to the park. It's so stuffy in here, no wonder we feel awful. We'll unpack later.'

'I hate my holiday,' Abbie says balefully as we leave the room. She slams the door and the room shakes.

Outside the weatherless limbo of Sandringham House a beautiful summer evening flourishes. We run most of the way to the Bayswater Road and fall into the wide green embrace of the park. At six thirty it's full of sunbathers, dog walkers, skateboarders, rich foreigners and poor natives. Abbie is straining like one of the dogs, pulling me towards a paved garden spouting with fountains. We sit on the edge of a fountain, its water a dazzling splash of crystal in the late sunlight.

'We could come and live here. It's much nicer than that dump of a hotel,' Abbie says.

'They lock this park at night, I'm afraid.'

'We could camp.' She stares fiercely at the park, inhaling space and freedom.

We have a picnic supper of bread and cheese and fruit and stay in the park until it closes at sunset. I indulge Abbie, push her on the swings, buy her ice creams and tell her stories, schmaltzy ones with moral signposts, as if to compensate for the amorality of our own story. She plays aggressively, desperately; plays at being a child.

All the time I'm thinking, how can this be the same park, the same city? Years ago, on one of our rare family outings, we visited Kensington Palace to see Queen Victoria's doll's house. Later, we sailed an expensive remote-controlled boat on the Round Pond. Abbie was a chubby, articulate five-year-old, bundled up in a red coat with a hood like a fat little dwarf, a parental giant on either side of her. Now we're something called a 'single-parent, emergency-homeless family', and tomorrow we might not even be that.

These bed-and-breakfast hotels are as bad as the slums where Lizzie and I grew up – worse, because here families with children, junkies, prostitutes and people who are mentally ill are all jumbled up together under one roof, whereas in turn-of-the-century Hoxton it was possible to be 'respectable' and live next door to a brothel. As we reluctantly walk back to Sandringham House I'm on the verge of telling Abbie the truth. But what is the truth? I don't want to terrify her with stories of demonic contracts and midnight transformations in case we wake up tomorrow morning looking just the same. After a few months as an emergency-homeless family we will have served our time, we'll become the deserving poor and will be given a flat of some kind. It will be harder than our old life, but I'll get a job and scavenge an education for Abbie.

At half past ten my daughter falls asleep in the lopsided double bed, one hand holding mine while the other clutches her koala bear. Sitting beside her in the dark, I gently loosen her fingers and wait for midnight. The thoughts I've been evading come flooding in as alarming noises come from the other rooms: babies crying, a woman screaming, the rhythmic thump of sex or violence, pop music, televisions, crockery smashing, voices arguing.

You said I might die. After all, I'm ninety-seven. Then Abbie will be taken into care, into what we used to call an orphanage. I don't suppose calling it care makes it any less horrible for the children. I must write to David, who is kind and, more likely than not, her father. If I die – but I can't, I *must* be here to see what happens next. I haven't had nearly enough of life yet, and if I hang around for a few more years science will catch up with magic and we'll all be able to cheat death. Another hour. I'll leave the letter to David ready to be posted just in case I'm not here in the morning. How will Abbie get to school without me – but I *will* be here, in some form or other.

Count sheep. Count corpses: Gerry, all those unknown people during the war, George, Nat, Hari, Katrina and her children, Toby, Charles . . . how many others I don't even know about? You've always resented Abbie; you think she's David's daughter. What were you doing that night, bending over her, performing some kind of operation with those other shadowy figures? You've been very generous to her and to me – no, mustn't think about that.

We couldn't have stayed in that life. Sooner or later Abbie would have defied you, irritated you, got in your way. You're so good at making it look like an accident, you would mourn and grieve as you did over Nat. The really frightening thing about you is that you're capable of both murder and compassion.

What is happening to that baby? I've never heard such horrendous noises. Half an hour to go. *That time may cease, and midnight never come* . . . you said the effect would be instantaneous. What was it Augustus said on his deathbed? 'Have I acted well in the farce?' I suppose I have, on the whole. How good it has been, compared with the poor, dull thing a life can be. I'm so glad I signed that crazy contract. I've developed as much in ninety years as some life forms do in millions; from a frightened, illiterate waif with only my body to sell to a woman who has done most things, grabbed an education, seized free will from the vaults of death. I'm thinking of myself in the past, writing my own obituary, but I must be here to watch over my child.

Ten minutes. I can feel the darkness thickening now, but if I put the light on I'll wake Abbie. How strong the past is in here tonight, I can feel my dead pulling at me, Ma and George and Lizzie. I don't want to die.

If I hold her hand like this I feel stronger. My fingers glide over Abbie's soft, straight light-brown hair, from the velvet of her hairband to the bulge of her forehead. Feathery eyebrows fly over her blue eyes, and her nose is a childish button. The curve of her mouth is like the wavy line that Abbie is still young enough to use to represent the sea in her pictures. Perhaps I'll never see Abbie's face or drawings again.

If I'm holding her whatever attacks me will hurt Abbie, too. So I drop her hand, hug her and then settle back into my solitary darkness, the smooth feel of Abbie's translucent skin tingling in my fingertips.

I open the curtains and the window. There, at least I'm not alone any more. I can see into the rooms opposite.

Two minutes. Abbie's still fast asleep. I want to look at her one last time. Something's at the window, in the room with me, at my throat. I can't breathe . . .

PART 2
Abbie in the Underworld

The Sandringham

I wake up when Mum opens the curtains and lie with my eyes shut. Maybe sleep will take me home. I think myself back to my garden and my paddling pool and the flower bed I planted myself and my trampoline. Johnny and me are lying together on the tartan rug. His curly golden-brown ears are tickling me, and exciting sounds come from the kitchen 'cause it's nearly my birthday and all my friends are coming to my party and I'll get lots of presents 'cause everybody likes me. I rub out everything that happened today and blow away the shavings. I lie back on my pillow and hold my koala to my ear to keep out the ugly noise.

Then my eyes are shocked open, and I sit up. There's a scream in the room, and Mum has vanished and there's a shrivelled old witch instead. I stare at her bald head and tree-root hands. This monster has stolen my beautiful mother. I jump out of bed and run to the door. The witch says in Mum's voice, 'Help me, Abbie. I can't see.'

That was weeks ago. You'd think we'd be dead by now, but we're still here. Mum used to tell me stories about this weird underworld, and now we're lost there. When I get up the bed slides off the books and I kick it. I hate this room, I hate the cockroaches and the heating that's always turned on although it's July and the floor that creaks and the taps that drip and the toilet that doesn't flush and the curtains that don't meet and the cracked mirror on the cupboard door that won't shut. Our suitcases and toys and books and clothes are piled all over the floor.

This old crone used to be my beautiful mother. I never knew that in just a few seconds skin could shrivel and hair could drop out and teeth go black. When it speaks I hear Mum's soft voice. She says, 'You must go to the shops, darling, to buy our supper. Then you can play in the park.'

'Come with me.'

'I can't. I'm too slow. I'm afraid of falling again. Soon I'll get used to walking by myself, and then I'll take you to school.'

I stare over her shoulder at the damp patch on the wall and try to see that morning in September when the two of us will walk across the park to my school and my old life and friends. Mum seems to believe in that picture, but I can't.

'Shall we just have a salad and bread and cheese and fruit again for supper?' she asks. I don't care. I look out of the dirty window. You can see all the other dirty windows and at the bottom there's a dirty glass shelf. When I was seven we stayed in a hotel near Florence in a white vaulted room. From the window you could see a cloister with a fountain and feathery trees. A proper hotel. I shut my eyes and want it to come back, but when I open them again I still see the same view. A window opens two floors down, and a black woman in a red dress climbs out over the glass shelf. She crawls to an empty cigarette packet, shakes it and climbs back through her window.

'Mum,' I ask, 'are cigarettes very expensive?'

'No, my darling. Anyway I don't smoke. Why?'

'Just wondered. The bed's on books, breakfast's in a bag, there's nowhere to cook and they'll do anything for a fag.'

'I like your little songs.' Her voice sounds all wrong.

'Better go to the shops, then,' I say. I take five pounds from Mum's wallet and put it in the pocket of my dungarees. But I don't kiss her like I used to. She smells.

'Have a nice time, darling,' Mum says.

No more nice times. Never. In the hot corridor the black-and-orange carpet wriggles with insects. Silver-fish they're called, like they're precious instead of disgusting. All the doors are closed. I was desperate to get out of our room, but now I'm alone I'm scared. I turn and run back to 325 and hammer on the door.

'Mum!'

'Did you forget something?'

'Goodbye.'

'Goodbye, darling.' That weird voice again. A bit mad, like a tea party in a jungle. I go back to the stairs, covered with rotting brown linoleum like mouldy chocolate. They stop suddenly like they don't have enough energy to go anywhere and turn into another stuffy corridor. Then a grand staircase sweeps down to the lobby, the kind Fred Astaire and Ginger Rogers might come dancing down. Every time I go down these stairs I want to bounce and skip; they have wonderfully slidy banisters, and Finn always seems to be polishing them.

He's here now, his piggy fingers holding a duster. His hand reaches through the black railings to touch my bum. Slug. I'd like to squish him under a stone and scrape him into the dustbin with a spoon. But

Finn's the only person in the hotel 'cept Mum who talks to me. Finn's white and flabby with wavy brown hair dripping with gel and an oozy voice.

'And where are you going, young lady?'

'To the shops.'

'Want a drink?'

'I've no money.'

'Tea, coffee, hot chocolate, tomato soup or Coke?' His Irish voice makes them all sound delicious, and I'm parched so I follow him to the drinks machine. It chugs and shines like something in a fairground. Then Finn's fat hands switch it off so it goes dark.

'I've to fill it up in any case. Will we get you a drink now while nobody's looking?' He gives me a Coke, and the red can cools me when I rub it against my cheek and it tastes wonderful.

'Come on, I'll show you around. Have you seen the ballroom yet?'

'The what?'

Finn stares at me again, his green eyes like hungry gooseberries. I think he wants my money. I put my hand in the pocket of my dungarees and squeeze my five pounds. I want to run off to the shops, but I also want to see what a ballroom looks like. It's a word from our old life, like chandelier and Gucci. Finn's hand grips the top of my arm, and we go back up the Hollywood stairs. He isn't Fred Astaire, he isn't even my friend, but at least he's somebody to talk to. People who pass us on the stairs give me mean looks like it's prison and I'm sucking up to one of the warders.

At the top of the stairs there's a locked door with a sign: PRIVATE. Finn takes out a huge bunch of keys – so he *is* a warder. The ballroom's ginormous, with a high ceiling and french windows. The orange curtains are drawn, and the carpet's gross yellow and green. I imagine all the insects dancing on it. On the ceiling naked fatties like the ones I saw in Italy lie around upside down. This used to be a house people wanted to live in and dance in. Finn shuts the door, then he lights a cigarette and offers me one.

'No, thank you. I don't want to die of cancer.'

'Cheerful little bugger, aren't you?'

'I'm only ten. You shouldn't offer me cigarettes.'

'Ten, is it? Thought you was older. Thought you'd be glad of a ciggy – most of you hotel kids are.'

I switch the light on. The horrible carpet stretches for miles. The ballroom's empty, 'cept at the far end where there's a row of little gold chairs and an electric kettle. Finn looks greedy, and the naked fatties look sad and old.

'See, didn't I tell you there was a ballroom? I bet they had some parties here!'

'But what's it used for now?'

'Well, I do some entertaining in here sometimes.' I don't like the way he says this, so I reach behind me for the doorknob. 'No, don't run away. What's your name again?'

'Abigail Mankowitz. I have to go to the shops now.' Finn lets me open the door. I want to go, only I remember I've got nowhere to go to and I sort of stay.

'That's a lot of name for a little girl. Can I call you Abbie?'

'All right. But I don't understand why this room's empty. What about us? What about all the children in the hotel with nowhere to play?'

'Oh, but we couldn't allow them in here. They'd wreck the place. Mr Taggart, the owner, would like to hire it out for conferences and that. Such a fine big room slap-bang in the middle of London. Trouble is, once you get the homeless in a hotel the businessmen and the tourists don't want to know.'

'We're not rats, you know, to be kept cooped up in cages till we go bonkers.'

'I'm not talking about you, now, Abbie with the long name. You're different. I saw that right away.'

'No I'm not!' I shout, although inside I'm pleased he's noticed. 'It's not fair! There ought to be a playroom! I'm going to complain. I'll write a petition and make everybody in the hotel sign it! I know all about petitions from Auntie Annette.'

Finn laughs. 'You just go ahead and do that, darling. You and your granny'll be thrown out of here the next day and put in a real slum. There's far worse hotels than this one, I can tell you.'

I cry. Finn's arms are around me, and one of his piggy hands strokes my hair while the other slips inside my dungarees and into my knickers. His thick lips clamp down on mine, and his tongue invades my mouth. He smells of old biscuits and cigarettes and sweat. I push him away. I feel power like a lift rising inside me, and I throw him across to the other side of the ballroom. He lies on the floor swearing at me.

I turn and run. At the top of the stairs I wipe my eyes and nose on the sleeve of my T-shirt. There's about twenty people in the lobby staring at me. You don't often see people talking at Sandringham House. Everyone's sad and silent, but Mum said to be careful, that gossip spreads like the fungus on the wallpaper and the insects on the carpets. I want to shout at them, 'I beat Finn up!' Then I think maybe I killed him. I could be sent to prison.

I just want to get out, but first I have to get past Eileen's sentry-box at the door. Eileen looks like Mrs Thatcher. She's hard as nails. She wears sugary-pink-and-apricot jumpers. She's always knitting them. I try to get to the front door without being told off. I stand on tiptoe to sign the register. It's kept chained on a high shelf, and the biro's on a chain, too, in case it escapes.

'Where's your granny today then?'

'I told you. She isn't my granny, she's my mum.'

'Correction.' (Eileen's so bossy when she says good morning she makes you feel like it's too good for you. Anyway, mornings here aren't good they're horrible. At eight o'clock Eileen hands out breakfast, that's paper bags full of starvation rations like they're Fortnum's hampers. You get a teabag, a slice of bread and miniature rations of margarine and jam. Mum gives me hers, but my tummy still rumbles all the time.) 'That old thing upstairs is not your mother. You arrived with your mother and smuggled in your granny a few days later. I'll have to speak to Mr Taggart. It's against the regulations, or would be if anyone had ever thought to do such a thing before. Your granny should be in a home, and you should be in care.'

I hate Eileen. She has fluffy orange hair that clashes with the soppy colours she wears like candy floss on arsenic. She makes me so nervous I can't speak. I just open the front door and run.

I stop at the corner and put my hand in my pocket to check my money's still there. It is, but nothing else seems to be in the right place. Big pale houses wobble on the dirty pavement and the trees gasp with pollution. The sun's hot. I look up at it, surprised it's still there. Mum can't see the sun. Can't see anything. I try to imagine how that feels. I was going to ask Eileen to help me find a doctor, but I'm afraid they'll take Mum away. She's still got all those bruises all over her face. Every time I think about them I feel sick. I think Daddy must have put them there. They must have had a big fight.

I want to cry again, but I'm too old. I walk to Queensway, but I can feel the hotel pulling me back. People on the pavements – mums with buggies and tourists and veiled Arab ladies – they all look like ghosts.

In Queensway there's a toyshop. On my tenth birthday I led Mum here. First and last time she's been out. She stumbled and swayed, clinging to me. It was a miserable birthday – no home, no Daddy, no dog, no friends, no party – so this walk with a blind witch just about finished it off. Everybody stared at us. Mum insisted on buying me a birthday present, so I chose a monkey with a silly grin wearing a tennis dress. It cost twenty pounds, same as our food allowance for four days, and on the way back to the hotel Mum fell over and hurt her legs. They're like knotted twigs. Now she just stays in Room 325 all the time and talks in that weird cheerful voice.

I used to like toyshops. I'm the only customer, and the sales lady watches me like she knows I'm a hotel child. I keep my hands in my pockets. If I don't touch anything she can't say I'm shoplifting.

I stop in front of an old-fashioned doll's house. There's a four-poster bed and a hip bath and a black stove. I press my nose against the glass. I love the teeny books and cutlery and knitting-needles. There's even a tiny ball of wool being chased by a one-inch kitten. The people in the doll's house are lovely, too. There's a maid in a black dress and frilly white apron and a lady in a long blue velvet dress and a man in a checked jacket with a watch chain and a boy and a girl wearing sailor suits. I used to have a doll's house, only it got left behind in my old bedroom. I never used to play with it, but now I would. I wish I lived in it.

There's music in the toyshop: 'It's a Small World'. No it isn't, it's a ginormous world, and me and my ancient blind mum don't belong in it. My breath steams a circle on the glass, and I spread out my hands on the cabinet. I want to break through to that wonderful house. Then the sales lady marches over with a cloth and a can of glass cleaner. I've left smeary marks all over the glass. I'm dirty now. Everyone can see it.

I go to a supermarket to buy bread and cheese and fruit. The basement kitchen at the hotel only opens a few hours each day. I went down there one day at lunchtime. Desperate mums were fighting to use the stoves and accusing each other of stealing food from the fridges. Women were cooking with babies on their hips. It was all smoky as they chopped and fried and stirred and shouted. Most of the little kids in the hotel have burns all over their arms and legs. I only know how to make chocolate brownies. I was too scared even to light the oven. So now we have picnics on the bed. In the summer in our tropical room cold food's nice. Mum says by the time winter comes we'll be out of the Sandringham.

When I finish shopping it's only four, and I don't want to go back to the hotel. Still five hours before we can go to bed. Five hours of using the bed as a sofa and a table and a playroom and a kitchen. We could sit on the floor to eat supper, but then the cockroaches will think we're *their* supper. All the hotel children are covered in red sores, but not the mums 'cause they're too tough.

Just the other side of the park is my real house where Daddy and Johnny must be living all alone missing me. Daddy must want to know what's happened to us. Johnny used to howl even if I went out for just a few hours. Daddy always has money. It grows in his pockets, and his black leather wallet is full of cards you can buy anything with. I'm going to tell him how awful it is at Sandringham House and about Mum going blind and Finn and Eileen and the cockroaches. In my pocket I find my last ten pence and go to the phone box on the corner and dial our old number. My heart thumps. I imagine Daddy walking over the polished floor to answer it and Johnny's ears twitching with hope. But there's the wrong sound: not beep-beep but a long bleak note. Unobtainable, unhome, unfather, undog.

Let Daddy and Johnny be alive and I don't care if I've murdered Finn. I'll go to prison. But Finn isn't dead. When I ring the bell he opens the front door and stands well away from me. I push past him and run upstairs.

We eat our bread and cheese on the bed as usual. Like children playing at mothers and fathers, Mum says with a silly laugh.

''Cept there aren't any fathers,' I say. 'Where is he?'

'I don't know.'

'I phoned our old house just now, and there's nobody.'

'He might be away. He usually is.'

'No, the phone's been cut off. Beeeeep.'

'How strange.'

'I'm going over there to have a look.'

'I'm sure he misses you.'

'We shouldn't of left. Why did we? Why can't you tell me?'

'We had to go. I honestly believed it was the best thing for you.'

'But it's horrible here. I hate it! Ever since we came here you've been old and ill and blind. How can you of got so old in just a few hours? Eileen doesn't believe you're my mum. She says you're my granny and she's going to put you in a home.'

Then Mum drifts away inside her head, like she's slammed a door and locked it in my face. Her eyes are shut, but she isn't asleep. I think she's going nuts as well as blind. She has this sort of conversation with herself:

'Well, if it isn't the eternal beauty.'

'It was your idea. You made me do it.'

'You look old enough to make up your own mind. Almost too old to have a mind.'

'You don't know how it feels. The terror of falling or being run over or looking stupid. Is that blur a person or a tree or a lamppost? As soon as I go outside this room I depend on my daughter. I can't expect her to be my guide dog.'

'"To be blind is not miserable; not to be able to bear blindness, that is miserable." Milton.'

'He had adoring women to look after him. Men always do.'

'He knew how to ask for help.'

'Can't do that. Can't stand it when people feel sorry for me.'

'Mum? What's Milton?' I ask. So then she stops talking and that's even worser. I hate the silence. Then I hear whispering, giggling, running in the corridor outside, and I jump up. I'm going out, I say. She doesn't say anything. I kiss Mum's shrivelled papery forehead. She smells like old seaweed.

I open the door just in time to join the children. I know they're all like me, running away from sad mums in ugly rooms, and I want to run away with them. We almost knock Finn over on the stairs, and then we laugh and run past Eileen and out of the door before she has time to tell us off.

We run to the park in a wild, screaming, laughing gang. There's about ten of us. Rosa's in charge. She's the oldest, and she carries the youngest, a baby, a bit like a cat with a kitten in its mouth. Rosa's really pretty. She's got spiky red hair and a thin white face and blue eyes.

She says, 'Right, let's see what ugly mugs are out there today. Shelley and Jason, you go for the tourists. Stick together, and if you meet any pervy old guys kick 'em in the balls and run. Karen, you washed your hair, you useless gimbot. Told you not to wear your new dress. Let's see if we can give you a black eye wiv a bit of dirt.' Rosa pushes them all off then looks at me. 'You're new, aren't you? How old are you?'

'Ten,' I say.

'No you're not; you're only eight and you haven't eaten since yesterday and your mum's on the game and this is your little brother what you have to look after all the time.' Rosa throws the baby at me. 'And don't talk too posh. I'm like your agent, see? Every pound you get, I get forty pence. S'only fair, innit?' Rosa gives me a shove. The baby feels warm and soft and lovely. It reaches out for my hair and sucks it. I've never carried a baby before. I smile at the fat little brown face, then try to look sad as I walk up to two old ladies sitting on a bench.

'Tell 'em you've been on the at-risk register eleven times,' Rosa whispers from the trees behind me.

I stand in front of the old ladies. They're wearing suits and straw hats like Molly. She isn't my grandma really, but she said I could borrow her.

'Is that your little brother, dear? You're a good little girl to look after him like that.' She sounds like Molly. My tears drip down on to the head of the baby. It cries, and the old ladies press pound coins into my hand and I run back to Rosa.

'Two quid? Wicked! You carry on like that, gel, and you'll be a star. I'll take one of them coins, give you the change later. Now, off you go and bovver that old geezer over there. See if you can turn your taps on again. We'll keep you for the granny market.'

Leo and David

Who shall I be now? I must say I never expected to run out of identities. I'm so tired. Drug barons and mafiosi and dictators are allowed to retire, usually into discreet luxury. War criminals evade arrest and die in their sleep. I could claim, as so many Nazis did at Nuremberg, that I was only obeying orders from above – or rather below – fulfilling my destiny as a do-badder. Nowadays reformed murderers are admired; instead of hanging you they form a support group around you, buy your film rights and pay you to write your story. There's a fashion for confessions, and mine would certainly be worth reading.

Abbie's dog, Johnny, sits at my feet, staring up with stupid, faithful eyes. I've always hated pets and the fuss people make over them, yet here I am, stuck with the ingratiating beast. He and a cupboard full of their possessions are the only evidence that the woman and the child weren't figments of my imagination. If only I could unimagine them.

These pains I get, I think they must be feelings. And dreams: my dreams have always been beautifully impersonal calculations and accurate prophesies. There's actually no magic involved in foretelling the future, you just appeal to people's basest instincts and expect the worst. But now I wake at four each morning, shivering with longing for her, my arms stiff as if she has just slipped out of them. I feel her presence in my room so powerfully that I look around for her, sometimes call her name. I thought it would be easier once I moved here. I deliberately got rid of our bed and most of our furniture to exorcize her. But even my new single bed is full of her. In the morning I lie here listening to the children playing. I have a tape of Abbie aged about two, which I listen to constantly. Her confident, breathless little voice tells Jenny the story of Cinderella. And in the background I'm whistling 'Oh, Oh, Antonio' from our music-hall period.

'And then she did go to the party.'

'And were her sisters pleased?'

'No. Nasty sisters. And she had boofil dress. And strawberries.' The 'aw' of the strawberries expands to four syllables as the little voice staggers. Eight years ago. All I can remember now about that year is these ten minutes preserved on plastic.

When I destroyed her contract I didn't know what would happen any more than she did. I was so angry with her I didn't care if she died. This silence is terrible. I don't know where she and the child are living or how or even if.

Intimations of normality. My small, dull, modern flat is above a newsagents near Fulham Broadway. I get up late, shave, have a bath, feed the dog and let him take me out for a long circuitous walk: Parsons Green, the North End Road market, the gentrifying Fulham Road. The longer the walk, the better I shall sleep tonight. I have breakfast in a café where passing women and children worship the dog and ignore me. Then I go to a bookshop in the Fulham Road and browse: poetry, theology, science fiction. I am the science fiction of the past, thousands of years of mythology embodied in an unemployed, solitary man who looks about thirty. Books are my only luxury now; they encrust my walls and make my rooms a little less empty.

All I have ever been is a projection of people's ideas and fears, a whipping boy for their guilt, a horror film that lasted for centuries. Now they no longer project anything on to me. My screen is blank.

I go to another café to read the newspaper with its usual catalogue of disasters, heartache, violence, torture, suicide, drugs and betrayal. I couldn't have arranged it better myself. Things are no worse than they were when I thought I mattered – which is quite bad enough. I tend to eat in the same cafés and restaurants. Routine is a kind of sanity. Today, as I eat my lunchtime bacon sandwich, feeding bits of bacon to Johnny, who is tied to my chair, a woman's voice breaks in on me. 'Leo!'

Outside on the pavement, waving at me coyly through the glass, is Oliver Cromwell, or Dr Olive Weller as she calls herself now. She bounces in and invites herself to join me. 'I'd never have expected to see you in such a shabby place,' she says loudly as the Greek waitress brings her coffee. 'And what on earth are you wearing? You *are* still called Leo, aren't you?' She pushes her cleavage across the table at me. Like so many ex-men she overdoes the femininity. Despite the cold, she's wearing a tight, low-cut black dress and a lot of gold jewellery that glitters in the drab café.

'Until I can think of a better name.'

'Where's that pretty girlfriend of yours?'

'I wish I knew.'

'Oh dear!' she laughs. 'Run off and left you with the dog?' She bends down and studies Johnny, who growls.

'He only likes one-lifers.'

'Must give you a hard time then.'

'He's used to me now.'

'So you mean he isn't . . .'

'Nope. Absolutely natural. Born of a cocker spaniel bitch four years ago in West Kensington.'

'Fascinating. Just what I was looking for. It must be an awful bore for you, having to look after a dog. How much would you like for him?'

'He's not for sale.'

'Oh, come on, Leo, I'll give him back in a couple of weeks.'

'And what will you have done to him in the meantime? A fifth leg? Wings? Green fur?'

'Nothing ugly or visible, I promise. Actually it's his brain I'm interested in. Animals don't have to be dumb any more. Wouldn't you enjoy his company more if he could talk to you?'

'No.'

'Where did you say you're living?'

'I didn't.'

'Well, wherever it is, let's go back and talk about this more comfortably.' I glance down at her beautifully pickled breasts. It might be relaxing to spend the afternoon with her. But who would I be in bed with? A gentleman squire, a revolutionary, a tyrant, a vamp or a distinguished scientist? 'Come on, Leo. I don't like being messed about. Bring the dog and we'll get a taxi back to my place.' The tyrant shows through the charm, makeup and three hundred years.

'No, sorry, Oliver . . . Olive.'

'But why not?'

'I'm gay. I've got my period. I'm a virgin.' She stares at me, white with rage. I remember, too late, that in this age lack of sexual interest is the one unforgivable sin. Better to confess to a million perversions.

After she walks out of the café I take my unmodified dog home and stare out of the window. Between three thirty and four the schoolchildren come past. Every day I look out for Abbie. I wish I'd been with her for her birthday and given her the present I'd bought: a bicycle. I still have it here, wrapped up in paper with teddy bears all over it. She is every child I see, and it's no comfort to remind myself that she couldn't really be my daughter. After Zeus populated Greece with unhappy hybrids, immortals were, of course, sterilized, which, long before anaesthetics, was a painful business. I still have the scars.

When she was little I watched for signs that Abbie might, after all, be my child, that she might have inherited some sixth or seventh sense that set her mysteriously apart from other children. Just once, as we flew above New York, I remember a curious tussle in mid-air. I wanted to return to the hotel and felt her will struggle against mine, surprisingly powerful for an ordinary child. Strange how lovable the ordinary can be.

I take the curly golden-brown idiot for another walk, feed him and have supper in an Italian restaurant. Food in England has improved. I remember the rubbery meat and tortured vegetables in cheap East End restaurants a century ago, when I used to lure people into opium dens and gin palaces. I love food. it's one of the chief pleasures of having a body, although I've never learnt to cook.

Returning to my flat, I listen at the door in case they've come home while I was out and check the answerphone to see if they've left a message, knowing full well that they haven't got my address or phone number any more than I have theirs. How humiliating to be so irrational.

Of course, it's never easy, the period of transition between one incarnation and another. It's a kind of death. But whereas death is a release from decisions my present state demands a million choices I haven't the energy to make. I'm stuck in an anteroom with a mirror, alone, staring at my reflection. I've only had a reflection for a few years, and I was happier without it. Looking at yourself in the mirror can only lead to vanity or self-disgust or an uncomfortable mixture of the two. In the past I picked new identities like a child in a sweetshop, becoming a magician or a pilot or a drug dealer, anything I thought would be fun and wouldn't attract too much attention. Women like flamboyant characters and I liked women, so I did my best to entertain them and myself. Now, for the first time in many centuries, my sexuality seems to be on hold.

In the mirror in my small white bathroom I stare at my face: long, pale, serious, the jaw line marked by a dark track of stubble where I can't be bothered to shave. My eyes gaze into themselves with suspicion, as well they might. Jenny used to make me wear denim to match their colour, but I've got rid of all my fashionable clothes, took them to the Oxfam shop in Kensington High Street and exchanged them for this wardrobe of a broken-down schoolmaster: baggy cords, V-necked sweaters and tweed jackets. I look older. I'm considering a trip to that man in San Francisco to have a few more wrinkles and bags inserted. I wonder if it would suit me to go bald? I want to be taken seriously for a change; I need gravitas and, like everything else, it can be bought. I could become an academic. I already have an encyclopaedic knowledge of theology and philosophy and could write remarkably vivid history. A few fake qualifications and references – no, I can't be bothered.

The friends Jenny and I had together, Katrina and Toby and Charles: all bubbles and illusions. I should have known it wasn't worth investing any emotion in one-lifers. I remember good old David, the only person who might know where Jenny is.

I've never met David, but the thought of him fills me with rage, as if he has stolen something from me. Jealousy? How banal. Over the years I've gathered information about him. Without asking Jenny direct questions about him I've hoarded every crumb that has dropped from her mawkish feast. So I make an appointment to see him and cycle over to Lincoln's Inn Fields.

I never could understand what Jenny saw in David, and when I finally meet him I'm more baffled than ever: a stocky middle-aged man with a red face. In his clear blue eyes and light-brown hair there is a resemblance to Abbie on steroids, and this chokes me with anger so that I can hardly speak.

He greets me with bland professional manners. 'Delighted to meet you. I hope you didn't have too much trouble parking.'

'I'm on a bike.'

'How very green of you!' But I can see he's perplexed by my shabbiness. He's used to clients who wear Armani suits and drive BMWs. 'Now, Mr Bishop, how can I help you?'

'I'm looking for Jenny.'

His face splits open and I see real feeling. Once I would have arranged for a thunderbolt or disembowelled him on the carpet, but now I don't. Or can't.

'You're *that* Bishop!' he gasps. 'Leo?'

'That's me.'

'But you seem in rather reduced circumstances. Has she . . . ? I do hope Jenny hasn't made rapacious demands?' Thank God I didn't marry her, he means, of course.

'I've enough money to pay your fee, if that's what you're worried about. She hasn't made any demands. She just disappeared with my, her, our daughter a month ago. Do you know where they are?'

Silently he takes an envelope from his pocket. Jenny has scrawled on a sheet torn from a child's sketchbook:

Dearest David

You're the only one I can write to, because what happened between us binds us for ever. It's nearly midnight, and in a few minutes I may be dead, or unrecognizable. If I die, you must look after Abbie, take her away from this awful place and bring her up with your children. After all, she could be your daughter. I hope she is. Leo's much worse than I realized. I made a terrible mistake. You must never let him anywhere near your life. Now I can't . . .

I examine the letter and its envelope for clues, while David examines me. 'I can't read the address she's scrawled at the top. Sandgem House?'

'That's what I thought. Some seaside boarding-house? It arrived in June. Can you read the postmark?'

'No, can't decipher that either.'

'Typical!' David says. 'Disappearing in this melodramatic way.'

'I can assure you, her accusations about me are wildly exaggerated.'

'Oh, she was always impossible. But we must find them.'

'And if we do? Would you really want to adopt Abbie?'

'But what about my wife? I can't just foist a third child on her. What am I supposed to say? "Jenny's been bumped off, so I thought we'd adopt Abbie. After all, she could be my daughter." Or, "You know how keen Ben was on getting a Romanian orphan for Christmas? Well, let's get him a British orphan instead. After all, my grandfather and her grandmother were lovers, so it's all in the family, so to speak."'

His sarcasm reassures me. 'If we do find Abbie I shall bring her up as my daughter, whether she is or not. As for Jenny – she probably isn't dead anyway. She's pretty indestructible.'

'Are you still living in that enormous house?' David asks, and then blushes.

'I'm selling it. Downscaling. I've moved to a small flat. Not so much a moral decision as a kind of breakdown. Without them, nothing seems to have much meaning.'

'You do love her!' David says with surprise.

'And you?'

'Oh, I did. Desperately. But I've been married to Muriel for twenty years now, and we have two children and – it's just not the same thing.'

'If Laura had been Petrarch's wife, would he have written sonnets all his life?'

'Exactly. You can't eat sonnets. But if I can help you to find them I will. Keep in touch.'

I don't want to go. I feel a pathetic urge to cling to him and talk about Jenny and Abbie. 'Can I come again soon?'

'Just phone my secretary. Now I'm afraid I must go. I have to visit my grandmother. Ninety-one, talking of indestructible. We've just had to put her in a nursing home. She wanted to stay in her own flat, but she refused to stop cooking. Food was always her passion, you see. She invited us around six months ago and made a great ceremony out of roasting a chicken for us. We kept hearing strange squeals and shrieks from the kitchen. Ben said, "Grandma, that chicken doesn't sound right to me." "Nonsense, darling, I'm sure it'll be delicious. I stuffed it with sage and onion." "You're sure it was dead?" my wife asked. Then there was this bloodcurdling screech from the kitchen, and we all rushed in. A chicken was sitting on the cat's plastic dish, and the face of the cat, poor old Ruddigore, wild with agony and rage, was squashed against the glass door of the oven. Muriel opened it just in time, the cat leapt out of the oven and out of the kitchen window, never to be seen again.

'A fortnight later Grandma set fire to her kitchen and had to be rescued by firemen. So we found this nursing home. Grandma's quite happy, seems to think she's living in a hotel. She probably could stay in a suite at the Dorchester for what we're paying.'

I can tell this is an anecdote David has polished at a dozen dinner parties. He tells it with affection and self-justifying complacency, assuming I share his family values. I don't. A pater that has lost my familias, I'm not sure whether I'm expected to laugh or cry at this vignette of one-liferdom. To lose your mind at only ninety-one! Jenny is ninety-seven – if she is still alive.

We go downstairs and shake hands. David gets into his Volvo and I cycle through the rain and the Friday rush-hour traffic. I'm surprised I can still cycle, because I feel as if I'm made of stone. A statue left out in the rain. Bitten into by time, its original form unrecognizable, eye sockets blank. And, deep inside, the birth of a new creature, hot, wet, sticky and bloody. And painful. Yes, I think these pains must be feelings.

The House in Phillimore Gardens

One night I couldn't sleep. I think I was two. I went to my bedroom window. I saw Mum and Daddy fly past. It wasn't a dream. I wasn't asleep. I really did see them. They didn't look at me. They looked at each other. They were happy. Then they disappeared over the rooftops. I was frightened they wouldn't come back and there'd be nobody to look after me. I cried. I wandered all over my house and put all the lights on, then I fell asleep on their ginormous bed. In the morning Mum and Daddy were there with me, and I was too little to explain, so I just pointed to the window and said, 'Bird!'

Mum hugged me. She said, 'You had a bad dream. The bird won't come again.' But I knew it wasn't a dream.

After that I often heard their fights and watched their flights from my window. The fights were worser. When I was four there was a big fight about which sort of school I should go to. Finally I was allowed to choose between a big house where the children had to wear an ugly grey uniform and sit in silent rows and a glassy building where children wore their own clothes and ran and shouted. I chose that one. I knew Daddy didn't like it. The first day at school I told the other children my mummy and daddy could fly. Then I realized that was a silly thing to say. But all mummies and daddies fight.

When I was little, about five, I used to dig in my garden. Mum used to tell me stories about another city under London, where there were dreams and monsters and treasure and marvels. I wanted to see it, so I was digging this tunnel. Suddenly I felt cold and tired. I wasn't sure if I really did want to have adventures after all. So I looked around for Mum and I couldn't see her, and all I could see was dark garden and empty windows. Then I looked up and saw Mum at the kitchen window smiling down at me, and it was all right again.

I liked school. I liked the way we all went there every morning like a river of children. My teacher asked me to draw my mummy and daddy and my house. I drew Mummy thin and smiley with long black hair holding hands with Daddy. He was thin and smiley, too. They stood in front of a house with a red triangle roof and five green windows under a smiley yellow sun. Mum said she loved my picture. She stuck it on the kitchen wall and I loved it, too, 'cause it looked like all the other children's pictures. I was glad I didn't draw the pictures that came into my head first of Mummy and Daddy flying past my window or Mummy hitting Daddy with a shopping bag or Daddy disappearing with a flash in the middle of supper or Mummy crying because Daddy didn't come home. Nobody would want those silly pictures on their wall.

We used to have relations. Not proper ones, but they wouldn't like it if they knew we were living at Sandringham House. Grandma Molly's very old. She has disgusting table manners, but I love the look on her face when she sees me. Like a lump of ice when you put it in front of a fire. I'm the fire. I didn't like it when she met me after school 'cause my friends said she smells, but now I wish she would come and meet me and take me back to her flat. She lets me eat sweets and crisps and play with Ruddigore, and she tells me stories about people in funny clothes in old photos.

Uncle David was at Molly's sometimes. I liked him. He was my friend. I used to sit beside him on the couch and talk to him.

'Doesn't she ever play?' Uncle David asked Grandma.

'Typical only child: five going on forty,' Grandma said.

I said, 'Don't talk about me as if I aren't here.'

Uncle David laughed. He said, 'Come to my house on Saturday. You can play with Alice and Ben.'

I was so excited. I imagined my wonderful cousins. They were bigger than me, and I thought they'd love me. Mum didn't want me to go, but I did anyway. But they didn't love me at all. We played in their garden. I had to be the piggy in the middle and the patient with Doctor Alice torturing me and the prisoner with Red Indians dancing and whooping around me.

I said to Auntie Muriel, 'It's not fair. Someone always gets left out of games like these and it's always me.'

She said, 'I'm afraid you'll just have to get used to other children.'

'You're spoilt,' Alice said. 'Only children are always difficult.'

Ben wouldn't talk to me, so I ran to Uncle David. I knew he was my friend.

If Johnny was here I wouldn't feel lonely. I got him when I was six. One day when Mum was out I went to see Daddy in his room.

'What do you want?' he asked. Daddy doesn't have a special voice for children. He sounded like I was a letter he didn't particularly want to open.

'Can I see your lav . . . lav . . .'

'Laboratory?'

'Can I? Please?'

'Where's your mother?'

'She's gone to see Auntie Annette. She'll be ages. Please, Daddy.'

'I'm working. You must be very quiet.'

Daddy's laboratory smelt of power and hot plastic and disinfectant. There were four computers and a fax machine and three telephones.

'Make the ceiling and the wall fall down,' I said.

'Oh, you saw that, did you? I thought you were asleep.'

'Are you cross with me?'

'I don't think you ought to be in here.'

'I love you, Daddy.' He looked surprised and pleased. I kissed his long thin hand. Daddy's skin is cool.

He looked down at me. 'Who do you look like, Abbie?'

'Nobody. Like me. What's your job?'

'Why?'

'My friends are always asking me.'

'I work for a bank.'

'Are we rich?'

'What do you think?'

'I think we're poor.'

'Why?'

'I'm not allowed to have sweets or a puppy or a baby brother, and Susie's got two brothers and three cats and she has sweets every day and her mummy hasn't even got a job and Susie hasn't got a daddy.'

'Would you like a puppy very much?'

'Yes. Can I really? And a brother?'

'Just a puppy. The trouble with babies is you never know where they come from.'

Then I climbed up and hugged him and covered his nose in kisses, and he smiled very slowly.

Next day me and Mum went to a flat in West Kensington. Five golden-brown puppies were with their mummy in a basket. They smelt lovely. I rubbed my face against them.

'Which one do you like best?' Mum asked.

I said, 'I love all of them. Stroke them, Mummy.'

'Choose one, darling. Don't let them lick you. You'll get spots.'

I rolled on the floor laughing. The puppies were so lovely; their soft bodies wriggled all over me. 'I want to get spots,' I said.

'Do you want a boy or a girl?' Mum asked.

'I want them all.'

'Don't be silly. Now, make up your mind. We have to go.'

'Won't the mummy dog be sad?'

'Animals don't have the same feelings as us. Now, hurry up. I have to meet a friend for lunch.'

'But you'd be sad?' I asked just to check.

'Now choose one, and let's go. That little shy one that keeps falling over is rather sweet.'

I wanted to take all of them so much I could feel screaming hiccuppy sobs rise from my heart to my throat. But tantrums don't work with Mum, so I chose a boy, the littlest, weakest one, and held him in my hands so my mouth touched his curly velvet ears.

'Why are you crying?'

'I want all of them.'

'Don't be ridiculous. Come on. Let's get a taxi. What are you going to call him?'

'Johnny.'

'Johnny's a name for people, not dogs. Why don't you call him Golden Syrup?'

Mum's really dumb sometimes. Johnny was the name of the brother I wanted and also a boy at school I used to stare at in assembly, only he just ignored me. Johnny's little warm body felt lovely in my arms. His heart was beating and his soft head was tucked under my chin. Mum never understood about Johnny. I think about him all the time.

Grandma Molly's flat smells of Ruddigore and pee and mouldy food, but I got used to it. Grandma never told me off for making a mess. There was already lots of mess. Johnny wasn't allowed to go with me to Molly's 'cause he annoyed Ruddigore. I liked it when Auntie

Annette and Auntie Muriel and Uncle David came to see Grandma. It was like we were all a proper family.

When I was eight I was there one day, and I pretended to be asleep so the grown-ups would forget about me and say things children aren't supposed to know.

Auntie Muriel said, 'She always seems to be here.'

Grandma whispered, 'Poor little thing. Are you awake, Abbie, darling?'

I kept my eyes and mouth shut, but my ears were open.

'Who did you say the father is?' Muriel said.

'Some chap called Leo. Rich as Croesus. I've never met him. They're not married.'

'Marriage is an atavistic ritual,' Auntie Annette said.

'We can't all be man-haters like you. Some of us rather like men. Don't we, Muriel?'

'Jenny certainly does.'

'And how is Jenny?' Uncle David asked.

Grandma whispered, 'That woman is absolutely incredible. She must be well into her forties, yet she could still pass for nineteen. If you ask me, it's uncanny.' The other grown-ups laughed, and Grandma said, 'You think I'm going gaga, don't you? Well, I'm not. There really is something mysterious and sinister about her, like a witch.'

Auntie Annette said, 'Grandma, I'm a socialist. You can't expect me to believe in witches and fairies and all that nonsense. I expect she spends a fortune on cosmetics and plastic surgery.'

'I've never liked her,' Auntie Muriel said.

Then I felt sorry for Mum 'cause they were being mean about her like they thought she was beautiful just to spite them. It wasn't Mum's fault they were all getting old and ugly. I didn't want them to say any more, so I pretended to wake up and looked around the room, and Uncle David was red. He was looking at me, and the other grown-ups all looked cross.

That year we went to Uncle David's house for Christmas. Daddy didn't come. Molly couldn't manage any more. Mum said she was losing her marbles. I saw my cousins again. Alice still didn't like me, but Ben did. He was twelve. He had floppy black hair and green eyes. We sat on the floor and talked about books. He'd read more than me. We talked and talked about everything, and then we went sliding in his garden and I got wet and cold, but I didn't cry. I knew Ben would go off me if I cried. I really liked him. I don't know where he is now.

Last Christmas I was nine. We went to New York. We stayed in a hotel with Daddy. We had a suite with a roof garden at the top of a glittering tower. I loved New York. It's brilliant. I wouldn't let Daddy's hand go. I was afraid he'd disappear again. He asked me what I wanted for Christmas.

'I want to fly, like you and Mum.'

'In a jet or a helicopter?'

'You know what I mean. Just fly at night like you two do. I've seen you often flying past my window.'

'You must have been dreaming.'

'I want to fly here over New York like Superman.'

'Superman can do anything he wants.'

'So can you.'

Later, when Mum was asleep, Daddy made me put on my coat, and we opened the doors to the roof garden. He asked me if I was frightened.

'I'll never be frightened if you're here.'

'Hold on to me very tight then.' Suddenly the hotel was a needle of light and we were flying through the frozen air. Daddy's arms were around me so I could lie back and see the black-and-yellow city. I could feel the power I always knew Daddy had and something inside me, too. I wanted all those people in the shining towers to look out and admire the marvellous Abbie-Leo bird as we flew into the future together.

Daddy asked if I was tired.

'No,' I said. 'I want to fly like this for ever.'

'They'll think we're terrorists.'

We swooped down to a cube of light. It was our roof garden. I tried to make Daddy stay up in the air, but I couldn't. Then I saw Mum on the other side of the glass doors yelling at us, banging on the glass, angry and frightened.

That was seven months ago – seems like centuries. All this remembering makes me sad, makes me miss Daddy and Johnny even more. I don't like asking people for money in the park. Most of them have dogs, and that reminds me of Johnny, too.

I have to see my house again. I run away from Rosa and the other kids. I pass the fairy tree. I used to believe that stuff. It's cold and raining, and I run past Kensington Palace where Princess Di lives with her two lucky little boys and no worries 'cept choosing a new dress. When the hotel children hear a helicopter fly past they say that's Princess Di going shopping.

On the Broad Walk cool kids with proper families are skateboarding and rollerblading. I run around the back of the Palace, cross Millionaires' Row and then Kensington Church Street. I know every shop, and I feel at home again. I imagine how happy Daddy and Johnny will be, how we'll get a taxi to Mum and then we'll all go back home together.

Then I stand outside my house and the windows look funny. There aren't any blinds or curtains. Then I see the sign: FOR SALE. I run up the steps and ring the bell. I imagine Daddy in his laboratory. Johnny will know it's me. He'll smell me and come to the door. Only he doesn't. So I knock on the door three times like a policeman. Then I yell through the letterbox, 'Daddy! It's me!'

I wait a long time, but my house looks, smells, feels empty. Then I cry. I can't help it. I stumble down the steps and nearly get run over 'cause I can't see. A car brakes screechily, and I think that's Uncle David at the wheel. But if it is I don't want him to see me cry. He'll think I'm a wimp and tell Ben and Alice. So I run back to the park, all the way to the fountain garden where us hotel children meet. Most of them haven't got daddies either. Rosa is there with her baby. He's called Kevin. Rosa was fourteen when he was born.

'Got any dosh for me, then?' Rosa holds out her hand.

'I haven't been begging. I just went for a walk.'

'You've been crying, love.' Rosa hugs me with Kevin. He needs changing, and I wriggle. Rosa says, 'What is it then, Abbie? Some bloke been having a go at you? Is it that Finn, dirty bugger?'

'No,' I say, but I can't stop crying.

'Never mind. You'll get a flat soon. So will I. My friend Michelle did the tarot cards for me, and there was this king and this bloody great house, so I'm gonna be rich. And soon Kev will be walking, and then we can go along to the toddlers'.'

'The what?' I ask.

'The mum-and-toddler group. It's a jammy dodger there. There's this bloody great room, all warm and full of toys and mums and kids and coffee and free biscuits. No more begging for us.'

'It sounds nice. Can I come?'

'Not you. You're too old, darling. Never mind. Maybe in a few years you'll have a baby, too, then you can be just like me.'

I'm cold and wet. It's nearly dark. 'I'm going back to the hotel,' I say.

'Hang on, we'll all come with you. You don't wanna go back there on your own, else Eileen'll have a go at you.' Rosa rounds up the children and takes her commission. Then we all go back to Sandringham House laughing and eating sweets and crisps. We're a gang. I don't feel so frightened of Eileen when I'm with them.

Rosa says, 'Soon as Eileen opens that door, you all rush in and get up them stairs fast as you can. Right?'

So I ring the bell, and this is my bell, my front door, just like the Phillimore Gardens one, and Mum's upstairs – old and blind but still Mum. I really don't understand.

Finn opens the door. He says, 'Well, if it isn't the karate kid.' He gives me a dirty look. We all scoot past him. Eileen's knitting, staring at us over her blue plastic glasses that stick out at the corners. We all rush in, but Eileen pulls me back. The others escape upstairs 'cept Rosa. She's my friend, so she waits for me.

'I want a word with you, Miss Abigail Mankowitz. You come back here, young lady. I've told you before you have to sign your name when you come in and out.'

'You didn't make the others sign.'

'Well, they're just kids, aren't they? Not like you with your tricks and your gran and your goings on. I've had a word with Mr Taggart about you, and there's a social worker coming soon to sort you out. Put you in care and your gran into a home. And you should be in care, too,' she says to Rosa. 'Or prison. I know what you get up to in that park.'

'We don't get up to nothing. Just playing. I do like your new glasses, Eileen, they really suit you,' Rosa says. Then we run upstairs. 'And I hope you die of it!' Rosa whispers, and we laugh.

'She's always saying she'll throw us out. Can she really, Rosa?'

'Nah. Mr Taggart doesn't give a fuck who's in his hotels. He gets money from the government, see, and the more people there is in a room the more he gets.'

'I hate Eileen.'

'Daughter of darkness and bride of Frankenstein rolled into one, that's Eileen. See ya tomorrow.'

Rosa's my friend. She's had a very interesting life. When she was thirteen she ran away from a children's home in Devon. Then she came to London and got pregnant with Kevin. His dad is sometimes an Arab prince, sometimes a drug dealer and sometimes a student.

Mum's really happy to see me. When she first got old I couldn't tell what she was feeling, but now I can. She hugs me. It's like being hugged by a spider. 'You're soaked. Where have you been?'

'I went back to our old house, but Daddy isn't there any more. It's empty. And just now Eileen went on again about putting me in care and you in a home.'

'We'll find somewhere else to go,' Mum says. But we're both frightened. She touches my tears, then she says, 'I had a dream. I was wandering through tunnels searching for you. You were lost, and I was terrified. I passed a starving cat and a cowering dog, but the animals made no sound. The silence was unbearable. I called out your name, and I opened the door of an empty room, and cold fetid air rushed at me. I shut that door and opened another. I was in a kind of cell with dirt and rubbish all over the floor. Eight sad little children sat on a filthy bed, but you weren't there. One of them said, "Our mummy isn't alive at the moment."'

'So?' I say. 'Have we got to go and live in tunnels now?'

This is the story Mum tells me at bedtime. She isn't a lot of use, but she does know lots of stories.

'Long, long ago there were three sexes, not just two: male, female and hermaphrodite. These people were round with four arms and four legs, one head with two faces, four ears and two hearts.'

'Did they have two bums?'

'Yes. They walked very fast on their four legs, and when they were in a hurry they turned cartwheels. Men came from the sun, women came from the earth and hermaphrodites from the moon. One day they had a revolution against the gods. Zeus was angry, but he didn't want to destroy them because then he wouldn't have anyone to worship him or make sacrifices to him. So to punish them Zeus sliced each one in half like an avocado. Then each person only had two legs. As he watched them stagger around Zeus said that if they rebelled again he'd slice them into four so they'd have to hop. When he saw how uncomfortable they were, Zeus took a little bit of pity on them but not much because Zeus wasn't a soppy god. He told Apollo to turn their faces around so they faced the other way and to pull their skin tighter and tie it in the middle to make a tummy button.'

'Did they have an anaesthetic?'

'No. They were very sore, and, even worse, their one heart was broken. They remembered how wonderful it was when they were joined together, and they wobbled off on their two legs. They wandered all over the world searching for their other half. So that's what love is. Are you awake, Abbie? If you find your lost twin you must never leave him.'

Sibyl

'The Metaphysical Bank. Can I take you through security?'

'No. Pastoral Care, please.'

'Did you wish to use our counselling service? Do you have a contract with us?'

'I invented the contracts.'

'May I have your identity number, please?'

'For the time being I have no identity, which is why I need counselling.' I swear under my breath as the baffled clerk disappears. I'm so nervous that my eye's twitching. I've never asked for help before. Then I recognize the voice of the branch manager, a stockbroker who jumped out of his Wall Street window in 1929. He should understand something about personal crises. 'Hello? Is that you, Carl? This is Leo – I mean this was Leo. I'm having problems – I don't know how to phrase this – deciding who to be next.'

The voice on the other side of the phone is bland as margarine. 'Why, Leo, it's good to hear from you. We were wondering what had happened to you. You weren't at the last directors' meeting. Which century did you wish your counselling to take place in?'

'I really don't know much about it. Which do you recommend?'

'Well, there's Roman therapy. They believe in opening your veins in a hot bath.'

'That's no use to me, I'd just have a few scars and exactly the same problems as I had before.'

'Well, you could try the Inquisition. We sometimes find it works in cases of extreme self-possession and persecution mania. They're not very caring, of course.'

'Haven't you got anything more – timeless?'

'We have a very respected oracle in a cave under the Earls Court Road. Classical, I'd say, rather than timeless. Speaks in doggerel and never washes.'

'Well, I suppose that'll have to do. How do I make an appointment?'

How I detest this time of year. I swear at myself every time I pass a Christmas tree or a cluster of fairy lights. Yes, I admit I've got into the habit of talking to myself lately. Six months since they disappeared. I walk down Redcliffe Gardens and into the Earls Court Road, turn right and ring the bell of an unprepossessing basement. The door is opened by a dark thick-set woman in a purple caftan and curlers.

'I was sent here by the Metaphysical Bank.'

'Ah, then you must be Leo. I'm Fatima. Haven't seen you since Derby Day, 1921. How's that pretty girl who was with you? Dead, I suppose.'

'Strangely enough, she's the reason I'm here.'

'I thought she might be.'

'Well. Good to see you.' We kiss guardedly on the doorstep, scrutinizing each other close up. I'm struck by the leathery texture of her skin. 'You did take out a contract with us, didn't you? If you don't mind my saying so, I wouldn't have known.'

'If you must know, my clients like me to look a little more mature. After all, the oracle's several thousand years old and looks it. We can't be vestal virgins for ever. Anyway, you're not looking particularly young or beautiful yourself – unshaven, seedy. You look like death warmed up, if you really want to know. Come in.' She leads me down a corridor with a linoleum floor, opens a door and brusquely lifts a trap-door in the floor. 'You can go straight down. There's no point in sitting around in the waiting-room. You'll only frighten our clients.'

The stone steps leading down to the cellar ooze with grease, and the stench that drifts up, of damp and unwashed wisdom and sacrificial bones, reminds me unpleasantly of my disastrous visit to the sibyl at Cumae sixteen hundred years ago. I half fall down the stairs into the darkness of the cave-like cellar, pick myself up and say irritably, 'I'm not sure this is a good idea. When they said "Classical" I didn't realize they meant you. You're pre-Christian. You couldn't possibly understand my problems.'

Silence. As my eyes adjust to the darkness I can just make out a cage swinging from the ceiling and a tiny figure – or a large bird? – crouched in it. There's a sound like wind stirring in a pile of leaves. Then a thin dry voice:

'Well? What is your question?'

'Who must I become next?'

'There is no must but only dust. There is no being only seeming. Find the child who once you lost. Restore the sight of the blind one dreaming. Invent a future you can bear.'

Another silence. Then I say impatiently, 'I dare say I'm being thick, but I haven't a clue what you're talking about. As for finding the child, I've been trying for months. But how? People don't talk in riddles nowadays, you know.'

'*I* do,' the voice says more robustly. 'Although I often wonder why I bother.'

'Is that it then? Is that my counselling? Can't I just talk to you? Sibyl, please, I desperately need a mother figure to confide in, and you're probably the last person around who's older than me.'

'Well why didn't you say so?' the voice says in a much warmer tone, with a faint Viennese accent. The door of the cage opens, and I can dimly see a tiny figure stepping out of it.

Then there's a flash, and I'm lying on a red velvet *chaise-longue* in a large, bright room. A small, elderly woman in a black trouser-suit sits behind a carved wooden desk, resting her chin on her folded hands and staring at me intently. The face above the hands is so deeply lined it appears to be tattooed, and she's staring at me out of dark, sunken eyes. The noxious smell of the cave has been replaced by polish and cologne. I close my eyes and talk as I've never talked to anyone before.

'That's better. Thank you. Do you know, I think I like this century better than any of the others. There's not much of it left, of course. But if only I could find Jenny and Abbie again I'd choose to stay here. It seems to me a lot of barriers are coming down. Between good and evil, men and women, people of different races and religions. Not between rich and poor, unfortunately, but I can't take responsibility for that. I'm here, I suppose, because I want to join the human race. I rather like them. I know they're weak and foolish and muddled and frequently destructive, but, still, they have their charm. I'm so bored with my own tricks and evasions. I want to be not honest exactly but no worse than anyone else. To forget my pasts and live quite simply. I don't suppose you've ever had a patient like me before,' I say with pride.

'You come to me in droves,' she says wearily.

'We do? You mean there are others like me?'

She opens her desk diary and waves it at me. 'My dear, there are more of you than I have hours in the day. Professional confidentiality forbids gossip, you will understand, but I can tell you that many of your colleagues – angels, devils, agents, franchisees, whatever we want to call them – are going through an identity crisis. And not only you, but the eternally young and rich come to me, too, weeping, groaning – I had one of them here only this morning. The most beautiful courtesan in the harem in Byzantium, still a top model, but she's had enough. She envied me my wrinkles. Tragic.'

'So I'm not alone?'

'Far from it. We could form a support group, but it would fill the Albert Hall.'

'Until the beginning of this century I'd say I was quite well adjusted. I seduced young girls, tempted thieves, handed weapons to psychopaths, led teetotallers to inns and loving husbands to brothels. The usual kind of thing. It was repetitive, but so are most jobs. My magic and alchemy had degenerated into cheap tricks in music halls. Then one day a young girl came to me, striking-looking but nothing special. Not particularly talented or intelligent.'

'Ah, Jenny!'

'But how do you . . . She's been here?'

'I'm not allowed to tell you that. But everyone knows about you and Jenny. It was one of the great love affairs of the century.'

'They do? How embarrassing.'

'You have let yourself become an Englishman. Be careful.'

'I don't want to rush around starting wars and causing droughts and famines any more. I'd like to resign from the board of the Metaphysical Bank, only I don't know how. I'd like to be the same person for ever, with the same woman and the same child. I know she can't really be my child, but I feel as if she was and I do miss her. Horribly. Can't you help me to find them?'

'That would be unprofessional. Do they want to find you?'

'I don't even know if they're alive!' I howl.

'One minute an English gentleman, the next a Transylvanian werewolf,' she says thoughtfully and makes notes.

'That's why I'm here. I really don't know who I am or want to become.'

'I see. What do you remember about your childhood?'

'I don't think I had one. My earliest memory is of playing the harp and singing –'

'A Marx Brothers movie?'

'No. I mean – before the revolution up there – I was quite musical. Ten thousand harps, can you imagine the noise? Now I can't stand that kind of music, it gives me a headache. But I wasn't a child. I was about the size I am now. We were all ageless, sexless. Anyway, that's all I remember: music, clouds, sunsets, sweetness, light.'

'And were you happy?'

I lower my voice. 'Well, actually, you weren't allowed to be unhappy. Any complaints and you were out. That was how the revolution started, in fact. A few of us got together and decided to ask questions. What were we supposed to be praising all the time? Why couldn't we go and help them if it was so awful down there? Why did children suffer and die? It was very exciting, but it didn't last long.'

'You were punished?'

'I'll say. They found out we'd been lusting after the daughters of men and that was the last straw. We were banished, excommunicated. All I remember is falling into this freezing chaotic darkness. I'd never seen the dark before. I was terrified.'

'And where were you? When were you?'

'In Greece. I'm not sure of the date,' I sigh.

'This was a very difficult time for you?'

'Well, of course, I've always been a survivor. I found a woman – my first – you can imagine. I can't remember her name, but we lived in a cottage on an island in the midst of olive groves. At night I would gaze up at the sky and speculate.'

'Did you long to return?'

'No. My only regret was that I didn't know where the others, my friends, had fallen to earth. I knew there were many of us, and I longed to talk to them.'

'Did you ever find out what had happened to them?'

'Gradually, over the centuries, some of us bumped into each other. Somehow I always recognized them. Belial commanded a pirate ship in the Aegean and terrorized the little fishing community where I was living. I noticed he had special powers – we all did – he could summon tempests and was quite indestructible. Even when all the men in the village caught him and set upon him with their axes he walked away unscathed.'

'And did he stop menacing you when he realized who you were?'

'Well, no, not exactly. I suppose I might as well be honest with you. I never have been with anybody else. As a matter of fact, I joined forces with him and we ended up controlling the whole coast. Then we met up with another fallen angel, running a string of bordellos in Asia Minor. Many of us went into business or crime, often both, sometimes the Church. As we got together we gradually formed an alternative power base. How else were we to manage? We made a bit of money as *tempestorii*, whipping up storms that spared the fields of the peasant who was paying us.

'Then – I think it must have been in the third century – priests were already doing a roaring trade in indulgences. Pieces of the true cross, feathers from the wings of the Archangel Gabriel, a twig of the bush from which the Lord spoke to Moses. We realized we had something to sell, too. So we negotiated the first contracts, and the Banca Metafisica was founded. We were really very innovatory; this was centuries before the Italians started in banking or the Templars started to arrange money transfers for pilgrims to the Holy Land. We were quite prepared to help them, too. We had nothing against Christians. Later we lent money for the Crusades and also, of course, to Saladin.'

'So you feel you had a good career?'

'Oh yes. Only it's gone on too long.'

'And do you ever feel guilty?'

'About what? Not about my Fall, I've had a far more interesting life than I would have had up there. Goodness is so – obvious. I suppose I was pretty brutal during the first few centuries, but most people were in those days, including popes.'

'How many deaths do you think you have been responsible for, Leo?'

'Statistics are so boring.'

'Haven't you ever asked yourself?'

'Never. You see it's so hard to calculate. I've lived so many lives in so many places I really don't know the answer. I've forgotten so much that happened to me. I wish now I'd kept a journal. I only started to be aware of myself in this century. And, as Dostoevsky said, "To be conscious is an illness – a real thoroughgoing illness."'

'And what is the cure?'

'For everybody else, death.'

'Would you die, if you could?'

'Oh yes. Most willingly. I've done everything, been everywhere. I only want to be human, and the great privilege they have – although, of course, they don't see it like that – is the option to die. A life without end is like the idyll I was expelled from: monotonous, exhausting, repetitive. These transition periods like the one I'm going through now . . . I can't go through this again.'

'You are right, it isn't easy to live for ever.'

'Of course, I forgot. You're in the same situation. Yet you seem so calm.'

'You don't get to be a sibyl if you are manic depressive.'

'Of course not. But – forgive my curiosity – how did it happen? Am I allowed to ask you questions?'

'Strictly speaking, no. But I will share my experience with you because I like you. No, not like that, I know I'm too old for you. I was born in Greece, in what they call the Golden Age, before immortals were sterilized. In those days many of us had immortal blood, and those of us who loved life and passionately wanted to work, as I did, went on and on. As people became more conventional I had to pretend to die, of course, every seventy years or so. But I had great vitality and I loved people, I wanted to help them, and I found I could. I was already over a thousand years old when Tiberius Claudius came to me – even older when you stumbled into my cave.'

'So it *was* you! You weren't very nice to me. You spat at me and came up with the most impenetrable riddle.'

'I had a few problems with men at the time.'

'Sorry. I didn't mean to interrupt. Please go on.'

'Then the Christians came, and they were a bunch of misogynists. That was the end of the sibyls like me, the old goddesses, the Mothers. We had to go underground for many centuries. People no longer came to us with gifts and respect; our strength was despised and feared. I refused to sell myself into a submissive marriage, but it was very hard to make a living. They still came to me for advice and reme-dies, but then they'd accuse me of being a witch and cheat me. I was always hiding, running away, looking for a place where I could be myself without being persecuted. I met the oracle from Delphi in ninth-century Paris chained up in a filthy tent, guessing the weight of cakes.

'I myself lived in huts, barns and often in the streets and fields. It was not so much the living conditions I minded – after all I'd lived in a cave for a thousand years – but the cruelty and ignorance all around me. I often despaired and cursed my immortality. Like you, I would have died if I'd been able to.

'In Westphalia in the fifteenth century I was hiding in the woods outside a little town. A merchant, Cristoph, came to hang himself because he'd been swindled out of all his money and was ashamed to go home to his family. I talked him out of it, talked him back into life and gave him some advice.

'When he took it and prospered he was grateful to me and even gave me a room in his house. My rage and bitterness left me as I became fond of him and of his family. They were Jews, and although they were rich they were also, like me, hated. After a year in their household I converted, thinking that I would at least share in their persecution. I didn't have to wait long. A few months later there was an outbreak of the plague, and the people of the town said the Jews had caused it by drinking the blood of Christian children. They locked us all in a tower and set fire to it. Cristoph and his family, my only friends, were incinerated. I smelt their flesh as it crackled and roasted, and I wept as I wished I could live and die as cleanly as them. That night I walked out of the burnt tower.

'Later the intolerance became even worse. I was burnt at the stake all over Europe, tortured, denounced as a heretic, as indeed I was. What is unique about the Christian story that gave them the right to hate all others in the name of universal love?

'But, like you, I have an affection for this century. Here we are in a room, talking to each other, trying to understand each other without a rack or a bonfire. The old forces are coming out again, not only you and I. The religions are flowing together, and women are allowed a voice once more. Do you know what my patients say to me, those who are rushing to do it all in only one life? They say things are much worse; they used to be so much better. All around I hear it, this crazy nostalgia for a past that never was. But you and I know, don't we, Leo, that sentimentality about history is a mug's game. Was history sentimental about me when I was rejected and tortured and hounded for all those centuries?'

'I agree it's better now. I also found it a great burden, being stereotyped as bad. Incidentally, I've always rather liked strong women. If the Church Fathers had let a few Mothers in, the whole system would have been more humane and balanced. Well, Sibyl, where will you and I be in another hundred years? That's what I really want to know. And don't give me an obscure riddle.'

'I speak in riddles because the future is ambiguous. It isn't fixed, it isn't a picture I can gaze into and describe to you. The past doesn't change; it can only be reinterpreted, but what you become is clay, and your hands are moulding it. So don't come to me like a young girl to a fortune-teller, asking if you'll meet your lover soon. It's not that simple, and neither are you.'

'No. But will I?'

'Will you see Jenny again? Ask yourself why she left you, why she took the extraordinary step of throwing away all that she had and putting her child in danger –'

'They *are* still alive then?'

'Leo, I can be some kind of friend to you, but I won't be your detective. Now I'm afraid I have another patient coming soon.'

'From the Metaphysical Bank? Another of the eternally rich?'

'I never discuss my patients, whether I see them in my cave or in my consulting-room.'

'You're throwing me out! Just when I thought I'd found someone I could confide in.' I stagger to my feet. 'Back to my lonely room. I don't suppose I'll talk to anyone for days now, except the dog. Couldn't you cancel your next appointment and let me stay another hour instead? I'll pay double, triple . . .'

'My God, anyone would think I was a prostitute!'

'I've had plenty of sex. It's talking I need.'

But she walks me firmly to the door, so tiny and bent that she hardly comes up to my waist. I look down in astonishment at this shrivelled creature, who scuttles like a crab and speaks with more eloquence and power than many angels I have known.

Down the Plughole

I wake up in this rickety double bed with Mum and try to believe I'm going to school. My school's just on the other side of the park. I could walk there in half an hour and be in time for the first lesson. My teachers and friends would be pleased to see me – they like me – but the little girl they liked isn't here any more. I can imagine as far as the door, but I can't imagine spending a whole day just listening, chatting, playing. I'd be worried about Mum and frightened the other children would find out where I'm living and laugh at me. Then I remember it's nearly Christmas. It's the holidays – it's always holidays now. I wonder if Grandma Molly would still like me. I think about her so much; I want to see her so much. I shake Mum. Her voice sounds young in her horrible face.

'What's the matter, darling?'

'Mum, we've got to go and see Grandma Molly. I'll help you downstairs and across roads. Let's walk across the park. It's a lovely sunny morning.'

'But why is it so important to see her today?' Mum hasn't been out since my birthday six months ago.

'I've just got to see Grandma. I'll burst if I don't.'

'Why do I have to come?'

'Because I need you. My head's splitting; my heart's splitting. I can't keep going out to the park on my own and pretending Daddy and Johnny and Grandma never happened.'

Then Mum realizes I'm desperate. I sort of know how she feels, how scary everything must be when you're blind. Mum's bones are so fragile that if she falls maybe she'll never ever walk again. So I take her arm, and we go downstairs very slowly. I expect Eileen to stop us, but she just glares at us.

'Are you all right, Mum?' I ask when we're in the street.

The air feels strange, as if my skin's been peeled off. Instead of just darkness I can see stripes of light.

'Ow!' she says when a car passes. Everything's so loud it hurts. She's really frightened, and so am I, so I keep talking to her. I hold her arm, and it feels like it might break.

'We're in the park now,' I say. 'It's really sunny, and there are squirrels everywhere. Mind that conker. There are millions of people here, little kids and tourists and skateboarders and people walking dogs. Loads of dosh. Rosa says old ladies are magic with punters. Shall we see if we can get enough money for our taxi home?'

'How would we do that?'

'Begging.'

'It's wrong to beg,' Mum says, and I wonder what she thinks I've been doing in the park.

The walk takes centuries. I can't run, and Mum has to sit down every five minutes. In daylight her skin looks sort of green, like a crocodile, and everyone stares at us. Finally we get to Kensington High Street, where we used to go shopping and go to restaurants. All the shops are full of Christmas stuff, but Mum can't see anything or do anything or buy anything. It's miserable.

Molly's home is like Sandringham House, only they're all old and

Mum says it's really expensive. It doesn't smell expensive. It smells of pee and pooh and disinfectant. I hope when I get old like Mum and Grandma I just die. A bossy lady tells me to sign the visitors' book. She's like Eileen. I've had enough of all that signing, so I just pretend to sign and lead Mum upstairs. You can tell which people are the visitors: they're all smiling 'cause they're so happy they can get out again. There are flowers and plants, but even they look old. We pass a room where all these old people sit on chairs in silence. Some of them are so tiny their feet don't touch the ground, like ancient children. They look like they're waiting for someone to ask them to dance. They look so sad. Suddenly I realize this is where Eileen wants to put Mum.

Grandma Molly's wearing a dirty pink dressing-gown and blue fluffy slippers. Her knotted blue-and-green legs look horrible. I want to cover them up. Lines cut across her face like roads on a map, and there's this sort of caked, powdery ditch between her nose and her mouth. I help Mum into a chair and run to hug Grandma.

'It's me, it's Abbie.' I bury my face in Grandma. I think I'll die if she doesn't recognize me. But she does. She's happy to see me.

'Abbie, darling – and who's this poor old thing?'

'That's my mum. She sort of had an accident.'

'Accident? Looks more like a cataclysm. You look older than God, Jenny. How old *are* you anyway?' Grandma squawks at Mum. She leans forward and pokes her face.

'Shush, Grandma, she's blind.'

Molly laughs. She used to be sensible but now she's talking absolute rubbish. 'Eugenie-bloody-Manette. Ha-ha-ha. Jenny-do-any-thing-for-a-penny. It *is* you, isn't it? You took us all in pretending to be young and luscious. How did you do it? That's what I want to know. Bitch! Whore!'

I didn't know old people knew words like that. But Mum just smiles.

'I'd say it's good to see you, Molly, only I can't. Not that I want to see myself now. Yes, it's me. I often wanted to tell you. It's like what they say about murderers. The urge to confess is almost unbearable. Endless youth is a heavy burden – anyway, it wasn't endless, as you see.'

'Does the child know?' Molly asks Mum.

'Know what? What are you talking about?' I yell.

'Not yet,' Mum says.

'So you're older than me, and now you look it. Lost your looks. Wish I could find them.' Molly laughs. It isn't a very nice laugh. 'Jenny and Abbie! Ha-ha-ha! Shabby fanny any cabby. Took us all in. And where did the little girl come from?'

'Stop it, Grandma. I'm Abbie. I'm her daughter.'

'Caught her? I'm not surprised.'

I don't like all this crazy stuff. It's scary. I want us to be a proper family again.

'Look, Grandma, I brought you that chocolate you like.'

'You must be very nice people to give me a present. Is it my birthday?'

'No, not until January. You'll be ninety-two,' Mum says in a funny voice, like she wants Molly to be even more older than she is.

'Will I really? I've never been as old as that before.'

I stare into Grandma's beaming, dribbling face as she gobbles the big bar of chocolate. A nurse comes in to change Grandma's nappy. In the bathroom we hear her talking to Grandma like she was Kevin. 'Now don't play naughty with me, Mrs Dumphry, my darling. Here is coming your granddaughter and your antique friend to visit you, isn't it?'

When Grandma Molly comes back into the room she stares at us like she's never seen us before. She says, 'Lovely to see you. Who did you say you were?'

'It's still me, Grandma. Abbie. And my mum.'

But Grandma Molly isn't there any more. I want her to come back, so I put my hands on her hands on the table, then I pull Mum to her feet and make her put her hands on top, the four old hands all mixed up like greenish-white claws. Grandma wears rings, but Mum has sold her jewellery. My hands are on top. Then Grandma takes her hands away and the hand mountain collapses, and Grandma stares at her telly like we're not there.

'We've got to go now, Grandma. It was lovely to see you. We'll come again soon. I think your room's really nice.' I sound like a grown-up, lying all the time. Then I lead Mum to the lift.

When we get back to Sandringham House we're exhausted. Mum can hardly walk. I just want to get up to our room and sleep, but Eileen catches us.

'You should've told me you was going out. I must've told you a million times about signing that register. Social Services has been here looking for you two. They want to talk to you about going into care – and they're after Rosa, too. That baby needs to be properly looked after, and so does your gran.'

'I *told* you. She's my mum not my gran.'

Then Rosa comes in with Kevin, and Eileen says it all again, waving her knitting-needles, her glasses glittering. Kevin wakes up and cries as Eileen looms over him.

'Yes, well might you cry, poor little thing. What hope is there for you with a mother like that?'

'If I want your opinion, Eileen, I'll pull the bloody toilet chain. Talk about Hitler, about dictation and that he had nothing on you. Well, you don't scare me!'

I think Rosa's really brave.

'They'll soon teach you to talk proper where you're going, young lady,' Eileen says.

Then we all go upstairs. I pretend not to be frightened, but I am. And then we all go to Room 325 and have a meeting.

'What are we going to do?' I ask Rosa.

'We'll find somewhere to go. They're not going to take Kevin away or your granny or whatever she is neither. There's places we can go, tunnels and that. I've heard stories.'

'Mum?'

'Sorry, darling, I was years away. I'm so tired.'

'Mum. Please. We've got to do something quickly.'

But she just lies on the bed and shuts her eyes. 'So this is old age. How right I was to avoid it. I'm nobody, nothing, nowhere. Less than the dust beneath your chariot wheels.'

'Whose chariot? What are you talking about, Mum?'

'I struggle like a fly in the syrup of my past. Once I had wings, but I'll never fly again. All that youth, beauty, money wasted! Never mind. Old people are allowed to give up. They'll take me away from you and give me a room and feed me and wash me and forget me like Molly. You'll be cared for, too, my darling. You'll go to school and be a child again with other children. Maybe it's all for the best.'

'Mum! Shut up! You can't die yet.'

'Yet? I'm not exactly a spring chicken. I'm nearly a hundred. I've had enough. I'm blind and poor and exhausted.'

'No! Remember how you felt when your mother left you? I'm younger than you were then. I need you.'

'Someone else can look after you now. Leo or the state or good old David.'

'No! You, you said you'd always be there for me. You promised!'

Then we hug, and we're both crying, and Kevin cries, too, and Mum says, 'Sorry, Abbie, you're right. I won't ever leave you.'

Then we see two letters have been pushed under the door, one for us and one for Rosa. I open it. This is what it says: 'Places have been found for Abigail Mankowitz in a children's home in Ealing and for her elderly relative Jenny Mankowitz in a residential home in Peckham. Transport will be organized for them both on the morning of

January 6th, and Abigail Mankowitz will start at her new school the following day.'

Rosa reads her letter. 'Well, Eileen can stick this up her arse. Says here they put Kevin on the at-risk register. That's a lie for a start. I never hit him, did I, my smelly angel?'

Suddenly Mum sounds younger, stronger. She says, 'We can't stay here. Now we've got to disappear, become unpersons. I've been one most of my life anyway. Tell me about these tunnels, Rosa.'

'There *is* tunnels, and I know there's kids down there, too, 'cause I've heard stories about them. Only it's cold and dangerous. You don't live in rooms like up here but in holes like rats. What I mean is – well, it's better to be honest, isn't it? – me and Abbie and Kevin's young, but you, Gawdalmighty, how old *are* you?'

'Ninety-seven.'

'Well, then, you're a bit old to go pot-holing, innit? Do your gran or whatever she is a favour, Abbie. 'Snot fair if we have to drag some old dinosaur around with us. She'll be much better off in a home. I know it's not the same as having your own place, but she'll be warm and safe and, I mean, she's not gonna live for ever, is she?'

'I'm not going anywhere without my mum.'

Mum's angry. 'Do you think only children like to be free? That I can't hear or feel just because I can't see? I don't know what you look like, Rosa, but I know how much you love Kevin, how you two need to be together. And that's even more important than being comfortable. So don't write me off.'

'OK, we'll take the old bat – I mean, we'll all go down there together. First sign of illness we dump her at the nearest hospital and run. Don't wanna be stuck with a fucking corpse, innit? No disrespect and that.'

Mum starts to sing in a funny high voice like she really is a bat. Don't go gaga on me, I think. This is her song: 'My baby as gawn dahn the plughole, / My baby as gawn dahn the drain. / The poor little fing was so skinny and thin, / 'E should have been washed in a jug.' Mum sings some more, then she says we're all going down the plughole like dead skin. But we aren't dead; we're very much alive.

So then me and Rosa go off to explore the tunnels, and that's our Christmas. All over London children are too excited to sleep and mums and dads are wrapping presents. There's parties and skiing holidays and pantomimes and concerts and ballet and lights and carols and brilliant trees. Most people in Sandringham House have gone home to families. Tomorrow there's a free Christmas dinner at the church. I was looking forward to it, but Mum and Rosa say we've got to leave now while the hotel's empty and nobody can follow us.

'Mum, don't die yet.'

'I'll try not to.' I hug her. I don't mind her smell now. Rosa hugs Kevin. We have to go, but I don't want to.

Mum's talking to Kevin. 'Never mind, my darling, we'll be all right. Takes more than bureaucracy and a few rats to kill me off. When I could see the light I'd have been far more frightened of plunging down into the darkness. Now I can't see the sky or the trees. But how will you grow up, little toad in a hole? I'm not giving up. I won't be shoved into an institution or let Abbie be brought up by strangers.'

And I wish I was little again. I wish I knew where Daddy was. I wish I was Kevin sitting on Mum's knee just laughing and crying and being sweet. But I'm not. I have to go down there with Rosa, and I'm terrified.

Finn used to let us play in the cellars when it was raining. There's a boiler-room, and that's where me and Rosa go. There's this tunnel behind the boiler. I don't want to go down there, but Rosa says beggars can't be choosers. We follow the tunnel. It's just big enough for me to stand up in, but a grown-up couldn't. Rosa's not much taller than me, but Mum would have to stoop. You can feel water all around you and the walls drip and there are all these weird noises. Every time a tube train goes past there's a hurricane, and you can hear crying and singing and animals snuffling. It's like you're in another world with just memories and echoes of London. I'm glad Rosa's with me, but we don't talk. It's freezing. The tunnel goes on and on. We don't know which direction we're going in or what time it is.

Suddenly there's water, and this man's shining a torch in our faces and yelling at us. I think he's a policeman arresting us. He opens a door at the top of the tunnel and shoves us through, and when I look down there's a river where we were standing.

We're in another tunnel, only this one's dry, and the man's wearing shiny black boots and a shiny black raincoat, like a bin bag on legs. And he yells at us again and says we're stupid. 'I'm fishing bodies out every day, and I'm sick of it. Used to be a nice peaceful job, but now it's like bloody Piccadilly Circus down here. Bad enough having to work Christmas Eve, never mind rescuing ruddy damsels in distress.'

Rosa whispers, 'Go on, Abbie, do your Oliver Twist number.'

So I tell him we've got nowhere to live and we've got to look after a baby and an old blind woman. At first he's suspicious. He asks if we're on the run from the police. Finally, he says there is somewhere safe we could stay. Says he'll help us if we don't tell anyone.

So we follow him for miles, until we come to a door in the wall of another tunnel. He takes this key off a ginormous bunch of keys jangling on his belt and opens the door, and we're in this room with bunks and posters on the wall and there's even a light. When he switches it on all you can see is dust.

"Snot Claridges, but you'll be safe here. They built this place as a bunker during the war long before you two was born. There's an air filter, and you get the warm air blowing in from the Central Line. I'm giving you this key, but if anyone catches you and asks how you got in here, you found it, right? Dunno why I'm doing this, but I'd rather think of you down here than in the morgue. You're lucky I've got daughters your age.'

Under his bin-bag hat he's got a real boozer's face with a cauliflower nose all red veins. He gives us the key, and me and Rosa hug him. He says we're under Marble Arch. He gives us this map of all the tunnels with red arrows marking the dangerous ones that flood. Then he shows us how to get up to the street. We pass all these people living in tunnels. He disappears, and we're standing in the Edgware Road, and it's eleven when we get back to the hotel.

Mum's asleep with Kevin, but we wake them up, and we all agree we've got to go, so we pack three bags.

Mum says to Rosa, 'You can choose a Christmas present.' Rosa kneels on the floor and rummages through all our clothes and books. She chooses a green silk scarf and a book of fairy-tales for Kevin. Mum says we must only take what we can use or sell. I stare at my teddies and the little plastic people I used to play with and the red silk dress Mum looked beautiful in at my birthday party when I was nine. We have to leave them all behind for Finn and Eileen.

Then Mum takes my arm, and we leave Room 325.

Lunch

I sit in the noisy, crowded pizza restaurant in Holborn and watch David and Annette approach my table. On the phone David sounded abrupt and suspicious, as if Jenny was an illness he'd recovered from and didn't wish to be reminded of. I'll bring my sister, he said, as if Annette was the twentieth-century equivalent of garlic and a crucifix.

David is formally dressed in a three-piece suit and looks more defensive than at our last meeting three years ago. His sister is wearing a tailored apricot-coloured suit and carries a smart black leather brief-case, exactly like her brother's. Her short wavy hair is determined to stay black, and her efficiently made-up face is tense with anxiety. I smile at them, wondering what they put in their briefcases and what they have to be so anxious about. I'm wearing a shabby black corduroy jacket, jeans and a grey polo-neck jumper. David's thick pink hand brushes against my fingers; he kisses his sister and puts up the menu as a barrier.

I set out to charm Annette, as David is obviously immune. 'How lovely to meet you at last. Jenny was so fond of you. I've heard so much about you – the papers are full of you. I must say, you're doing awfully well. A friend of mine was saying just the other day perhaps you'll be the first woman to become a Labour prime minister.'

Flattery always works. 'Well, there's a long way to go. Homelessness is one of my main concerns. There are lots of these dreadful bed-and-breakfast hotels being used to house homeless families in my constituency, and I want to see an end to it. Far too much council housing has been sold off. There shouldn't be any beggars or homeless people on our streets.'

'I'm sure there won't be, if you have any power.'

'Yes, quite.'

'This year East Plumford, next year the whole country.'

'Yes,' Annette replies, without any sense of irony. 'Now we've got these bloody Tories out, and we'll see some real socialism in action. I can't wait.'

'Did you get that ministerial job?' David asks his sister, flushed with sibling rivalry and family pride. He wants me to know they're important, not to be trifled with.

'No. Maybe next time. I'm a bit old now, although they don't tell you that, of course.'

'Old?' I say. 'Rubbish. Politicians and popes go on for ever. It must be very exciting to be part of the ruling party.'

'I don't seem to do much ruling. Mostly it's chairing meetings in my constituency and helping to organize this wonderful party at the Dome.'

'Ah yes, the pride of the new millennium.'

Determination is etched into Annette's unflinching brown eyes, her stubborn mouth and firm jaw line. She might go far, if there's anywhere worth travelling to in this feeble democracy. Her brother has a less developed public face, but I sense his hostility. Fool. Jenny can't really have been interested in him.

'I know how busy you both are. Thanks so much for coming along. Now, we haven't got long, so let's get straight to the point. Annette, any luck?'

'I'm afraid not.' She snaps opens her briefcase, and I glance at the interior of neatly organized layers of documents in crisp, geometric leather pockets. 'I asked my friend at Kensington and Chelsea Social

Services, Verity, to look out for them, but all she could find is this letter. They should have been taken into local-authority care, but they seem to have disappeared from the hotel at Christmas 1994. It must be them; the names are right, although I can't understand why Jenny is described as elderly.'

'She might have aged,' I say. The brother and sister turn to me, and I feel I'm on trial between these two lawyers.

'Jenny's about my age,' Annette says, 'and when I last saw her, four years ago, she looked considerably younger. Are you suggesting she might have some mysterious illness that ages her prematurely?'

'Something like that.' I decide it would be a waste of time to try to explain the laws of my universe to this formidable one-lifer. 'This is a photo of my – of Abbie, taken just before they disappeared. Perhaps you could give it to the police and to your friend in social services?'

'That's pointless,' David says. 'My daughter, Alice, changed beyond recognition between the ages of nine and twelve. Let me just see that – yes, I think it must have been her.'

He stares at the photograph and my hope almost chokes me as I ask, 'You've seen Abbie?'

'It must have been about three years ago. I was visiting my grandmother, and I parked near your old house – Phillimore Gardens . . .' David blushes, emotion floods his face like water in a rusty tap, and I wonder again what the two of them got up to there. 'A little girl ran in front of my car, her face covered in hair and tears, like a maenad. I nearly knocked her down, but I braked just in time.'

'Why didn't you talk to her? Follow her?'

'I wasn't sure it was her. I wasn't wearing my glasses, and I was in a hurry –'

'How could you just let her go?' My voice is naked with rage, and they stare at me in surprise. From that moment our civilized lunch becomes a battle.

'And what have you been doing? Have you been to the police?' David glares at me.

'No.'

'Your common-law wife and daughter disappeared three years ago, and you made no attempt to find them?'

'There were special circumstances.'

'Then I think you'd better tell us what they were, or you might find yourself the subject of a murder investigation.'

'Jenny and I had a quarrel.'

'What about?'

'I don't think that's any of your business.'

'It is if you want to stay out of prison.' Annette looks at her brother in astonishment. The tables are packed close together in the restaurant, and people around us are riveted.

'You're married, aren't you, David?'

'What's that got to do with it?'

'How long have you been married?'

'Twenty years.'

'Jenny and I lived together for twenty-five. Sometimes we were happy, and sometimes we infuriated each other, just like you and your wife, I expect.'

'Was it a violent quarrel?'

'I never hit Jenny or Abbie. Jenny decided to leave me and take her daughter with her.'

'Then why didn't you make a proper settlement and make sure they were all right? You're rolling in money.'

I struggle to stay calm. I know that antisocial things happen when I lose my temper. 'There wasn't time. As you must both realize, having known her for so long, Jenny's very impulsive. One day I thought we were a family, the next she announced she couldn't bear to spend another night under my roof. She went off to pick Abbie up from school and never came back.'

'And what the fuck did you do about it?'

'Calm down, you two, the age of duelling is past. Let's just agree that we want to find them now. Show me this note Jenny sent you, David.' He snaps open his own briefcase, revealing another meticulous leather interior, and hands Annette the note, which she reads slowly while David and I avoid each other's eyes. 'What is all this melodramatic rubbish? *Is* Abbie your daughter, David?'

'I wish I knew,' David says.

'And what does she mean about not letting Leo anywhere near your life? *Are* you so evil?' she asks me with an amused grin.

'The devil incarnate.' I smile back.

'God, what a mess you heterosexuals make of your lives! But you know – at the time I didn't take it seriously – last time I visited Grandma she burbled something about Jenny. Said she'd been to see her with Abbie and Jenny looked a hundred. But Grandma's gaga, poor old thing.' Annette looks at her watch and says abruptly, 'Well, I really don't see what I can do about it. I've got to get back to the House for PMQs.'

'No! Don't go. We need to plan some kind of campaign.' David doesn't want to be left alone with me. 'Let's have a coffee and think about what we should do next.'

'But it's quite hopeless. They could be anywhere. It's no good being irrational and emotional about this. Jenny could easily have just disappeared. The National Missing Persons' helpline takes eighty thousand calls every year. She could have married and settled in Australia or South America. Knowing her, she probably has. She always was obsessed with men.'

'Could we give Abbie's photo to Interpol?' I ask.

'But she will have changed. And they'd only be interested if there's a suspicion of foul play, which you claim there isn't.' David glowers at me.

'I'd hardly have got in touch with you if I had anything to hide, would I?'

'Honestly, David, I think you've been reading too many thrillers. Women leave their partners every day. They're not obliged to tell anyone where they've gone. Perhaps she had some reason to think Leo would get custody of Abbie. I'm afraid we can only find her if she wants to be found. Perhaps we should advertise, making it clear that it would be to her financial advantage to turn up again. I assume it would be?' she asks me.

'Of course. I can't bear to think of them living in some sleazy squat. Even if Jenny doesn't want to live with me I could buy them a flat and support them.'

'Fair enough. Which papers does Jenny read?'

'None,' David and I say together and then avoid each other's eyes.

'I see she hasn't changed. The last of the nineteenth-century heroines. Apolitical, unemployable and addicted to romantic love. Poor Abbie.'

'Jenny is quite tough,' I say after a pause, feeling I should defend her against the cold blast of Annette's judgement.

'So was Emma Bovary, and look where it got her. Well, I have a country to run.' Annette stands up, prompting a competition between David and me to pay for lunch. My gold card wins. David clings to his sister. 'I'll help you get a taxi, Annette.'

'I'm quite capable of getting my own taxi.'

'No, really, we need to talk. We don't see enough of each other these days.'

'I think we see quite enough of each other.'

I kiss Annette's cheek, bow to David and stride off into the crowds of Holborn. David and Annette are walking just in front of me, and I hear their conversation.

'Well, I think he's absolutely charming. Jenny was very lucky. What was the matter with you?'

'Women are so gullible. It's quite obvious he's a sadistic, phoney bastard. I bet he treated Jenny badly even if he didn't actually bump them off. And he's so pretentious. Did you see the way he bowed to me? Nobody bows nowadays.'

'He's intelligent, stylish and handsome. There's no evidence he's a sadist. I'd fancy him myself if he wasn't a man.'

I let them walk ahead, leaving me alone with my visceral hatred of David. Everything about him irritates me: his voice, clothes, face – can this be jealousy? But my *alter ego* is Harlequin, the heartless trickster, not Pantalone, that pathetic old cuckold. Confused, I get on a bus and sit upstairs, staring out of the window as we swoop down Oxford Street and Park Lane. I remember when Tyburn stood at Marble Arch. In the old days I would have sorted David out with a flash of lightning or a dose of the plague. What's the matter with me? He virtually called me a murderer; I could sue for slander. But I don't want to be vindictive. I just want to find them. Annette's right. They could be anywhere.

Mothers

Abbie must be the same age as Jenny was when I first met her. Bright, beautiful, trouble.

Today when I return to my lonely flat there's a note from Sibyl, in ancient Greek, inviting me to the Institute of the Mothers. What can she mean? Jam and knitting hardly seem to be her kind of thing. Perhaps I mistranslated. Anyway, it's in Eaton Square, so it obviously pays to be motherly. I'm going there on Friday for lunch. I'm rather looking forward to some home cooking and some pleasant female company.

I turn up in the smartest clothes I still possess: a navy suit, red silk tie and clean white shirt. The gilded cage of a lift opens straight into a drawing-room done up in bordello Renaissance style with gold elephants, pink tart's-knickers curtains and shiny hunks of furniture jostling to impress. I'm surrounded by women of a certain age, expensively overdressed.

I act delight, turn on my charm and circulate, kissing hands and complimenting sagging allures. Far from feeling allured, I'm desperately wondering what they want from me. The names of these women mean nothing to me, although once or twice I vaguely recognize a flash in a much-mascara'd eye or brooding power in a lipstick-smothered mouth. My confusion is increased by the champagne to which I help myself. For a moment it seems as if the circle of women around me is distinctly menacing, and as each one approaches me with gracious coos

I feel like the blindfolded victim of blind man's buff, being spun around and tossed between his persecutors.

Then I spot Sibyl, who is, or so I think, a friend. Over these last few difficult years, as I have tried to turn myself into an ordinary man, she has been my style consultant. I've spent hours on her couch, and she has been marvellous; her only limitation is her tendency to talk about herself. Normally, when I see her, I'm horizontal. Her size, or lack of it, always surprises me. She barely comes up to my elbow as she stands beside me in her black silk suit, her tiny hands bulging with gold and jewels like a kleptomaniac toddler. 'Sibyl,' I hiss, 'what is all this about?'

But she continues to smirk and says in a loud voice, 'After lunch we'll have a private screening.'

'A film? How nice. Holiday snaps?' I ask, stifling a yawn and furious with myself for not inventing an urgent two o'clock appointment.

'You could call it a family film,' Sibyl says with a gracious smile.

Lunch is a magnificent buffet. On these occasions you have to choose between eating or talking, and I'm afraid I shamelessly go for the greedier option, refilling my plate again and again. I exclaim with delight as I recognize tastes I haven't experienced for centuries: a dormouse stuffed with pine kernels; a boar's head with tusks of macaroni and prunes for eyes; sparrows pickled with fermented rice; chrysanthemum leaves with walnut dressing; ostrich brains; *gefilte* fish; Caribbean crab cake; salmagundi; almond flummery; honeyed quinces; and Aztec chocolate with chillies. I must say that transhistorical globalization has its moments. I realize that these women have moved far beyond the rice puddings one might expect at a Mothers' Institute meeting. Then I notice that the magnificent centrepiece is a marzipan subtletie, something I haven't seen since the court of Louis XIV. It seems to represent the final scene of *Don Giovanni*. 'Most ingenious,' I beam as I break off the Commendatore's head and eat it.

My friend Byron used to say that an old man's senses are all in his stomach, and as the world contracts to the enchanted circle of my overflowing plate I hear the background chatter of women's voices. Gushing, I imagine, about grandchildren and clothes and recipes.

I'm just digesting my second cup of coffee when there is a flash and the room tilts. You might think it would be impossible for an old ham like me to be surprised by such tricks, but I *am*. There are not many earthquakes in Belgravia.

The ostentatious reception room vanishes, and we appear to drop, painlessly, down through several floors to a mouldy cave-like place. We are in one of those corridors of lost time hidden beneath the blandness of late-twentieth-century London. Our mass-produced clothes are replaced by flowing dark robes, and the circle of women who surround me have that unmistakable Walpurgisnacht look. Their makeup has camouflaged faces of terrifying power, and they are all staring at me. My hand rises defensively to my stubbly chin and shaggy hair – a sort of eternal seediness has crept in since I became a solitary – as I fiddle with what was once my tie.

Sibyl steps towards me. Not the tiny caged oracle or the elegant Viennese shrink but a third persona, fierce and angry, a prophetess. Her voice becomes husky and resonant, full of terrible certainty. 'Sisters, daughters of Chaos, we have come together today to forget the low-key moans and grumbles of an age when nobody believes in anything. You all know Leo – most of you have slept with him . . .' (I look more closely at the faces glowing in the strange greenish light. I recognize an Egyptian priestess I had an affair with when cats were still sacred and the abbess of a great convent near Siena, who captivated me in the eleventh century. In fact, they are all vaguely familiar. I feel like an old roué – or, rather, an old ruin. As I listen to Sibyl and watch the faces around me I realize that all my most important experiences have happened with women, through women, because of women. If anything has battered me it is the forces of sex and, more recently and painfully, love. I stop wondering why they have invited me.) '. . . Others have encountered him at the Metaphysical Bank. For four years now Leo has been my patient, if one can use that word of such an impatient and fundamentally selfish man. How often over those years I have tried to share my experience with him, to show that I understand. As I don't have to tell you, we're all immortals under the skin. If you prick us we don't bleed, and if you stab us we don't die – can't die. But Leo doesn't want fellowship with me or with anyone else. He feels he has been ill-treated by Jenny, a flighty young woman of a hundred and two. It is the fate of all of us to depend on the creatures we create, and this has happened to him. Jenny, tired of his vanity and frightened by his underworld connections, fled with her daughter, and Leo wants to know what has happened to them.'

Sibyl pauses. I feel absolutely sure that she does know what has happened to Jenny and Abbie and that she could have told me at any time in these last four years – if I'd grovelled a bit more. Women always talk about masculine vanity as if they had none themselves. I know the film show is about to begin and have a horrible suspicion that I am to be its star.

'Leo has been going through a crisis. Like all of us he has changed form many times over the centuries, but now he has lost his nerve. We are all accomplished at parthenogenesis. Without wishing to boast, I have given birth to myself a hundred and twenty-seven times, in as many different languages, in every part of the world. In a few years it will be time to be born again, and I'm toying with various ideas – a New Age prophet in India? A scientist in Antarctica? You will find a suggestion box in the hall. I am hardly an *ingénue*, but I do still have an appetite for life.

'Leo, however, feels that he has had enough. I don't have to tell you how innately conservative men are. The old monks who persecuted us for so long used to say women and the devil were the same. What we do, perhaps, have in common is a certain curiosity and enthusiasm for change. Well, Leo has lost that. He wants one life, one woman. He has fallen in love, not just with a very ordinary woman but with this troubled and faithless age.

'I have brought you all here today because I don't know what to do with him. Has an immortal the right to choose mediocrity? In the old days, of course, he would have been chained to a rock and vultures would have pecked out his liver for eternity. But in these wishy-washy liberal times crime and punishment are as muddled as everything else. Now we're going to watch a few scenes from his long and questionable life, and I'm going to ask you to be the judges of whether Leo should be allowed to abdicate his immortality.'

I look around for some kind of screen. What do I expect? A sort of immorality play, I suppose, for what can only be described as a hardcore audience. I wouldn't want to try to shock any of these women, and I'm not exactly Disgusted of Tunbridge Wells myself. Anyway, how can a man be scandalized by his own life?

This is what appears to happen, as we stand in a circle in that metropolitan cave. Jenny appears. Seeing her again, I'm so moved that I want to rush up to her, but Sibyl, standing beside me, whispers harshly, 'If you touch her you'll never see her again.'

Jenny is very young. Of course, she never looked very old, but there is an adolescent gawkiness about her as she stands, twisting a shiny black corkscrew of hair around her finger, tears dripping down her face on to the corset that bites into her firm, young body with the savagery clothes used to manifest towards women. She's standing on a dusty stage, and I inhale again that smell of sweaty costumes, dirty props, greasepaint and hot gas lamps. Standing over her, glaring down distastefully at her crumpled face, is a thin young man in an evening suit. Me and not me.

'I just want to go home. I'm so tired. We'll start again in the morning.'

'Stop snivelling, I can't hear a word you say when you whine and sob like that. Your diction is bad enough to begin with. Now blow your nose and get it right this time. Bertie has gone home, but you can do it without the piano. Remember, you want them to go; you're happy for them. The song rather loses its point if you're dissolving into tears as you sing "Goodbye-ee, don't cry-ee". Now pick up your props, that's right, white feather in your left hand and the flag in your right. Come on, hurry up, it's two o'clock in the morning.'

'What about you, Leo? Which one shall I give you?'

'I don't know what you're talking about.'

'You can't wait to shove our brave boys off to be slaughtered.'

'They're not going to die. You've been listening to defeatist propaganda.'

'I know what happens in wars. My father told me about the Boer War – anyway if you're such a blooming patriot how come you're not buggering off to France?'

'Really, Jenny, how ungrateful you are. What would you do without me?'

'I'd be better off without you, bullying and yelling at me all the time. Might find a fella what cares about me.'

'*Who*, not what. Well. I'm really rather shocked by your heartlessness. I'd like to join up, of course I would, but unfortunately I had TB a few years ago. I have a medical certificate.'

'You've got a bloody great chest of 'em. Medical, birth, marriage – well, they can't stop a girl from thinking.'

'I certainly wouldn't wish to do that. Your intellectual life must be a great strain.'

'See, there you go again. Sarcastic bastard. Think I'm stupid, don't you?'

'What thoughts you have, Jenny, were put there by me. That's right. Blow your nose. Tears accomplish nothing.'

'I'm only crying 'cause I'm so bloody angry.'

'Your nose is red; you look hideous. Now get on with your routine. You'll never be much good, but you may at least learn to sing in tune and dance in a less ridiculous fashion.'

At this point I step forward into the shadows between the phantom Leo and Jenny, who vanish as I protest, 'I never said that! I got impatient, of course I did; she was lazy. But I was never cruel to her.'

'He's in denial,' one of the Mothers remarks wearily.

'She should have dumped him then instead of hanging around for another seventy-five years,' the ex-abbess agrees.

Sibyl pulls me firmly back into the ring of watching, judging women.

'You don't help yourself by barging in like that. You can't change the past.'

'But that wasn't the past, that's the whole point. I never said those things.'

'How do you know? These are projections of Jenny's memories. Why should you remember that scene more accurately than she does?'

'So she is alive!'

'Shut up and watch.'

Jenny reappears, and I feel again that hot soreness in my eyes, that clutch of pain where my heart would be. The pain of mortality, which I'm asking these pagan harpies, these subterranean goddesses, to grant me. For a few hours they have put on recognizable forms to lull me, as Sibyl has done for the last four years. I look around for her and see her, tiny, at my elbow.

Jenny is not quite so horribly young this time. A few years of working the halls and sleeping with me and dozens of others have coarsened her a little. Twenty-one? 1918? About the time the naïve and ridiculous George appears on the scene. I don't remember resenting him in the least. I have never suffered from jealousy, one of the sillier mortal failings. However, here I am, or here my illusion is, in my old Harlequin costume, bending over the beautiful girl in white.

That period when women suddenly changed shape, lost their curves, grew legs like stalks out of the mystery of the long skirts that had enveloped them for so long. Even to a jaded palate like mine the emergence of long, silky legs and arms is exciting. And Jenny's are so beautiful. Watching my phantom self stroke her leg as he peels her stocking off, I can feel again that soft place behind her knee where the blue veins meet like tributaries of a river in the white estuary of her flesh. My hand twitches out, craving her remembered geography, but Sibyl slaps it down.

'Do you let him do this?'

'Who?' Her voice is not yet elocutionized; it still has the flat, hard vowels of the East End. A gritty, resilient voice, not a victim at all, as I want to point out to the watching judges.

'Your dozy law student. He's waiting out there again in the street; he's probably been waiting all night. I never saw such a booby. Just as well he was too young to go to France for more than a few months. A sitting duck if ever I saw one.'

'He loves me. You *would* think that's daft.'

'How can you say that, Jenny? Haven't I devoted myself to you for years now, day and night. Specially night.'

'Only because you think I might be a star and earn you a few bob.'

'Is that what you think? That I'm after your non-existent money? No, my dear, you'll never be a great variety artiste. At best you'll struggle in the provincial halls and revues. Your best performances aren't in public at all but in private, in bed, with me . . . What's the matter?'

She jumps up, kicks me in the balls and leaves me doubled up in agony, foolishly clutching her stocking. Even if he is only a misremembered Leo I feel the pain and humiliation again, her power over me. Jenny rushes out, not caring that one of her legs is bare or that her elderly landlady is watching as she runs downstairs and out of the house. 'There, you see, she was the bully, not me,' I insist to Sibyl as the images fade. 'She was always attacking me, leaving me . . .'

But instead of sympathy I hear a savage howl of laughter. All the Mothers are cackling at me, even Sibyl, their faces wild masks of contempt and mockery. I want to run away, but I can't break out of their circle.

Finally, between gasps of hysteria, Sibyl speaks. 'Oh, Leo, thank you. I haven't laughed like that for centuries. You can go. We don't have to sit through seventy years of domestic cliché.'

'It may be cliché to you, but to me those scenes with Jenny are the central experience of my life – a life almost as long as yours.'

'Exactly. What use is immortality to such a banal fellow?'

'What use has he ever been? Roaming the centuries like a rutting stag.'

'He deserves to be a human being.'

'Let him die in the arms of his girl, his old girl, if that's what he wants.'

'You're wasting our time, Sibyl. If I didn't have such aeons of it I would be quite angry with you.'

They all turn away from me, and I'm afraid they'll disappear before I can ask the question that has been disturbing me for many years. 'Before you go – I don't suppose we'll ever meet again – please tell me, am I Abbie's father?'

I long for some oracular answer. Instead, their figures grow dim and fade until I'm alone in that cave-like place, surrounded by damp mist. I feel a wave of panic and rage, as if they are, all of them, really my mothers and have just abandoned me. Then the cave revolves, so fast that it makes me feel sick.

I find myself standing in a grey concrete tunnel, its walls covered with graffiti. I am alone except for a ragged old woman who sits on the ground on a filthy sleeping-bag, wheezing on a mouth organ. I stoop to give her a pound coin and follow the tunnel up a ramp into the bright afternoon of Hyde Park Corner.

Lost Children

Nowadays you'd hardly know Mum is blind. She looks after the kids and moves around the tunnels so confidently, like she's come to a private arrangement with the air to suspend the laws of gravity. She never falls over as she glides swiftly, tapping her stick so fast it sounds like a machine. She used to go on talking to people after they left the room – in the days when we lived in rooms – but now she seems to know exactly whom she's talking to.

For the first year we thought they'd come and evict us from our bunker. Them, the people up there with capital letters and bossy voices who tell people like us where and how to live. I know about London property prices, I stare at the windows of estate agents every day. Even subterranean dumps like this must be worth a fortune. We never again saw the man who gave me and Rosa the key. If this bunker belongs to the Underground, maybe they have no use for it. Or maybe it belongs to nobody, a forgotten scrap of the city that sweeps past us, above us, leaving us down here among the rats and the lost children. Or maybe we're allowed to squat here in return for looking after all these children the local authorities don't want to pay for. Most of the time we're too busy to think about it.

It's not exactly Buckingham Palace, although that might be their sewers we can hear. It's really damp, and you can hear tube trains and buried rivers roaring and gurgling just the other side of the wall. Our décor is minimal: scarred and mouldy concrete, grey with patches of green on it. There are thirty-six triple bunks, and the space between them is plastered with faded posters reminding us that careless talk costs lives and a day out in Margate is a treat for all the family, so we're still fighting some kind of war down here, and I don't think we're winning. The floor's covered with sleeping-bags and mattresses we've scavenged from skips, with a few gas stoves and camping lamps and, in one corner, a chemical loo. Beside it, in big cardboard boxes, there's our clothes bank. You have to dig into it every morning to find something that more or less fits. Now, after four years, the rats stay away most of the time, discouraged by the clean floor.

But kids keep turning up. They've run away from children's homes or from families where they've had three stepfathers or, like Jonathan, from brothels. Several kids have only one kidney, after being kidnapped and operated on by body terrorists. The toughest ones don't stay. Rosa left very soon; she's squatting in a house at Crystal Palace. Kevin's five now; he lives with us part of the time. Rosa often comes to see us, and last time she came, Wednesday I think it was, she read us a story in a tabloid newspaper headed URBAN MYTH? It said gangs of feral children roam London, organized by an evil, ancient, blind hag from a labyrinth under Mayfair. Something ought to be done about it, the article said. But nothing has been done. We're still here.

All these kids have been through some kind of hell, but Jonathan is the most badly damaged. He's fourteen, so battered by the outside world he thinks this place is wonderful. When Jonathan was six his mum, who was drowning in debt, sold him into 'adoption' – actually a children's brothel in Tooting, where for five years he was so viciously sexually abused that now he refuses to take his clothes off, even when he's asleep and shakes whenever he has to talk to an adult male. When he was eleven the brothel was raided by the police and Jonathan was put in a home where the abuse, he says, was almost as bad and the food worse. Six months ago he found his way to us. Mum usually says this place is only for children, because there's not much space, but I don't think she'll ever be able to throw Jonathan out. He does more than any of us, makes me feel lazy. When he first came to live with us Mum asked what Jonathan looked like, and I said, 'Like a broken angel.' He's really fit, tall and slim with coppery skin and green eyes with thick lashes and gorgeous curly black hair – wish I had his looks. But he's frightened of everybody, and he jumps about six feet if you touch him, and he's always screaming in the middle of the night.

Jonathan organizes the children into begging gangs, like Rosa used to, and leads them all over London. Mum doesn't exist as far as the authorities are concerned, so she can't claim any kind of benefit. The children's daily explosion on to the streets of the city feeds and clothes us all and keeps us in camping lamps, candles and paraffin. Each morning Jonathan rounds them up like a sheepdog, about forty kids, although there are only thirty-six bunks. A few extra kids always manage to sneak in and sleep on the floor. Jonathan's nervous voice becomes more confident as he bosses the younger children, reminding them which streets and areas of the park they have to cover and what time they're to meet him at McDonald's. I know Jonathan needs to pretend to be a kid again, to hide in this gang of kids.

But I don't want to any more. Kevin sits beside me and watches me watch Mum. It's like living in a school, only it's always break and the kids never go home. They're fighting over a bag of crisps, screaming for the attention of the only teacher, who happens to be my mother. Can't remember the last time I had a proper conversation with Mum. Even in the middle of the night there's always a kid who's sick and another one banging on the door, crying to be let in. God, I hate kids. I'm glad I'm not one any more, and I'm never going to have any.

'Shut it, Kevin. I told you. She'll be here some time today.'

'Will she bring me a present?'

'I dunno, do I? I expect so.' Rosa usually stops at Hamleys to shop-lift an expensive toy.

Fifteen already, and I never meet any good-looking blokes. All these runaways, running to my mother, but what about me? Where do I run to? It's awful having a saint for a parent, specially when everyone thinks she's my great-grandma. I hate it when other grown-ups tell me she's wonderful. She's got two kids on her lap and another wound around her neck.

I go over to the communal clothes and hunt through the stale smelly heap of musty jumpers, jeans and T-shirts, pulling at them angrily. I hate these clothes that belong to everybody and are loved by nobody. I remember the fitted wardrobe in my old bedroom, the ironed dresses, skirts, jackets and coats, shelves neatly stacked with underwear, jumpers and tops, dozens of pairs of shoes poised on the touchline at the bottom, as if they were about to dance off. Finally my fingers touch the slippery Lycra of a swimming costume. It's a lurid pink, as far as I can tell – colours never look the same down here – and it looks too small, but it'll stretch. I roll it up into a sausage, stuff it into the front of my dungarees and try to slip out of the door, which is supposed to be locked but is usually left open during the day.

Kevin wants to follow me, but I scream at him, 'I never want to see another bloody kid in my life!' So he joins the group around Mum. She's trying to organize breakfast, the usual stale biscuits and muffins donated by local cafés when they're past their sell-by dates. Sometimes the food makes us all ill, but that's better than starving. For Mum's hundredth birthday party, two years ago, a big hotel in Park Lane gave us a box of rancid profiteroles and a crate of overripe melons.

I grab an almond croissant, break off the greenish bit and pick my way through the debris of mattresses, sleeping-bags and discarded clothes to the door. Then I run off up the tunnels before the screaming kids can follow me. I want to run through the park, dart in and out of the shops. Perhaps I'll sneak into a hotel and have a free bath or shower in an empty room when nobody's looking. Don't know what they'd do to me if they caught me. Anyway I can take care of myself: Finn, that mugger in the park, that drunken businessman who tried to rape me in an underground car park last month – I don't really understand how it happens. I'm scared I'll kill someone one day.

I run through the underground labyrinth, passing cardboard boxes and tents and concrete patches neatly furnished with tables and chairs found in skips. Everybody I pass knows me; they all nod or say a few words. Me and Mum have been down here longer than anybody. People don't exactly move, but they *are* moved on or disappear to visit relations or join squats. These are my people. They might fight and drink and take drugs, but they look out for each other; they're tolerant because they've seen it all. They despise the nerds who live and work up there, in what they sneeringly call the 'real world', where money and cars and mortgages and jobs rule the idiots who imagine they are free.

Maybe they hate all that because they've never had it. It's different for me. When Mum tells me stories about our life, the point's supposed to be that she was right to throw it all away and come down here. And because I love her and she's a good storyteller I used to want to believe her. But what's so great about being poor and smelly and hungry and cold like us? Whatever she says now, we were perfectly happy in that house. She was young and beautiful then, and Dad was rich and good-looking and our house was like something out of a movie. If that was hell and this is heaven, then it's all gone pear-shaped.

I push open the metal door that leads to the pedestrian subway under Marble Arch. On the ramp that leads up towards the park I stand in a patch of sun and hold my face up to it, closing my eyes. The sun wakes up my skin as I sniff the grass, traffic fumes, hot dogs and dog shit. I inhale the heat and cool spray from the fountains above and stretch out my arms. Then I'm off again, darting up to Speakers' Corner where the nutters, many of them my friends, are ranting.

I look around for someone to finance my afternoon. A lot of kids my age and younger give blow jobs to dirty old sods for cash. Yuck. I do want a boyfriend, only he's got to be young and beautiful and rich. Mum's told me stories about adoring men who used to hang around outside the theatre when she was young, waiting to take her out to dinner in expensive restaurants. One of them would do very nicely.

I go up to a well-dressed tourist of about forty who's taking photos of a Muslim fundamentalist loudly demanding Sharia law for England. Best smile. 'Excuse me, my wallet has been stolen. Would you mind lending me five pounds so I can get home? I wouldn't normally dare to ask, but you look so kind. If you give me your address I'll return it to you, of course.'

'Are you student?' he asks with a German accent.

'I'm an art student actually. But I'm an orphan, and I have to work in a restaurant every night to support myself. I live in Barnet, miles away.' He shrugs and hands me a ten-pound note and his business card with an address in Frankfurt. 'That's very kind of you. I'll send you the money next week. Goodbye, and thanks.' Rosa's training. Tell them what they want to hear, never tell the truth if a lie will do; men are a softer touch than women. If I had another tenner I could take some food back for the others this evening.

I'll still be in time to catch the morning rush-hour crowds pouring through Marble Arch Station. I buy a can of Coke to moisten my throat and stand near the main exit. I feel like singing that Spice Girls hit I heard in the Virgin shop yesterday, but that won't melt any hearts or loosen any wallets, so I gaze soulfully ahead and sing it again and again – cheesy but good for business – 'Let me take you by the hand / And lead you through the streets of London . . .'

Some of them ignore me; others mutter 'Fucking scrounger!' or 'Why don't you get yourself a job?' A middle-aged prat in a suit hovers near me, licking his lips nervously, staring at my tight T-shirt like he's never seen tits before. I glare at him, and he slinks off. About a quarter of the punters throw ten- and fifty-pence pieces and even one-pound coins into the baseball cap at my feet. A guy in a grey suit smiles at me and throws down a foil-wrapped pack of sandwiches.

When I'm singing like this I always hope I'll see my dad. Five years now I've been looking for him all over London. I don't know where he went after he left Phillimore Gardens. He'll walk around that corner wearing a blue silk shirt the same colour as his eyes, with Johnny on a lead. And Johnny will recognize me, and Dad will fall down on his knees and I'll tell him to get up and forgive him and Johnny will lick me with his stinky tongue and I'll lead them back to Mum and we'll get a taxi back to our old house and Rosa and the others will come and visit us and I'll become an MP like Auntie Annette and I'll make the government build proper houses for everyone. Only he never does come.

Just when my throat's beginning to hurt I see a policeman barging over to demand to see my busking licence, so I pick up my takings and dart through the tunnels back to the park.

I unwrap the sandwiches. Ham salad on granary bread – not bad. Then I count the coins in my baseball cap: nine pounds sixty-five, enough to buy chips and chicken nuggets to take back to the bunker later, and I've still got dosh to spend on myself. I buy another Coke at a kiosk and sit on the grass with my picnic, wallowing in London. Later I'll buy an ice cream and window-shop all over Oxford Street and Bond Street. I won't have to sneak into a hotel for a bath now, I can pay to go for a swim at the Serpentine lido and have a shower and a hair wash afterwards. Then I'll go and read in the library until it closes at seven. It's not education exactly. I just read whatever takes my fancy: newspapers, novels, art books, poetry. Happy, I lie on my back on the grass, my eyes shut, the sunlight filtering through my lashes.

'Hiya, darling.' Talk about a weird couple. I stare up at Mum and

Rosa arm in arm, and it's Beauty and the Beast. Please put me down like an old dog when I get to forty. Rosa glows with health – you'd think she was all innocent if you didn't know her – and Mum looks like an old witch who's come creeping out of the shadows to turn her into a frog. If Rosa were a frog she'd set up a business selling slime to the other frogs. Rosa's a real looker now; must have another rich bloke after her. She's got her red hair done in little curls, really short and glossy, and she's wearing this awesome dress I saw in the window of a shop in Bond Street, two hundred squids, creamy linen with little red-and-black flowers all over it. Mum's taller than Rosa, her scraggy white hair's pulled back into a bun and her chalk-white face is almost transparent. I don't often see her in daylight. Her black jumper and long black skirt are full of holes and loose threads, and she's got bare feet in huge leather lace-up shoes. I'm so scared she'll die on me. She looks bloodless, and when I stand up and hug them both I notice she smells of ancient damp.

Rosa takes an atomizer of perfume out of her bag and squirts her. 'Thought your mum needed a bit of air.'

I can feel Mum's bones through her clothes. I try to make a joke of it. 'There's not much meat on you, is there? If you were ninety years younger you could be a model.'

'I thought I'd just sit here in the sun and listen to some Bach,' Mum says. She sits on a bench with the Walkman I nicked for her birthday, and me and Rosa fuss around her, bring her a cappuccino and a cinnamon Danish. We all sit on the bench in a row, munching and talking, and Rosa does her big-sister act. 'You want to watch it, Abbie. It's crack city round here.'

'I can look after myself.'

'Any hard drugs down in that bunker and I'll murderate you. Kevin gone off with the others then?'

'They left about half an hour ago. You might still be able to catch them up.'

'Why don't you go with them any more?'

'I'm too old. I don't want to spend all my time with a bunch of screaming kids.'

'Guess what. I'm getting married again Saturday.'

'Who is it this time?'

'Some old Algerian geezer, Omar's uncle. Needs the passport. Two thousand squids in cash, and I don't even have to spend the night with him.'

'Rosa, that's bigamy, or is it trigamy? They'll catch you and put you in prison.'

'Can't catch me. I'm the gingerbread woman.'

'What happened to your last husband?'

'I left him, innit?' Rosa laughs, a big warm laugh that carries you along with it. What I like about Rosa is she never gives up. 'Tell you what, though, I'm going to save for the deposit on a house, with cable TV and a dishwasher and a shower and central heating and that. And you and me and Kevin and your mum's going to live life to the Reilly till she dies, poor old blind bat.'

'What about all these other kids?'

'We'll squeeze the little buggers in somehow. Get you in on this marriage scam soon as you're eighteen.'

'I don't want to marry some horrible old man.'

'Nah, we won't then. Tell you what, next time I get married I'll pay for you to have singing lessons. You've got a gorgeous voice and you're really pretty. You'll do all right, Abbie, love. And my Kevin's not stupid neither, although he's about as much use as a chocolate teapot.'

'He's only five.'

'Don't they take a long time growing up, though?'

'Not long enough,' Mum says sadly, and I realize she's been listening to us instead of Bach. 'Still, come to think of it, I didn't have much childhood either.'

'Abbie says you was stunning when you was young. Ain't ya ever going to change that skirt?'

'It doesn't matter what I look like now. But I do worry about you, Abbie. There's no point in nagging you all the time and cross-examining you – what can I do, after all? – but you're so young and gentle and London's such a dangerous place.'

'Gentle? Your Abbie?'

'What do you mean?'

'She might talk posh and look cute, but she's well able to look after herself. I wouldn't want to mess with your Abbie. The karate kid, Finn used to call her.'

'Karate?'

'One of them martian arts. Once, years ago when Kevin was a baby and we was all living in Eileen's dungeons, we was in the park after a good day, sharing out our dosh, when this big guy comes up and pulls a knife on us. I was ready to hand it over and run, but your gentle little daughter, she just stares at him – doesn't even touch him, honest – and this six-foot bloke backs away, looking absolutely terrified. This bloody great knife he's been pointing at us is pointing at him. Thought he was gonna commit hurry-curry right there on the grass.'

'Did he?'

'Dunno. Didn't look. Couldn't get away fast enough. But she's no wet lettuce.'

'You never told me that, Abbie.'

'Thought you'd be frightened.'

'I am.'

'Look, darling, worrying about Abbie ain't worth a spit on a grave. You look after yourself. You look like something Dracula's cat brought in.'

'I'm scared to go out since that article appeared. What if there are policemen or journalists looking for me?'

'Don't you worry, love. If anyone bothers you I'll sort them out. I'll do my classy voice and say we're just on our way to Harrods and you're my grandmama. One of them rich eccentric old bags. I should be so lucky. Tell you what, though, I did go through Harrods on the way over here. Bloody amazing, innit?'

'I haven't been there for years.'

'Shall we go there now? Oh, I forgot, you can't see. Well, there's mountains of toys, about five thousand different sorts of teddies and the most gorgeous dolls you ever saw. I'd love to get them all for my Kevin. Downstairs, there's every kind of food in the world. I'd get fat as a pig, me, if I could shop there every day.'

'I hope you didn't nick anything.'

'Couldn't, could I? They've got security blokes with eyes in the backs of their heads. Cameras everywhere. Nearly picked up a sugar daddy in the perfume department, only his fucking wife turns up.'

Time Bites

So I'm one of them now, a hairless monkey. I wonder if those women who made such a fool of me really were the original Mothers poor old Faust was so frightened of. Sibyl was distinctly menacing that day, not a benignly listening shrink after all but a shape-shifter.

I can feel my own shape shifting, and this time it's final. How exciting to think that if I fall under a lorry tomorrow that will be it. Of course, I can't be sure, it's not as if I have a certificate of mortality. Yet I *do* feel different. Weaker, more emotional and irrational. I must have been longing for death for years to be so titillated by the prospect now. I spend hours gazing at myself in the mirror.

Over the last few weeks the reflection that I first began to notice in the mirror fifteen years ago has clarified and developed. I don't know if I like what I see, but to see it at all seems rather wonderful. The very texture of my skin has coarsened, I'm more hirsute, and lines have appeared around my mouth and eyes. Minor ailments I never suffered from before queue up for my attention: headaches, indigestion, a nagging tooth. These details fascinate me as if I were my own homunculus, every bulging vein and tiny mole the surprising outcome of self-experiment. It's good to have a body that can suffer and perish. But what if I die before I find Jenny and Abbie? I'm quite sure that they are both still alive. They didn't tell me directly of course; prophetesses and oracles and sphinxes never do. Ambiguity is their trade.

The dog responds to me differently now. Instead of staring at me shiftily it gazes at me with devotion, licks me and climbs up on to the bed to sleep at my feet. I lie here, a nightly knight on my last crusade, my monument the blue-and-white striped duvet I once shared with her. I sleep and eat less than I used to do, fuelled by a dry, feverish, nervous energy that fires volleys of memory into the air. In the morning I feel heavy and am often unable to remember if I have slept at all. The dog bounces up with moronic optimism, whines for breakfast and wags its tail, insisting that the day is worth having. It drags me out for long walks, and I let it pull me for miles in all directions. There is always the possibility it will find them, sniffing their chemicals like truffles in the city dirt.

Now I have no more power over her, no magical privileges to glide me through the urban labyrinth. Just as my body feels coarser, so the city itself seems bigger, heavier, more formidable. This is a crazy task, a hopeless quest.

Another week trudging the hot streets. But now I see only the solid mass of bricks and mortar. Doors and windows no longer dissolve to show me vignettes from other lives. I get blisters and the pollution makes my eyes red and sore as I'm pulled by Johnny, driven by memory. There are so many London streets I've walked down with Jenny at one time or another. Memory itself has changed. Just as my skin has become thinner and more sensitive, so the tissue of my past life has become translucent. I see through the aggressive chic of this King's Road to the old, dark, grim street dominated by the Chelsea Palace; through the cars and buses of Gower Street to her room above the horse-drawn traffic where we spent our first nights together. And these memories are painful, like a bloodstained plaster ripped off a wound. I realize now that all those years when I thought I was living for ever I was half dead, protected from the vivid entrails of experience.

As I walk with the dog across the park from Knightsbridge to Bayswater I'm accosted by a gang of screaming kids, about twenty of them, begging ferociously. I hand out a few coins and flee. Then I turn back to stare after them, wondering if Abbie could have been among them. Fifteen now, but she might look younger. If Jenny suddenly looked like the nonagenarian she was after I destroyed her contract, then she probably wasn't able to work or look after Abbie. They would have sunk very quickly to that social level conveniently ignored by politicians and directors of the Metaphysical Bank: people who sit in doorways, sleep in cardboard boxes and eat food that has been thrown away by the rest of us.

A month ago this screaming flock of children would merely have disgusted me. Now they make me feel uncomfortable, and I even wonder what right I have to my bulging wallet and the Chinese lunch in Queensway I'm looking forward to. Have I become one of those ineffectual hypocritical ninnies, a *bien pensant* liberal who shakes his head at the status quo, does very nicely out of it and sheds crocodile tears over misfortunes he has no intention of alleviating? Seeing that anarchic little army of homeless kids makes me realize just how cut off I really am from the life of the city I'm trying to penetrate: streetdumb, streetblind, streetdeaf. I understand no more about those children than about the pigeons in my roof.

How uncomfortable this mortality is. No wonder they complain all the time. Already I've lost my perfect complexion and the natural heavenly fragrance women used to admire so much. The sun has reddened my nose, and insects, which used to stay away from me because my signals were all wrong, have been devouring me, leaving hideous red lumps all over my arms. As I stride off on my marathon walks I sweat and my sweat stinks. Although I've spent a fortune in Boots on remedies for all these repulsive little problems, I'm stuck inside this big, smelly, clumsy, hypersensitive lump of a body.

I sit down to write my letter of resignation to the Metaphysical Bank. There's no tradition of retirement; I'm the first and probably the last. It's illegal for a mortal to be a director, and I wouldn't want to be pursued by the lawyers of the Metaphysical Bank who are, quite literally, Furies.

So here I sit, toying with words at my grubby desk in my seedy room. I used to be able to write fluently in both Latin and Greek, but something has happened to my mind. All that comes out now is a rather stilted English, a sort of grovelspeak: Greetings to the Eternally Wise, my illustrious Fellow Directors of the Supreme Economic Mysteries . . . Even when I take out the capital letters it looks odd.

They'll find out anyway, of course. I've already skipped three board meetings. There's plenty of money, particularly since I sold the house. I could simply move it to an ordinary bank; there'll be quite enough to see me out. I would like to leave Abbie something, if only I could find her. Age is catching up with me rapidly. Every time I look in the mirror I see new lines, broken veins, grey hairs. If I look like this on the outside, who knows what state my internal organs are in? I might have a stroke or heart attack any minute now.

As well as this new hypochondria, I catch myself feeling afraid for the first time. After all, my fellow directors of the Metaphysical Bank aren't corporate pussycats, they are Nero, Boudicca, Genghis Khan, Lucrezia Borgia, not people to trifle with. Of course, those aren't the names that appear on our letterhead, just their most successful incarnations. What if they revive some medieval clause that allows them to confiscate all my money? How I wish now I'd studied law instead of alchemy and conjuring.

The sheet of paper in front of me has turned into a love letter to Jenny. Suddenly my pen flies, and I know exactly what I have to say: this is the letter I never wrote you in all those years we were together. Somewhere in the universe there's probably a sort of poste restante black hole where our unexpressed feelings and unspoken words go. Here is an undelivered letter to join them. Knowing you will never read this, I'm freed of shame and embarrassment. I'm experiencing love backwards, you see, as a searchlight, dazzling and transforming our mutual past. I was disingenuous when I said you won't read this. Actually, I believe you will and that we will die in each other's arms. At this moment that's the height of my ambition. Are you laughing, Jenny? Oh well. Love *is* absurd, I quite agree. I have to see you again so that we can have a good laugh about it together. When I think how seriously I used to take myself, with my transhistorical investments and my multinational deals, fussing over what to wear and what kind of bathroom and kitchen to have. No wonder you left me.

But I've changed, Jenny, I really have. I know you have, too. I picture the gawky little girl from Hoxton, your raw, pale face with huge dark eyes burning with vitality like dark ponds in a snowy landscape. It was that energy of yours that persuaded me, ten years later, that you deserved a stab at immortality. Until very recently, you see, I never doubted that immortals were better, and better off, than mortals. We were the universal grown-ups, watching benevolently as you poor little creatures with your pathetically short life spans and infantile self-importance strutted around your sandpit.

But when you renounced your immortality you made me question thousands of years of complacency.

I see you in the hallway of our perfect house, that morning you came back from the Metaphysical Bank, your face covered with scratches and bruises. When you waved your contract at me I thought you were stupid and ungrateful. I didn't love you or Abbie enough to interfere with what I knew was a form of suicide. That night I used my bag of alchemical tricks to destroy your contract. At midnight, alone in the house, I told myself you were dead and Abbie was lost to me for ever. I went into her room and stared at all her clothes and toys: that magnificent doll's house, probably much grander than any house she will ever live in again; the rows of toys staring at me reproachfully; the books that were to guarantee her cleverness; and the cupboard full of miniature designer clothes. All the paraphernalia of the late-twentieth-century princess I had intended her to be.

I often looked for her as I walked or cycled around London, but after a few months I accepted that you would both have changed. For the first time since you were fifteen I had no control over who or where or what you were.

Who am I looking for now as I blunder down the streets of London? An old woman of a hundred, perhaps, accompanied by a young girl. I'm sure you're out there somewhere. Pretty soon, my darling, I'll look as ancient as you and we can totter towards death together. When I find you. If I find you.

Abbie in Love

After meeting Mum and Rosa in the park I have a swim in the Serpentine. The lido's as hot as Oxford Street and just as crowded. I love swimming underwater, but goggles are expensive, so I shut my eyes and launch myself in a sitting dive down into the murky, greasy water. Shouts and laughter are switched off, and I'm sealed in watery consciousness, moving blindly. I love being invisible like this, silent, alone in the forest of legs. My path through the water is blocked by something. I open my eyes and mouth in surprise, and the water attacks my lungs, flows up my nostrils and forces me to come up, spluttering, still entangled with the thing, which turns out to be a boy.

'Sod off,' I yell. I'm sort of disappointed when he does because he's about my age, too young to be a dirty old man. He sits on the grass looking worried, his white legs dangling in the tepid brown water. His eyes keep swivelling back to me, and I keep pretending not to look at him. I mess about a bit, do somersaults and handstands in the water, wanting him to go on looking at me, feeling his eyes slithering all over me like the sunlit water. Then I turn and swim towards him. As his face comes closer I see that he's smiling and really fit, with dark hair and green eyes and this long, slim body. He leans towards me and says, 'I think you need a new swimming costume.'

'I know. I'll ask Daddy to get me one tomorrow.'

'Is your father here with you?'

'Oh no. Daddy doesn't like me coming here, he wants me to join this incredibly expensive health club, but I think it's more fun here.' Funny thing is, he believes it. I don't overdo it, don't do a silly voice like those yah girls me and Rosa used to want to strangle when they came out of Harvey Nichols with all their bags. He's not thick; he just thinks all kids our age have homes to go to.

After we've showered we meet and walk together towards Knightsbridge. I tell him I'm at Benenden and I've just taken my GCSEs. I want to see how much I can get away with. Then I ask him questions.

'Well, it's a long story. Why don't we go for a walk and I'll tell you. I hope you're not shockable.'

'Right. Shock me,' I say. We sit down with our backs against a tree that shades us from the hot afternoon and share his bottle of water.

'I bet your daddy wouldn't like it if he knew you were talking to someone like me. What's your name?'

'Charlotte.'

'I'm Steve. Do you know why I came swimming?'

'To pick up girls?'

'To get clean. I've been sleeping rough for the last year, ever since I ran away from school.'

'Why don't you go home?'

'I haven't really got one. My parents died in a plane crash when I was twelve. My father was a diplomat, so we were always moving around, from one cocktail party to another. After they died I was sent to this really strict public school where they beat me and tried to make me join the cadets. I'm a pacifist. During the holidays I had to stay with my uncle in Yorkshire. He's terribly religious, and whenever I listened to my Walkman he said I'd go to hell and there was no TV, and he was always accusing me of telling lies. He really hated me because I was in love with my cousin, you see, his daughter. Guinevere. We used to go up on the moors together and ride our ponies and go for walks. Then she got pregnant, well, you can imagine, there's not much else to do up on the moors with no TV. He knew it was me, and he threw me out of the house. So last summer instead of doing my A-levels I ran away and came to London. It's hard sleeping out. I nearly froze to death last winter. You need a lot of drugs and booze to keep going. I don't get much to eat, and I've been beaten up a few times.' What a load of bollocks. I stare at his clear eyes and skin, clean T-shirt and jeans and new, expensive trainers. 'I expect you'll bugger off now. You wouldn't want anything to do with somebody like me, I'm your parents' worst nightmare of a boyfriend.'

'There's only my father. Mummy went off with the chauffeur when I was six. She lives in Malibu now. They surf all the time. She's one of the most beautiful women in the world. She's been offered lots of parts in movies; film producers come and queue up around her swimming pool, trying to get her to sign a contract, but all she wants to do is surf and make love to Johnny. He used to be Daddy's chauffeur, but now he's her second husband. He's well gorgeous; you wouldn't believe his pecs. I went to stay with them once, but she was embarrassed to have such an old daughter; she kept pretending to everyone that I was her niece. Then she said Johnny was after me – well, he was, but nothing happened.'

'And your father hasn't married again?'

'He's still in love with Mummy. And he says I look just like her, so he's terribly possessive. When he's away on business he pays this private detective to follow me around . . .' I look over my shoulder, and he looks terrified. 'But I think I managed to lose him in Harrods.'

'What does your father do?'

'Buys and sells things. Houses. Oil. Movies.'

'Really? I bet you live in an amazing house.'

'Well, it is quite big, considering it's in the middle of London. There's the indoor pool and the library and the billiards room and the ballroom. I have my own suite, of course.'

'Maybe you could smuggle me in some time.'

'I think that might be dangerous. Daddy's heavies are all over the house. And they're really heavy. Like, guns and hand grenades – I don't think you'd stand a chance if they caught you.'

'So how come you're sitting under a tree talking to a creep like me?'

'I just have to get away sometimes. It's all too much: the formal meals even when I'm on my own, the personal shopper waiting outside my door each morning, the charge cards, the dinner invitations.'

'Sounds awful. I would have thought you'd be away at this time of year.'

'Well, of course, I could have gone on a cruise or to Thailand with Daddy or to stay with our friends in Cans.'

'Where?'

'Cans. It's in the south of France.'

'I don't think you pronounce the "s".'

'You do if you live there.'

There's a brief silence. Then he leans towards me, smiling gently, and puts his hand on the back of my neck. Just as well I smell of shampoo for once. He smells of soap and old money; last time he saw a cardboard box was when he pulled his new computer out of it. He kisses my neck and then my mouth. It's not too disgusting. He doesn't fumble in my knickers, just puts his arm around me. 'Shall I walk you home?'

'Better not. Someone might see you and shoot you. I have to go. We have dinner at eight. Horse dervrers and three courses. It's such a bore, and I have to change into an evening dress.'

'Will you meet me here tomorrow at two?'

'OK.' I try to sound cool and walk off in the direction where my house is supposed to be. That's the odd thing about lying; you almost convince yourself. Later, I turn back to the bunker where I lie awake all night thinking about him.

The next day I don't really expect him to be there. I think he must have seen through my Charlotte story, must know I live in a squalid hole and don't even go to school and always wear the same clothes because I haven't got any others. He'll disappear, like all good things.

The tree is in a straight line from the bandstand nearest to Knights-bridge; you can just about see the Serpentine from it. I've no idea what kind of tree it is: a love tree, a happiness tree. I'm not in love. Don't be silly, I hardly know him, can hardly even remember what he looks like: tall, thin, dark straight hair, green eyes. It's his voice I remember, warm and funny, and the hardness of his body whenever we not quite accidentally touched. There are lots of boys in the park who look like him, and all the trees look the same, too. I panic and imagine us waiting by different trees, missing each other, never finding each other again.

Then I see him a few yards away, smiling at me through the trees. I run up to him. I want to fling myself into his arms, but I stop a few inches away. It looks so easy in films.

'I didn't think you'd come,' he says.

'Is this the same tree?'

'Yup. Nineteen from the bandstand. I counted yesterday.'

We smile at each other and slide down, our backs to the tree. 'You're looking smart. Got an ironing board in your cardboard box?'

'No, it's a new shirt – I mean I nicked it.'

'Yeah, right. Bet you're a master criminal.'

'Well, I looked up your dad's company last night, and it doesn't exist.' We catch each other's eyes and grin. We sit and talk until our throats are so dry we have to go to a kiosk to buy drinks. Then we go back to our tree and talk some more until it's nearly dark. Can't remember what we said, only that I felt completely relaxed beside him, watching his long fingers play with the grass. We don't exactly tell the truth but stop telling quite such elaborate lies. As the last daylight disappears he says, 'I will walk you home anyway. Wherever it is.'

I jump up nervously. 'No. Really, it's OK. See you here tomorrow?' And then I disappear. I wonder if he feels as abandoned as I do. As if the sun's blood in the Serpentine comes from my own arteries.

The next day he kisses me again. We become one of those couples who lie on the grass panting and groping, couples I found absolutely gross until this summer. His body feels so strange at first, firm and leathery, prickly where he hasn't shaved. When we touch each other I realize there really is this huge exciting difference between men and women; blokes aren't just girls with knobs on, as Rosa used to say. Then I find it's cold, even in the sun, if his arms aren't around me. When I come back here alone each night to lie in my bunk, my nerves scream with need. Withdrawal symptoms. I thought I was tough but it hasn't taken long to hook me completely. I still don't know much about him; we're still calling each other Steve and Charlotte. We don't actually make love. We're too shy or something. Both virgins as it turns out. For a week it's as if London, the whole world, shrinks to that patch of grass under a tree. Just us two, our bodies and voices.

'I want to go to bed with you and stay there for ever. Come home with me.'

'So you do have a home?'

'OK, I admit it. But my family are away for another two weeks. We could go there together.'

'Where is it?'

'Kew. It's a very boring house.'

Boring means central heating, a bathroom, a fridge stashed with food in a kitchen you can cook in, comfortable beds, television, video, his own room. 'Are your parents rich? What does your dad do?'

But he won't answer. In the end we don't go back to his house that night but stay under our tree, falling into each other's arms as darkness falls. The hot summer night in the park, full of lovers' groans and grunts, a sort of invisible orgy: couples climbing in and out over the fence, black and white and brown, gay and straight, picking each other up. Every night we stay longer it's harder to let go of each other, and I have to run away, he's so determined to see me home. I don't think it occurs to him that I don't have one, that what was for him a romantic fantasy is my whole existence. He thinks I'm middle class like him because of the way I talk and the books I've read, doesn't realize homeless doesn't mean mindless, doesn't realize I read those books in public libraries and haven't been to school since I was nine.

That tree. We never should have left it. We were safe and happy there. Even that one afternoon it rained we just sat there. We should have stayed there until the September winds came. It was my fault. I kept thinking how amazing it would be to spend the whole night together, doing all the things other people do: eating proper food, sitting on a sofa, watching a movie, having a bath, sleeping in a bed. His boring house was my idea of heaven, and I went on and on about it until late one afternoon he says, 'Let's go then.'

'Where?'

'Back to my house. I can't stand watching you disappear into the trees again. I hate waking up from dreams of you and finding you're not there, as if you were a nymph and lived in this tree and couldn't leave it.'

We stand up, and he brushes the grass out of my hair very gently. The park gates are still open, so we don't have to climb out. He buys us hot dogs and Diet Cokes – he always has money. I watch him take the pound coins and five-pound notes out of his pocket, so casually. He has no idea what some kids have to do for a pound, let alone five. After we've eaten we run, holding hands and laughing, dancing across the traffic at Hyde Park Corner, on a crazy high because we're together and we've finally left the park.

We sit upstairs at the front of the bus, wound around each other, laughing and talking, drunk on each other. After a bit I realize he's talking non-stop because he's nervous. When we get to his house I don't ask any questions, mainly because I don't want to answer any. I treat his house like a hotel, just glance at the kitchen and living-room, which are quite scruffy, not half as stylish as the house I lived in when I was little.

'Shouldn't you phone your dad?'

I gawp, suddenly realizing he believes my story – or at least some of it.

'Oh no, it's OK. He doesn't worry about me.'

'Do you mean you usually stay out all night?'

'No!' I see the word 'slapper' flashing behind his eyes and realize I have to phone my non-existent father just to reassure Steve I'm not going to give him AIDS or a dose of crabs. So I go to the phone, which is on the other side of the room, luckily, and punch the first eleven numbers that come into my head. It rings and a bad-tempered old lady squawks, 'Who is it?'

'Hi, Daddy, it's me, Charlotte. Just to let you know I'm spending the night at Julie's. I'll be back in the morning. Lots of love. It was his answerphone.' I slam the phone down on the querulous old lady.

'Are you hungry?' He opens the kind of fridge I knew they'd have, big enough to live in, enough food to feed an army. We sit at the kitchen table and stuff ourselves with bread and cheese and salami and beer and chocolate ice cream. It's cosy, and I'm looking at him all the time, so I don't even notice the family photographs all around.

Then we go upstairs and he says, 'We might be more comfortable in my parents' bedroom.'

It isn't comfortable at all, dingy and a bit grubby, but at least there's a huge bed and we fall into it. We've never really been alone together before. In the park I was always worried we'd be arrested or get our bare bums bitten by police dogs or be gang-banged by one of the groups of crack freaks that roam the parks at night or get kidnapped by body terrorists. So I never really let go.

But here, alone with him in the dark room in the silent house, we discover each other for the first time. All of each other, without having to excavate through jeans or stop at the last minute because we don't have a condom. One night in the park we wasted a whole packet because neither of us knew how to use one. Ten of them lying on the grass like moth-eaten pink balloons.

I never really noticed I had a body before. I'd masturbated, of course, but not much because it makes my bunk creak and Mum sleeps in the one below. I thought sex was something furtive and nasty that happened in locked rooms and public loos. It was forced on you or you did it for money.

He's just as nervous as me. He's shaking as he finishes undressing and rolls towards me, his eyes shut. The body he presses into my arms is soft and clumsy and thin, like mine, not the heavy hairy thing I'd always imagined a man's body to be. We're like two children clinging together all night. That first night we hardly sleep. We talk, whispering at first because it all feels so mysterious. Then, as we realize we really are alone in the house, we talk and laugh aloud. We begin to get the hang of being naked and dance around the room. When I was little, friends used to come and play in my garden on hot summer afternoons and Mum used to spray us with the garden hose. That's the sort of mood he and I are in, wild and exultant.

At about three in the morning we go down to the kitchen to get some cans of beer and make some toast and peanut butter, and at five we have a shower together, our wet soapy bodies and greedy mouths sliding all over each other. 'I've been wanting to do this ever since I first saw you in the water,' he says. 'You looked so sexy.'

'What, in my swimming costume three sizes too small?'

'That's what was so erotic. You were bursting out of it, the elastic cut into your buttocks and squashed your tits and when you did hand-stands these long brown legs came shooting up, and then you stood up and all this thick dark blonde hair fell down over the fragile curve of your neck and your shoulder blades . . .' And he kisses the bits of me he's talking about and I feel completely loved. I catch sight of us in the steamed-up bathroom mirror, our bodies the same height and colour; don't know where I begin and he ends, like that story Mum told me about the creatures who lost their other halves and wandered around the world searching for them.

Then we borrow his parents' bathrobes and go down to the garden to see the dawn. We sip mugs of coffee and stare at each other, faces again now, not just bodies. Steam from his coffee winds around him in a kind of mist. I can see his beautiful throat, strong and vulnerable, and the triangle of his chest where his father's white bathrobe begins. I'll never forget him, standing there in the early morning garden. His house, like all the houses overlooking the garden, is so solid and sure of itself. It's easy to get out of bed in a house like that. Last winter there were mornings in our bunker when it was so damp and cold that our sleeping-bags and all our clothes felt like they'd just been washed and put away in a fridge.

'Are we shocking your neighbours, do you think?'

'Hope so. They're so fucking smug. I suppose you'd better phone your father. He'll be worried about you.'

Caught in my own tangled bloody web again. I stare at him, only wanting to get back into bed with him to sleep and make love and talk until some time in the next century. 'It's a bit early to phone. I'll go back soon. But – I wish I could stay here. When do your parents get back?'

'Next Wednesday. Won't your father be furious if you stay here?'

'Would you like me to?'

'Of course. It's amazing to see you here. As if two worlds had merged, my dreary old family and that magic, poetical dream world we made under our tree. Will you come back tonight, then?'

I nod and come up with the old chestnut about leaving my purse at home to get two quid out of him. I don't like scrounging money off him but don't fancy walking all the way to Marble Arch. He comes to the bus stop with me, and we kiss, and the minute I step on to the bus I start to miss him. I arrive back at the bunker at about eight, crawl into my sleeping-bag and don't wake up until five.

When I tell Mum I'll be out for the next few nights she just strokes my face with those weirdly sensitive fingers, like insect wings. Do insects think with their wings? She does, or at least it feels like it as her dry, cool fingers brush over my eyes, sucking out my feelings. As far as I can gather she was the toast of London by the time she was my age, so she probably thinks I'm a bit retarded. She doesn't say any of the obvious things, like be careful or use a condom, so I wind up saying them myself. 'Don't worry. I'll be fine. He's really nice. Definitely not a psychopath. Be back Wednesday at the latest.'

I get on the bus and fly across London. Don't think I've ever been so happy. Never will be again. I'm even pleased *he* isn't on the bus with me because I can concentrate on thinking about him, enjoy my trance as I remember every moment. I don't even worry about what's going to happen when his parents come back from holiday and find us installed in their bed. It all seems so clear. We've found each other. We'll always be together now.

From the bus stop it's a long, gloomy walk to his house. Those suburban streets with their sinister peace and insulting prosperity. When you haven't got a home yourself you hate people like that, with their two cars and matching china and spoilt brats who'll never have to beg. But I'm in such a good mood I don't even want to throw bricks through their twee windows or set fire to their naff Neff kitchens.

There's a glass panel in his front door, and we stare at each other through it, making faces. Suddenly I'm in that mood he puts me in, light and funny and happy. We kiss, pretend to fight for the only deckchair in the garden, drink a few beers on the lawn. When it's nearly dark we move inside his house. Doors and windows are open, filling the rooms with the smell of grass and soil and flowers that have been baked in the sun all day. At sunset his kitchen and living-room blaze, and I feel triumphant, because this is the point at which I used to up and run. Now I don't have to, we're settling in together for the night and we'll wake up together in the morning. By the time it's dark we're heaving around on the sofa, unbuttoning and unzipping each other. 'You don't even know my real name,' he mutters into my ear as he kisses it.

'Doesn't matter. Don't tell me. I don't want to know.'

'It's Ben. What's yours?' I open my eyes and pull away from him. Ben and Kew are too much of a coincidence. I need time to think. Then, somehow, thinking is the last thing I want to do and I slide back on to the sofa with him. 'Well? What *is* your real name?'

'You'll have to guess it. Like Rumpelstiltskin.'

'Yeah? And what do I get when I guess right?'

'The miller's daughter.'

'Don't fancy her. I'll have you instead.'

So we leave the lights out and play these very sexy games. I think we make love in every room in the house that night – on the living-room floor, on the stairs, in the shower, in his room when he's showing me his poetry. Before I can read even one poem he has his hands down my knickers again. 'At it like rabbits,' I say dreamily. 'I don't want a litter of baby rabbits. Where are the condoms?'

He stops for just long enough to say, 'We've run out. Sorry. But if you do get pregnant I'll look after you.' Every so often he comes up with a list of girls' names: 'Jane? Jemima? Jessica? Jezebel? Jeannie? Janet? Juliet? Jade? Jamila? Jill? Jewel? Jacqueline? Jocasta? You've got to tell me if I guess the right one.'

'You're miles out.' I can't call him Ben. I want his identity, like the house, shrouded in darkness. Later that night we end up in his parents' bed again, my head resting on his shoulder as we talk. He's relaxed, happy, absolutely sure of me. I pretend to float away with him on this cloud of ecstasy, but really I just don't want to talk, don't want to see the pieces he keeps sneaking into the jigsaw.

'So you're determined to go on being a mystery woman?'

'I'm just sleepy.' My head is between his legs, an incredibly comfortable place to lie.

'Have a sleep then. Do you ever wake up in the night? I often do, at about four in the morning.'

'Next time that happens it'll be me waking you up, lying between your legs. I like it here.'

I nearly drift off to sleep, but his voice is relentless. 'I thought you might like to meet my sister, when they all get back from Italy. She must be about your age. How old are you? Oh, so you're not going to tell me anything. Fine.' There's an edge to his voice now; he knows he's doing all the talking. Mystery was great under the tree, but now he wants a real person. Not me. All I can think is, please don't tell me your sister's name is Alice. 'I didn't hurt you, did I? I got a bit carried away, you see. You're so beautiful, I think I'm a bit in love with you. A lot in love with you. Only I think you're overdoing the enigma thing. Is it a really embarrassing name, like Hepzibah or Maud?'

'Nope.'

'Will you stay tomorrow night, too? Please. We can just laze around in the garden – I'll try and keep my hands off you. I've worn you out, haven't I? Go to sleep now. Darling. I've always hated that word when my parents use it. It sounds so phoney. But I've got to call you something. Let's go to sleep like this, in each other's arms.'

He does, and I pretend to. We're both lying on our sides, and he's behind me, curved to fit my spine and bum, his arms wrapped around me, his hands on my tits. Comforting, heavenly, perfect, as if my body is finally in the right place. I lie awake remembering all the stuff I want to forget, the bitchy thoughts that crash into your head at four in the morning. Last winter I was moaning on about never seeing Dad again when Mum suddenly said, 'He probably isn't your real father anyway.'

'Now she tells me! So who is?'

'Well, possibly, probably, your Uncle David. Sorry. I always meant to tell you.'

'But you're not supposed to sleep with relations.'

'He and I aren't related. But we did fall in love with each other – twice – the second time was the summer before you were born. So . . .'

'But he was married. He had kids. Mum, you old slag!'

'Old, certainly. Too old to worry about what people think. Only as you grow up you do look more and more like David and not a bit like Leo – his genes are an unknown quantity. I'd rather not think of you as half Leo. I think David would help you if anything happens to me.'

'So why didn't you tell me all this sooner?'

'Because it's all so vague, we'll never really know. Because today I realized I can't last much longer. Perhaps it doesn't matter – neither of your possible fathers is around anyway – but I just wanted to clarify things.'

'Well, you didn't. I'm totally confused.'

So here I lie beside my – brother, cousin? If I get pregnant the baby would be my niece or nephew – Mum's double grandchild. Oh God, I can't handle this, it's doing my head in. His breath on my back, his sperm inside me, his voice in my ears for ever. Nobody else's hands will ever do. We fit together like the branches of a candlestick, like two puppies curled together in a basket.

Morning sneaks between the curtains and we haven't stirred, although in my head I've given birth to his baby and spent the rest of my life with him. I turn towards him inside his arms, and stare at his face, sleeping so innocently and peacefully. Impossible to believe that anything we've done could have been wrong. But I remember there's a legal side to it – his dad who might be my dad is a solicitor after all – the authorities who wanted to put me into care and Mum into a home, who say, Thou must not sleep with a girl under sixteen, specially not if she's your sister. And if thou doesn't know if she's thy sister? Thou shouldst find out, plonker.

I slide out of his arms, back into the cold, lonely, Benless morning. He doesn't wake up, and I'm not sure I want him to. Don't want him to see me crying. I go downstairs and force myself to look at the photographs on the walls and the shelves I've worked so hard at not seeing. There's Uncle David, of course, collecting his degree; and Grandma

Molly before she went bonkers, sitting in that room where I used to read and cut up pictures from magazines; and that little bitch Alice, looking shifty in a party dress; none of me and Mum – not surprising, I bet Muriel hates our guts; and Auntie Annette, looking all Great Dictatorish. I'd been in that house a couple of times before, last time when I spent Christmas there, but now I allow myself to see it I remember it perfectly well. So, of course, I have to get out.

I hesitate in front of their lavish fridge. I'm not hungry, but I know I'll remember that fridge later when I am and wish I'd helped myself to some cheese and yoghurt and ham. If I steal anything he'll think that was all I ever wanted from him. Not at first, for a few days it will hurt like hell. But after a week or two he'll find reasons not to love me.

I don't take anything. Just walk out of his front door.

In the Bunker

Can't sleep, can't eat, can't talk. My body and mind have floated off and left me here on my bunk. Can't live without him. And now I've got to.

Mum's hand comes up like an old lizard and touches mine. She's talking to me, perhaps she's been talking for some time. 'I'm here if you do want to talk.' What's the point? How could she understand the first thing about love? Silence is like another bunker where I shelter. 'Never give all the heart,' she says.

My voice comes back from Planet Ben. 'What was that about heart?'

'Never give all the heart. It's a poem by Yeats, very sound advice. Or, as Dorothy Parker said, "Don't put all your eggs in one bastard."'

Reluctantly I giggle. 'Mum? Can I ask you something?'

'Of course.'

'You once said Leo wasn't my real dad. So who was? Was it Uncle David?'

'This is going to sound crazy, but I don't know.'

'But he could have been, right?'

'Yes, it's possible. Why do you ask me that?'

'Because it's suddenly become the most important question in my life.' Before I can explain Jonathan rushes in with his flock of screaming, laughing kids.

Night after night I lie awake, vaguely aware of the others sleeping around me and Mum tossing with useless sympathy in the bunk below. It's all your fault. I've inherited your problems and your crazy, impossible story, and now you're going to go and die and leave me even more alone. Ben's the one thing I've ever really wanted, and I can't have him because of you. I hear the first tube trains rumble and roar on the other side of the wall. Strange how I always know when it's morning, even down here. I feel weak and dizzy, but I have to keep going back to the tree where we used to meet.

I pull on my clothes and go out before the others are awake. The morning is dark, Marble Arch seethes with rush-hour traffic and the park is carpeted with soggy leaves and conkers. Usually autumn is my favourite season, but this year there's no beauty anywhere. As I approach our tree the cool sun is rising. I shiver and wish I'd pinched a second jumper from the communal box. I sit on damp leaves, my back against the tree, and cry for him. Every day I have to go back to the tree to check there's nothing there. The rain would have soaked through letters anyway. But there aren't any letters. Ben doesn't know where I live, and I've no idea what he is doing. Probably gone off to university like middle-class kids do. Left home, left London, gone to a new park with new girls in it.

I sit with Rosa in a café in North Audley Street. 'But you can't just do nothing on millennium night. Go on, Abbie, love, do yourself a favour, have another muffin. Well, I'm going to, anyway, it's screaming "Eat me." Never seen you look so scraggy. You used to be quite pretty. Tell ya what, you come out with me and Ali millennium night. We'll watch the fireworks, river of blood – sounds like fucking Hannibal Lector, innit? Then I'll fix you up with one of Ali's friends and we'll go clubbing down Brixton. You listening, Abbie? Gawd almighty, that cappuccino must taste like chicken soup, all that salt water you're dripping into it. What is it, darlin'? You don't want to get yourself all of a trauma 'bout some bloke. You pregnant? Want me to help you get rid of it? Mind you, might be an idea to hang on to it. Be a bit of company for you when your gran finally kicks the bucket, and if you've got a baby they'll have to give you a flat. Kids are great, I love Kevin to bits now he's grown up a bit. Might have some more babies with Ali – wouldn't mind having a football team. He's all right, Ali is, treats me like a fucking lady. Sixth time lucky. You ought to try this marriage scam like me. Oh, Abbie, stop crying. It's like talking to Viagra Falls.'

I see Rosa, hear her and feel her sympathy but can't form any words. She gives me a fiver – Rosa's always generous when she does have money. I get on the bus. I'm shivering in my denim jacket, the warmest garment in the communal box that still fits me. I've had a cold and a sore throat for weeks. From the top of the bus I gaze down on shops tarted up for Christmas, on the city I have no place in.

Last time I did this journey it was a summer evening and I was full of health and trust and hope. It's raining when I get off the bus and walk down the quiet suburban road. He can afford to despise it. I'm afraid I won't recognize his house in the dark. It looks exactly like all the others yet somehow shrieks at me. Bikes and cars outside, these people have so many possessions. Mum and I could move with a couple of carrier bags – if we had anywhere to go – but Ben and his family would need a fleet of lorries. Soaking wet, coughing, I stand outside his house. All the curtains are drawn, five windows gawp back unhelpfully. His room is the middle window upstairs, the dark one. I just stand there staring up at his window, don't know what I want – I want him. If there was a light on up there I'd throw stones up and make him see me, make him let me in. Perhaps they're all downstairs, sitting around a fire in a room as full of winter evening as it was once full of summer and us. Leading their proper family life in their proper family house. If Ben has gone out he might come back and see me and then somehow it'll be all right and Uncle David will understand and they'll let me in.

I stand there for hours, freezing, getting wetter and wetter, not thinking at all really, just feeling. But his window stays dark and he doesn't come.

When I get back to the bunker late that night I feel really ill, and it's such a relief. Too ill to have to help with the kids or go out singing or think about Ben. It's like being little again and letting go of everything except that all-powerful grown-up hand. Mum's been nursing me. She says I've been ill all through Christmas. I had a fever, and I think I must have talked about Ben. Mum seems to know all about him, and that's a relief, too.

This morning I wake up feeling like I have a brain. A tiny, mouldy, shrivelled thing floating in the sea of snot and tears and gunk inside my head. Anyway, I feel able to talk, and we can because Jonathan's taken the kids out and me and Mum are alone in the icy bunker. She piles up all the sleeping-bags on her bunk and we lie there together, both so skinny we can fit into the narrow bunk and so filthy we don't mind each other's smells.

That weird feeling as Mum's fingers flutter, walking over my face, extracting me like juice from an orange. 'You've been very ill. Your cheeks have lost their childhood curves, your cheekbones and nose feel quite sharp now.'

'Bet I look a right old ratbag. Red eyes, greasy hair – thank God we haven't got a mirror down here.'

'We used to be beautiful,' she says in a puzzled voice, like beauty is a place and she's forgotten how to get there.

'Mum, am I stupid to love him so much?'

'I think it's the people who can't love who are stupid – or to be pitied.'

'Did you ever love a bloke so much you felt a part of him?'

'Oh yes.'

'Who? Dad? Which one?'

'When I was your age I fell in love with Leo.'

'How did you meet him?'

And she tells me this story, so strange that for a few minutes I forget about my broken heart and imagine her falling in love with the magician or con artist or whatever he was. Lying beside the ancient crone I shut my eyes and see the beautiful young girl, and I can almost shake hands with her across the years.

'Jesus, if you're really over a hundred you must remember 1900.'

'I can see this image of two tiny girls in white frilly pinafores welcoming the new century. It might have been me and my sister Lizzie, or a film I saw once. Memory's a scavenger, swooping over you with titbits in its beak that might be succulent fruit or the entrails of the dead. I've stopped wondering if things are true or if all this can have happened to the same woman. Too late to worry about identity now.'

'So have you been happy, Mum, whoever you are?'

'I never even ask myself that now. The happiness I once knew, that mixture of love and narcissism and joy in the outside, visible world, will never come again. Sometimes it seems that being too busy to ask the question *is* a kind of happiness. But it doesn't really matter about me any more. Abbie. If you really love this boy you must find a way of being with him.'

'But I've got to look after you.'

'No you haven't. Seize the day, my darling, before it seizes you. Anyway, I'm going to die soon. But first I have to find Leo.'

'Why can't we find him?'

'I haven't really wanted to, or tried to, until now. I've never stopped wanting him and missing him, but I needed to escape from him. Now I see that wasn't fair on you. The confusion about your birth is a kind of curse that has to be lifted before I can die.' I hate the way she talks about dying in that matter-of-fact way.

Then the kids come screaming in, and Mum gets up to look after them. Around us the hullabaloo of millennium fever rages as they make their plans for tonight. There's going to be a giant street party all over London, with fireworks and music and a fair in the Mall. Even

Kevin is planning to stay up all night, and they're waiting for Rosa, who has promised to take all the children out in a gang.

I cough, can't stop. I sit up, feeling breathless again, that horrible, gasping dry retching that leaves me drained, then I sink back down under the sleeping-bags. But I can't afford to miss the prosperous crowds that will fill London. I'll have to sing for my supper, and I haven't sung for weeks. My voice is a croak.

Flashback

A life sentence is better than immortality, but I still find the days too long. Anxiously, I examine my face in the mirror each morning in the glum yellowish light of my bathroom. There are lines around my eyes and mouth, a thoughtful-looking furrow between my eyes – deceptive, because I can hardly even concentrate on a book any more. The thought of all the books that have been printed since that pushy Caxton decided to spread the affliction of literacy depresses me. I look about forty now. If that's my biological age I might have to glare at myself in the mirror for another forty years.

The Metaphysical Bank has done very well out of my early retirement. My substantial holdings as a director have been haggled away to a life pension, index-linked, and a solid portfolio of Pasts (1837 railway shares, 1492 shares in Nicholas Jenson's printing press in Venice and 1620 shares in the East India Company) as well as some promising Futures (Intergalactic Efinance, Fly Me To The Moon and Grow-Your-Own-Kidney Bags). Anyway, I have more than enough to live on. If this can be considered living.

Strange how the days are longer now they're numbered. I can't be bothered to make any new friends, and two thousand years of energetic lechery have left me indifferent to the flesh. I find my own repulsive, other people's unappetizing. The dog looks gloomy, too, as it sighs and farts and drools, ageing like me. I'm glad it's dumb. I couldn't stand a talkative companion.

If not for Johnny's whining I would never go out. I feel like another old dog, or perhaps a wolf, loping around London. Once I do get out I realize that I like walking. It soothes my worst moods and tires me out so that I am able to sleep without the pills I've become dependent on recently. He drags me to the open-air drawing-room of Holland Park, saturated with memories of them both; to the wilds of Hampstead Heath, where she stayed with George and Molly after she returned from Italy in the sixties. Most of all, Hyde Park draws us like a magnet. Day after day, the dog walks me up the North End Road, turns into High Street Kensington, across Kensington Gardens to the Serpentine and then over to Marble Arch and Bayswater. It gets dark early now, and I still prefer night to day. Slinking through the crepuscular trees, I feel pulled as if the dying vegetation is willing me to stay. Dangerous? Then you haven't understood what a release it would be to feel the mugger's knife at my throat and to know that, this time, death is real.

Today cafés and pubs and buses are humming with people making plans for millennium eve. Not another one! My last. At midday Johnny drags me from Hyde Park to Marble Arch, and we pass through one of the pedestrian tunnels under the road. As I walk down the concrete ramp the dog strains at the lead and starts to bark and yelp hysterically. I hear the last few lines of 'The Streets of London', sung in a husky girl's voice. I used to hate music, except the raucous bawling of music-hall songs and the most nihilistic rock and pop, but recently I've noticed it has an extraordinary effect on me. This sweet, melancholy young voice goes through me as if I was a field of wheat and her song was a wind bearing compassion. The voice must belong to the seedy-looking girl sitting under a blanket. Although she has stopped singing by the time I pass, I put a pound coin in the green baseball cap beside her. The beauty of the girl's singing seems all the more poignant when I see how frail and skinny and apathetic she looks. I try to walk on, but Johnny won't let me. The dog is almost strangling himself as he strains towards the girl, who stares back at him in disbelief and then glances up at me.

An old woman is standing near by. At a second glance I see that she's grotesquely old, dressed in an odd assortment of clothes: a man's tweed jacket, a pair of green jogging trousers, disintegrating trainers, a scarlet baseball cap and a bright yellow scarf. She holds herself very erect and looks as if she might break out into poetry, a speech of Hecuba's, perhaps. Then I notice that my curiosity is being ignored and something in the milkiness of her eyes tells me she's blind. I stop beside her.

'Who is it?' she asks in a surprisingly youthful and educated voice.

'Nobody – a friend. Are you hungry?' I desperately want to hear her voice again.

Instead of replying she stretches out her hands and brushes my face with light, dry fingers. There is unexpected power in her touch, as if she is moulding the clay of my face, not just learning it. As she explores my face I stare into hers, into leathery folds and wrinkles edged with dirt, a toothless mouth, deep lines running from its edges up to the bony hill of her nose. The sightless eyes have once been dark, sunken now into bowls of shadow.

She laughs. 'You're waiting for me to make the first move, Leo. You always did.'

The girl under the blanket says, 'Hello, Daddy.'

They are in my arms, and the reality of their bodies is a shock. I've been alone for so long that I've forgotten how other people feel – and smell. They do stink. And there is so much to say that we walk up the concrete ramp together in silence, towards the swelling daylight.

I buy them lunch in an Italian café in Park Street. Although it's crowded, nobody wants to sit at our table. Jenny perks up over the meal, as soon as she has some hot soup and a glass of wine inside her, and we reminisce about our music-hall days. Abbie hardly says a word. Johnny sits between her knees and she reaches down to touch him occasionally, looking bewildered.

We stand on the pavement outside the café. We've talked over lunch, but it isn't enough, it will never be enough. Abbie clutches her blanket in exactly the same way as she used to hold her panda when she was three. She has hardly spoken or eaten during lunch, and her white, traumatized face worries me even more than the gargoyle that has been carved out of Jenny's beauty. 'Well. Two o'clock. The children will wonder where we are.' Jenny turns away from me, reaching out for Abbie's shoulder.

'No! You can't just go like this. I'm coming with you. I can't let you disappear again.'

Jenny shrugs, and Abbie gives me another of those terrible blank looks. I take Jenny's arm firmly – like a policeman, I think uncomfortably – and Abbie walks in silence on her other side. Jenny stinks of urine and decaying unwashed flesh. She stumbles a few times on the unfamiliar pavement. We walk back through the subway where I found them, across Speakers' Corner and down to a labyrinth of tunnels hidden beneath Marble Arch, where I've never been before. The buskers and beggars who congregate here all greet Jenny and Abbie warmly and look at me suspiciously. In the café I felt that I was a respectable citizen generously feeding two derelict and none too fragrant females, but down here I feel that I'm the outsider. Johnny's lead is held by Abbie now, and I feel oddly bereft.

Abbie takes a key out of her pocket, opens a door marked Emergency Exit and leads us down a dark corridor. Long before we reach the bunker I'm disorientated and nervous, half expecting to be attacked in this darkness seething with transient life. I still hold Jenny's arm with one hand and with the other clutch my wallet in the breast pocket of my corduroy jacket. After a long walk Abbie unlocks another door and we enter a dark, cold space, more like a cave than a room.

We've left daylight far behind us in the world above. My eyes make sense of the new space by the feeble yellowish light of a camping lamp. Bunks line the walls, which drip with condensation, and there is no other furniture. Only children, swarming like maggots, shouting and laughing and playing. When they see Jenny the maggots run up to her and bear her off to one of the bunks. Abbie, still silent, sets about preparing some kind of repulsive instant soup in dozens of plastic cups. I hover in the doorway, reluctant to be swallowed up by this subterranean chaos.

They seem to have forgotten about me, absorbed in this horrible life they have made without me. Down here is everything I've always despised and avoided: poverty, ugliness, discomfort, squalor. I feel a wave of nausea. Over the last five years I've so often imagined the triumphant moment when I find them. The next frame is a triple embrace, followed by their happy return to my flat. Of course, I realized that Abbie would be adolescent and Jenny – if she was alive at all – might be dangerously old and fragile, but it never once occurred to me that the embrace would be followed by separation, that they wouldn't want to be rescued by me.

Superfluous in the doorway, I watch Abbie bustle around, still silent and apathetic, while Jenny sits on a lower bunk surrounded by children demanding hugs, stories, attention, love. What about me? I hug myself bleakly, cross my arms over my chest in an attempt to ward off the infection and misfortune that are in the air. At first the children ignore me, but after twenty minutes some of the bigger ones begin to give me threatening glances. I sidle over to where Jenny is sitting, trying to be invisible. But I've lost the knack. I feel enormous, looming over the maggots, my green corduroy suit far too smart. I grip my wallet firmly as I push through the swarming children and touch the hand of the old crone who was once my beautiful Jenny, the hand I've kissed and been stroked by and, occasionally, hit by. Memories flood in, a gallery of Jennies and Leos.

'Still here?' she asks coolly.

'It's taken me five years to find you.' I hold the old root I remember as smooth intimate flesh. 'I can't just let go of you. I must see you again. We have to talk about Abbie.'

'Yes, we do. I'll meet you at eight in the subway where we met this morning.'

And the hideous old beggar woman dismisses me. Johnny stays

behind with Abbie. They've collapsed together on to one of the bunks and appear to be asleep, the curly golden-brown idiot in the arms of the girl who used to be my daughter. As I shuffle back through the tunnels I feel abandoned, lonelier than ever. I miss the feel of the rough leather lead that connected me with Johnny.

I found them, I found them, I keep reminding myself, but I'm afraid of what I've found, afraid of their dark underworld. I return to the city of light and trees and crowds that know where they belong and where they're going. The last short afternoon of the century is almost over, and the weather is mild, grey and still, as if London is holding her breath. People from all over the country are surging into the capital, and there's a mood of collective euphoria I can feel but can't share. My brain is muffled, and I can hardly walk.

I stagger into a café in the Edgware Road and order a coffee, then another. Four o'clock. Already, our meeting at lunchtime seems dream-like. I'm worried that Jenny won't turn up, that I will lose her again. I wish I was alone in my flat so that I could lie down and give in to this wave of shock. But I have to stay upright at this table in this crowded café swirling with people preparing to throw themselves joy-fully into the future. Like me, these millions of people on the streets have only one life, yet they seem to think the millennium matters, whereas I know it's just another nought clocked up on the heartless dial of history.

The subway is horribly empty when I arrive at eight. At last I hear the tapping of a stick and the bizarre figure comes down the ramp towards me. I touch her arm and feel sick again at the stench that bounces off her. 'Where's Abbie?'

'Still asleep.' Jenny tells me about Abbie and Ben. At the end she says, 'Of course, I know girls her age are reduced to idiocy by love. I was myself. But this is serious. She's changed so much in the last few months. She has been really ill and now she's like a zombie.'

'Haven't you taken her to the doctor?'

Jenny laughs bitterly. 'Doctors don't want to know about people like us. We're homeless, hopeless, we're not part of the nation so we don't deserve the National Health. We live in the sewers and die in the gutter.'

'Well, what do you want me to do?'

'*Are* you her father?'

'I don't know. Neither does David. I asked him.'

A leathery blush floods the face opposite, clashing with her scarlet baseball cap. I'm furious. 'Did you see him? How was he? Still married?'

'Seemed to be.'

'Did he mention me?'

'We talked about nothing else.'

'Oh, good.'

'Jenny, even if you live to be two hundred you'll still be a vain old flirt. I thought you'd changed, sobered up.'

'God knows I get few enough opportunities to flirt at the moment. We were supposed to be talking about Abbie.'

'There's only one person who can tell us who her real father is. Sibyl, *the* sibyl I should say.'

'Not that repulsive old hag in the cave at Earls Court? I sometimes forget, I'm a repulsive old hag, too.'

'So you did go and see her! She's very good, you know.'

'But she talks in gibberish.'

'She can be a bit ambiguous.'

'And how come she knows more about our family history than we do?'

'It's her job to know everything. Whether she wants to or not.' I dial a number on my mobile. 'Sibyl? It's Leo. Well, yes, I was angry at the time but I've forgiven you . . . Oh, it's wonderful. I stare at myself in the mirror every day and count my wrinkles and bags. I'm looking forward to my funeral immensely. But I'm really calling because I've found Jenny . . . Yes, both of them. Well, she's not a little girl any more, that's what we need to talk to you about . . . In an hour? Thanks . . . No, *don't* beam us up to your consulting-room. No flashes or tricks, please. We're feeling a bit fragile. We'll get a taxi.'

In the taxi Jenny looks confused. 'Are you all right?' I keep asking her. Obviously she isn't; she looks as if she might die at any minute, before I can use science to restore what magic once preserved. She sinks back in the shadowy seat, and I describe everything to her, where we're going and why.

'It's so strange to be sitting opposite you again, to hear your voice. I'm lurching from memory to memory. I feel not so much travel sick as time sick, time weary. You've appointed yourself narrator, Leo, but I'm not sure I want my world to be interpreted by you again. Wasn't that how all the trouble started?'

'Interpret your own world, but at least let me help you.'

Getting her out of the taxi and up to Sibyl's consulting-room is a long and painful process. At any minute she might fall, collapse, have a stroke or a heart attack, beat me to the finishing post of death. Then we stand, arm in arm, on the threshold of Sibyl's room, and my hands are clasped by tiny, shrivelled fingers.

'To see you together! My dears, come and sit on my couch. Jenny, you don't look a day over a hundred. You could be his grandmother. Leo, you have a few lines and wrinkles now, you'll soon catch up . . .'

Jenny says, 'He won't catch up because I'll be dead. I could die any day now. I haven't come so that you can tell us what a lovely couple we make. I know we don't. I've come because my daughter has fallen in love with a boy who could be her half-brother, and we have to know if Leo is her father or not.'

Even when we both sit down Jenny and I are taller than Sibyl, who stands in front of us wearing her black trouser-suit, her face and hands like three strangely engraved leather bags, her bald head covered with a rather chic black wig.

'Father? But, Leo, you must have been around when they brought in compulsory sterilization for immortals. Gods, angels, devils, the lot. Enough is enough, they said, no more half-and-half freaks; they make good stories but bad citizens.'

'So he couldn't possibly be Abbie's father?'

'Ah well, of course, as with all methods of contraception there are loopholes. At least I remember a few superstitions.'

'Such as?' I demand impatiently.

'Well, the Witch of Endor, who ran one of the first abortion clinics, used to say that if an immortal fell deeply in love with an ant – as we called them, being unable to distinguish between them – a child would be born. But I never heard of such a case.'

'Can't we have something a bit more scientific to go on?'

'Science is only magic that works. Do you want me to use the old method? It's rather messy: goats' entrails, toads' blood, virgins, you know the sort of thing.'

'I don't know where you'd find a virgin in Earls Court.'

'Exactly. The only other thing I can suggest, my dears, is the flash-back.'

'Does it hurt?' Leo asks.

'Not physically. But as Jenny can't see, and this is visual magic, you will have to describe it for her. When was Abbie born?'

'Twenty-seventh of June 1984.'

'Nine months takes us back to – now, tell me what you see.'

There's a flash. On the red carpet in front of us a bed appears. 'It's our bedroom at Phillimore Gardens,' I murmur to Jenny. 'The walls are transparent and we're making love – Sibyl, this is very explicit stuff.'

'What you see is what you got, but so long ago that you have per-haps forgotten it. The flashback method,' Sibyl continues in her driest voice, 'selects the most intense moments of the subject's past and replays them. This method is frequently therapeutic and cathartic. There is no soundtrack available, but the speed is variable.'

'Slow that down a bit, could you?' I say in a strangled voice. I thought I'd lost interest in sex. 'I can't believe we really – Jenny, you were amazing. We were both completely carried away. God, we were so young!' I pause, unable to speak for a few moments.

Jenny says impatiently, 'Yes, but what about Abbie?'

'Well, I suppose there might be some connection.' To my surprise, I feel a certain pride that there could have been a result to my millions of sexual experiments. 'Oh, that's incredible! Sibyl, how did you do that? They – or we – are transparent now, and I can see you close up, Jenny. What an exquisite body. Even your digestive tract is beautiful. Oh, Jenny, how could you . . . ? Ah well. Something's happening inside you, a sort of fizzing – could you slow it down a bit more, please? Now all I can see is your internal ocean, tadpoles swimming up inside you, a race. Yes – one of them's ahead – the winner gets through! Sibyl, how can we be sure that tadpole turned into Abbie?'

'Do you want to see Jenny's belly a few weeks later?'

'A little walnut, crouching in your underwater cave.' I reach out for Jenny's filthy talon. 'Then a fish, an alien, a blob, a caricature. Now I can see a baby sitting inside you . . .'

'I remember the indigestion!' Jenny says. 'And wanting to pee all the time. Can you see her face?'

'No, it still has no sex or identity. How vague and gentle a face looks with its eyes shut. Now there's something of Abbie around the mouth. She's kicking you! She's yawning. Another bed – oh, Jenny, we're at the hospital. I think we'll fast-forward this bit. Oh! There she is! A little miracle shooting out of you – Sibyl, has something gone wrong with the speed? I'm sure we can't have been rushing around like that.'

'You asked me to fast-forward it.'

'Yes, but not to Buster Keaton. This is the most extraordinary moment of my life – our lives – I want to linger over it. You're laughing, Jenny. You've got Abbie in your arms, she's searching for your nipple with her blind little mouth, and I'm sitting on the side of your bed hugging both of you. We were so happy.'

'Do you want me to stop now while it's still schmaltzy?' Sibyl asks.

The figures on the carpet disappear, and I turn with a sigh back to the present. Beside me Jenny is silent.

'Are you convinced?' Sibyl asks briskly.

'I am. I must always have been a closet human being. What shall we tell Abbie? Jenny?'

'We'll tell her you're her father. She can have her lover, much good it'll do her.'

'And you'll come back to me?'

'I can't leave the children. I'll stay with them until I die, which won't be long.'

'Bring the children. We'll buy a huge house, two huge houses, just say you'll come. Into his habitation wheresoever . . .'

'What? Listen, Leo, I don't want any more of that crap about contracts.'

I kneel at the disintegrating shoes of the ancient, filthy, grim-faced woman. Sibyl watches enviously.

'Is this supposed to be a happy ending? It's too late, Leo. I'm too old and tired.'

'Who said anything about ending?'

PART 3
An Island in the Moon

2075

'Good evening, metamortals. This is your hourly feel-good update. Fighting, floods and plague continue to rage on earth. The city of Venice, Italy, was today covered by water just a few hours after historians completed the virtual replica. This week's world president was assassinated this afternoon when rebels bombed the Washington Archipelago. Four million organicists died, but no metamortals were reported injured. The weather will be whatever you want it to be . . .' I turn her off, the bland voice of compulsory joy. We have made our Utopia, and we must lie in it. Yet there are moments when honesty tugs at my heartstrings and I have to speak to my daughter.

In the courtyard of our house there's a pool. During the day we swim at least a hundred lengths to keep our plastimuscles toned, and in the evenings we use our pool for virtual visiting. The synthetic blue-green waves make a beautiful frame to grim visions of the battered earth.

I walk through my English country garden in the artificial sunset, staged each evening to make us exiles from earth feel at home. Then I watch the planetary tantrum that precedes the purple night of Luna Minor, our exclusive retirement colony for metamortals, a cylinder city that orbits the moon. It's always dark on the moon, but the lifestyle engineers who designed Luna Minor knew that we'd need light and views and so they have created them. I gaze out at a vast panorama of stars and planets, among them the one on which I was born.

Even now, years after my sight was restored, it still moves me very much to see Abbie, who is sitting in the shabby wooden hut that is all that remains of our mansion near Primrose Hill, above the flooded ruins of London. The house Leo bought so that we could all be together again. My two-year-old great-great-granddaughter Ella sits placidly on Abbie's knee, and as she becomes aware that I'm watching her my daughter reaches up to smooth her coarse grey bun.

Her wrinkled brown eyes are calm as she stares back at the masterpiece that is my face.

I do find these virtual visits a strain; I often wish she didn't have eternity on her hands. From my window I can see the moon, which still looks poetic but is in fact completely colonized. I'm glad the journey is still too tedious to tempt my indefatigable mother very often.

'You look tired, my darling. No more plagues?'

'We heard rumours of an outbreak of radiation flu, but we're OK.'

'With all those small children around – why don't you send them up here for a few months? We could get a special visa for Terrestrial Victims. We'd love to have them.'

'I know you would, but they'd come back so lunified it would take them six months to adjust back to life here.'

'And what are great-great-grandparents for if not to spoil children?'

'You have to admit you and Leo are confusing for them. For a start, you look sixty years younger than me.'

'There's no need to sound so resentful. I've always told you, I'll pay for you to have everything done. All you'd accept is that little brain implant . . .'

I sigh and touch the side of my head. I often wish I could tear out this bloody implant, which allows my mother to intrude whenever she wants to, so that I can't avoid seeing her holographic image and hearing her voice. 'You used to be so attractive, darling. And you could still leave here looking fabulous. It would probably give a new boost to your career.'

'What career? You know my voice has cracked, and anyway there aren't any more theatres or concert halls. I just sing for friends and family sometimes.'

'Well, up here science has caught up with mythology, and I think you're crazy not to make the most of it.'

'Let's not start that again. Please. We want to live and die down here, naturally, that's all.'

'But there's no need to die at all!' Her reconstructed face, a marvel of smooth pale curves – as long as you don't look too closely – peers anxiously, as if she expects to see an aggressive virus carry me off.

'It's no use looking at me like that. I don't want to be like you two.'

She sighs. 'How's Ben?'

'Old and tired, like me,' I say with satisfaction. 'And when we're on our deathbeds I don't want you sneaking down here injecting us with resurrection juice or whatever it is – oh, stop crying! All that glop you spray on your face instead of skin will congeal.'

'Of course I'm crying. I dedicate myself to the pursuit of eternal happiness and you don't want anything to do with it. You're determined to break my heart by dying an anachronistic and unnecessary death. What about your children? Don't you want to live for them?'

'They're all in their fifties and sixties, for God's sake. They'll miss me and Ben, I suppose. It'll be sad. But there's no room for us all, Mum. Only in your crazy little heaven. Down here there's barely enough food, the floods come every spring, we've no real medicine since all the governments and multi-nationals abandoned the planet –'

'Oh, don't start lecturing me again about your heroic pioneer spirit.'

'Pioneers start something, we're in at the end. Pretty soon after Ben and I die people will either flee to other planets as refugees or choose to die with the poor old earth.'

'London used to be such a fabulous city.'

'There are lots of fables about it. But there are no theatres, shops, restaurants or parks now, Mum. Anyway, if you remember, our life here wasn't always so fabulous.'

'Is that what made you so bitter and perverse? I wish now I'd never destroyed that contract and dragged you down into squalor.'

'It was the only real thing you ever did.'

'And what's so wonderful about reality?'

Ben comes in, and raises his eyebrows when he realizes we have a virtual visitor.

Then, as if she senses his presence, she says, 'Abbie, tell me about Ben. I can't hear him or see him but I assume he's there. Is he still writing poetry?'

'He never stops writing, although there aren't any readers left. He writes for a couple of hours each morning and then goes to help in the fields or strengthen the dam. I wish you could see how red and blistered his hands are.'

She shudders. 'Don't make me think about raw hands, grizzled hair or aging faces.'

I'm glad they can't see or hear each other as I turn to him and say, 'She's been trying to persuade us to go and join them on Planet Narcissus.'

'Don't think we'd fit in. We're too old and ugly. Tell her we're just about to eat.'

I say goodbye.

'Goodbye, my darling,' she replies.

I'm close to tears as their images fade. Always now, I'm afraid it will be the last time I see my daughter. When the pool is empty I look down at my own reflection in it and see a tall, slim woman in a long, dark dress, the night sky behind me shimmering in the ripples of water. Around me is the ingenious Mediterranean summer night of Luna Minor: the fireflies shimmering in the mild, seductive air, the softly illuminated fountains in the gardens where metamortals walk and talk and flirt. There are no mosquitoes or thunderstorms or tourists.

As I enter our transparent dome-shaped house the door asks me what I want for supper and reminds me to renew my cell-regenerating implant. Inside, a Chopin waltz plays as the artificial candles on the marble dining-table light themselves, the partition between the dining- and living-rooms slides back and the house becomes a planetarium. The telescopic lenses in the transparent walls of our house produce wonderful effects as the stars dance.

On Luna Minor the eye is always tricked and delighted. I often wonder how I'd feel about living here if I hadn't had my sight restored by ultrasound waves and tiny cameras in my retina soon after I returned to Leo. If I was still blind, locked in my inner life – which proved to be a surprisingly well-furnished secret room – I might have become an organicist like my daughter. So many people who were once homeless have chosen to stay down there; the poor *have* inherited the earth, simply because the rich no longer want it. The homeless and the dispossessed found their voices for the first time; they came pouring out of tunnels, roaring and bellowing, and overpowered the city. Now they're all over the world, and they're hungry for the future. Their anger was like the hum of ten million bees, and they were a force that cut across race and government and nationality. The have-nots decided they'd had enough.

Sometimes I can imagine an alternative life, in which I stayed down there with Abbie and Ben and their children, dying naturally. But simplicity has never appealed to me for longer than a daydream. So I joined Leo up here, where beauty and artifice and ingenuity have almost routed that bitch nature.

When the first global-warming disasters struck, causing famine all over Asia and Africa and flooding all the low-lying cities of the world, when the wars that nobody wanted destroyed London and New York and Paris and Berlin, those of us who had power and money weren't unprepared. It turned out that the space programmes governments had been mysteriously engaged in for decades made it possible for a small international élite to flee the dying planet. Once it became clear that nature was turning on people even more viciously than they could have turned on each other, Leo began to bring brochures home to the big house near Primrose Hill where we had lived for more than thirty years.

There was a military colony on Pluto, where murderers and psychopaths were exiled to fight out wars vicariously, like medieval champions; a group of redundant international politicians were fleeing on a starcruiser to another galaxy, so far away that it would take over a century to reach their destination. They had volunteered to be put into a state of hibernation, but while they were waiting they kept arguing about who would be president of their new galaxy and assassinating each other, so there were empty places on their starcruiser; various multinationals had combined to create Planet Joy, where exiles from earth could live in oxygen-regulated capsules and be fed intravenously with perfectly balanced nutrients and drugs that kept them in a state of permanent ecstasy while their brains were attached to interactive pornodreams.

Luna Minor was the most comfortable of the ex-planetary colonies. Many of the directors of the Metaphysical Bank were sibyls and magi who had known for centuries that the earth would become uninhabitable and had devoted their vast resources to planning and building their island in the moon. 'Not the cheapest or the most accessible of the new worlds. Only those with strong links with the Metaphysical Bank will be considered, and preference will be given to those with an association of at least five hundred years. But if you are successful we guarantee you an eternity of gracious civilization. Luna Minor. The best of all possible worlds.' As the floodwaters lapped against the windowsill of our kitchen in Primrose Hill I was seduced by the vibrant baritone of the sales video and agreed to accompany Leo.

I know Abbie despises the way I live – the fact that I'm alive at all – but, then, who wants to be natural and dead? There are still moments when my pleasure in life is as intense as it has ever been. When I'm invited to lecture in the Metaphysical Theatre to the other spareparters on Infinite Vitality, I whisper to my adoring audience that my secret is to enjoy small things every day. Then I raise a laugh by ending my lecture with one of my old dance routines, 'Roses in Picardy'. Yes, little daily pleasures: after dinner tonight we'll watch a series of spectacular volcanic eruptions on Io, Jupiter's moon. I've selected three Greek taverna meals, as Pierre is staying to supper after he and Leo finish their chess game.

Leo comes hobbling downstairs with Pierre, who was a barber-surgeon in Paris before the French Revolution and is now one of the most successful trackless-robot surgeons in the universe. Leo is complaining, as usual.

'It's the El Cid factor,' Pierre explains. 'You and Jenny are spareparters. It's not your fault. You were already mature when they began genetic screening at birth. So of course bits of you need replacing all the time.'

'For two thousand years I never had so much as a headache; now I'm a decaying mass of aches and pains. Could you do me a new spine?'

'There's nothing wrong with your back. You should just swim more. You're such a hypochondriac,' I say affectionately. Leo, like me, is a handsome patchwork, just about recognizable as the man I met before the First World War. Pierre opted to have one of the first triple-brain transplants, and his medical, musical and mathematical knowledge bulge like an extra ribcage in his forehead, above his long, pale face.

'It is, of course, possible to replace every inch of you every few years, like a Japanese temple, but at a certain point you might as well give up on the dubious privilege of being human, as I have done, and accept the superiority of machine life. I haven't a single cell or organ that was in me in Paris in the 1790s. Some of us are thinking of suing the Metaphysical Bank for a misleading description in our contract. After all, eternity *should* mean eternity. These new kids who've been genetically screened since birth are still only in their seventies, so it's too soon to say if they'll really live for ever.'

'Eternity. For ever,' Leo says gloomily. 'I don't know why we bother. What you get isn't really life at all. Look at this olive. Greek taverna, my foot. This olive bears no resemblance to the ones I used to eat on Crete a couple of thousand years ago. Might as well be made of plastic. It probably is. And this retsina tastes like bleach.'

I defend my skill with the meal-selector button. 'Considering how far away we are from Greece, it's not too bad.'

'Ah, Greece. I miss the earth, you know. Sometimes I think those organicists like Abbie and Ben have got it right: suffer and work and eat real food for a few years and then die.'

'They will. Quite soon,' I say, my eyes full of tears.

'I'm going to start a revolutionary movement here: dying is good for you. This place needs a few funerals to liven things up. Jenny?'

'What? Will I join you on your revolutionary funeral pyre? No thanks, there are still lots of things I enjoy.' I suddenly realize we've been leaving Pierre out of the conversation. 'Who won your chess game?'

'Me, of course. My brain capacity is equal to six chess champions, and I can do as many operations in a day as the old city hospitals could in a week. Yet when you talk and laugh like that I don't understand. Shall I demonstrate my social skills by telling you a joke?'

'That would be nice,' I say politely.

'It's not very funny. What do you call a dysfunctional interplanetary pilot?'

'I don't know,' I say in an encouraging voice. 'What *do* you call a dysfunctional interplanetary pilot?'

'Albert. You didn't laugh. Nobody ever does. I know two thousand four hundred and seventy-two more jokes.'

'Let's save them for another night. In a few moments Io will be erupting. I've maximized the telescopic lenses so we can see. Look! Isn't that fantastic?' We stare in silence through the transparent roof at the stunning display of white-hot lava swirling with dazzling colours. 'There's a starcruiser full of artists moored just outside the radiation belt of Jupiter. We'll have to buy some of their pictures when they come back. Tomorrow night there's another earthquake in Japan. We can watch that, too. Did you see the hurricane in Florida last week? That was incredibly beautiful. More coffee, Pierre?'

'No thank you. My caffeine and alcohol levels are high enough. I must go home now.'

'He was more fun before his brain was perfected,' I say as soon as the door slides shut.

'He was a lot more fun in 1815 when I first met him as an abortionist in Whitechapel – come to think of it, *I* was more fun in 1815, too.'

'Well, I wasn't even born then.' I'm still proud of being several thousand years younger than my lover. 'You're miserable tonight.' I reach out to hold his hands, which, like my own, are seamed with rope-like veins. When we touch there is still a sexual charge between us; Leo reaches out to stroke the curve of my shapely plastibuttocks.

'I'm not really unhappy. How could I be? My health monitor would simply raise my serotonin level. Yet this place brings out my most perverse and bloody-minded side. I don't know why.'

'Perhaps it's because you're a sort of illegal immigrant here. You only got in by lying about your past. Strictly speaking you ought to be up on Pluto, fighting out proxy wars with all the other criminals and psychopaths.'

'I wasn't that bad, was I? I forget.'

'Oh, Leo, how convenient your memory implants are. I wish I could forget as much as you do.'

'I'd have gone mad long ago if I had to keep remembering it all.'

'Murder, swindling, drug dealing . . .'

'Well, we're none of us perfect. Do you wish you'd never met me?'

'No, I've never wished that.'

I try to relive my own feelings: the fear and disgust that drove me to steal my contract from the vaults beneath the Metaphysical Bank eighty years ago. Rather than stay with Leo I was prepared to risk death and expose Abbie to terrible danger. I can see myself in the hotel room, my beauty suddenly demolished, the horror of realizing I was blind – I remember it all, can't pretend like Leo to have forgotten. These pictures are with me for ever, but the feelings, complexities and doubts behind them are lost. My past is a story I've told myself too often, tidying and justifying. If you live for ever you also lie for ever, desperately adjusting your self-image until you find one that is bearable. I look down at our four hands, clasped together in the volatile present.

Organicists

Since Ben's death I have envied him and cursed my inheritance. I'm glad I embarked on this great adventure in the ruins of London. But I'm tired now. I've had enough.

When Jenny and Leo told me I couldn't be Ben's sister there was a family conference. David and Muriel wanted their son to stay at university, and Jenny and Leo expected me to resume my apprenticeship as a princess. Leo bought the mansion that backed on to Primrose Hill and showed it to me with a flourish. But Ben and I didn't want their world, so we ran away together. We ran from London and childhood, from home and homelessness and education. The anger against my mother that I couldn't show when she was poor and blind and helpless flowed out of me in a great tidal wave that carried me with Ben to India and South America.

For years Ben and I were so fired by the heat of the forge in which we were reinventing ourselves that we never wrote to our parents or even telephoned them. We travelled furiously, sleeping rough or staying in farming cooperatives. When we were hungry we didn't ask our daddies for money but sang the songs we wrote. At first we were paid in rice and maize and free beds, but then we were invited to sing at the first anti-globalization events. It turned out that being against multinational companies and banks – metaphysical and otherwise – meant that we were part of a movement, although I always felt we were joining on false pretences: when I sang about eternal youth and midnight transformations and global conspiracies they all praised my brilliant imagination.

Our life was peripatetic. Often we had to go into hiding, and we trusted nobody except each other. I remember a night when we clung together in a granary in Afghanistan, buried under sacks. Inches away, we could hear soldiers searching for us, paid by the local warlord who resented a song we'd been singing about his drug and weapon deals. Lying in the dark with Ben's heart beating next to my own I wondered if my special powers, my 'martian arts' as Rosa used to call them, had any existence outside a little girl's fantasy. We were unarmed, and the soldiers tramping towards us had guns and knives.

When the soldiers left Ben and I were violently sick. We weren't heroes, we didn't want to fight or die. Ben wanted to learn how to farm so that the poor – us included – could eat. Those years of travelling nourished in me a fierce, almost perverse, simplicity. I wanted to dig and burrow into the earth my parents had skimmed above, to live with my face and body as it was, to love one man with all my heart.

In my late twenties, when I became pregnant, my childhood came rolling back like a ball I had chucked away over a high wall. Ben and I were singing at an open-air concert in Africa, where farmers had realized indigenous landowners were just as good at exploiting them as colonials. The crowd was dancing and swaying, and Ben and I were high on the dangerous illusion that art changes the world. The night throbbed with music and colour and a thousand people singing of love and peace and hope.

The first shots sounded like fireworks. Then I heard screams and saw blood spread across the white cotton dress of a woman who had been dancing a yard away from the stage. She slid to the floor as Ben and I registered what was going on and heard more shots and screams.

Well, as I said, I never was a heroine. My voice shook and fled before my legs followed it. Ben dropped his guitar as we held hands and ran to hide under the jeep we had arrived in. I clutched Ben, and the baby swelling under my breasts, and the British passport that meant the mad dictator's soldiers might think for a second before they killed me. We lay and watched as feet that had been dancing a few minutes ago were dragged into a pyramid, doused with paraffin and barbecued. Don't let me die, I prayed all night from my worm's-eye hiding place. Prayed to my mother, whom I hadn't seen for fifteen years, who might in fact be dead – although staying alive had always been her most noticeable attribute.

The next morning Ben and I were arrested. We were abject by then, dizzy with hunger, sick at the stench of charred human flesh, terrified that the baby inside me would be bayoneted out.

After two days in a filthy cage we were collected by a British diplomat, our man in Hades. He knew my father, who had phoned him and explained that his daughter and her boyfriend were playing silly buggers.

Ben and I were loaded on to a plane, then another, still shaking with dysentery and terror. At Heathrow we were met by my parents and an ambulance that rushed me to the Royal Free Hospital.

So I held my daughter in my arms when I sat up in bed and stared at my mother. She looked about my age. Her face was like a rare and valuable vase that has been shattered and then mended, not quite invisibly. Her features were all there – the large dark eyes, the strong but elegant nose, the generous mouth, the harmonious curves of her lovely cheekbones and jaw line. She even had her shining black hair again, thick waves of it tickling my cheek and brushing against the bald head of my baby. She was the mother whose beauty I had longed to inherit when I was a little girl, whose clone I had fervently wanted to be. She was embracing us, three generations together, and I gave myself to her arms until I opened my eyes and saw the cameras and microphones surrounding my hospital bed.

Suddenly I was aware of my ratty hair, blotchy unmade-up skin and the blood and vomit stains on my hospital gown. I pushed her away, and she tottered backwards on her stiletto heels, smiling as she posed one more time for the cameras, twirling to show them her tailored orange-linen suit with its very short skirt. 'She's a little overwrought,' Jenny murmured to the assembled journalists and cameramen. 'Perhaps you should come back later.'

The room emptied. Then I saw Leo, who also had that newly cobbled look. The opposite of youth isn't age but metasurgery. My father sat beside my bed, kissed my brow and nervously held out a finger to his granddaughter. Ben came forward, looking pale and exhausted and real. I held out my arms to him and sheltered in our private, unphotogenic love.

'I didn't ask them to come, darling. They insisted. So I thought we might as well sell the story to Beautiful People and put the money in trust for – is it a boy or a girl?'

Inside the warm circle of my lover and baby I felt strong enough to face my mother. 'Girl. Gina. You can see,' I said with wonder.

She smirked, showing off her spiky dark eyelashes. 'Leo's been so sweet. He just couldn't bear to let me go. So we got my eyes done in Switzerland, my kidneys and heart in Acapulco, my face in San Francisco. Leo's had quite a few ops, too, haven't you, darling? When it came to the point we realized we'd been foolish to throw away eternal youth. Old age and death are really only for failures and masochists.'

'Don't worry about anything,' Leo said benevolently. 'We'll look after you now.'

And they did. This house was still a modernized Victorian mansion then, much photographed by glossy magazines. Leo and Jenny were famous for being rich, glamorous and fashionably philanthropic. Leo kept his promise and allowed abandoned children to move in with us. Jenny's original lost children had grown up and disappeared, but there were always more. Half of their enormous house was a refuge for home-less kids. Ben and I lived there, and our children – I had four eventually – grew up thinking that communal life was natural.

Many of the rich followed Jenny's and Leo's example. Their houses were less likely to be burgled or looted, and there was even a word for it: compassionalization. There were tax breaks and compassionalized houses were safer, even if they were rather overcrowded. By the 2030s overcrowding was a comfort. It was the bodies of solitary men, women and children that you found floating on the waters or stranded like garbage on rooftops when the floods went down.

When I was about forty I had an infuriating conversation with my mother, who offered to remake me in her image. She sobbed that she couldn't bear to see my grey hairs and cellulite and stretch marks. I stared back at her, at the face and body I had longed for as a little girl, which she was now offering to buy for me. Perhaps I became an organicist at that moment. Although – as Ben used to tease me – I did accept this damned brain implant, so that in a sense I've always remained Mummy's and Daddy's girl, living in their house, my life saved on numerous occasions by their intervention. My final gesture of independence will be to be allowed to die.

For years none of us heard from Annette. She lost her seat at East Plumford, resigned from the Labour Party and quarrelled with every-body. There were rumours that she was living alone in a house near the sea in Dorset. Jenny and I searched for her and found her at last in a tiny house outside Weymouth, living alone and drinking heavily. She was old and lonely and incoherent. As I watched her make us tea with shaking hands, I thought, she'll never change the world now. We stayed for an awkward hour, but her conversation – self-pity and bitterness punctuated with incoherent prophecies – was so disturbing that we were relieved to escape.

Then, five years later, her book was published, and it was a revel-ation. Every great movement needs its bible, and *Life After Government* brilliantly combined anarchism, ecology and feminism. It managed to be both critical and hopeful, and for millions it became a blueprint for how we should live in a disintegrating world. She coined the word organicist to describe someone who 'channels her energy and intelli-gence into living with, not opposed to, nature in all her capricious moods'. Annette advocated huge non-violent protests against war, tax, pollution, debt and the global economy and insisted that resources, rather than employment, should be taxed. She ransacked history to find quotes and slogans, such as this one from the seventeenth-century Diggers: 'This earth we will make whole so it can be a common treasury for all,' which Ben and I turned into a successful song. Soon after Annette's death her book became an international best-seller, just before all the bookshops disappeared. The following year my parents decided to abandon the planet.

Nobody knows how many died in the wars against terrorism or the accidental nuclear wars or the cyberwars or the catastrophes the earth threw at us, like a mother who has lost her temper with her children. People just disappeared – Rosa, Kevin, Jonathan, Alice and dozens of other friends and relations. Ben and I were instinctive anarchists, and at first there was a kind of joy in our new freedom. No more taxes, statistics, banks, schools, police, television, newspapers, supermarkets or public transport. The infrastructure didn't melt away at once but so gradually that it was almost poetic, a slow ballet of decay. Rumours spread in frantic emails on the computers many of us still kept even after the cyberwars and via the crackly local radio stations that sprang up. The tube stations all closed, although they were covered with signs that said they would reopen as soon as possible. Then those signs went, too, and we knew the tunnels were flooded with sewage, the rails rusted, rats and maggots feasting on the last commuters.

I remember the last time I took my grandchildren, Jack and Ahmed, to school, one April morning when the floodwater shimmered from the fields of Regent's Park to the broken, ragged eggshell of St Paul's. It should have been a fifteen-minute walk, but there were potholes and bomb craters in the roads and pavements and our way was blocked by abandoned cars, buses and lorries. Beggars and refugees mobbed us when they saw we were carrying bags and wearing clothes that had once been expensive. We arrived at the playground – minus the children's lunch-boxes and Jack's trainers – to find a notice telling us the school would be closed 'until the end of the emergency'. The mob that had followed us shrieked with delight, and in a few minutes they occupied the empty playground and school buildings. As far as I know they're still there.

It's years since I've ventured that far. Ben and I were so close that sometimes even our children and grandchildren were jealous. We all lived here comfortably enough, a self-sufficient community. The house has a huge garden where Ben, who loved gardening, grew vegetables. Suddenly your survival depended on something as arbitrary as whether you lived in a basement in Lambeth or a top-floor flat in Muswell Hill. Estate agents tried to advertise London as the New Venice, with its quaint watery streets and flotillas of rowing boats and dinghies. Then the houseboats and floating houses began to appear. Some of them are just corrugated-iron shacks bolted to rotting wooden platforms; others are floating palaces used as holiday homes by Lunies.

Those of us who lived on the high ground built higher and higher walls and stockpiled food and weapons. Non-violent direct action was all very well, but those of us who thought we were liberals found we were quite capable of killing to protect our children and ourselves. Our extended family was a kind of ready-made community – or tribe – or private army.

Even after the house was bombed we stayed here and built huts and shacks in the ruins. We looked after each other and laughed at the politicians who tried to control us. After computer voting was exposed as a scam there were no more elections or nation states. Now that there is no transport, the world, that used to be as small as it was in the song I once heard in a toy shop, has become unimaginably big again. Last winter a group of refugees came from Highgate, with tales of starvation and fever. We let them stay, in return for help in the fields, as they were all skilled people and able to build their own shelters. As for further afield, for all I know there be dragons in France and India and the United States. My mother tells me of endless wars and bloodshed – she watches our disasters as after-dinner entertainment. I suspect that most people, like me, are delighted to have got rid of their beloved leaders and are quite capable of organizing their own modest resources. Individuals are kind, but governments are callous, or so I've always believed. So we survive. Only I don't want to any more.

'Darling, you mustn't give up.'

'Why shouldn't I? And how dare you listen in to my thoughts like that!'

'I'm so worried about you. Of course, I understand how much you must miss Ben. He was a sweet boy –'

'He was ninety-five.'

'But you could go on for ever, like me.'

'I don't want to be like you!'

'I can't bear to think of you dying. I'm coming, Abbie. I'm getting the first shuttle. Leo will come with me. You must come back here with us, have a break from all that squalor. You've been overdoing it. You need to see how beautiful life can be. Have a facial refurbishment, a jab of amnesiac, a hormonal renaissance – anything.'

'No!'

I hold my head to stop her voice from splitting it, rocking with pain and grief. Around my chair the younger people bustle, preparing supper and putting children to bed. From the window of the hut I can see the moon, threatening me. They will come; she's probably packing at this moment. Her virtual visits are bad enough, but this time she'll be physically here, criticizing my life and flirting with her great-grandsons. Her voice has gone, but I can feel her will, and Leo's, quivering in the moonlight.

Once I loved my parents, but they are not real, and I can't love unreality. I love my children and grandchildren and great-grandchildren, but they don't need me any more. All my deepest feelings are concentrated on Ben, and he is dead.

Tonight I decided to die.

Down to Earth

Pierre warned me that I might feel ill as I re-entered the earth's atmosphere, but I'm not prepared for this assault of vomiting, headaches, dizziness, anxiety.

'You're such a valetudinarian!' Jenny says as she strokes my forehead.

Her arm is the only part of her she can move. We lie side by side like two hieratic figures on a tomb, strapped down, bristling with tubes that feed us intravenously and bags that catch our fluids.

'Don't you feel ill? You're so tough!'

'I'd put up with anything to see Abbie. We must persuade her to come back with us. I've tried talking to her, but it's not the same. She has to see us to realize how marvellous life can be. I want to show her our house and the gardens and the fountains, introduce her to some charming people. Perhaps she'll find a new partner and stay up there with us. For years now she's known nothing but suffering, grief, disease, poverty. Naturally she's depressed, but we can soon fix that.'

I gaze at the other horizontal figures on the shuttle. Most of them are metamortals, who have been sent down by their therapists to remind them how happy they really are. They will be shuttled from war zone to flood to ruined city; they will see and even, if they can bear it, touch the diseased and starving refugees. The more intrepid ones will leave the ship for a week on a Local Colour houseboat moored on a lake in what used to be London or New York. They will all be forced to holiday until they beg to be allowed to return to Luna Minor, refreshed and rejuvenated, ready to enjoy a few more centuries of pleasure.

One of the interplanetary nurses makes us all do exercises for our circulation and muscles. The other passengers look at us suspiciously. When we were questioned by the Perpetual Police at the terminal at Luna Minor we admitted that we were going down to earth to visit family, and the news that we are actually going to stay with the natives has produced a *frisson* of shock. I know the story that I loved Jenny so much that we gave birth to a child has become a popular legend – it was turned into a genetic opera and performed at the Metaphysical Theatre only last year – but our visceral connection with the old world is not at all romantic. I see several of the women stare at Jenny in disgust; not only did she allow a flesh-and-blood baby, a nature brat, to pollute her body, but she is returning to her primitive and unhygienic origins.

Jenny has never cared what other people think. We gather our bags of food and presents and ignore the stares that follow us to the escape chute. They whisper fastidiously as the shuttle hovers above the green hill seething with tents, huts, vegetable patches, children and animals. A nervous titter spreads as the ship flies so low that we can see a woman in a green dress breast-feed her baby, surrounded by people in rags who stare up, shouting and pointing – a gratifyingly dramatic entrance.

There's no longer enough technology down here to build a terminal, so we are simply dumped, like manna in the wilderness. These biblical associations still pop into my head occasionally. Actually, a more appropriate simile is a helter-skelter on Brighton Pier. One sunny afternoon in about 1920 Jenny and I climb a dark wooden ladder, sniff the aroma of hot dust and seaweed and doughnuts and fried onions, sit on a couple of coconut mats and propel ourselves out and around and around, in exuberant spirals of sea beach and sky. She is between my knees, where I can bury my nose in her glossy black hair and the delicate curve of her neck and feel her lovely arse press against my cock, which twitches with the knowledge that in an hour we'll go back to our sleazy boarding-house and make love. Jenny's youth is an incantation that preserves a cheap fairground ride in poetic aspic.

We sit at the top of another chute and, again, Jenny sits in front of me. There is still an erotic charge between us, even if a hundred and fifty years have nibbled at her charms. The other passengers watch distastefully as we launch ourselves down to brutality.

A smell of fresh grass and shit; wind in a frighteningly uncontrolled sky; uncultivated faces coming nearer, gawping, yelling; Jenny between my knees and in my arms as we collapse on to the inflated bags at the bottom of the chute. We roll over on to the grass as the shuttle draws the contaminated chute back into its metal belly, like an aristocratic lady who has trodden in sewage, and takes off again.

I have to remind myself that some of these little barbarians are my descendants. I feel no connection with any of them but maintain my visiting-dignitary smile as I pull Jenny to her feet and face a barrage of impertinence.

'Greedy-weedy Lunies, fled to the moony, live for ever, think you're clever, greedy-weedy Lunies.'

'The goons in the moon send us all their typhoons . . .'

'Why did you steal our resources?'

'Why did you steal our future?'

'Why didn't you stop the wars?'

'Why don't you send us food?'

'Why don't you help us clean up the water supply?'

They surround us, their faces vibrating with spite. If they really are related to us they're surprisingly ugly. I still can't speak, I'm suffering from Earth Returnee Trauma: the smells and sights and emotions and noise down here are, literally, unspeakable.

But Jenny, beside me, sounds quite composed. 'We're Abbie's parents and we want to see her.'

They all start to yell again, and some of the faces grow wet and red and blotchy. They move even closer, we try to back away, but there's no escape from their stinking pressing bodies.

Silently I hold out the bags of food, medication and warm clothing we have brought with us. I had planned a dignified aid-presentation ceremony, but I'm afraid we'll be torn apart if we don't distract these ferocious creatures.

For a few minutes it works. They stop taunting us and turn their brief attention spans to the exquisitely wrapped packages that they tear open, hurling the contents on to the grass where pills, powerfood, sweaters, coats and shoes rapidly disappear. There are more people than presents, and they start to fight, rolling on the ground and chasing each other, tearing and breaking and crushing the objects of their desire.

Jenny and I stand at the periphery of this riot our goodwill has caused. We look around for our daughter. No doubt she has been coarsened by her years in this appalling place yet she is still . . . I never expected to feel sentimental about a substance as gross as blood, but I do long to see Abbie.

I remember walking with her on this hillside, just after she and Ben returned from their travels, when she was a young mother and Primrose Hill was one of the green oases of a prosperous bourgeois city, when we used to stand here with her little daughter Gina and Johnny's successor and look back at the walled mansion I had bought for us all. I wanted to live there for ever, or for as long as science granted me – a well-preserved patriarch, surrounded by my grandchildren, enthroned with Jenny who, satisfyingly, owed me everything again. Sharing my wealth with the homeless Jenny and Abbie were so eccentrically obsessed with seemed a marvellous way of having it all. Smug? Well, I certainly got my comeuppance. I can hardly bear to look around at this shanty town, let alone at the rest of London.

The Zen-like calm that encases me at home on Luna Minor has been shattered by the unsubtle chaos of earth. Memories assault me like these children's voices and the oafish weather they have down here. I remember Abbie as a little girl, coming into my laboratory and staring up at me. She used to hug me, kiss me, talk to me as if I was human. I love you, Daddy. In this gallery of memories I am always in the same frame while Abbie changes from detested baby to beloved child to desperately missed adolescent runaway. With a deep breath I prepare to meet her in her hideous old age. The virtue of virtual visiting is that all this ghastly emotion is edited out.

I turn to Jenny. But while I've been grazing on the past something has happened. Her face is a distorted mask of grief, and the children are dancing around us again.

'Dead.'

'She was old.'

'She couldn't walk properly.'

'You two can't be her mum and dad. You're not old enough.'

'The Earthkeeper will take her away.'

'Before she starts to stink.'

'Earthkeeper come, take away stinkybum. Earthkeeper say, death come for you some day.'

Then Jenny collapses in my arms and I think I collapse, too. The children whoop and snap at our ankles as they lead us to the hut where Abbie lies.

Much later a middle-aged woman brings us bowls of vegetable stew and flat bread. 'I'm Gina,' she says, standing awkwardly in the doorway of the hut.

Another child grown tastelessly old. I used to bath her when she was about three, in the green-tiled bathroom at the top of the house that stood where this hut is now, before these houses were bombed by the Sharia Faithful or the Christian Fundamentalists or the Hampstead Separatists. Gina doesn't look as if she baths much now.

The three of us sit on the earth floor around the table where my daughter is laid out and have a macabre picnic.

'I think she wanted to die. She missed my father and she was tired. She hated to think she'd be dependent on us all. My mother was a wonderful person but very proud; she couldn't stand being pitied. By the way, I'm sorry if the children gave you a hard time. They are a bit wild.'

I almost choke on my soup at this understatement and glance at

Jenny who sits beside me, cross-legged on the floor. She hasn't touched her food or said a word since we entered the hut.

Gina touches her arm nervously. 'I'm sorry, Grandma.'

Jenny reaches out for Gina's hand and kisses it, staring hungrily at this dumpy, brown-eyed, middle-aged woman who vaguely resembles Abbie. As Jenny kisses the coarse red hand her tears begin. She and Gina embrace, and it looks as if Jenny is hugging her mother.

I go outside the hut, leaving them together. I have changed, but, really, family clinches are not my thing. I have my own way of mourning Abbie.

In the farmyard encampment to which my real-estate investment has dwindled, children and adults and pigs and cows and hens are settling down to sleep in huts and tents and treehouses. They go to bed with the sun like medieval peasants – my descendants *are* medieval peasants. Restlessly, I pick my way among the shelters, dung, vegetable patches and compost heaps to the top of the hill.

This new London shimmers in the light of a full moon that is surrounded by a rainbow-like halo. One of those tricks played by the intemperate skies of this planet – on Luna Minor we can choose the sky that suits our mood. Down here, now that there is no electricity, stars can be seen again; they have reclaimed the sky as plants and water and animals have reclaimed the streets. Reflected in the floodwater that surrounds the hill is the ragged silhouette of the new skyline: broken towers, bombed-out terraces, heaps of rubble. Although there is no traffic the night is full of cries and screams and yells that could be human or animal or both. I can smell shit and grass and – surely another sort of grass, as well?

A cough behind me makes me whirl around. A tall young man is standing on the concrete platform where the ack-ack guns stood during the Second World War. He's pointing a gun that looks at least a hundred years old at me and smoking a joint. 'Sorry, mate. Thought you was a looter.'

'What do they loot?'

'Food, animals. They call us the fat cats; everyone wants to live up here.'

'Really,' I reply sceptically. We stare at each other. He must be about the age I look, and the resemblance is absurd, except that he's much darker-skinned than me.

He passes me the joint and nods amiably. 'Ahmed. Dunno what to call you really. Grandma always said I looked just like you.'

'Is Ahmed a common name now?'

'Dad got gang-banged by one of them Muslim-Feminist mobs. Left him unconscious, and nine months later a baby was left at the bottom of the hill: me.'

'I'm so sorry.'

'Not your fault. Well, of course, in a way it's all your fault.'

'Is that what you think?'

'Well, it's true, innit? All that messing about with staying young and buggering off to the moon and that. Not natural, is it?'

'No, I've never wanted much to do with nature.'

'Mind you, Grandma was way up there above the floods.'

'Is that a compliment?'

'She wouldn't take no diss. Once when I was little I wouldn't go to bed, and I bit her, and there was this sort of explosion, and it pushed me right through the wall of the hut. Still got a scar on my cheek. See? Special powers she had. Everyone said so.'

'What about you? Do you have special powers?'

'Don't think so. I'm just ordinary. We heard about you, though. Flying and doing magic stuff.'

'Do people still remember that?' I ask, flattered.

'All our bedtime stories was about you and Jenny. She's still a bit of a looker. Must be going on for two hundred, innit?'

'Oh yes. She's a remarkable experiment.'

''Course, she's Grandma's mum. Can't get my head round that. Doesn't look like a mum, somehow.'

'I think she feels like one tonight.'

'I'll miss the old bag.'

'So will I.'

Later I return to the hut where Abbie is laid out. Jenny is lying on a heap of old blankets, her eyes wide open, still weeping. I lie beside her and take her in my arms. Our wake is wordless but the night seethes with memories of our daughter. At first light Jenny falls asleep.

I get up and wander back up the hill which is misty now, floating above the water and the shadowy blue ruins. I tap Ahmed on the shoulder. 'You can go to bed now. I'll take over.'

'You sure? Fuckin' animals, some of them looters. Wouldn't want you to get hurt.'

'It's not likely. Go and get some sleep.'

'Well – take care.' He hands me the rusty old rifle and a half-smoked joint. 'Earthkeeper'll be here soon.'

It is pleasant to be alone as I watch the sun rise over the shattered breast of St Paul's. The skyline is gilded with illusory prosperity and smoke rises as the morning begins. A little barefoot girl with huge black eyes and Jenny's thick black curls runs up from the shanty town to give me a warm biscuit and a mug of herbal tea. Disconcerting, all these genetic mosaics. I dread being confronted with Abbie as she was when she was about seven. I love you, Daddy. Really, these memories are most disturbing, I shall have to talk to Pierre about editing them out.

Something squelches out of the water at the bottom of the hill and moves towards me. A tiny dark creature scurries up the hill. A child looter? I point the rifle and hope I won't have to use it. As it comes closer I see the figure is old, of indeterminate sex, wrapped in soaking-wet brown robes. Out of a leathery walnut face sharp black eyes stare at me. 'Good morning, Leo.'

'Sibyl! What are you doing here?'

'I might ask you that. I live here.'

'You mean you stayed in London all these years? I always half expected you to turn up on Luna Minor. You should come. We have marvellous parties and entertainments up there. We have a beautiful house and garden – as we say up there, all the fruits of the earth without any of the worms. I'm sure you'd love it.'

'I'd hate it.' She folds her withered arms and glares up at me, blasting me with foul breath. Her robes are filthy, edged with green slime.

'I see you're determined to be organic.'

'You think the earth is a fashion, to be abandoned when the whim takes you? I wouldn't have bothered helping you and Jenny if I'd known how trivial-hearted you were. Narcissism burrows inwards, and yours has drilled right through you.'

'There's no need to be insulting. I have feelings.'

'Not many.'

'I hope you're not going to come up with some obscure, depressing prophecy.'

'I don't do that any more. No riddles, no couches. These people have suffered terribly. They have to fight to survive, but they're used to that – these are the people who fell through the bottom of the old society – and then, when they've finished fighting, they must die.'

'Abbie has died.'

'I know. That's why I'm here.'

'So you're the Earthkeeper?'

'One of my names.'

'Well, I think I preferred you when you were Sibyl. It seems to me you've become very insensitive. Jenny and I are devastated by her death. Poor Jenny has been beside herself with grief all night.'

'She'll soon get over it, soon find another child.'

'How do you know?'

'I can't help knowing.'

'So, what's this earthkeeping you do?'

'I give people hope when they're desperate or sick or dying. I warn them against the old ideas and the old technology and try to teach them new ones. I try to stop them killing each other, and, when they do die, I take the bodies to the water and help the people who loved them to say goodbye.'

'So you're inventing a new religion. And you have the nerve to accuse *me* of hubris!'

'People need ritual and hope. It doesn't matter what you call them.'

I follow her down the hill where my descendants greet her warmly and lead her to the hut where Abbie lies. When I come from the sunlit hillside into the hut my eyes are at first dazzled. For a few seconds I think there is only one woman in there, an animated corpse with three heads, whispering in the dark. Then my eyes adjust and I see that Jenny and Sibyl are washing Abbie. Her body is old, scraggy, covered with wrinkles and moles and sagging pouches of grey skin. I mourn the beautiful princess she could have been. For ever.

Jenny seems calmer now, as if Sibyl has comforted her. The children spend the day weaving dry twigs into a stretcher, and the adults prepare food – it smells most unappetizing, but I suppose I'll have to eat it. After years of eating clean food, grown indoors in giant bacteria baths, it disgusts me to think of vegetables being grown in the earth, in all its filthy debris of sewage and decomposed bodies.

At sunset we all gather and carry Abbie, on the stretcher, down the hill. There are about a hundred of us, and I can't help feeling a glimmer of patriarchal pride as I glance at their faces. Many of them wear odd features of mine or Jenny's, like beads in a kaleidoscope making unexpectedly interesting patterns. At first I thought them all ugly, but I'm getting used to their faces now.

It's windy, the oil-dark water churns and billows as we kneel beside it, Jenny and I and Gina in front of the others, to lay Abbie's corpse at the edge of the water. Each of us in turn kisses her or murmurs a few words. Some of the children tuck wild flowers and pebbles into her long white robes. There are no speeches or sermons. As the last rays of the sun disappear behind the shattered buildings and drown in the floodwater we launch her. There's a burst of sound, a chanting, wailing song full of grief and pain. Jenny and I kneel side by side, silent. We don't know the tune; we don't know the words.

Sibyl melts away into the darkness, and the rest of us go back for the funeral feast, which is as unpalatable as I feared: nettle stew and burnt oatcakes. Yet these people do have qualities I like: they are robust and honest. An idea begins to form. Jenny and I sleep in the same hut, where the table is now horribly bare. Before we fall into exhausted sleep I whisper my plan to her.

Perhaps I should have said something to Gina before I gathered them all together to make my announcement this morning. 'Dear descendants – no, friends. I've come to appreciate you during these days we've spent together, mourning my beloved daughter. The horror of death, so final, so unnecessary. Some of you perhaps thought that Jenny and I and our eternal delight in each other were legends, tales told to children at bedtime. But as you see we are as real as you are – although, frankly, a lot more attractive.

'Soon our shuttle will return and take us back to Luna Minor. To our transparent dome, where delicious food and exquisite music can be summoned at the press of a button, where there are perfectly controlled gardens and fountains and pools – nothing so crude as weather. Others like us, the eternally young, talk and frolic and entertain themselves and each other. Sometimes we even look down on you, on your ghastly catalogue of disasters, and wish we could do more to help you.

'Jenny and I have thought of something we *can* do. We want you to choose one of the children you breed so prolifically to be adopted by us. Of course, we'd love to take more than one, but, as you'll appreciate, immigration has to be controlled rather strictly. The younger the better, as it will be easier to wipe out traumatic memories of life down here. Boy or girl, the choice is up to you. If it's a boy we'll call him Ulysses because this time he will have made the right decision, choosing to live without ageing or death on a magic island.'

I realize this last bit is above their heads and sit down. Silence. I glance at Jenny, who is staring hungrily at the tiny children playing in the dirt and clinging to their filthy mothers. They all gasp and mutter, and I think they are overwhelmed by my generosity.

Suddenly they erupt into a wild barbarous stampede, even worse than the riot when we arrived. Jenny and I cling to each other and gaze up at the sky, willing the shuttle to come and rescue us. I realize I was a fool to expect rational discourse.

Our last few minutes on earth are rather confused. Perhaps Jenny and I don't behave as well as we might. We are both grief-stricken, after all, battered by days of unrefined emotion, discomfort, awful food and, now, terrified by the threat of actual violence.

They chase us to the top of the hill, screeching and pushing and spitting. For a moment I think they're going to shove us over the edge. Of course, we'd just roll to the bottom, but, still, it would be most undignified. I have my arm around Jenny's shoulder, but she's stretching out her arms to our attackers, in supplication, I think. There's a roar above our heads, and we get ready to return to civilization. The chute is lowered towards us, and there's a rush of cold air as the vacuum prepares to rapture us up.

Jenny makes a lunge into the mob, grabs two-year-old Ella from Gina's arms and runs with her back to the chute of the shuttle. I help her to bundle the screaming, wriggling child in. After a few seconds of grief the child will be immeasurably better off. For ever. I admit this is an impulsive gesture, imperfectly considered. A mistake, in other words. The Welcome Machine at the threshold sniffs doubtfully at the nature brat. Ella's germs, dirt, tears and yells send the needles wild. They are designed to measure suitability for metalife, and as Jenny and I squeeze past into the cabin of the shuttle the Welcome Machine delivers its terrible judgement on Ella. Metal pincers reach out to force her back down the chute, out of the purified air, back into the arms of her grandmother.

Genetic Love

We made good time coming home. This time I was glad of the injection that allowed me to sleep dreamlessly throughout the journey. Long after it wore off I lay with my eyes shut, not wanting to face the curious eyes of the other passengers. I didn't want to talk to anyone, not even you.

Home. I shall never go down there again. The gap between us is so much wider than when Abbie was alive. We use the pool for swimming, now. Nobody down there has a brain implant, one of many things that died with Abbie. I thought of offering one to Gina so that she could see and hear my virtual visits, but I don't suppose she'd want to.

Since our return our little paradise seems different. I'm reminded of the period just after my sight was restored. For years I'd lived inside my head, among shapes that were imagined and guessed at and half remembered. I'd learnt to find my way around my head and to negotiate the outer world as well, tapping my stick. And when I first opened my sighted eyes again it was a terrible shock. I couldn't distinguish the objects around me, the flat expanse of meaningless patches of darkness, light and colour. I kept falling over and bumping into furniture that wasn't where my memory had placed it.

Now, again, I have that sense of displacement. The asteroid and meteor spectacles, the concerts and genetic art exhibitions at the Metaphysical Theatre, the dinner parties amid the fountains – somehow they're not as marvellous as they were. I tell my therapist I'm mourning my daughter, and she offers to wipe out all memory of Abbie. But I want those memories, I say, as she smiles at me pityingly. You keep telling me to stop living in my past.

But there's so much of it. I come out here alone to sit beside my pool. Up here they all despise the dead for dying, but I can't help loving them and Abbie most of all. I even let myself remember the years when she didn't love me at all – hated me probably.

Her disappearance was like a rehearsal for my bereavement now. So sudden, so brutal. As if I had to choose between you and Abbie, as if it was impossible for us all to live contentedly together. Of course, we had her tracked – there was a Metaphysical agent in Paraguay and others in Kabul and Nairobi – tracked her movements but not her feelings. I still don't know how much she resented me. Perhaps it doesn't matter. Parents have to be rejected – Sibyl would say – and children have to be loved. For fifteen years I followed every twist and turn of my daughter's adolescent rebellion, and when we were reunited I never reproached her.

You come out and sit beside me. We dangle our long brown legs in the turquoise ripples of the pool and my finger traces the taut curve of your cheekbone beneath your clear, deep-blue eyes. Still young, like me. The artificial waves lap gently at our bare feet as we talk.

'Still missing her?'

'Of course. Don't you?'

'She was my daughter, too.'

'I wish now we'd had more children. And taken the others up here so that we could keep them with us for ever.'

'It's not too late.'

'What do you mean?'

'I have a complete set of her genes.'

'But that's impossible!'

'Not at all. When she was about nine, when we were living in Phillimore Gardens and I realized you were going to leave me, I got the Metaphysical surgeons to come round and extract genes from both of you. Something to remember you by.'

I remember my nightmare visions of figures in white surrounding Abbie's bed and mine. 'So you weren't carrying out evil experiments, after all.'

'Reports of my evil were always vastly exaggerated.'

'But, Leo, after all you did . . .'

'People change. That's the marvellous thing about them . . . us. Now, what kind of baby would you like?'

'A girl, like Abbie.'

'Exactly like her?' I shut my eyes and remember the feel of her in my arms that first morning, the tiny, waxen face with the eyes that prefigured her unique personality. I can't speak.

'You can have any kind of baby you like. Unnatural selection. I have your genes, too, of course, so she could have your hair, for instance.' You stroke it. It's made of extruded squirrels but feels very soft.

'No, I don't want her to look like me, I want her to look exactly like herself. I even want to call her Abbie.'

'A clone?'

'Yes.'

'A little genetocrat. Character?'

'Just like . . . Well, actually, perhaps she could be just a bit less obstinate. After all, if she hadn't been so intransigent she'd still be here with us.'

'Intelligence?'

'Enough to cultivate and appreciate the beauty of our life here but not enough to keep asking awkward questions about life down there. Perhaps she could have a talent for singing, too?'

'We can download Abbie's mind from our metacomputers and modify it slightly. I suppose you want her to be healthy?'

'Oh yes. Perhaps just a few childhood illnesses so that we can show her how much we love her.'

'And how do you want her to be born?'

'Out of me.'

'Really? A nature brat?'

'Yes. I want to feel her heart beat under mine, to feel her kick, to feel the squelching astonishment as she shoots out of me.'

'All that blood and mess and pain?'

'Oh yes.'

'What a primitive you still are, Jenny. It will cause quite a scandal, but I'll talk to Pierre about it. Would you like our baby for the anniversary of our contract on the twelfth of October?'

'That's only eight months. That might affect her development. I want to carry her to term.'

'I'll try not to be so jealous this time.'

'Yes, this time it will be perfect.'